THE BANE CHRONICLES

Also by Cassandra Clare

THE MORTAL INSTRUMENTS

City of Bones

City of Ashes

City of Glass

City of Fallen Angels

City of Lost Souls

City of Heavenly Fire

THE INFERNAL DEVICES

Clockwork Angel

Clockwork Prince

Clockwork Princess

THE SHADOWHUNTER'S CODEX
With Joshua Lewis

The Bane Chronicles

CASSANDRA CLARE

SARAH REES BRENNAN

MAUREEN JOHNSON

Margaret K. McElderry Books

NEW YORK LONDON TORONTO SYDNEY NEW DELHI

MARGARET K. McELDERRY BOOKS
An imprint of Simon & Schuster Children's Publishing Division
1230 Avenue of the Americas, New York, New York 10020
This book is a work of fiction. Any references to historical events, real people, or real places are used fictitiously. Other names, characters, places, and events are products of the author's imagination, and any resemblance to actual events or places or persons, living or dead, is entirely coincidental.

Book design by Mike Rosamilia and Nicholas Sciacca
The text for this book is set in Dolly.
Manufactured in the United States of America
2 4 6 8 10 9 7 5 3
Library of Congress Cataloging-in-Publication Data
Clare, Cassandra. [Short stories. Selections]
The Bane chronicles / Cassandra Clare, Sarah Rees Brennan, Maureen Johnson. p. cm.
Summary: A collection of eleven short stories, previously published online, that illuminate the life of the enigmatic, flashy, and flamboyant High Warlock of Brooklyn, Magnus Bane, a character in The Mortal Instruments series.
ISBN 978-1-4424-9599-9 (hardcover)
ISBN 978-1-4424-9566-1 (eBook)
1. Short stories. [1. Supernatural—Fiction. 2. Demonology—Fiction. 3. Magic—Fiction. 4. Vampires—Fiction. 5. New York (N.Y.)—Fiction. 6. Horror stories. 7. Short stories.] I. Brennan, Sarah Rees.
II. Johnson, Maureen, 1973-
PZ7.C5265Ban 2014
[Fic]—dc23
2014013230
ISBN 978-1-4814-3131-6 (export paperback)

This is for the people—they know who they are—who write letters and e-mails, and come up at signings, and say Magnus and Alec mean a lot to them.

Like Magnus, you are magical
and you are heroes.

THE BANE CHRONICLES

CONTENTS

What Really Happened in Peru

By Cassandra Clare and Sarah Rees Brennan

So he kept at it with the charango, *despite the fact that he was forbidden to play it in the house. He was also discouraged from playing it in public places by a crying child, a man with papers talking about city ordinances, and a small riot.*

As a last resort he went up to the mountains and played there. Magnus was sure that the llama stampede he witnessed was a coincidence. The llamas could not be judging him.

—What Really Happened in Peru

It was a sad moment in Magnus Bane's life when he was banned from Peru by the High Council of Peruvian warlocks. It was not just because the posters with a picture of him that were passed around Downworld in Peru were so wildly unflattering. It was because Peru was one of his favorite places. He had had many adventures there, and had many wonderful memories, starting with the time in 1791 when he had invited Ragnor Fell to join him for a festive sightseeing escape in Lima.

1791

Magnus awoke in his roadside inn just outside Lima, and once he had arrayed himself in an embroidered waistcoat, breeches, and shining buckled shoes, he went in search of breakfast.

Instead he found his hostess, a plump woman whose long hair was covered with a black mantilla, in a deep, troubled conference with one of the serving girls about a recent arrival to the inn.

"I think it's a sea monster," he heard his hostess whisper. "Or a merman. Can they survive on land?"

"Good morning, ladies," Magnus called out. "Sounds like my guest has arrived."

Both women blinked twice. Magnus put the first blink down to his vivid attire, and the second, slower blink down to what he had just said. He gave them both a cheery wave and wandered out through wide wooden doors and across the courtyard into the common room, where he found his fellow warlock Ragnor Fell skulking in the back of the room with a mug of *chicha de molle*.

"I'll have what he's having," Magnus said to the serving lady. "No, wait a moment. I'll have three of what he's having."

"Tell them I'll have the same," said Ragnor. "I achieved this drink only through some very determined pointing."

Magnus did, and when he returned his gaze to Ragnor, he saw that his old friend was looking his usual self: hideously dressed, deeply gloomy, and deeply green of skin. Magnus often gave thanks that his own warlock's mark was not so obvious. It was sometimes inconvenient to have the gold-green, slit-pupilled eyes of a cat, but this was usually easily hidden with a small glamour, and if not, well, there were quite a few ladies—and men—who didn't find it a drawback.

"No glamour?" Magnus inquired.

"You said that you wanted me to join you on travels that would be a ceaseless round of debauchery," Ragnor told him.

Magnus beamed. "I did!" He paused. "Forgive me. I do not see the connection."

"I have found I have better luck with the ladies in my natural state," Ragnor told him. "Ladies enjoy a bit of variety. There was a woman in the court of Louis the Sun King who said none could compare to her 'dear little cabbage.' I hear it's become quite a popular term of endearment in France. All thanks to me."

He spoke in the same glum tones as usual. When the six drinks arrived, Magnus seized on them.

"I'll be needing all of these. Please bring more for my friend."

"There was also a woman who referred to me as her sweet peapod of love," Ragnor continued.

Magnus took a deep restorative swallow, looked at the sunshine outside and the drinks before him, and felt better about the entire situation. "Congratulations. And welcome to Lima, the City of Kings, my sweet peapod."

After breakfast, which was five drinks for Ragnor and seventeen for Magnus, Magnus took Ragnor on a tour of Lima, from the golden, curled, and carved façade of the archbishop's palace to the brightly colored buildings across the plaza, with their practically mandatory elaborate balconies, where the Spanish had once executed criminals.

"I thought it would be nice to start in the capital. Besides, I've been here before," Magnus said. "About fifty years ago. I had a lovely time, aside from the earthquake that almost swallowed the city."

"Did you have something to do with that earthquake?"

"Ragnor," Magnus reproached his friend. "You cannot blame me for every little natural disaster that happens!"

"You didn't answer the question," Ragnor said, and sighed. "I am relying on you to be . . . more reliable and less like you than you usually are," he warned as they walked. "I don't speak the language."

"So you don't speak Spanish?" Magnus asked. "Or you don't speak Quechua? Or is it that you don't speak Aymara?"

Magnus was perfectly aware he was a stranger everywhere he went, and he took care to learn all the languages so he could go anywhere he chose. Spanish had been the first language that he had learned to speak, after his native language. That was the one tongue he did not speak often. It reminded him of his mother, and his stepfather—reminded him of the love and the prayer and despair of his childhood. The words of his homeland rested a little too heavily on his tongue, as if he had to mean them, had to be serious, when he spoke.

(There were other languages—Purgatic and Gehennic and Tartarian—that he had learned so that he could communicate with those from the demon realms, languages he was forced to use often in his line of work. But those reminded him of his blood father, and those memories were even worse.)

Sincerity and gravity, in Magnus's opinion, were highly overrated, as was being forced to relive unpleasant memories. He would much rather be amused and amusing.

"I don't speak any of the things that you just said," Ragnor told him. "Although, I must speak Prattling Fool, since I can understand you."

"That is hurtful and unnecessary," Magnus observed. "But of course, you can trust me completely."

"Just don't leave me here without guidance. You have to swear, Bane."

Magnus raised his eyebrows. "I give you my word of honor!"

"I will find you," Ragnor told him. "I will find whatever chest of absurd clothes you have. And I will bring a llama into the place where you sleep and make sure that it urinates on everything you possess."

"There is no need to get nasty about this," Magnus said. "Don't worry. I can teach you every word that you need to know right now. One of them is '*fiesta*.'"

Ragnor scowled. "What does that mean?"

Magnus raised his eyebrows. "It means 'party.' Another important word is '*juerga*.'"

"What does that word mean?"

Magnus was silent.

"Magnus," said Ragnor, his voice stern. "Does that word also mean 'party'?"

Magnus could not help the sly grin that spread across his face. "I would apologize," he said. "Except that I feel no regret at all."

"Try to be a little sensible," Ragnor suggested.

"We're on holiday!" said Magnus.

"You're always on holiday," Ragnor pointed out. "You've been on holiday for thirty years!"

It was true. Magnus had not been settled anywhere since his lover died—not his first lover, but the first one who had lived by his side and died in his arms. Magnus had thought of her often enough that the mention of her did not hurt him, her remembered face like the distant familiar beauty of stars, not to be touched but to shine in front of his eyes at night.

"I can't get enough adventure," Magnus said lightly. "And adventure cannot get enough of me."

He had no idea why Ragnor sighed again.

* * *

Ragnor's suspicious nature continued to make Magnus very sad and disappointed in him as a person, such as when they visited Lake Yarinacocha and Ragnor's eyes narrowed as he demanded: "Are those dolphins *pink*?"

"They were pink when I got here!" Magnus exclaimed indignantly. He paused and considered. "I am almost certain."

They went from *costa* to *sierra* seeing all the sights of Peru. Magnus's favorite was perhaps the city of Arequipa, a piece of the moon, made of sillar rock that when touched by the sun blazed as dazzling and scintillating a white as moonlight striking water.

There was a very attractive young lady there too, but in the end she decided she preferred Ragnor. Magnus could have lived his whole long life without becoming involved in a warlock love triangle, or hearing the endearment "adorable pitcher plant of a man" spoken in French, which Ragnor did understand. Ragnor, however, seemed very pleased and for the first time did not seem to regret that he'd come when Magnus had summoned him to Lima.

In the end Magnus was able to persuade Ragnor away from Arequipa only by introducing him to another lovely young lady, Giuliana, who knew her way in the rain forest and assured them both that she would be able to lead them to *ayahuasca*, a plant with remarkable magical properties.

Later Magnus had cause to regret choosing this particular lure as he pulled himself through the green swathes of the Manu rain forest. It was all green, green, green, everywhere he looked. Even when he looked at his traveling companion.

"I don't like the rain forest," Ragnor said sadly.

"That's because you are not open to new experiences in the same way I am!"

"No, it is because it is wetter than a boar's armpit and twice as smelly here."

Magnus pushed a dripping frond out of his eyes. "I admit you make an excellent point and also paint a vivid picture with your words."

It was not comfortable in the rain forest, that much was true, but it was wonderful there all the same. The thick green of the undergrowth was different from the delicate leaves on trees higher up, the bright feathery shapes of some plants gently waving at the ropelike strands of others. The green all around was broken up by sudden bright interruptions: the vivid splash of flowers and the rush of movement that meant animals instead of leaves.

Magnus was especially charmed by the sight of the spider monkeys above, dainty and glossy with long arms and legs spread out in the trees like stars, and the shy swift spring of squirrel monkeys.

"Picture this," said Magnus. "Me with a little monkey friend. I could teach him tricks. I could dress him in a cunning jacket. He could look just like me! But more monkey-shaped."

"Your friend has gone mad and giddy with the altitude sickness," Giuliana announced. "We are many feet above sea level here."

Magnus was not entirely sure why he had brought a guide, except that it seemed to calm Ragnor down. Other people probably dutifully followed their guides in unfamiliar and potentially dangerous places, but Magnus was a warlock and fully prepared to have a magical battle with a jaguar demon if that was required. It would be an excellent story, which might impress some of the ladies who were not inexplicably allured by Ragnor. Or some of the gentlemen.

Lost in picking fruit and in the contemplation of jaguar demons, Magnus looked around at one point and found himself separated from his companions—lost in the green wilderness.

He paused and admired the bromeliads, huge iridescent flower-like bowls made out of petals, shimmering with color and water. There were frogs inside the jewel-bright recesses of the flowers.

Then he looked up into the round brown eyes of a monkey.

"Hello, companion," said Magnus.

The monkey made a terrible sound, half snarl and half hiss.

"I begin to rather doubt the beauty of our friendship," said Magnus.

Giuliana had told them not to back down when approached by monkeys, but to stay still and preserve an air of calm authority. This monkey was much larger than the other monkeys Magnus had seen, with broader bunched shoulders and thick, almost black fur—a howler monkey, Magnus remembered they were called.

Magnus threw the monkey a fig. The monkey took the fig.

"There," said Magnus. "Let us consider the matter settled."

The monkey advanced, chewing in a menacing fashion.

"I rather wonder what I am doing here. I enjoy city life, you know," Magnus observed. "The glittering lights, the constant companionship, the liquid entertainment. The lack of sudden monkeys."

He ignored Giuliana's advice and took a smart step back, and also threw another piece of fruit. The monkey did not take the bait this time. He coiled and rattled out a growl, and Magnus took several more steps back and into a tree.

Magnus flailed on impact, was briefly grateful that nobody was watching him and expecting him to be a sophisticated warlock, and had a monkey assault launched directly to his face.

He shouted, spun, and sprinted through the rain forest. He did not even think to drop the fruit. It fell one by one in a bright cascade as he ran for his life from the simian menace. He heard it in hot pursuit and fled faster, until all his fruit was gone and he ran right into Ragnor.

"Have a care!" Ragnor snapped.

"In my defense, you are quite well camouflaged," Magnus pointed out, and then he detailed his terrible monkey adventure twice, once for Giuliana in Spanish, and again for Ragnor in English.

"But of course you should have retreated at once from the dominant male," Giuliana said. "Are you an idiot? You are extremely lucky he was distracted from ripping out your throat by the fruit. He thought you were trying to steal his females."

"Pardon me, but we did not have the time to exchange that kind of personal information," Magnus said. "I could not have known! Moreover, I wish to assure both of you that I did not make any amorous advances on female monkeys." He paused and winked. "I didn't actually see any, so I never got the chance."

Ragnor looked very regretful about all the choices that had led to his being in this place and especially in this company. Later he stooped and hissed, low enough so Giuliana could not hear and in a way that reminded Magnus horribly of his monkey nemesis: "Did you forget that you can do *magic*?"

Magnus spared a moment to toss a disdainful look over his shoulder.

"I am not going to ensorcel a monkey! Honestly, Ragnor. What do you take me for?"

Life could not be entirely devoted to debauchery and monkeys. Magnus had to finance all the drinking somehow. There was always a Downworlder network to be found, and he had made sure to make the right contacts as soon as he'd set foot in Peru.

When his particular expertise was called for, he brought Ragnor with him. They boarded the ship in the Salaverry harbor together, both dressed in their greatest finery. Magnus was wearing his largest hat, with an ostrich feather plume.

Edmund García, one of the richest merchants in Peru, met them on the foredeck. He was a man with a florid complexion, dressed in an expensive-looking cassock, knee breeches, and a powdered wig. An engraved pistol hung from his leather belt. He squinted at Ragnor. "Is that a sea monster?" he demanded.

"He is a highly respected warlock," said Magnus. "You are, in fact, getting two warlocks for the price of one."

García had not made his fortune by turning his nose up at bargains. He was instantly and forevermore silent on the subject of sea monsters.

"Welcome," he said instead.

"I dislike boats," Ragnor observed, looking around. "I get vilely seasick."

The turning green joke was too easy. Magnus was not going to stoop to make it.

"Would you care to elaborate on what this job entails?" he

asked instead. "The letter I received said you had need of my particular talents, but I must confess that I have so many talents that I am not sure which one you require. They are all, of course, at your disposal."

"You are strangers to our shores," said Edmund. "So perhaps you do not know that the current state of prosperity in Peru rests on our chief export—guano."

"What's he saying?" Ragnor asked.

"Nothing you would like, so far," Magnus said. The boat lurched beneath them on the waves. "Pardon me. You were talking about bird droppings."

"I was," said García. "For a long time the European merchants were the ones who profited most from this trade. Now laws have been passed to ensure that Peruvian merchants will have the upper hand in such dealings, and the Europeans will have to make us partners in their enterprises or retire from the guano business. One of my ships, bearing a large quantity of guano as cargo, will be one of the first sent out now that the laws have been passed. I fear attempts may be made on the ship."

"You think pirates are out to steal your bird droppings?" Magnus asked.

"What's going on?" Ragnor moaned piteously.

"You don't want to know. Trust me." Magnus looked at García. "Varied though my talents are, I am not sure they extend to guarding, ah, guano."

He was dubious about the cargo, but he did know something about Europeans swooping in and laying claim to everything they saw as if it were unquestionably theirs, land and lives, produce and people.

Besides which, he had never had an adventure on the high seas before.

"We are prepared to pay handsomely," García offered, naming a sum.

"Oh. Well, in that case, consider us hired," said Magnus, and he broke the news to Ragnor.

"I'm still not sure about any of this," Ragnor said. "I'm not even sure where you got that hat."

Magnus adjusted it for maximum jauntiness. "Just a little something I picked up. Seemed appropriate for the occasion."

"Nobody else is wearing anything even remotely like it."

Magnus cast a disparaging look around at all the fashion-challenged sailors. "I feel sorry for them, of course, but I do not see why that observation should alter my current extremely stylish course of action."

He looked from the ship deck across to the sea. The water was a particularly clear green, with the same shading of turquoise and emerald as in a polished green tourmaline. Two ships were visible on the horizon—the ship that they were on their way to join, and a second, which Magnus suspected strongly was a pirate ship intent on attacking the first.

Magnus snapped his fingers, and their own ship swallowed the horizon at a gulp.

"Magnus, don't magic the ship to go faster," Ragnor said. "Magnus, why are you magicking the ship to go faster?"

Magnus snapped his fingers again, and blue sparks played along the weather-worn and storm-splintered side of the ship. "I spy dread pirates in the distance. Ready yourself for battle, my greenish friend."

Ragnor was loudly sick at that and even more loudly unhappy about it, but they were gaining on the two ships, so Magnus was overall pleased.

"We are not hunting pirates. Nobody is a pirate! We are safeguarding cargo and that's all. And what is this cargo, anyway?" Ragnor asked.

"You're happier not knowing, my sweet little peapod," Magnus assured him.

"Please stop calling me that."

"I never shall, never," Magnus vowed, and he made a swift economical gesture, with his rings catching the sunshine and painting the air in tiny bright brushstrokes.

The ship Magnus insisted on thinking of as the enemy pirate ship noticeably listed to one side. It was possible Magnus had gone slightly too far there.

García seemed extremely impressed that Magnus could disable ships from a distance, but he wanted to be absolutely sure the cargo was safe, so they drew their vessel alongside the larger ship—the pirate ship was by now lagging far, far behind them.

Magnus was perfectly happy with this state of affairs. Since they were hunting pirates and adventuring on the high seas, there was something that he had always wanted to try.

"You do it too," he urged Ragnor. "It will be dashing. You'll see."

Then he seized a rope and swung, dashingly, across fathoms of shining blue space and over a stretch of gleaming deck.

Then he dropped, neatly, into the hold.

Ragnor followed him a few moments later.

"Hold your nose," Magnus counseled urgently. "Do not breathe in. Obviously someone was checking on the cargo, and left the hold open, and we both just jumped directly in."

"And now here we are, all thanks to you, in the soup."

"If only," said Magnus.

There was a brief pause for them both to evaluate the full horror of the situation. Magnus, personally, was in horror up to his elbows. Even more tragically, he had lost his jaunty hat. He was simply trying not to think of what substance they were mostly buried in. If he thought very hard of anything other than the excrement of tiny winged mammals, he could imagine that he was stuck in something else. Anything else.

"Magnus," Ragnor said. "I can see that the cargo we're guarding is some very unpleasant substance, but could you tell me exactly what it *is*?"

Seeing that concealment and pretense were useless, Magnus told him.

"I hate adventures in Peru," Ragnor said at last in a stifled voice. "I want to go home."

It was not Magnus's fault when the ensuing warlock tantrum managed to sink the boat full of guano, but he was blamed just the same. Even worse, he was not paid.

Magnus's wanton destruction of Peruvian property was not, however, the reason he was banned from Peru.

1885

The next time Magnus was back in Peru, he was on a job with his friends Catarina Loss and Ragnor Fell. This proved Catarina had, besides magic, supernatural powers of persuasion, because Ragnor had sworn that he would never set foot in Peru again and certainly never in Magnus's company. But the two had had some adventures together in England during the 1870s, and Ragnor had grown better disposed toward Magnus. Still, the whole time they were walking into the valley of the Lurín River with their client, Ragnor was sending Magnus suspicious little glances out of the corner of his eye.

"This constant air of foreboding that you have when you're around me is hurtful and unwarranted, you know," Magnus told Ragnor.

"I was airing the smell out of my clothes for years! Years!" Ragnor replied.

"Well, you should have thrown them out and bought clothes that were both more sweetly scented and more stylish," Magnus said. "Anyway, that was decades ago. What have I done to you lately?"

"Don't fight in front of the client, boys," Catarina implored in her sweet voice, "or I will knock your heads together so hard, your skulls will crack like eggs."

"I can speak English, you know," said Nayaraq, their client, who was paying them extremely generously.

Embarrassment descended on the entire group. They reached Pachacamac in silence. They beheld the walls of piled rubble, which looked like a giant, artful child's sculpture made of sand.

There were pyramids here, but it was mostly ruins. What remained was thousands of years old, though, and Magnus could feel magic thrumming even in the sand-colored fragments.

"I knew the oracle who lived here seven hundred years ago," Magnus announced grandly. Nayaraq looked impressed.

Catarina, who knew Magnus's actual age perfectly well, did not.

Magnus had first started putting a price on his magic when he was less than twenty years old. He'd still been growing then, not yet fixed in time like a dragonfly caught in amber, iridescent and everlasting but frozen forever and a day in the prison of one golden instant. When he was growing to his full height and his face and body were changing infinitesimally every day, when he was a little closer to human than he was now.

You could not tell a potential customer, expecting a learned and ancient magician, that you were not even fully grown. Magnus had started lying about his age young, and had never dropped the habit.

It did get a little embarrassing sometimes when he forgot what lie he'd told to whom. Someone had once asked him what Julius Caesar was like, and Magnus had stared at him for much too long and said, "Not tall?"

Magnus looked around at the sand lying close to the walls, and at the cracked crumbling edges of those walls, as if the stone were bread and a careless hand had torn a piece away. He carefully maintained the blasé air of one who had been here before and had been incredibly well dressed that time too.

"Pachacamac" meant "Lord of Earthquakes." Fortunately, Nayaraq did not want them to create one. Magnus had never created an earthquake on purpose and preferred not to dwell on unfortunate accidents in his youth.

What Nayaraq wanted was the treasure that her mother's mother's mother's mother, a beautiful noble girl living in the Acllahausi—the house of the women chosen by the sun—had hidden when the conquerors had come.

Magnus was not sure why she wanted it, as she seemed to have money enough, but he was not being paid to question her.

They walked for hours in sun and shadow, by the ruined walls that bore the marks of time and the faint impressions of frescoes, until they found what she was looking for.

When the stones were removed from the wall and the treasure was dug out, the sun struck the gold and Nayaraq's face at the same time. That was when Magnus understood that Nayaraq had not been searching for gold but for truth, for something real in her past.

She knew of Downworlders because she had been taken by the faeries, once. But this was not illusion or glamour, this gold shining in her hands as it had once shone in her ancestor's hands.

"Thank you all very much," she said, and Magnus understood and for a moment almost envied her.

When she was gone, Catarina let her own glamour fall away to reveal blue skin and white hair that dazzled in the dying sunlight.

"Now that that's settled, I have something to propose. I have been jealous for years about all the adventures you two had in Peru. What do you say to continuing on here for a while?"

"Absolutely!" said Magnus.

Catarina clapped her hands together.

Ragnor scowled. "Absolutely not."

"Don't worry, Ragnor," Magnus said carelessly. "I am fairly certain nobody who remembers the pirate misunderstanding is still alive. And the monkeys definitely aren't still after me. Besides, you know what this means."

"I do not want to do this, and I will not enjoy it," Ragnor said. "I would leave at once, but it would be cruel to abandon a lady in a foreign land with a maniac."

"I am so glad we are all agreed," said Catarina.

"We are going to be a dread triumvirate," Magnus informed Catarina and Ragnor with delight. "That means thrice the adventure."

Later they heard that they were wanted criminals for desecrating a temple, but nevertheless, that was not the reason, nor the time, that Magnus was banned from Peru.

1890

It was a beautiful day in Puno, the lake out the window a wash of blue and the sun shining with such dazzling force that it seemed to have burned all the azure and cloud out of the sky and left it all a white blaze. Carried on the clear mountain air, out over the lake water and through the house, rang Magnus's melody.

Magnus was turning in a gentle circle under the windowsill when the shutters on Ragnor's bedroom window slammed open.

"What—what—what are you doing?" he demanded.

"I am almost six hundred years old," Magnus claimed, and Ragnor snorted, since Magnus changed his age to suit himself every few weeks. Magnus swept on. "It does seem about time to learn a musical instrument." He flourished his new prize, a little stringed instrument that looked like a cousin of the lute that the lute was embarrassed to be related to. "It's called a *charango*. I am planning to become a *charanguista*!"

"I wouldn't call that an instrument of music," Ragnor observed sourly. "An instrument of torture, perhaps."

Magnus cradled the *charango* in his arms as if it were an easily offended baby. "It's a beautiful and very unique instrument! The sound box is made from an armadillo. Well, a dried armadillo shell."

"That explains the sound you're making," said Ragnor. "Like a lost, hungry armadillo."

"You are just jealous," Magnus remarked calmly. "Because you do not have the soul of a true artiste like myself."

"Oh, I am positively green with envy," Ragnor snapped.

"Come now, Ragnor. That's not fair," said Magnus. "You know I love it when you make jokes about your complexion."

Magnus refused to be affected by Ragnor's cruel judgments. He regarded his fellow warlock with a lofty stare of superb indifference, raised his *charango,* and began to play again his defiant, beautiful tune.

They both heard the staccato thump of frantically running feet from within the house, the swish of skirts, and then Catarina came rushing out into the courtyard. Her white hair was falling loose about her shoulders, and her face was the picture of alarm.

"Magnus, Ragnor, I heard a cat making a most unearthly noise," she exclaimed. "From the sound of it, the poor creature must be direly sick. You have to help me find it!"

Ragnor immediately collapsed with hysterical laughter on his windowsill. Magnus stared at Catarina for a moment, until he saw her lips twitch.

"You are conspiring against me and my art," he declared. "You are a pack of conspirators."

He began to play again. Catarina stopped him by putting a hand on his arm.

"No, but seriously, Magnus," she said. "That noise is appalling."

Magnus sighed. "Every warlock's a critic."

"Why are you doing this?"

"I have already explained myself to Ragnor. I wish to become proficient with a musical instrument. I have decided to devote myself to the art of the *charanguista*, and I wish to hear no more petty objections."

"If we are all making lists of things we wish to hear no more . . . ," Ragnor murmured.

Catarina, however, was smiling.

"I see," she said.

"Madam, you do not see."

"I do. I see it all most clearly," Catarina assured him. "What is her name?"

"I resent your implication," Magnus said. "There is no woman in the case. I am married to my music!"

"Oh, all right," Catarina said. "What's his name, then?"

His name was Imasu Morales, and he was gorgeous.

The three warlocks were staying near the harbor, along the shoreline of Lake Titicaca, but Magnus liked to see and be part of life in a way that Ragnor and Catarina, familiar with quiet and solitude from childhood on account of their unusual complexions, did not quite understand. He went walking about the city and up into the mountains, having small adventures. On a few occasions that Ragnor and Catarina kept hurtfully and unnecessarily reminding him of, he had been escorted home by the police, even though that incident with the Bolivian smugglers had been a complete misunderstanding.

Magnus had not been involved in any dealings with smugglers that night, though. He had simply been walking through the Plaza Republicana, skirting around artfully sculpted bushes and artfully sculpted sculptures. The city below shone like stars arranged in neat rows, as if someone were growing a harvest of light. It was a beautiful night to meet a beautiful boy.

The music had caught Magnus's ear first, and then the laughter. Magnus had turned to look and saw sparkling dark eyes and rumpled hair, and the play of the musician's fingers. Magnus had a list of favored traits in a partner—black hair, blue eyes, honest—but in this case what drew him in was an individual response to life. Something he hadn't seen before, and which made him want to see more.

He moved closer, and managed to catch Imasu's eye. Once both were caught, the game could begin, and Magnus began it by asking if Imasu taught music. He wanted to spend more time with Imasu, but he wanted to learn as well—to see if he could be absorbed in the same way, create the same sounds.

Even after a few lessons, Magnus could tell that the sounds he made with the *charango* were slightly different from the sounds Imasu made. Possibly more than slightly. Ragnor and Catarina both begged him to give the instrument up. Random strangers on the street begged him to give the instrument up. Even cats ran from him.

But: "You have real potential as a musician," Imasu said, his voice serious and his eyes laughing.

Magnus made it his policy to listen to people who were kind, encouraging, and extremely handsome.

So he kept at it with the *charango*, despite the fact that he was forbidden to play it in the house. He was also discouraged from playing it in public places by a crying child, a man with papers talking about city ordinances, and a small riot.

As a last resort he went up to the mountains and played there. Magnus was sure that the llama stampede he witnessed was a coincidence. The llamas could not be judging him.

Besides, the *charango* was definitely starting to sound better. He was either getting the hang of it or succumbing to auditory hallucinations. Magnus chose to believe it was the former.

"I think I really turned a corner," he told Imasu earnestly one day. "In the mountains. A metaphorical, musical corner, that is. There really should be more roads up there."

"That's wonderful," Imasu said, eyes shining. "I can't wait to hear it."

They were in Imasu's house, as Magnus was not allowed to play anywhere else in Puno. Imasu's mother and sister were both sadly prone to migraines, so many of Magnus's lessons were on musical theory, but today Magnus and Imasu were in the house alone.

"When can we expect your mother and sister back?" Magnus asked, very casually.

"In a few weeks," Imasu replied. "They went to visit my aunt. Um. They didn't flee—I mean, leave the house—for any particular reason."

"Such charming ladies," Magnus remarked. "So sad they're both so sickly."

Imasu blinked.

"Their headaches?" Magnus reminded him.

"Oh," Imasu said. "Oh, right." There was a pause, then Imasu clapped his hands together. "You were about to play something for me!"

Magnus beamed at him. "Prepare," he intoned, "to be astounded."

He lifted the instrument up in his arms. They had come to understand each other, he felt, his *charango* and he. He could make music flow from the air or the river or the curtains if he so chose, but this was different, human and strangely touching. The stumble and screech of the strings were coming together, Magnus thought, to form a melody. The music was almost there, in his hands.

When Magnus looked at Imasu, he saw Imasu had dropped his head into his hands.

"Er," Magnus said. "Are you quite all right?"

"I was simply overcome," Imasu said in a faint voice.

Magnus preened slightly. "Ah. Well."

"By how awful that was," Imasu said.

Magnus blinked. "Pardon?"

"I can't live a lie any longer!" Imasu burst out. "I have tried to be encouraging. Dignitaries of the town have been sent to me, asking me to plead with you to stop. My own sainted mother begged me, with tears in her eyes—"

"It isn't as bad as all that—"

"Yes, it is!" It was like a dam of musical critique had broken. Imasu turned on him with eyes that flashed instead of shining. "It is worse than you can possibly imagine! When you play, all of my mother's flowers lose the will to live and expire on the instant. The quinoa has no flavor now. The llamas are migrating because of your music, and llamas are not a migratory animal. The children now believe there is a sickly monster, half horse and half large mournful chicken, that lives in the lake and calls out to the world to grant it the sweet release of death. The townspeople believe that you and I are performing arcane magic rituals—"

"Well, that one was rather a good guess," Magnus remarked.

"—using the skull of an elephant, an improbably large mushroom, and one of your very peculiar hats!"

"Or not," said Magnus. "Furthermore, my hats are extraordinary."

"I will not argue with that." Imasu scrubbed a hand through his thick black hair, which curled and clung to his fingers like inky vines. "Look, I know that I was wrong. I saw a handsome man, thought that it would not hurt to talk a little about music and strike up a common interest, but I don't deserve this. You are going to get stoned in the town square, and if I have to listen to you play again, I will drown myself in the lake."

"Oh," said Magnus, and he began to grin. "I wouldn't. I hear there is a dreadful monster living in that lake."

Imasu seemed to still be brooding about Magnus's *charango* playing, a subject that Magnus had lost all interest in. "I believe the world will end with a noise like the noise you make!"

"Interesting," said Magnus, and he threw his *charango* out the window.

"Magnus!"

"I believe that music and I have gone as far as we can go together," Magnus said. "A true artiste knows when to surrender."

"I can't believe you did that!"

Magnus waved a hand airily. "I know, it is heartbreaking, but sometimes one must shut one's ears to the pleas of the muse."

"I just meant that those are expensive and I heard a crunch."

Imasu looked genuinely distressed, but he was smiling, too. His face was an open book in glowing colors, as fascinating as it was easy to read. Magnus moved from the window into Imasu's space and let one hand curl around Imasu's callused fingers, the other very lightly around his wrist. He saw the shiver run through Imasu's whole body, as if he were an instrument from which Magnus could coax any sound he pleased.

"It desolates me to give up my music," Magnus murmured. "But I believe you will discover I have many talents."

That night when he came home and told Ragnor and Catarina that he had given up music, Ragnor said, "In five hundred years I have never desired the touch of another man, but I am suddenly possessed with a desire to kiss that boy on the mouth."

"Hands off," said Magnus, with easy, pleased possessiveness.

The next day all of Puno rose and gathered together in a festival. Imasu told Magnus he was sure the timing of the festival was entirely unrelated. Magnus laughed. The sun came through in slants across Imasu's eyes, in glowing strips across his brown skin, and Imasu's mouth curled beneath Magnus's. They did not make it outside in time to see the parade.

Magnus asked his friends if they could stay in Puno for a while, and was not surprised when they agreed. Catarina and Ragnor were both warlocks. To them, as to Magnus, time was like rain, glittering as it fell, changing the world, but something that could also be taken for granted.

Until you loved a mortal. Then time became gold in a miser's hands, every bright year counted out carefully, infinitely precious, and each one slipping through your fingers.

Imasu told him about his father's death and about his sister's love for dancing that had inspired Imasu to play for her, and that this was the second time he had ever been in love. He was both *indígena* and Spanish, more mingled even than most of the mestizos, too Spanish for some and not Spanish enough for others. Magnus talked a little with Imasu about that, about the Dutch and Batavian blood in his own veins. He did not talk about demonic blood or his father or magic, not yet.

Magnus had learned to be careful about giving his memories with his heart. When people died, it felt like all the pieces of yourself you had given to them went as well. It took so long, building yourself back up until you were whole again, and you were never entirely the same.

That had been a long, painful lesson.

Magnus had still not learned it very well, he supposed, as he found himself wanting to tell Imasu a great deal. He did not only wish to talk about his parentage, but about his past, the people he had loved—about Camille; and about Edmund Herondale and his son, Will; and even about Tessa and Catarina and how he had met her in Spain. In the end he broke down and told the last story, though he left out details like the Silent Brothers and Catarina's almost being burned as a witch. But as the seasons changed, Magnus began to think that he should tell Imasu about magic at least, before he suggested that Magnus stop living with Catarina and Ragnor, and Imasu stop living with his mother and sister, and that they find a place together that Imasu could fill with music and Magnus with magic. It was time to settle down, Magnus thought, for a short while at least.

It came as a shock when Imasu suggested, quite quietly: "Perhaps it is time for you and your friends to think of leaving Puno."

"What, without you?" Magnus asked. He had been lying sunning himself outside Imasu's house, content and making his plans for a little way into the future. He was caught off guard enough to be stupid.

"Yes," Imasu answered, looking regretful about the prospect of making himself clearer. "Absolutely without me. It's not that I have not had a wonderful time with you. We have had fun together, you and I, haven't we?" he added pleadingly.

Magnus nodded, with the most nonchalant air he could manage, and then immediately ruined it by saying, "I thought so. So why end it?"

Perhaps it was his mother, or his sister, some member of Imasu's family, objecting to the fact that they were both men. This would not be the first or the last time that happened to Magnus, although Imasu's mother had always given Magnus the impression he could do anything he liked with her son just so long as he never touched a musical instrument in her presence ever again.

"It's you," Imasu burst out. "It is the way you are. I cannot be with you any longer because I do not want to be."

"Please," Magnus said after a pause. "Carry on showering me with compliments. This is an extremely pleasant experience for me, by the way, and precisely how I was hoping my day would go."

"You are just . . ." Imasu took a deep, frustrated breath. "You seem always . . . ephemeral, like a glittering shallow stream that passes the whole world by. Not something that will stay, not something that will last." He made a small, helpless gesture, as if letting something go, as if Magnus had wanted to be let go. "Not someone permanent."

That made Magnus laugh, suddenly and helplessly, and he threw his head back. He'd learned this lesson a long time ago: Even in the midst of heartbreak, you could still find yourself laughing.

Laughter had always come easily to Magnus, and it helped, but not enough.

"Magnus," said Imasu, and he sounded truly angry. Magnus

wondered how many times when Magnus had thought they were simply arguing, Imasu had been leading up to this moment of parting. "This is exactly what I was talking about!"

"You're quite wrong, you know. I am the most permanent person that you will ever meet," said Magnus, his voice breathless with laughter and his eyes stung a little by tears. "It is only that it never makes any difference."

It was the truest thing he had ever told Imasu, and he never told him any more truth than that.

Warlocks lived forever, which meant they saw the intimate, terrible cycle of birth, life, and death over and over again. It also meant that they had all been witness to literally millions of failed relationships.

"It's for the best," Magnus informed Ragnor and Catarina solemnly, raising his voice to be heard above the sounds of yet another festival.

"Of course," murmured Catarina, who was a good and loyal friend.

"I'm surprised it even lasted this long; he was much better looking than you," mumbled Ragnor, who deserved a cruel and terrible fate.

"I'm only two hundred years old," said Magnus, ignoring his friends' mutual snort at the lie. "I can't settle down yet. I need more time to devote myself to debauchery. And I think—" He finished his drink and looked speculatively around. "I think I am going to ask that charming young lady over there to dance."

The girl he was eyeing, he noted, was eyeing him back. She had lashes so long they were almost sweeping her shoulders.

It was possible Magnus was a little bit drunk. *Chicha de molle* was famous for both its swift effects and the horrible hangovers that followed.

Ragnor twitched violently and made a sound like a cat whose tail has been stepped on. "Magnus, please, no. The music was bad enough!"

"Magnus is not as bad at dancing as he is at the *charango*," Catarina remarked thoughtfully. "Actually, he dances quite well. Albeit with a certain, er, unique and characteristic flair."

"I do not feel even slightly reassured," Ragnor said. "Neither of you are reassuring people."

After a brief heated interlude, Magnus returned to the table breathing slightly hard. He saw that Ragnor had decided to amuse himself by hitting his own forehead repeatedly against the tabletop.

"What did you think you were doing?" Ragnor demanded between gloomy thumps.

Catarina contributed, "The dance is a beautiful, traditional dance called El Alcatraz, and I thought Magnus performed it—"

"Brilliantly," Magnus suggested. "Dashingly? Devastatingly attractively? Nimbly?"

Catarina pursed her lips in thought before selecting the appropriate word. "Spectacularly."

Magnus pointed at her. "That's why you're my favorite."

"And traditionally the man gyrates—"

"You did gyrate spectacularly," Ragnor observed in a sour voice.

Magnus made a little bow. "Why, thank you."

"—and attempts to set fire to his partner's skirts with a candle," Catarina continued. "It's a wonderful, vibrant, and rather gorgeous dance."

"Oh, 'attempts,' is it?" Ragnor asked. "So it is not traditional for someone to utilize magic, actually set the woman's skirts and his own ostentatious coat on fire, and keep dancing even though both the dance partners involved are now actually spinning towers of flame?"

Catarina coughed. "Not strictly traditional, no."

"It was all under control," Magnus declared loftily. "Have a little faith in my magic fingers."

Even the girl he'd danced with had thought it was some marvelous trick. She had been enveloped in real, bright fire and she had tipped back her head and laughed, the tumble of her black hair becoming a crackling waterfall of light, the heels of her shoes striking sparks like glittering leaping dust all over the floor, her skirt trailing flame as if he were following a phoenix tail. Magnus had spun and swung with her, and she'd thought he was marvelous for a single moment of bright illusion.

But, like love, fire didn't last.

"Do you think that eventually our kind becomes far enough removed from humanity that we transform into creatures that are untouchable and unlovable by humanity?" Magnus asked.

Ragnor and Catarina stared at him.

"Don't answer that," Magnus told them. "That sounded like the question of a man who doesn't need answers. That sounded like the question of a man who needs another drink. Here we go!"

He lifted a glass. Ragnor and Catarina did not join him, but Magnus was happy to make the toast on his own.

"To adventure," he said, and drank.

Magnus opened his eyes and saw brilliant light, felt hot air drag across his skin like a knife scraping across burned bread. His whole brain throbbed and he was promptly, violently sick.

Catarina offered him a bowl. She was a muddle of white and blue in his blurred vision.

"Where am I?" Magnus croaked.

"Nazca."

So Magnus was still in Peru. That indicated that he had been rather more sensible than he'd feared.

"Oh, so we went on a little trip."

"You broke into a man's house," Catarina said. "You stole a carpet and enchanted it to fly. Then you sped off into the night air. We pursued you on foot."

"Ah," said Magnus.

"You were shouting some things."

"What things?"

"I prefer not to repeat them," Catarina said. She was a weary shade of blue. "I also prefer not to remember the time we spent in the desert. It is a mammoth desert, Magnus. Ordinary deserts are quite large. Mammoth deserts are so called because they are larger than ordinary deserts."

"Thank you for that interesting and enlightening information," Magnus croaked, and tried to bury his face in his pillow, like an ostrich trying to bury its head in the sand of a mammoth desert. "It was kind of you both to follow me. I'm sure I was pleased to see you," he offered weakly, hoping that this would lead to Catarina's bringing him more liquids and perhaps a hammer with which he could smash in his skull.

Magnus felt too weak to move in quest of a liquid, himself. Healing magic had never been his specialty, but he was almost certain that moving would cause his head to topple from his shoulders. He could not allow that to happen. He had confirmation from many witnesses that his head looked superb where it was.

"You told us to leave you in the desert, because you planned to start a new life as a cactus," Catarina said, her voice flat. "Then you conjured up tiny needles and threw them at us. With pinpoint accuracy."

Magnus chanced another look up at her. She was still very blurry. Magnus thought this was unkind. He'd believed they were friends.

"Well," he said with dignity. "Considering my highly intoxicated state, you must have been impressed with my aim."

"'Impressed' is not the word to use to describe how I felt last night, Magnus."

"I thank you for stopping me there," Magnus said. "It was for the best. You are a true friend. No harm done. Let's say no more about it. Could you possibly fetch me—"

"Oh, we couldn't stop you," Catarina interrupted. "We tried, but you giggled, leaped onto the carpet, and flew away again. You kept saying that you wanted to go to Moquegua."

Magnus really did not feel at all well. His stomach was sinking and his head was spinning.

"What did I do in Moquegua?"

"You never got there," Catarina said. "But you were flying about and yelling and trying to, ahem, write messages for us with your carpet in the sky."

Magnus had a sudden vivid memory, wind and stars in his hair, of the things he had been trying to write. Fortunately, he didn't think Ragnor or Catarina spoke the language he had been writing in.

"We then stopped for a meal," Catarina said. "You were

most insistent that we try a local specialty that you called *cuy*. We actually had a very pleasant meal, even though you were still very drunk."

"I'm sure I must have been sobering up at that point," Magnus argued.

"Magnus, you were trying to flirt with your own plate."

"I'm a very open-minded sort of fellow!"

"Ragnor is not," Catarina said. "When he found out that you were feeding us guinea pigs, he hit you over the head with your plate. It broke."

"So ended our love," Magnus said. "Ah, well. It would never have worked between me and the plate anyway. I'm sure the food did me good, Catarina, and you were very good to feed me and put me to bed—"

Catarina shook her head. She seemed to be enjoying this, like a nightmare nurse telling a child she did not especially like a terrifying bedtime story. "You fell down on the floor. Honestly, we thought it best to leave you sleeping on the ground. We thought you would remain there for some time, but we took our eyes off you for one minute, and then you scuttled off. Ragnor claims he saw you making for the carpet, crawling like a huge demented crab."

Magnus refused to believe he had done any such thing. Ragnor was not to be trusted.

"I believe him," Catarina said treacherously. "You were having a great deal of difficulty walking upright even before you were hit with the plate. Also, I believe the food did not do you much good at all, because then you flew all over the place exclaiming that you could see great big monkeys and birds and llamas and kitty cats drawn on the ground."

"Gracious," Magnus said. "I progressed to full hallucinations? It's official. That sounds like . . . almost the most drunk I have ever been. Please don't ask questions about the most drunk I have ever been. It's a very sad story involving a birdcage."

"You were not hallucinating, actually," Catarina said. "Once we stood on the hills yelling 'Get down, you idiot,' we could see the vast drawings in the ground as well. They're very grand and beautiful. I think they were part of an ancient ritual to summon water from the earth. Seeing them at all was worth coming to this country."

Magnus still had his head sunk deep in the pillow, but he preened slightly.

"Always happy to enrich your life, Catarina."

"It was not grand or beautiful," Catarina said reminiscently, "when you were sick all over those mystical and immense designs from a civilization long gone by. From a height. Continuously."

He briefly felt regret and shame. Then he mostly felt the urge to get sick again.

Later, when he was soberer, Magnus would go to see the Nazca Lines, and commit to memory the trenches where gravel had been cut away to show naked clay in sprawling, specific patterns: a bird with its wings outstretched in soaring flight, a monkey with a tail whose curves Magnus thought positively indecent—obviously, he approved—and a shape that might have been a man.

When scientists discovered and spent the 1930s and 1940s investigating the Nazca Lines, Magnus was a little annoyed, as if shapes scored in stone were his own personal property.

But then he accepted it. That was what humans did: They

left one another messages through time, pressed between pages or carved into rock. Like reaching out a hand through time, and trusting in a phantom hoped-for hand to catch yours. Humans did not live forever. They could only hope what they made would endure.

Magnus supposed he could let the humans pass their message on.

But his acceptance came much, much later. Magnus had other things to do the day after he first saw the Nazca Lines. He had to be sick thirty-seven times.

After the thirtieth time Magnus was ill, Catarina became concerned.

"I really think you might have a fever."

"I have told you again and again that I am most vilely unwell, yes," Magnus said coldly. "Probably dying, not that either of you ingrates will care."

"Shouldn't have had the guinea pig," said Ragnor, and he cackled. He seemed to be bearing a grudge.

"I feel far too faint to help myself," Magnus said, turning to the person who cared for him and did not take unholy joy in his suffering. He did his best to look pathetic and suspected that right now his best was really excellent. "Catarina, would you—"

"I'm not going to waste magic and energy that could save lives to cure the ill effects of a night spent drinking excessively and spinning at high altitudes!"

When Catarina looked stern, it was all over. It would be more use to throw himself on Ragnor's tender green mercies.

Magnus was just about to try that when Catarina announced

thoughtfully, "I think it would be best if we tried out some of the local mundane medicines."

The way mundanes in this part of Peru practiced medicine, it appeared, was to rub a guinea pig all over the afflicted sufferer's body.

"I demand that you stop this!" Magnus protested. "I am a warlock and I can heal myself, and also I can blast your head clean off!"

"Oh, no. He's delirious, he's crazed, don't listen to him," Ragnor said. "Continue applying the guinea pig!"

The lady with the guinea pigs gave them all an unimpressed look and continued to go about her guinea pig business.

"Lie back, Magnus," said Catarina, who was extremely open-minded and always interested in exploring other fields of medicine, and apparently willing to have Magnus serve as a hapless pawn in her medical game. "Let the magic of the guinea pig flow through you."

"Yes indeed," put in Ragnor, who was not very open-minded at all, and giggled.

Magnus did not find the whole process as inherently hilarious as Ragnor did. As a child he'd taken *djamu* many times. There was bile of goat in that (if you were lucky—bile of alligator if you weren't). And guinea pigs and *djamu* were both better than the bloodletting someone had tried on him in England once.

It was just that he generally found mundane medicine very trying, and he wished they would wait until he felt better to inflict these medical procedures on him.

Magnus tried to escape several times, and had to be forcibly restrained. Later Catarina and Ragnor liked to act out the time he tried to take the guinea pigs with him, reportedly shouting "Freedom!" and "I am your leader now."

There was a distinct possibility that Magnus was still a tiny bit drunk.

At the end of the whole horrific ordeal, one of the guinea pigs was cut open and its entrails examined to see if the cure had been effected. At the sight of it Magnus was promptly sick again.

Some days later in Lima, after all the trauma and guinea pigs, Catarina and Ragnor finally trusted Magnus enough to let him have one—just one, and they were watching him insultingly closely—drink.

"What you were saying before, on That Night," said Catarina.

Catarina and Ragnor both called it that, and in both cases Magnus could hear them using the capitals for emphasis.

"Don't fret," Magnus said airily. "I no longer want to go be a cactus and live in the desert."

Catarina blinked and winced, visibly having a flashback. "Not what I was referring to, but good to know. I meant about humans, and love."

Magnus did not particularly want to think about whatever he had been babbling piteously about on the night when he'd gotten his heart broken. There was no point in wallowing. Magnus refused to wallow. Wallowing was for elephants, depressing people, and depressing elephants.

Catarina continued despite the lack of encouragement. "I was born this color. I did not know how to wear a glamour as a newborn. There was no way to look like anything but what I was then, all the time, even though it was not safe. My mother saw me and knew what I was, but she hid me from the world. She raised me in secret. She did everything she could to keep me safe. A great wrong was done to her, and she gave back love. Every human I heal, I heal in her name. I do what I do to honor her, and to know that when she saved my life she saved countless lives through the centuries."

She turned a wide, serious gaze to Ragnor, who was sitting at the table and looking at his hands uncomfortably, but who responded to the cue.

"My parents thought I was a faerie child or something, I think," Ragnor said. "Because I was the color of springtime, my mother used to say," he added, and blushed emerald. "Obviously it all came out as a bit more complicated than that, but by then they'd gotten fond of me. They were always fond of me, even though I was unsettling to have around the place, and Mother told me that I was grouchy as a baby. I outgrew that, of course."

A polite silence followed this statement.

A faerie child would be easier to accept, Magnus thought, than that demons had tricked or hurt a woman—or, more rarely, a man—and now there was a marked child to remind the parent of their pain. Warlocks were always born from that, from pain and demons.

"It is something to remember, if we feel distant from humans," Catarina said. "We owe a great deal to human love. We live forever by the grace of human love, which rocked strange children in their cradles and did not despair and did not turn away. I know which side of my heritage my soul comes from."

They were sitting outside their house, in a garden surrounded by high walls, but Catarina was always the most cautious of them all. She looked around in the dark before she lit the candle on the table, light springing from nothing between her cupped hands and turning her white hair to silk and pearls. In the sudden light Magnus could see her smile.

"Our fathers were demons," said Catarina. "Our mothers were heroes."

That was true, of course, for them.

Most warlocks were born wearing unmistakable signs of what they were, and some warlock children died young because their parents abandoned or killed what they saw as unnatural creatures. Some were raised as Catarina and Ragnor had been, in love that was greater than fear.

Magnus's warlock's mark was his eyes, the pupils slit, the color lucent and green-gold at the wrong angles, but these features had not developed immediately. He had not been born with Catarina's blue or Ragnor's green skin, had been born a seemingly human baby with unusual amber eyes. Magnus's mother had not realized his father was a demon for some time, not until she had gone to the cradle one morning and seen her child staring back at her with the eyes of a cat.

She knew, then, what had happened, that whatever had come to her in the night in the shape of her husband had not been her husband. When she had realized that, she had not wanted to go on living.

And she hadn't.

Magnus did not know if she had been a hero or not. He had not been old enough to know about her life, or fully comprehend her pain. He could not be sure in the way Ragnor and Catarina looked sure. He did not know if, when his mother knew the truth, she had still loved him or if all love had been blotted out by darkness. A darkness greater than the one known by his friends' mothers, for Magnus's father was no ordinary demon.

"And I saw Satan fall," Magnus murmured into his drink, "like lightning from Heaven."

Catarina turned to him. "What was that?"

"Rejoice that your names are written in Heaven, my dear," said Magnus. "I am so touched that I laugh and have another drink so that I may not weep."

After that he took another walk outside.

He remembered now why he had told them, on that dark drunken night, that he wanted to go to Moquegua. Magnus had been to that town only once before, and had not stayed long.

Moquegua meant "quiet place" in Quechua, and that was exactly what the town was, and exactly why Magnus had felt uneasy there. The peaceful cobbled streets, the plaza with its wrought-iron fountain where children played, were not for him.

Magnus's life philosophy was to keep moving, and in places like Moquegua he understood why it was necessary to keep moving. If he did not, someone might see him as he really was. Not that he thought he was so very dreadful, but there was still that voice in his head like a warning: *Keep in bright constant motion, or the whole illusion will collapse in on itself.*

Magnus remembered lying in the silver sand of the night desert and thinking of quiet places where he did not belong, and how sometimes he believed, as he believed in the passage of time and the joy of living and the absolute merciless unfairness of fate, that there was no quiet place in the world for him, and never would be. *Thou shalt not tempt the Lord thy God.*

Nor was it wise to tempt angels, even of the fallen sort.

He shook the memory off. Even if that were true, there would always be another adventure.

You might think that Magnus's spectacular night of drunken debauchery and countless crimes must be the reason he was banned from Peru, but that is not in fact the case. Amazingly, Magnus was allowed back into Peru. Many years later he went back, this time alone, and he did indeed find another adventure.

1962

Magnus was strolling through the streets of Cuzco, past the convent of La Merced and down the Calle Mantas, when he heard the man's voice. The first thing he noticed was how nasal said voice was. The next thing he noticed was that he was speaking English.

"I don't care what you say, Kitty. I maintain that we could have gotten a bus to Machu Picchu."

"Geoffrey, there are no buses to Machu Picchu from New York."

"Well, really," said Geoffrey after a pause. "If the National Geographic Society is going to put the wretched place in their paper, they might at least have arranged a bus."

Magnus was able to spot them then, wending their way through the arches that lined the street once you were past the bell tower. Geoffrey had the nose of a man who never shut up. It was peeling in the hot sun and arid air, and the once-crisp edges of his white trousers were wilting like a sad, dying flower.

"Another thing here is the natives," said Geoffrey. "I had

hoped we could get some decent pictures. I expected them to be so much more colorful, don't you know?"

"It's almost as if they are not here for your entertainment," said Magnus in Spanish.

Kitty turned around at the sound, and Magnus saw a small mocking face and red hair curling underneath the brim of a very large straw hat. Her lips were curling too.

Geoffrey turned when she turned.

"Oh, well spotted, old girl," he said. "Now, he's what I call colorful."

That much was true. Magnus was wearing more than a dozen scarves all in different colors and carefully arrayed to swirl about him like a fantastic rainbow. He was not too impressed by Geoffrey's powers of observation, however, since Geoffrey was apparently unable to imagine that anyone with brown skin could possibly be a visitor like himself.

"I say, fellow, do you want to have your picture taken?" asked Geoffrey.

"You're an idiot," Magnus told him, smiling brightly.

Magnus was still speaking in Spanish. Kitty choked on a laugh and turned it into a cough.

"Ask him, Kitty!" said Geoffrey, with the air of one prompting a dog to do a trick.

"I apologize for him," she said in halting Spanish.

Magnus smiled and offered his arm with a flourish. Kitty skipped over the flagstones, worn so smooth by time that the stone was like water, and seized his arm.

"Oh, charming, charming. Mother will love to see these shots," said Geoffrey enthusiastically.

"How do you put up with him?" Magnus inquired.

Kitty and Magnus beamed like actors, toothy, ecstatic, and entirely insincere.

"With some difficulty."

"Let me offer an alternate proposition," Magnus said between the locked teeth of his smile. "Run away with me. Right now. It will be the most amazing adventure, I promise you that."

Kitty stared at him. Geoffrey turned around, in quest of someone who could take shots of them all together. Behind Geoffrey's back Magnus saw Kitty begin, slowly and delightedly, to smile.

"Oh, all right. Why not?"

"Excellent," said Magnus.

He spun and seized her hand, and they ran, laughing, together down the sunlit street.

"We'd better go pretty quickly!" Kitty shouted, voice breathless as they rushed. "He's bound to notice soon that I stole his watch."

Magnus blinked. "Pardon?"

There was a noise behind them. It sounded disturbingly like a ruckus. Magnus was, through hardly any fault of his own, somewhat familiar with the sound of the police being summoned and also the sounds of a hot pursuit.

He pulled Kitty into an alleyway. She was still laughing, and undoing the buttons of her blouse.

"It will probably take them a little longer," she murmured, the mother-of-pearl buttons parting enough to show the sudden rich flash of emeralds and rubies, "to realize that I also stole all his mother's jewels."

She gave Magnus a little saucy smile. Magnus burst out laughing.

"Do you con a lot of annoying rich men?"

"And their mothers," said Kitty. "I could probably have taken them for the whole family fortune, or at least the silver, but a handsome man asked me to run away with him, and I thought, *What the hell.*"

The sound of pursuit was closer now.

"You are about to be very glad you did," Magnus told her. "Since you showed me yours, I believe it's only fair I show you mine."

He snapped his fingers, making sure to trail blue sparks to impress the lady. Kitty was clever enough to realize what was going on as soon as one of the first pursuers glanced down the alleyway and ran on.

"They can't see us," she breathed. "You turned us invisible."

Magnus raised his eyebrows and made a gesture of display. "As you see," he said. "And they don't."

Magnus had seen humans shocked and scared and amazed by his power. Kitty flung herself into his arms.

"Tell me, handsome stranger," she said. "How do you feel about a life of magical crime?"

"Sounds like an adventure," said Magnus. "But promise me something. Promise we will always steal from the irritating and spend the cash on booze and useless trinkets."

Kitty pressed a kiss to his mouth. "I swear."

They fell in love, not even for a mortal lifetime but for a mortal summer, a summer of laughing and running and being wanted by the law in several different countries.

In the end Magnus's favorite memory of that summer was an image he had never seen: that last picture on Geoffrey's camera, of a man trailing bright colors and a woman hiding them beneath a white blouse, both smiling because they knew a joke he did not.

Magnus's sudden turn to a life of crime, shockingly enough, was not the reason he was banned from Peru either. The High Council of Peruvian warlocks met in secret, and a letter was sent to Magnus several months later announcing that he had been banned from Peru, on pain of death, for "crimes unspeakable." Despite his inquiries, he never received an answer to the question of what he had been banned for. To this day, whatever it is that actually got him banned from Peru is—and perhaps must always remain—a mystery.

The Runaway Queen

By Cassandra Clare and Maureen Johnson

On the word "Axel," she froze. This was all he needed. He shoved her backward out the window. The balloon, bumped back by the force, shifted a foot or so away from the window—so she landed half in, half out.

—The Runaway Queen

THUMP
THMP
WAK
THUMP
YOUR MAJESTY, YOU MUST STOP. YOU MUST LISTEN TO ME.
AXEL-
gasp
...
PUSH
EEEK!

Paris, June 1791

There was a smell to Paris in the summer mornings that Magnus enjoyed. This was surprising, because on summer mornings Paris smelled of cheese that had sat in the sun all day, and fish and the less desirable parts of fish. It smelled of people and all the things that people produce (this does not refer to art or culture but to the baser things that were dumped out of windows in buckets). But these were punctuated by other odors, and the odors would shift rapidly from street to street, or building to building. That heady whiff of a bakery might be followed by an unexpected flush of gardenias in a garden, which gave way to the iron-rich pong of a slaughterhouse. Paris was nothing if not alive—the Seine pumping along like a great artery, the vessels of the wider streets, narrowing down to the tiniest alleys . . . and every inch of it had a smell.

It all smelled of *life*—life in every form and degree.

The smells today, however, were a bit strong. Magnus was taking an unfamiliar route, one that took him through quite a rough patch of Paris. The road here was not as smooth. It was brutally hot inside his cabriolet as it bumped its way along. Magnus had animated one of his magnificent Chinese fans, and it flapped ineffectively at him, barely stirring the breeze. It was, if he was completely honest with himself (and he did not want to be), a bit too hot for this new striped blue-and-rose-colored coat, made of taffeta and satin, and the silk faille waistcoat embroidered with a scene of birds and cherubs. The wing collar, and the wig, and the silk breeches, the wonderful new gloves in the most delicate lemon yellow . . . it was all a bit *warm*.

Still. If one could look this fabulous, one had an obligation to. One should wear *everything*, or one should wear nothing at all.

He settled back into his seat and accepted the sweat proudly, glad that he lived by his principles, principles which were widely embraced in Paris. In Paris people were always after the latest fashion. Wigs that hit the ceiling and had miniature boats in them; outrageous silks; white paint and high, blushed cheeks on the men and the women; the decorative beauty spots; the tailoring; the colors . . . In Paris one could have the eyes of a cat (as he did) and tell people it was a trick of fashion.

In a world such as this, there was much work for an enterprising warlock. The aristocracy loved a bit of magic and were willing to pay for it. They paid for luck at the faro table. They paid him to make their monkeys speak, to make their birds sing their favorite arias from the opera, to make their diamonds glow in different colors. They wanted beauty spots in the shapes of hearts, champagne glasses, and stars to spontaneously appear on their cheeks. They wanted to dazzle their guests by having fire shoot from their fountains, and then to amuse those same guests by having their chaise longues wander across the room. And their lists of requests for the bedroom—well, he kept careful notes on those. They were nothing if not imaginative.

In short, the people of Paris and the neighboring royal town of Versailles were the most decadent people Magnus had ever met, and for this he revered them deeply.

Of course, the revolution had put a damper on some of this. Magnus was daily reminded of that fact—even now, as he pulled back the blue silk curtains of the carriage. He received a few penetrating looks from the *sans-culottes* pushing their carts or selling their cat meat. Magnus kept apartments in the Marais, on the rue Barbette, quite near the Hôtel de Soubise, home of his old (and recently deceased) friend the Prince of Soubise. Magnus had an open invitation to wander the gardens or entertain himself there anytime he chose. In fact, he could walk into any number of great houses in Paris and be warmly greeted. His aristocratic friends were silly but mostly harmless. But now it was problematic to be seen in their company. Sometimes it was problematic to be seen at all. It was no longer a good thing to be very rich or well connected. The unwashed masses, producers of the stink, had taken over France, overturning everything in their unwashed path.

His feelings about the revolution were mixed. People *were* hungry. The price of bread was still very high. It did not help that the queen, Marie Antoinette, when told that her people could not afford bread, had suggested that they eat cake instead. It was sensible to him that the people should demand and receive food, and firewood, and all the basic needs of life. Magnus always felt for the poor and the wretched. But at the same time, never had there been a society quite as wonderful as that of France at its dizzying heights and excesses. And while he liked excitement, he also liked to have some sense of what was going on, and that feeling was in short supply. No one quite knew who was in charge of the country. The revolutionaries squabbled all the time. The constitution was always being written. The king and queen were alive and supposedly still somewhat in power, but they were controlled by the revolutionaries. Periodically there would be killings, fires, or attacks, all in the name of liberation. Living in Paris was like living in a powder keg that was stacked on top of several other powder kegs, which were in a ship tossing blindly at sea. There was always the feeling that one day the people—the undefined *people*—just might decide to kill everyone who could afford a hat.

Magnus sighed and leaned back out of the range of prying eyes and put a jasmine-scented cloth to his nose. Enough stink and bother. He was off to see a balloon.

Of course, Magnus had flown before. He'd animated carpets and rested upon the backs of migrating flocks of birds. But he'd never flown by a human hand. This ballooning thing was new and, frankly, a little alarming. Just shooting up into the air in a fabulous and garish creation, with the whole of Paris staring at you . . .

This, of course, was why he had to try it.

The hot air balloon craze had largely passed him by when it had first been the rage of Paris, almost ten years before. But just the other day, when Magnus had had perhaps a little too much wine, he'd looked up and seen one of the sky-blue, egg-shaped wonders drifting past, with its gold illustrations of zodiacal signs and fleurs-de-lis, and all at once he'd been overcome with the desire to get into its basket and ride over the city. It had been a whim, and there was nothing Magnus attached more importance to than a whim. He'd managed to track down one of the Montgolfier brothers that very day and had paid far too many *louis d'or* for a private ride.

And now that Magnus was on his way to take said ride on this hot afternoon, he reflected back on just how much wine he had drunk on the afternoon when he had set this all up.

It had been quite a lot of wine.

His carriage finally came to a stop near the Château de la Muette, once a beautiful little palace, now falling apart. Magnus stepped out into the swampy afternoon and walked into the park. There was a heavy, oppressive feel to the air that made Magnus's wonderful clothes hang heavily. He walked along the path until he came to the meeting spot, where his balloon and its crew awaited him. The balloon was deflated on the grass—the silk just as beautiful as ever, but the overall effect not as impressive as he had hoped. He had better dressing gowns, when it came down to it.

One of the Montgolfiers (Magnus could not remember which one he had hired) came rushing up to him with a flushed face.

"Monsieur Bane! *Je suis désolé*, monsieur, but the weather . . . today it will not cooperate. It is most annoying. I have seen a flash of lightning in the distance."

Sure enough, as soon as these words were spoken, there was a distant rumble. And the sky did have a greenish cast.

"Flight is not possible today. Tomorrow, perhaps. Alain! The balloon! Move it at once!"

And with that, the balloon was rolled up and carried to a small gazebo.

Dismayed, Magnus decided to have a turn around the park before the weather deteriorated. One could see the most fetching ladies and gentlemen walking there, and it did seem to be a place that people came to when they were feeling . . . amorous. No longer a private wooded area and park, the Bois de Boulogne was now open to the people, who used the wonderful grounds for growing potatoes for food. They also wore cotton and proudly called themselves *sans-culottes*, meaning "without knee breeches." They wore long, workmanlike pants, and they cast long, judgmental looks at Magnus's own exquisite breeches, which matched the rose-colored stripe in his jacket, and his faintly silver stockings. It really was getting difficult to be wonderful.

Also, the park seemed singularly devoid of handsome, love-struck persons. It was all long trousers and long looks and people mumbling about the latest revolutionary craze. The more noble sorts all looked nervous and turned their gazes to the path whenever a member of the Third Estate walked by.

But Magnus did see someone he knew, and he wasn't happy about it. Coming toward him at great speed was Henri de Polignac, dressed in black and silver. Henri was a darkling of Marcel Saint Cloud's, who was the head of the most powerful clan of vampires in Paris. Henri was also a terrible bore. Most subjugates were. It was hard to have a conversation with someone who was always saying, "Master says this" and "Master says that." Always groveling. Always lingering about, waiting to be bitten. Magnus had to wonder what Henri was doing out in the park during the day—the answer was certainly something bad. Hunting. Recruiting. And now, bothering Magnus.

"Monsieur Bane," he said, with a short bow.

"Henri."

"It's been some time since we've seen you."

"Oh," Magnus said airily. "I've been quite busy. Business, you know. Revolution."

"Of course. But Master was just saying how long it's been since he's seen you. He was wondering if you'd fallen off the face of the earth."

"No, no," Magnus said. "Just keeping busy."

"As is Master," Henri said with a twisted little smile. "You really must come by. Master is having a party on Monday evening. He would be very cross with me if I did not invite you."

"Would he?" Magnus said, swallowing down the slightly bitter taste that had risen in his mouth.

"He would indeed."

One did not turn down an invitation from Saint Cloud. At least, one didn't if one wanted to continue living contentedly in Paris. Vampires took offense *so* easily—and Parisian vampires were the worst of all.

"Of course," Magnus said, delicately peeling one of his lemon-yellow gloves from his hand, simply for something to do. "Of course. I would be delighted. Most delighted."

"I will tell Master you will be in attendance," Henri replied.

The first drops of rain began to fall, landing heavily on Magnus's delicate jacket. At least this allowed him to say his good-byes quickly. As he hurried across the grass, Magnus put up his hand. Blue sparks webbed between his fingers, and instantly the rain no longer struck him. It rolled off an invisible canopy he had conjured just over his head.

Paris. It was problematic sometimes. So political. (Oh, his shoes . . . his shoes! Why had he worn the silk ones with the curled toes today? He had *known* he'd be in a park. But they were new and pretty and by Jacques of the rue des Balais and could not be resisted.) Perhaps it was best, in the current climate, to consider retiring to somewhere simpler. London was always a good retreat. Not as fashionable, but not without its charms. Or he could go to the Alps. . . . Yes, he did love the clean, fresh air. He could frolic through the edelweiss and enjoy the thermal baths of Schinznach-Bad. Or farther afield. It had been too long since he'd been to India, after all. And he could never resist the joys of Peru. . . .

Perhaps it was best to stay in Paris.

He got inside the cabriolet just as the skies truly opened and the rain drummed down so hard on the roof that he could no longer hear his thoughts. The balloon-maker's assistants hurriedly covered the balloon works, and the people scurried for cover under trees. The flowers seemed to brighten in the splash of the rain, and Magnus took a great, deep breath of the Paris air he loved so well.

As they drove off, a potato hit the side of his carriage.

The day, in a very literal sense, appeared to be a wash. There was only one thing for it—a long, cool bath with a cup of hot lapsang souchong. He would bathe by the window and drink in the smoky tea, and watch the rain drench Paris. Then he would recline and read *Le Pied de Fanchette* and Shakespeare for several hours. Then, some violet champagne and an hour or two to dress for the opera.

"Marie!" Magnus called as he entered the house. "Bath!"

He kept as staff an older couple, Marie and Claude. They were extremely good at their jobs, and years of service in Paris had left them completely unsurprised by anything.

Of the many places he had lived, Magnus found his Paris house to be one of the most pleasing abodes. Certainly there were places of greater natural beauty—but Paris had *unnatural* beauty, which was arguably better. Everything in the house gave him pleasure. The silk wallpaper in yellow and rose and silver and blue, the ormolu tables and giltwood armchairs, the clocks and mirrors and porcelains . . . With every step he took farther into the house, to his main salon, he was reminded of the good of the place.

Many Downworlders stayed away from Paris. There were certainly many werewolves in the country, and every wooded glen had its fey. But Paris, it seemed, was the terrain of the vampire. It made sense, in many ways. Vampires were courtly creatures. They were pale and elegant. They enjoyed darkness and pleasure. Their hypnotic gazes—the *encanto*—enchanted many a noble. And there was nothing quite as pleasurable, decadent, and dangerous as letting a vampire drink your blood.

It had all gotten a bit out of hand during the vampire craze of 1787, though. That's when the blood parties had started. That's when all the children had gone missing and some other young people first returned home pale and with the absent look of the subjugate. Like Henri, and his sister, Brigitte. They were the nephew and niece of the Duke de Polignac. Once beloved members of one of the great families of France, they now lived with Saint Cloud and did his bidding. And Saint Cloud's bidding could be a strange thing indeed. Magnus didn't mind a little decadence—but Saint Cloud was evil. Classic, straightforward evil of the most old-fashioned type. The Shadowhunters of the Paris Institute seemed to have little effect on the goings-on, possibly because in Paris there were many places to hide. There were miles of catacombs, and it was extremely easy to snatch someone from the street and drag them below. Saint Cloud had friends in places high and low, and it would have been very difficult to go after him.

Magnus did all he could to avoid the Parisian vampires and the vampires who appeared on the edges of the court at Versailles. No good ever came of an encounter.

But enough of that. Time for the bath, which Marie was already filling. Magnus kept a large tub in his main salon, right by the window, so he could watch the street below as he bathed. When the water was ready, he submerged himself and began reading. An hour or so later he had dropped his book bathside and was watching some clouds pass overhead while absently thinking about the story of Cleopatra dissolving an invaluable pearl in a glass of wine. There was a knock on his chamber door, and Claude entered.

"There is a man here to see you, Monsieur Bane."

Claude understood that in Magnus's business it was not necessary to take names.

"All right," Magnus said with a sigh. "Show him in."

"Will monsieur be receiving his visitor in the bath?"

"Monsieur is considering it," Magnus said, with an even deeper sigh. It was annoying, but professional appearances had to be kept. He stepped out, dripping, and put on a silk dressing gown embroidered on the back with the picture of a peacock. He threw himself petulantly into a chair by the window.

"Claude!" he yelled. "Now! Send him in!"

A moment later the door opened again, and there stood a very attractive man with black hair and blue eyes. He wore clothes of an obviously fine quality. The tailoring was absolutely delicious. This was thc sort of thing Magnus wanted to happen more often. How generous the universe could be, when she wanted to be! After denying him his balloon ride and giving him such an unpleasant encounter with Henri.

"You are Monsieur Magnus Bane," the man said with certainty. Magnus was rarely misidentified. Tall, golden-skinned, cat-eyed men were rare.

"I am," Magnus replied.

Many nobles Magnus had met had the absentminded air of people who had never had to take care of any matters of importance. This man was different. He had a very erect bearing, and a look of purpose. Also, he spoke French with a faint accent, but what kind of accent, Magnus could not immediately place.

"I have come to speak to you on a matter of some urgency. I wouldn't normally . . . I . . ."

Magnus knew this hesitation well. Some people were nervous in the presence of warlocks.

"You are uncomfortable, monsieur," Magnus said with a smile. "Allow me to make you comfortable. I have a great talent in these matters. Please sit. Have some champagne."

"I prefer to stand, monsieur."

"As you wish. But may I have the pleasure of learning your name?" Magnus asked.

"My name is Count Axel von Fersen."

A count! Named Axel! A military man! With black hair and blue eyes! And in a state of distress! Oh, the universe had outdone herself. The universe would be sent flowers.

"Monsieur Bane, I have heard of your talents. I can't say whether I believe what I've heard, but rational, intelligent, sensible people swear to me that you are capable of wonderful things beyond my understanding."

Magnus spread his hands in false modesty.

"It's all true," he said. "As long as it was wonderful."

"They say you can alter a person's appearance by some sort of . . . conjuring trick."

Magnus allowed this insult to pass.

"Monsieur," von Fersen said, "what are your feelings on the revolution?"

"The revolution will happen regardless of my feelings on the matter," Magnus said coolly. "I am not a native son of France, so I do not presume to have opinions on how the nation conducts itself."

"And I am not a son of France either. I am from Sweden. But I do have feelings on this, very strong feelings. . . ."

Magnus liked it when von Fersen talked about his very strong feelings. He liked it very much.

"I come here because I must, and because you are the only person who can help. By coming here today and telling you what I am going to tell you, I put my life in your hands. I also risk lives much more valuable than mine. But I do not do so blindly. I have learned much about you, Monsieur Bane. I know you have many aristocratic friends. I know you have been in Paris for six years, and you are well liked and well known. And you are said to be a man of your word. Are you, monsieur, a man of your word?"

"It really depends upon the word," Magnus said. "There

are so many wonderful words out there . . ."

Magnus silently cursed himself on his poor knowledge of Swedish. He could have added another witty line. He tried to learn seductive phrases in all languages, but the only Swedish he had ever really needed was, "Do you serve anything aside from pickled fish?" and "If you wrap me in furs, I can pretend to be your little fuzzy bear."

Von Fersen visibly steadied himself before speaking again. "I need you to save the king and queen. I need you to preserve the royal family of France."

Well. That was certainly an unexpected turn. As if in reply, the sky darkened again and there was another rumble of thunder.

"I see," Magnus replied after a moment.

"How does that statement make you feel, monsieur?"

"Quite the same as always," Magnus replied, making sure to keep his calm demeanor. "With my hands."

But he felt anything but calm. The peasant women had broken into the palace of Versailles and thrown out the king and queen, who now lived at the Tuileries, that broken-down old palace in the middle of Paris. The people had produced pamphlets detailing the supposed crimes of the royal family. They seemed to focus quite heavily on Queen Marie Antoinette, accusing her of the most terrible things—often sexual. (There was no way possible she could have done all of the things the pamphleteers claimed. The crimes were too gross, too immoral, and far too physically challenging. Magnus himself had never attempted half of them.)

Anything relating to the royal family was bad and dangerous to know.

Which made it as appealing as it was frightening.

"Obviously, monsieur, I've just taken a great risk in saying that much to you."

"I realize that," Magnus said. "But save the royal family? No one has harmed them."

"It is only a matter of time," von Fersen said. His emotion brought a flush to his cheeks that made Magnus's heart flutter a bit. "They are prisoners. Kings and queens who are imprisoned are generally not freed to rule again. No . . . no. It is only a matter of time before the situation grows very dire. It is already intolerable, the conditions under which they are forced to live. The palace is dirty. The servants are cruel and mocking. Every day their possessions and natural entitlements are diminished. I am certain . . . I am quite, quite certain . . . if they are not freed, they shall not live. And I cannot live with that knowledge. When they were dragged from Versailles, I sold everything and followed them to Paris. I will follow them anywhere."

"What is it you want me to do?" Magnus said.

"I am told you can alter a person's appearance through . . . some kind of . . . marvel."

Magnus was happy to accept *that* description of his talents.

"Whatever price you wish, it shall be paid. The royal family of Sweden will also be informed of your great service."

"With all due respect, monsieur," Magnus said, "I do not live in Sweden. I live here. And if I do this . . ."

"If you do this, you do the greatest service to France. And when the family is restored to their proper place, you will be honored as a great hero."

Again, this made little difference. But what did make a difference was von Fersen himself. It was the blue eyes and the dark hair and the passion and the obvious courage. It was the way he stood, tall and strong . . .

"Monsieur, will you stand with us? Do we have your word, monsieur?"

It was also a very bad idea.

It was a terrible idea.

It was the worst idea he had ever heard.

It was irresistible.

"Your word, monsieur," Axel said again.

"You have it," Magnus said.

"Then I will come again tomorrow night and lay the plan out in front of you," von Fersen said. "I will show you what must happen."

"I insist we dine together," Magnus said. "If we are to undertake this great adventure together."

There was a momentary pause, and then Axel gave a sharp nod.

"Yes," he said. "Yes. I agree. We will dine together."

When von Fersen left, Magnus looked at himself in the mirror for a long time, looking for signs of madness. The actual magic involved was very simple. He could easily get himself in and out of the palace and cast a simple glamour. No one would ever know.

He shook his head. This was Paris. Everyone knew everything, somehow.

He took a long sip of the now warm violet champagne and swished it round his mouth. Any logical doubts he had were drowned out by the beating of his heart. It had been so long since he'd felt the rush. In his mind now there was only von Fersen.

* * *

The next night, Magnus had dinner brought in, courtesy of the chef at the Hôtel de Soubise. Magnus's friends permitted his use of the kitchen staff and their excellent foodstuffs when he needed to set an especially fine table. Tonight he had a delicate pigeon bisque, turbot, Rouen duckling with orange, spit-roasted veal, green beans au jus, artichokes, and a table full of cream puffs, fruit, and tiny cakes. The meal was simple enough to arrange—getting dressed, however, was not. Absolutely nothing was right. He needed something that was flirtatious and fetching, yet businesslike and serious. And at first it seemed that the lemon-yellow coat and breeches with the purple waistcoat fit the bill precisely, but these were discarded for the lime-green waistcoat, and then the violet breeches. He settled on an entire ensemble in a simple cerulean blue, but not before he had emptied out the entire contents of his wardrobe.

Waiting was a delicious agony. Magnus could only pace, looking out the window, waiting for von Fersen's carriage to appear. He made countless trips to the mirror, and then to the table Claude and Marie had so carefully laid before he'd sent them away for the evening. Axel had insisted on privacy, and Magnus was happy to oblige.

At precisely eight o'clock a carriage stopped in front of Magnus's door, and out he stepped. Axel. He even looked up, as if he knew that Magnus would be looking down, waiting for him. He smiled a greeting, and Magnus felt a pleasant kind of sickness, a panic. . . .

He hurried down the steps to admit Axel himself.

"I've dismissed my staff for the evening, as you asked," he said, trying to regain his composure. "Do come in. Our dinner is ready for us. You'll excuse the informality of my service."

"Of course, monsieur," Axel said.

But Axel did not linger over his food, or allow himself the pleasures of sipping his wine and taking in Magnus's charms. He launched right into the business at hand. He even had maps, which he unrolled on the sofa.

"The escape plan has been developed over several months," he said, picking an artichoke from a silver dish. "By me, some friends of the cause, and the queen herself."

"And the king?" Magnus asked.

"His Majesty has . . . removed himself from the situation somewhat. He is very despondent over the state of things. Her Majesty has assumed much responsibility."

"You seem to be very . . . fond of Her Majesty," Magnus noted carefully.

"She is to be admired," Axel said, dabbing at his lips with his napkin.

"And clearly she trusts you. You must be very close."

"She has graciously allowed me into her confidence."

Magnus could read between the lines. Axel didn't kiss and tell, which made him only more attractive.

"The escape is to be made on Sunday," Alex went on. "The plan is simple, but exacting. We have arranged it so the guards have seen certain people leaving by certain exits at certain times. On the night of the escape, we will substitute the family for these people. The children will be woken at ten thirty. The dauphin will be dressed as a young girl. He and his sister will be removed from the palace by the royal governess, the Marquise de Tourzel, and will walk to meet me at the Grand Carrousel. I will be driving the traveling carriage. We will then wait for Madame Elisabeth, sister of the king. She shall leave by the same door as the children. When His Majesty finishes his *coucher* for the evening and is left alone, he will leave as well, disguised as the Chevalier de Coigny. Her Majesty . . . will escape last."

"Marie Antoinette will leave *last*?"

"It was her decision," von Fersen said quickly. "She is extremely courageous. She demands to go last. If the others are discovered missing, she wishes to sacrifice herself in order to aid their escape."

There was that frisson of passion in his voice again. But this time when he looked at Magnus, his gaze stayed there for a moment, fixed on the catlike pupils.

"So why do you want only the queen glamoured?"

"Partially it has to do with timing," Axel said. "The order in which people must be seen coming and going. His Majesty will be with people right up until his *coucher*, and he departs instantly after that. Only Her Majesty will be alone in the palace for some time. She is also more recognizable."

"Than the king?"

"But of course! His Majesty is not . . . a handsome man. Gazes do not linger on his face. What people recognize are his clothes, and carriage, all the external signs of his royal status. But Her Majesty . . . her face is known. Her face is studied and drawn and painted. Her style is copied. She is beautiful, and her face has been committed to many a memory."

"I see," Magnus said, wanting to move away from the subject of the queen's beauty. "And what will happen to you?"

"I will drive the carriage as far as Bondy," he said, his gaze still fixed on Magnus. He continued to list details—troop movements, stations to change the horses, things of that nature. Magnus had no interest in these details. They could not hold his attention like the way the elegant ruff of shirt fabric brushed Axel's chin as he spoke. The heavy plumpness of his lower lip. No king or queen or palace or work of art had anything that could compare with that lower lip.

"As for your payment . . ."

These words drew Magnus back in.

"The matter of payment is quite simple," Magnus said. "I require no money—"

"Monsieur," Axel said, leaning forward, "you do this as a true patriot of France!"

"I do this," Magnus continued calmly, "to develop our friendship. I ask only to see you again when the thing is done."

"To see me?"

"To see you, monsieur."

Axel's shoulders drew back a bit, and he looked down at his plate. For a moment Magnus thought it was all for nothing, that he had made the wrong move. But then Axel looked back up, and the candlelight flickered in his blue eyes.

"Monsieur," he said, taking Magnus's hand across the table, "we shall be the closest of friends evermore."

This was precisely what Magnus wanted to hear.

On Sunday morning, the day of the escape, Magnus woke to the usual clamor of church bells ringing all over Paris. His head was a bit thick and clouded from a long evening with the Count de —— and a group of actors from the Comédie-Italienne. It seemed that during the night he had also acquired a monkey. It sat on the footboard of his bed, happily eating Magnus's morning bread. It had already tipped over the pot of tea that Claude had brought in, and there was a pile of shredded ostrich feathers in the middle of the floor.

"Hello," Magnus said to the monkey.

The monkey did not reply.

"I shall call you Ragnor," Magnus added, leaning back against the pillows gently. "Claude!"

The door opened, and Claude came in. He did not appear in the least bit surprised about Ragnor's presence. He just immediately set to work cleaning up the spilled tea.

"I'll need you to get a leash for my monkey, Claude, and also a hat."

"Of course, monsieur."

"Do you think he needs a little coat as well?"

"Perhaps not in this weather, monsieur."

"You're right," Magnus said with a sigh. "Make it a simple dressing gown, just like mine."

"Which one, monsieur?"

"The one in rose and silver."

"An excellent choice, monsieur," Claude said, getting to work on the feathers.

"And take him to the kitchen and get him a proper breakfast, will you? He'll need fruit and water, and perhaps a cool bath."

By this point Ragnor had hopped down from the foot of the bed and was making his way toward an exquisite Sevres porcelain vase, when Claude plucked him up like he'd been monkey-plucking all his life.

"Ah," Claude added, reaching into his coat, "a note came for you this morning."

He made his quiet exit with the monkey. Magnus tore open the note. It read:

There is a problem. It is to be delayed until tomorrow.
—Axel

Well, that was the evening's plans ruined.

Tomorrow was Saint Cloud's party. Both of these obligations needed to be met. But it could be done. He would take his carriage to the edge of the Tuileries palace, attend to the business with the queen, get back into the carriage, and get to the party. He'd had busier nights.

And Axel was worth it.

Magnus spent far more of the next day and evening worrying about Saint Cloud's party than about his business with the royal family. The glamour would be easy. The party would likely be fraught and uncomfortable. All he had to do was put in an appearance, smile, and chat for a bit, and then he could be on his way. But he couldn't escape the feeling that somehow this evening was going to go wrong.

But first, the small matter of the queen.

Magnus took his bath and dressed after dinner, and then quietly left his apartments at nine, instructing his driver to take him to the vicinity of the Tuileries garden and return at midnight. This was a familiar enough trip. Many people went to the garden for a "chance encounter" amongst the topiaries. He walked around for a bit, making his way through the shadowy garden, listening to the snuffling noises of lovers in the shrubbery, occasionally peeking through the leaves to have a little look.

At ten thirty he made his way, by following Axel's map, to the outside of the apartments of the long-departed Duc de Villequier. If all went to plan, the young princess and dauphin would be exiting those unguarded doors soon, with the dauphin disguised as a little girl. If they did not exit, the plan was already foiled.

But only a few minutes later than expected, the children came out with their nurses, all in the disguises. Magnus followed them quietly as they walked through the north-facing courtyard, down the rue de l'Échelle, and to the Grand Carrousel. And there, with a plain carriage, was Axel. He was dressed as a rough Parisian coachman. He was even smoking a pipe and making jokes, all in a perfect low Paris accent, all traces of his Swedishness gone. There was Axel in the moonlight, lifting the children into the carriage— Magnus was struck speechless for a moment. Axel's bravery, his talent, his gentleness . . . it tugged on Magnus's heart in a way that was slightly unfamiliar, and it made it very difficult to be cynical.

He watched them drive away, and then returned to his task. He would enter through that same door. Even though the door was unguarded, Magnus needed his glamour to protect him, so that anyone looking over would see only a large cat sneaking into the palace through a door that seemed to blow open.

With thousands of people coming in and out—and no royal staff of hundreds of cleaners—the floors were grimy, with clumps of dried mud and footprints. There was a musty smell about the place, a mix of damp, smoke, mold, and a few unemptied chamber pots, some of which sat in the halls. There was no light, save what was reflected from windows, off mirrors, and weakly amplified with crystal chandeliers that were thick with spiderwebs and dimmed by soot.

Axel had given Magnus a hand-drawn map with very clear instructions on how to get through the seemingly endless series of arches and largely empty grand rooms, their gilded furnishings either absent or having been roughly appropriated by guards. There were a few secret doors hidden in the paneling, which Magnus quietly passed through. As he went deeper into the palace, the rooms grew a bit cleaner, the candles a bit more frequent. There were smells of cooking food and pipe smoke and more people passing by.

And then he arrived at the royal chambers. At the door he'd been instructed to enter, a guard sat by, idly whistling and kicking back on his chair. Magnus sent up a small spark in the corner of the room, and the guard got up to examine it. Magnus slipped the key into the lock and entered. These rooms had a velvety silence about them that felt unnatural and uncomfortable. He smelled smoke from a recently extinguished candle. Magnus was not cowed by royalty, but his heart began to beat a bit more quickly as he reached for the second key Axel had given him. Axel had a key to the queen's private rooms. The fact was both exciting and unsettling.

And there she was—Queen Marie Antoinette. He'd seen her image many times, but now she was in front of him, and altogether human. That was the shock of it. The queen was a human, in her sleeping dress. There was a loveliness about her. One part, no doubt, was simply the training she had had—her regal bearing and small, delicate footsteps. The pictures had never done justice to her eyes, though, which were large and luminous. Her hair had been carefully coiffed in a halo of light curls, over which she wore a light linen cap. Magnus remained in the shadows and watched her pace her room, going from bed to window and back to bed again, clearly terrified about the fate of her family.

"You notice nothing, madame," he said quietly. The queen turned as he said this and looked at the corner of the room in confusion, then returned to her pacing. Magnus drew closer, and as he did so, he could see how the strain of things had taken its toll on the woman. Her hair was thin, and pale, turning brittle and gray at points. Still, her face had a fierce, determined glow that Magnus quite admired. He could see why Axel felt for her—there was a strength there he never would have expected.

He wiggled his fingers, and blue flames crackled between them. Again the queen turned in confusion. Magnus passed his hand by her face, changing her visage from the familiar and royal to the familiar and ordinary. Her eyes diminished in size and grew dark, her cheeks became plumper and heavily flushed with red, her nose increased in size, and her chin receded. Her hair became more limp and darkened to a chestnut brown. He went a little further than was absolutely necessary, even altering her cheekbones and ears a bit until no one could mistake the woman in front of him for the queen. She looked as she was supposed to look—like a Russian noblewoman of a different age, a different life altogether.

He created a noise near the window to draw her attention away, and when her back was turned, he exited. He left the palace through a heavily trafficked exit behind the royal apartments, where the queen kept a gate open for Axel's nightly entrances and exits.

It was altogether simple and elegant, and a good night's work. Magnus smiled to himself, looked up at the moon hanging over Paris, and thought of Axel, driving around in his coach. Then he thought of Axel doing other things. And then he hurried on. There were vampires to see.

It was a fortunate thing that vampire parties always started so late. Magnus's carriage drew up to Saint Cloud's door after midnight. The footmen, all vampires, helped him from his carriage, and Henri greeted him by the door.

"Monsieur Bane," he said, with his creepy little smile. "Master will be so very pleased."

"I'm so glad," Magnus said, barely concealing his sarcasm. Henri's eyebrow flicked just a bit. Then he turned and put his arm out to a girl of similar age and appearance—blond, glassy-eyed, dull of expression, and very beautiful.

"You know my sister, Brigitte?"

"Of course. We've met several times, mademoiselle, in your . . . previous life."

"My previous life," Brigitte said with a little, tinkling laugh. "My previous life."

Brigitte's previous life was an idea that continued to entertain her, as she kept giggling and smiling to herself. Henri put his arm around her in a way that was not entirely brotherly.

"Master has very generously allowed us to keep our names," he said. "And I was most pleased when he permitted me to return to my former home and bring my sister back here to live. Master is most generous in this way, as he is in all ways."

This caused Brigitte to have another fit of giggles. Henri gave her a playful pat on the bottom.

"I'm absolutely parched," Magnus said. "I think I'll find some champagne."

Unlike the dreary and poorly lit Tuileries, Saint Cloud's house was spectacular. It didn't quite qualify as a palace, in terms of size, but it had all of the opulence of the décor. It was a veritable jungle of patterns, with paintings packed frame to frame up to the ceilings. And all of Saint Cloud's chandeliers sparkled and were full of black candles, dripping black wax onto the floor. The wax was then instantly scraped up by a small army of darklings. A few mundane hangers-on were draped over the furniture, most holding wineglasses—or bottles. Most slumped with their necks exposed, just waiting, begging to be bitten. The vampires stayed on their own side of the room, laughing amongst themselves and pointing, as if choosing what to eat from a table laden with delicacies.

In mundane Parisian society the large powdered wig had recently gone out of fashion, in favor of more natural styles. In vampire society the wigs were bigger than ever. One female vampire wore a wig that was at least six feet high, powdered a light pink, and supported by a delicate latticework of what Magnus suspected was the bones of children. She had a bit of blood at the corner of her mouth, and Magnus could not figure out if the slashes of red on her cheeks were blood or extreme streaks of blush. (Like the wigs, the Paris vampires also favored the slightly passé makeup styles, such as the sharp spots of blush on the cheeks, possibly in mockery of the humans.)

He passed an ashen-faced harpist who had—Magnus noted grimly—been shackled to the floor by his ankle. If he played well enough, he might be kept alive for a while to play again. Or he could be a late-night snack. Magnus was tempted to sever the harpist's chain, but just at that moment there was a voice from above.

"Magnus! Magnus Bane, where have you been?"

Marcel Saint Cloud was leaning over the rail and waving down. Around him, a cluster of vampires peered at Magnus over their fans of feather and ivory and bone.

Saint Cloud was, though it pained Magnus to admit it, strikingly beautiful. The old ones all had a very special look about them—a luster that came with age. And Saint Cloud was old, possibly one of Vlad's very first vampire court. He was not as tall as Magnus, but was very finely boned, with jutting cheekbones and long fingers. His eyes were utterly black, but caught the light like mirrored glass. And his clothes . . . well, he used the same tailor as Magnus, so of course they were wonderful.

"Always busy," Magnus said, managing a smile as Saint Cloud and his cluster of followers descended the steps. They clung to his heels, altering their pace to fall in line with his. Sycophants.

"You've just missed de Sade."

"What a shame," Magnus replied. The Marquis de Sade was a decidedly eerie mundane, with the most perverse imagination Magnus had ever come across since the Spanish Inquisition.

"There are some things I want to show you," Saint Cloud said, putting a cold arm around Magnus's shoulders. "Absolutely wonderful things!"

One thing Saint Cloud and Magnus had in common was a rich appreciation for mundane fashion, furniture, and art. Magnus tended to buy his, or receive them as payment. Marcel traded with the revolutionaries—or with the street people who had raided great houses and taken the pretty things from inside. Or his darklings handed over their possessions. Or things just arrived in his house. It was best not to ask too many questions but simply to admire, and admire loudly. Marcel would take offense if Magnus didn't praise every item.

Suddenly, a chorus of voices from an outside courtyard was calling for Saint Cloud.

"Something seems to be going on," Marcel said. "Perhaps we should investigate."

The voices were high, excited, and giddy—all tones Magnus didn't want to hear at a vampire party. Those tones meant very bad things.

"What is it, my friends?" Marcel said, walking toward the front hall.

There was a tangle of vampires standing at the foot of the front steps, with Henri at the head. A few of them were holding a struggling figure. She made high-pitched squeals from a mouth that sounded covered, though it was impossible to see her in the throng.

"Master . . ." Henri's eyes were wide. "Master, we have found . . . You will not believe, Master . . ."

"Show me. Bring it forward. What is it?"

The vampires ordered themselves a bit and threw the human into the cleared space on the ground. It was all Magnus could do not to make a sound of alarm, or give away anything at all.

It was Marie Antoinette.

Of course, the glamour he had applied did not affect the vampires. The queen was exposed, her face white with shock.

"You . . . ," she said, addressing the crowd in a shaky voice, "what you have done . . . You will—"

Marcel raised a silencing hand, and to Magnus's surprise, the queen stopped speaking.

"Who brought her?" he asked. "How did this happen?"

"It was I, monsieur," said a voice. A dapper vampire named Coselle stepped to the front. "I was on my way here, coming down the rue du Bac, and I absolutely could not believe my eyes. She must have gotten out of the Tuileries. She was just on the street, monsieur, looking panicked and lost."

Of course. The queen would not have been accustomed to being out on the streets on her own. And in the dark it was easy to go the wrong way. She had made a wrong turn and crossed the Seine somehow.

"Madame," Marcel said, walking down the stairs. "Or should I say 'Your Majesty'? Do I have the pleasure of addressing our beloved and most . . . illustrious queen?"

A low snicker from around the room, but aside from that no noise at all.

"I am she," the queen said, rising to her feet. "And I demand—"

Marcel put up his hand again, indicating silence. He descended the rest of the steps and walked to the queen, stood in front of her, and examined her closely. Then he gave a small bow.

"Your Majesty," he said. "I am thrilled beyond words that you could attend my party. We are all thrilled beyond words, are we not, my friends?"

By now, all the vampires who could fit had crowded into the doorway. Those who could not were leaning out of the windows. There were nods and smiles, but no reply. The silence was terrible. Outside Marcel's courtyard wall, even Paris itself seemed to have fallen silent.

"My dear Marcel," Magnus said, forcing a laugh. "I do *hate* to disappoint you, but this is not the queen. This is the mistress of one of my clients. Her name is Josette."

As this statement appeared to be plainly and glaringly false, Marcel and the others remained silent, waiting to hear more. Magnus walked down the steps, trying to look like he was amused by this turn of events.

"She's very good, isn't she?" he said. "I cater to many tastes, much like you. And I happen to have a client who wishes to do to the queen what she has been doing to the French people for many years. I was hired to do a complete transformation. And I must say, at the risk of sounding immodest, that I have done an excellent job of it."

"I have never known you to be modest," Marcel said without a hint of a smile.

"It's an overrated quality," Magnus replied with a shrug.

"Then how do you explain the fact that this woman claims she is, in fact, Queen Marie Antoinette?"

"I am the queen, you monster!" she said, her voice now hysterical. "I am the queen. I am the queen!"

Magnus got the impression that she was saying this not as a way of impressing her captors but as a way of assuring herself of her own identity and sanity. He stepped calmly in front of her and snapped his fingers in front of her face. She fell unconscious at once, slumping gently into his arms. "Why," he said, calmly turning toward Marcel, "would the queen of France be wandering down this street, unattended, in the middle of the night?"

"A fair question."

"Because she wasn't. Josette was. She had to be complete in every way. At first my client wanted her only to look like the queen, but then he insisted on the entire package, as it were. Appearance, personality, all of it. Josette absolutely believes she is Marie Antoinette. In fact, I was doing a bit of work on her in this very regard when she became afeared and escaped from my apartments. Perhaps she followed me here. Sometimes my talents get the better of me."

He set the queen gently on the ground.

"It also appears she has a light glamour on her," Marcel added.

"For mundanes," Magnus said. "You can't have a woman who looks exactly like the queen passing through the streets. It's quite a light one, like a summer shawl. She was not supposed to leave the house. I was still working."

Marcel squatted down and took the queen's face in his hand, turning it from side to side, sometimes looking at the face itself, sometimes at the neck. A long minute or two passed in which the entire assembled group waited for his next utterance.

"Well," Marcel said at last, standing back up. "I must congratulate you on an excellent piece of work."

Magnus had to brace himself in order that his sigh of relief would not be seen.

"All of my work is excellent, but I accept your congratulations," he said, flicking a careless hand in Marcel's direction.

"A marvel such as this, it would be such a success at one of my gatherings. So I really must insist that you sell her to me."

"Sell her?" Magnus said.

"Yes." Marcel leaned down and traced his finger down the queen's jawline. "Yes, you must. Whatever your client paid you, I'll double it. But I really must have her. Quite stunning. Whatever you like, I will pay."

"But, Marcel . . ."

"Now, now, Magnus." Marcel slowly waggled a finger. "We all have our weaknesses, and our weaknesses must be indulged if they are to flourish. I will have her."

It wouldn't do to imply that this fictional client was more important than Marcel.

Think. He had to *think*. And he knew that Marcel was watching him think."If you insist," Magnus replied. "But, as I said, I was still working. I just had a few finishing touches left to do. She still has a few unfortunate habits left over from her previous life. All of those Versailles mannerisms—there are so many of them—they all had to be stitched in like fine embroidery. And I hadn't yet signed the work. I do like to sign my work."

"How long would this take?"

"Oh, not long at all. I could bring her back tomorrow . . ."

"I would prefer she stayed here. After all, how long does it take you to sign your work?" Marcel asked with a light smile.

"It can take time," Magnus said, responding with his own knowing smile. "I have an exquisite signature."

"While I deal in used goods, I do prefer ones in pristine condition. Don't be long about it. Henri, Charles . . . take Madam upstairs and put her in the blue room. Let Monsieur Bane complete his signature. We are looking forward to seeing the final product shortly."

"Of course," Magnus said.

Slowly he followed the prostrate queen and the darklings back inside.

After Henri and Charles put the queen on the bed, Magnus locked the door and slid a large wardrobe to block it. Then he threw open the shutters. The blue room was a third-floor room, a sheer drop down to the receiving courtyard. That was the only way out.

Magnus allowed himself a few moments of swearing before shaking his head and taking stock of his situation again. He could probably get himself out of this, but to get both himself and the queen . . . *and* to return the queen to Axel . . .

He looked out the window again, to the ground below. Most of the vampires had gone back inside. A few servants and darklings remained to greet the carriages, though. Down would not work, but *up* . . .

Up, in a balloon, for instance.

Magnus was certain of one thing—this work was going to be very difficult. The balloon itself was on the other side of Paris. He reached out with his mind and found what he was looking for. It was rolled up still, in the gazebo in the Bois de Boulogne. He rolled it to the grass, he willed it to inflate, glamoured it invisible, and then he lifted it from the ground. He felt it lift, and he guided it up, over the trees of the park, over the houses and the streets, carefully avoiding the spires of the churches and cathedrals, over the river. It was strongly buoyant and was pulled easily by the wind. It wanted to go straight up into the sky, but Magnus held on.

At some point he would run dry of power, and then he would lose consciousness. He could only hope that this would happen late enough in the process, but there was really no telling. As the balloon drew nearer, he did his best to glamour it completely, making it invisible to even the vampires just below. He watched it come to the window, and as carefully as he could, he guided it close. He leaned out as far as he could and caught hold of it. The basket had a small door, which he managed to get open.

When one steals a flying balloon and animates it to fly over

Paris, one should, ideally, have some idea how said balloon normally works. Magnus had never been interested in the mechanics of the balloon—his only interest was that the mundanes could now fly in a colorful piece of silk. So when he discovered that the basket contained a fire, he was dismayed.

Also, the queen herself was probably not heavy, but her dress—and whatever she had concealed or sewn into the dress for her escape—certainly was, and Magnus had no energy to spare. He snapped his fingers, and the queen woke. Just in time he drew a finger across her lips and silenced the scream that was about to come from her mouth.

"Your Majesty," he said, the exhaustion weighing his voice. "There is no time to explain, and no time for introductions. What I need you to do is—as quickly as possible—step out of that window. You cannot see it, but there is something out there that will catch you. But we must be quick."

The queen opened her mouth and, finding that she could not speak, began to run around the room, picking up objects and hurling them at Magnus. Magnus cringed as vases hit the wall next to him. He managed to lash the balloon to the window with the curtain and grabbed the queen. She began to pummel Magnus. Her fists were small and she was clearly unused to this sort of activity, but her blows were not entirely ineffective. He had very little strength left, and she seemed to be running on raw fear, which quicksilvered her veins.

"Your Majesty," he hissed. "You must stop. You must listen to me. Axel—"

On the word "Axel," she froze. This was all he needed. He shoved her backward out the window. The balloon, bumped back by the force, shifted a foot or so away from the window—so she landed half in, half out. She hung there, terrified and grasping at something she could feel but not see, her slippered feet kicking into the air and smacking into the side of the building. Magnus had to accept a few flurried kicks in the chest and face before he was able to roll her over into the basket. Her skirts tumbled over her head, and the Queen of France was reduced to a pile of cloth and two flailing legs. He jumped into the basket himself, closed the basket door, and released the hold on the basket with a deep sigh. The balloon went straight up, shooting above the rooftops. The queen had managed to flip herself over and scramble to her knees. She touched the basket, her eyes wide with a childlike wonder. She drew herself up slowly and peered over the side of the basket, took one look at the view below, and fainted dead away.

"Someday," Magnus said, looking at the crumpled royal person at his feet, "I must write my memoirs."

This was not the balloon ride Magnus had hoped for.

For a start, the balloon was low and suicidally slow, and seemed to like nothing more than dropping suddenly onto roofs and chimneys. The queen was shifting and groaning on the floor of the basket, causing it to sway back and forth in a nausea-inducing way. An owl made a sudden assault. And the sky was dark, so dark that Magnus had largely no idea where he was going. The queen moaned a bit and lifted her head.

"Who *are* you?" she asked weakly.

"A friend of a friend," Magnus replied.

"What are we—"

"It's best if you don't ask, Your Majesty. You really don't

want the answer. And I think we're being blown south, which is the completely wrong direction."

"Axel . . ."

"Yes." Magnus leaned over and tried to make out the streets below. "Yes, Axel . . . but here's a question . . . If you were trying to find, say, the Seine, where would you look?"

The queen put her head back down.

He managed to find enough strength to restore the glamour on the balloon, rendering it invisible to the mundanes. He did not have the energy to completely glamour himself in the process, so some people were treated to the view of Magnus's upper half sailing past their third-story window in the dark. Some people didn't spare the candles, and he got one or two very interesting views.

Eventually he caught sight of a shop he knew. He pulled the balloon down the street, until more and more looked familiar, and then he caught sight of Notre Dame.

Now the question was . . . where to put the balloon *down?* You couldn't just land a balloon in the middle of Paris. Even an invisible one. Paris was just too . . . spiky.

There was only one thing for it, and Magnus already hated it.

"Your Majesty," he said, prodding the queen with his foot. "Your Majesty, *you must wake up*."

The queen stirred again.

"Now," Magnus said, "you won't like what I am about to say, but trust me when I say it is the best of several terrible alternatives. . . ."

"Axel . . ."

"Yes. Now, in a minute we are going to land in the Seine—"

"What?"

"And it would be very good if you perhaps held your nose. And I'm guessing your dress is full of jewels, so . . ."

The balloon was dropping fast, and the water was coming up. Magnus carefully navigated them to a spot between two bridges.

"You may get—"

The balloon simply dropped like a stone. The fire went out, and the silk immediately came down on Magnus and the queen. Magnus was almost out of strength, but he managed to find enough to rend the silk in two so it didn't trap them. He swam on his own power, pulling her under his arm to the bank. They were, as he'd hoped, quite close to the Tuileries and its dock. He got her over to the steps and threw her down.

"Stay here," he said, dripping wet and panting.

But the queen was unconscious again. Magnus envied her.

He trudged up the steps and back up onto the streets of Paris. Axel would probably have been circling the area. They had agreed that if anything went wrong, Magnus was to send a blue flash into the sky, like a firework. He did it. Then he sank to the ground and waited.

About fifteen minutes later a carriage pulled up—not the simple, plain one from before but a massive one, in black and green and yellow. One that could easily carry half a dozen or more people for several days, in the grandest of possible styles. Axel hopped down from the driver's seat and rushed to Magnus.

"Where is she? Why are you wet? What has happened?"

"She's fine," Magnus said, putting up a hand. "*This* is the carriage? A *berline de voyage?*"

"Yes," von Fersen said. "Their Majesties insist. And it would be unseemly for them to arrive in something less grand."

"And impossible not to be noticed!"

For the first time von Fersen looked uncomfortable. He had clearly hated this idea and had fought it.

"Yes, well . . . this is the carriage. But . . ."

"She's on the steps. We had to land in the river."

"Land?"

"It's a long story," Magnus said. "Let's just say things got complicated. But she is alive."

Axel got to his knees in front of Magnus.

"You will never be forgotten for this," Axel said in a low voice. "France will remember. Sweden will remember."

"I don't care if France or Sweden remembers. I care if you remember."

Magnus was genuinely shocked when it was Axel who instigated the kiss—how sudden it was, how passionate, how all of Paris, and all the vampires, and the Seine and the balloon and everything fell away and it was just the two of them for one moment. One perfect moment.

And it was Magnus who broke it.

"Go," he whispered. "I need you to be safe. Go."

Axel nodded, looking a bit shocked at his own action, and ran to the dock steps. Magnus got up, and with one last look started to walk.

Going home was not an option. Saint Cloud's vampires were probably at his apartments right now. He had to get inside until dawn. He spent the night at the *petite maison* of Madame de ——, one of his more recent lovers. At dawn he returned to his apartments. The front door was ajar. He made his way inside cautiously.

"Claude!" he called, carefully staying in the pool of sunlight by the door. "Marie! Ragnor!"

"They are not here, monsieur," said a voice.

Henri. Of course. He was sitting on the staircase.

"Did you hurt them?"

"We took the ones called Claude and Marie. I don't know who Ragnor is."

"Did you *hurt* them?" Magnus said again.

"They are beyond hurt now. My master asked me to send his compliments. He said they made for excellent feasting."

Magnus felt sick. Marie and Claude had been good to him, and now . . .

"Master would like very much to see you," Henri said. "Why don't we go there together, now, and you can speak when he wakes this evening."

"I think I'll decline the invitation," Magnus said.

"If you do, I think you will find Paris a most inhospitable place to live. And who is that new gentleman of yours? We'll find his name eventually. Do you understand?"

Henri stood, and tried to look menacing, but he was a mundane, a darkling of seventeen.

"What I think, little darkling," Magnus said, stepping closer, "is that you forget who you're dealing with."

Magnus allowed some blue sparks to flick between his fingers. Henri backed up a step.

"Go home and tell your master that I've gotten his message. I have given offense that I did not mean to give. I will leave Paris at once. The matter can be considered closed. I accept my punishment."

He stepped away from the door and extended his arm, indicating that Henri should exit.

* * *

As he'd expected, everything was a shambles—furniture overturned, burn marks up the walls, art missing, books shredded. In his bedchamber wine had been poured onto his bed and his clothes. . . . At least he thought it was wine.

Magnus didn't take long to pick through the wreckage. With the flick of his hand, the marble fireplace moved away from the wall. He retrieved a sack heavy with *louis d'or*, a thick roll of *assignats*, and a collection of wonderful rings in citrine, jade, ruby, and one magnificent blue topaz.

This was his insurance policy, should the revolutionaries have raided his house. Vampires, revolutionaries . . . it was all the same now. The rings went on his fingers, the *assignats* into his coat, and the *louis d'or* into a handsome leather satchel, which had also been stored inside the wall for this very purpose. He reached back farther into the opening and produced one last item—the Gray Book, bound in green velvet. This he carefully placed in the satchel.

He heard a tiny noise behind him, and Ragnor crawled out from under the bed.

"My little friend," Magnus said, picking up the frightened monkey. "At least you survived. Come. We'll go together."

When Magnus heard the news, he was high in the Alps, resting by a stream, crushing some edelweiss under his thumb. Magnus had tried to avoid all things French for weeks—French people, French food, French news. He had given himself over to pork and pounded veal, thermal bathing, and reading. For most of this time he had passed his days alone—with little Ragnor—and in the quiet. But just that morning an escaped nobleman from Dijon had come to stay at the inn where

Magnus was living. He looked like a man who liked to talk at length, and Magnus was in no mood for such company, so he'd gone to sit by the stream. He was not surprised when the man followed him there.

"You! Monsieur!" he called to Magnus as he puffed and huffed up the hillside.

Magnus flicked some edelweiss from his fingernail.

"Yes?"

"The innkeeper says you recently came from Paris, monsieur! Are you my countryman?"

Magnus wore a light glamour at the inn, so he could pass as a random noble French refugee, one of hundreds that were flowing over the border.

"I came from Paris," Magnus said noncommittally.

"And you have a monkey?"

Ragnor was scampering around. He had taken to the Alps extremely well.

"Ah, monsieur, I am so glad to find you! For weeks I have not spoken to anyone from my land." He wrung his hands together. "I hardly know what to think or do these days. Such terrible times! Such horrors! You have heard about the king and queen, no doubt?"

"What about them?" Magnus said, keeping his face impassive.

"Their Majesties, God protect them! They tried to escape Paris! They made it as far as the town of Varennes, where it is said a postal worker recognized the king. They were captured and sent back to Paris. Oh, terrible times!"

Without a word Magnus got up, scooped up Ragnor, and returned to the inn.

* * *

He had not wanted to think of this matter. In his mind Axel and the family had been safe. That was how he'd needed it to be. But now.

He paced his room, and finally wrote a letter to Axel's address in Paris. Then he waited for the reply.

It took three weeks, and came in an unfamiliar hand, from Sweden.

Monsieur,

Axel wishes you to know he is well, and returns the depth of feeling. The King and Queen, as you know, are now imprisoned in Paris. Axel has been moved to Vienna to plead their case to the Emperor, but I fear he is determined to return to Paris, at the risk of his life. Monsieur, as Axel seems to hold you in high esteem, won't you please write to him and discourage this enterprise? He is my beloved brother, and I worry for him constantly.

There was an address in Vienna given, and the note was signed simply "Sophie."

Axel would return to Paris. Of that, Magnus was sure.

Vampires, fey folk, werewolves, Shadowhunters, and demons—these things made sense to Magnus. But the mundane world—it seemed to have no pattern, no form. Their quicksilver politics. Their short lives . . .

Magnus thought once again of the blue-eyed man standing in his parlor. Then he lit a match and burned the note.

Vampires, Scones, and Edmund Herondale

By Cassandra Clare and Sarah Rees Brennan

It was then that the fair-haired Shadowhunter that Magnus had spotted at the Institute somersaulted from the top of a wall and landed gracefully in the street before him.

—Vampires, Scones, and Edmund Herondale

AFTER ALL
ATTRACTIVE AND INTERESTING PERSONS DO NOT SIMPLY DROP OUT OF THE SKY.
!!
DEVASTATING ENSEMBLES MADE ON BOND STREET WITH RED BRO-CADE WAISTCOATS DO NOT SIMPLY DROP OUT OF THE SKY!
I BEG YOUR PARDON?

London, 1857

Ever since the unfortunate events of the French Revolution, Magnus had nursed a slight prejudice against vampires. The undead were always killing one's servants and endangering one's pet monkey. The vampire clan in Paris was still sending Magnus rude messages about their small misunderstanding. Vampires bore a grudge longer than any technically living creatures, and whenever they were in a bad temper, they expressed themselves through murder. Magnus generally wished his companions to be somewhat less—no pun intended—bloodthirsty.

There was also the fact that sometimes vampires committed crimes worse than murder. They committed crimes against fashion. When one was immortal, one tended to forget the passing of time. Still, that was no excuse for wearing a bonnet last fashionable in the era of Napoléon I.

Magnus was beginning, however, to feel as if he might have been a trifle hasty in dismissing *all* vampires.

Lady Camille Belcourt was a terribly charming woman. She was also attired in the absolute height of fashion. Her dress had a darling hoop skirt, and the fall of blue taffeta in seven narrow flounces about her chair made it appear as if she were rising from a cascade of gleaming blue water. There was not very much material at all around her bosom, which was as pale and curved as a pearl. All that broke the perfect pallor of the curve of bosom and the column of neck was a black velvet ribbon and the thick shining ringlets clustered about her face. One gold ringlet was long enough so that it rested in the delicate curve of her collarbone, which led Magnus's eyes back once again to—

Really, all roads led back to Lady Camille's bosom.

It was a wonderfully designed dress. It was also a wonderfully designed bosom.

Lady Camille, as observant as she was beautiful, noticed Magnus noticing, and smiled.

"The marvelous thing about being a creature of the night," she confided in a low voice, "is that one need never wear anything but evening clothes."

"I had never considered that point before," said Magnus, much struck.

"Of course I adore variety, so I do seize any opportunity to change costumes. I find there are many occasions during an adventurous night for a lady to divest herself of her garments." She leaned forward, one pale, smooth elbow resting against the

Shadowhunters' mahogany table. "Something tells me that you are a man who knows something about adventurous nights."

"My lady, with me, every night is an adventure. Pray continue your discourse on fashion," Magnus urged her. "It is one of my favorite subjects."

Lady Camille smiled.

Magnus lowered his voice discreetly. "Or if you choose, pray continue your discourse on disrobing. I believe that is my most favorite subject of all."

They sat side by side at a long table in the Shadowhunters' London Institute. The Consul, a dreary Nephilim heading up the proceedings, was droning on about all the spells they wished warlocks to make available to them at cut-rate prices, and about their notions of proper behavior for vampires and werewolves. Magnus had not heard a single way in which these "Accords" could conceivably benefit Downworlders, but he could certainly see why the Shadowhunters had developed a passionate desire to ratify them.

He began regretting his agreement to make the voyage to London and its Institute so that the Shadowhunters could waste his valuable time. The Consul, who Magnus believed was called Morgwhatsit, seemed passionately in love with his own voice.

Though, actually he had stopped talking.

Magnus glanced away from Camille to find the far less pleasant sight of the Consul—his disapproval writ across his face, as stark as the runes on his skin—staring at him. "If you and the—the vampire woman could cease your flirtation for a moment," he said in acid tones.

"Flirting? We were merely indulging in a little risqué

conversation," Magnus said, offended. "When I begin to flirt, I assure you the entire room will know. My flirtations cause sensations."

Camille laughed. "What a clever rhyme."

Magnus's joke seemed to liberate the restless discontent of all Downworlders at the table.

"What else are we to do but talk amongst ourselves?" asked a werewolf stripling, still young but with the intense green eyes of a fanatic and the thin determined face of a fanatic who was actually competent. His name was Ralf Scott. "We have been here for three hours and have not been given the chance to speak at all. You Nephilim have done all the talking."

"I cannot believe," put in Arabella, a charming mermaid with charmingly placed seashells, "that I swam up the Thames, and consented to be hauled out by pulleys and put in a large glass aquarium, for *this*."

She spoke quite loudly.

Even Morgwhatsit looked taken aback. *Why*, Magnus wanted to know, were Shadowhunter names so long, when warlocks gave themselves elegant family names of one syllable? The long names were sheer self-importance.

"You wretches should be honored to be in the London Institute," snarled a silver-haired Shadowhunter by the name of Starkweather. "I wouldn't allow any of you in my Institute, unless I was carrying one of your filthy heads on a pike. Silence, and let your betters speak for you."

An extremely awkward pause ensued. Starkweather glared around, and his eyes dwelled on Camille, not as if she were a beautiful woman but as if she might be a fine trophy for his wall. Camille's eyes went to her leader and friend, the pale-haired vampire Alexei de Quincey, but he did not respond to her mute appeal. Magnus put out his hand and took hers.

Her skin was cool, but her fingers fit his very neatly. He saw Ralf Scott glance over at them and blanch. He was even younger than Magnus had thought. His eyes were huge and glass green, transparent enough for all his emotions to shine through, in his thin face. They were fixed on Camille.

Interesting, Magnus thought, and filed the observation away.

"These are meant to be peace accords," Scott said, deliberately slowly. "Which means we are all meant to have a chance to have our voices heard. I have heard how peace will benefit Shadowhunters. I wish now to discuss how it will benefit Downworlders. Will we be given seats on the Council?"

Starkweather began to choke. One of the Shadowhunter women stood up hastily. "Gracious, I think my husband was so excited by the chance to deliver a speech that he did not offer refreshments," she said loudly. "I am Amalia Morgenstern." *Oh, that's it,* Magnus thought. *Morgenstern. Awful name.* "And is there anything I can offer you?" the woman continued. "I will ring for the maid in a trice."

"No raw meat for the dog, mind," Starkweather said, and sniggered. Magnus saw another Shadowhunter woman titter silently behind her hand. Ralf Scott sat, pale and still. He had been the moving force behind assembling Downworlders here today, and had been the only werewolf willing to come. Even his own young brother, Woolsey, had stayed away, parting from Ralf on the front steps of the Institute with an insouciant toss of his blond head and a wink at Magnus. (Magnus had thought, *Interesting,* about that, too.)

The faeries had flatly refused to attend, the queen having

set herself against the idea. Magnus was the only warlock who had come, and Ralf had been forced to hunt him down, knowing his connections to the Silent Brothers. Magnus himself had not had high hopes about this attempt to forge a peace with Shadowhunters, but it was a shame to see the boy's airy dreams come to this.

"We are in England, are we not?" asked Magnus, and he bent a charming smile on Amalia Morgenstern, who looked rather flustered. "I would be delighted if we could have some scones."

"Oh, certainly," said Amalia. "With clotted cream, of course."

Magnus gazed upon Camille. "Some of my fondest memories include lashings of cream and beautiful women."

Magnus was enjoying scandalizing the Shadowhunters. Camille rather looked as if she were enjoying it too. Her green eyes were heavy-lidded for a moment with amused satisfaction, as if she were a cat who had already had her fill of cream.

Amalia rang the bell. "While we wait for scones, we can hear the rest of dear Roderick's speech!"

There was an appalled silence, and in the stillness the mutter outside the door rang out, loud and clear.

"Merciful Angel, give me strength to endure. . . ."

Roderick Morgenstern, who Magnus thought truly deserved to have a name that sounded like a goat chewing gravel, stood up happily to continue his speech. Amalia attempted to rise unobtrusively from her seat—Magnus could have told her that hoop skirts and stealth together were a lost cause—and made her way to the door, which she threw open.

Several young Shadowhunters tumbled into the room like puppies falling over one another. Amalia's eyes rounded in comic surprise. "What on earth—"

Despite Shadowhunters having the swiftness of angels, only one managed to land with grace. It was a boy, or rather a young man, who ended his fall on one knee before Amalia, like Romeo proposing to Juliet.

He had hair the color of a coin that was pure gold, no base metal, and the lines of his face were as clean and elegant as a profile etched on one of those princely coins. His shirt had become disarranged at some point during the eavesdropping, the collar pulled open to reveal the edge of a rune drawn on his white skin.

The most remarkable thing about him were his eyes. They were laughing eyes, at once both joyous and tender: they were the radiant pale blue of a sky slipping toward evening in Heaven, when angels who had been sweet all day found themselves tempted to sin.

"I could not bear to be parted from you a moment longer, dear, dearest Mrs. Morgenstern," said the young man, possessing himself of Amalia's hand. "I yearn for you."

He made play with his long golden eyelashes, and Amalia Morgenstern was forthwith reduced to blushes and smiles.

Magnus had always had a decided preference for black hair. It appeared as though fate were determined that he should broaden his horizons. Either that or the blonds of the world had formed some sort of conspiracy to be good-looking all of a sudden.

"Excuse me, Bane?" said Roderick Morgenstern. "Are you attending?"

"I'm so sorry," Magnus said politely. "Somebody incredibly attractive just came into the room, and I ceased to pay attention to a word you were saying."

It was perhaps an ill-judged remark. The Shadowhunter elders, representatives from the Clave, all appeared horrified and dismayed at any Downworlder expressing interest in one of their youths. The Nephilim also had very decided opinions on the subject of inverts and deviant behavior, since as a group their chief occupations were waving large weaponry about and judging everybody they met.

Camille, meanwhile, looked as if she found Magnus even more interesting than she had before. She looked back and forth between him and the young blond Shadowhunter boy, and covered her smile with a gloved hand.

"He *is* delightful," she murmured to Magnus.

Magnus was watching as Amalia shooed out the young Shadowhunters—the blond boy; an older young man with thick brown hair and significant eyebrows; and a dark-eyed, birdlike little girl, barely more than a toddler, who looked over her shoulder and said, "Papa?" in a clear questioning voice to the head of the London Institute, a grave dark man called Granville Fairchild.

"Go, Charlotte. You know your duty," said Fairchild. Duty before all; that was the warrior's way, Magnus reflected. Certainly duty before love.

Little Charlotte, already a dutiful Shadowhunter, trotted obediently away.

Camille's low voice recalled Magnus to attention. "I don't suppose you'd like to share him?"

Magnus smiled back at her. "Not as a meal, no. Was that what you meant?"

Camille laughed. Ralf Scott made an impatient noise, but was shushed by de Quincey, who muttered at him in annoyance;

while over that noise rose the discontented grumblings of Roderick Morgenstern, a man who clearly wished to continue with his speech—and then finally the refreshments arrived, carried in on silver tea trays by a host of maids.

Arabella the mermaid lifted a hand, sloshing energetically in her aquarium.

"If you please," she said. "I would like a scone."

When Morgenstern's interminable speech was finally done, everybody had lost all will to converse and simply wished to go home. Magnus parted from Camille Belcourt with deep reluctance and from the Shadowhunters with deep relief.

It had been some time since Magnus was last in love, and he was beginning to feel the effects. He remembered the glow of love as brighter and the pain of loss as gentler than they had actually been. He found himself looking into many faces for potential love, and seeing many people as shining vessels of possibility. Perhaps this time there would be that indefinable something that sent hungry hearts roving, longing and searching for something, they knew not what, and yet could not give up the quest. Every time a face or a look or a gesture caught Magnus's eye these days, it woke to life a refrain in Magnus's breast, a song in persistent rhythm with his heartbeat. *Perhaps this time, perhaps this one.*

As he walked down Thames Street, he began to plot ways in which to see Camille again. He should pay a call upon the vampire clan in London. He knew de Quincey lived in Kensington.

It was only civil.

"After all," Magnus remarked aloud to himself, swinging

his monkey-headed cane, "attractive and interesting persons do not simply drop out of the sky."

It was then that the fair-haired Shadowhunter that Magnus had spotted at the Institute somersaulted from the top of a wall and landed gracefully in the street before him.

"Devastating ensembles made on Bond Street with red brocade waistcoats do not simply drop out of the sky!" Magnus proclaimed experimentally to the Heavens.

The young man frowned. "I beg your pardon?"

"Oh, nothing, nothing at all," said Magnus. "May I help you? I do not believe I have had the pleasure of making your acquaintance."

The Nephilim stooped and picked up his hat, which had fallen onto the cobblestones when he'd made his leap. He then took it off in order to flourish it in Magnus's direction. The effect of the smile and the eyelashes together was like a small earthquake of attractiveness. Magnus could not blame Amalia Morgenstern for her giggling, even if the boy was far too young for her.

"No fewer than four of my esteemed elders told me I was on no account to ever converse with you, so I vowed that I would know you. My name is Edmund Herondale. May I ask your name? They referred to you only as 'that disgraceful one-warlock show.'"

"I am deeply moved by that tribute," Magnus told Edmund, and made his own bow. "Magnus Bane, at your service."

"Now we are acquainted," Edmund said. "Capital! Do you frequent any low dens of sin and debauchery?"

"Oh, now and then."

"The Morgensterns said you did, while they were throwing

away the plates," Edmund said, with every sign of enthusiasm. "Shall we go?"

Throwing away the plates? It took Magnus a moment to comprehend, and when he did, he felt cold inside. The Shadowhunters had thrown away the very plates Downworlders had touched, afraid their china would be corrupted.

On the other hand, that was not Edmund's fault. The only other place Magnus had to go was the mansion he had perhaps rashly purchased in Grosvenor Square. A recent adventure had caused him to become temporarily wealthy (a state he despised; he usually tried to get rid of his money as soon as he had it), so he had decided to live in style. The *ton* of London were referring to him, he believed, as "Bane the nabob." This meant a great many people in London were anxious to make his acquaintance, and a great many of them seemed tiresome. Edmund, at least, did not.

"Why not?" Magnus decided.

Edmund glowed. "Excellent. Very few people are willing to have real adventures. Haven't you found that out, Bane? Isn't it sad?"

"I have very few rules in life, but one of them is to never decline an adventure. The others are: to avoid becoming romantically entangled with sea creatures; to always ask for what you want, because the worst thing that can happen is embarrassment but the best thing that can happen is nudity; to demand ready money up front; and to never play cards with Catarina Loss."

"What?"

"She cheats," Magnus explained. "Never mind that one."

"I would like to meet a lady who cheats at cards," Edmund

said wistfully. "Aside from Granville's aunt Millicent, who is a terror at piquet."

Magnus had never truly considered that the high-and-mighty Shadowhunters ever played cards, let alone cheated at them. He supposed he had imagined that their leisure activities consisted of weapons training and having discussions about their infinite superiority over everyone else.

Magnus ventured to give Edmund a hint. "Mundane clubs do generally frown upon patrons who have, purely for random example, an abundance of weaponry about their person. So that might be an impediment."

"Absolutely not," Edmund promised him. "Why, I have the most paltry assortment of weapons on me. Only a few miserable daggers, a single stiletto knife, a couple of whips—"

Magnus blinked. "Hardly an armory," he said. "Though, it sounds like a most amusing Saturday."

"Capital!" said Edmund Herondale, apparently taking this for approval of his company on Magnus's excursion. He looked delighted.

White's club, on St. James's Street, had not changed outwardly at all. Magnus regarded the pale stone facade with pleasure: the Greek columns and the arched frames to the higher windows, as if each window were a chapel unto itself; the cast-iron balcony, which bore an intricate swirling pattern that had always made Magnus think of a procession of snail shells; the bow window out of which a famous man had once looked, and bet on a race between raindrops. The club had been established by an Italian, had been the haunt of criminals, and had been the irresistible bane of English aristocrats for more than a hundred years.

Whenever Magnus heard anything described as a "bane," he felt sure he would like it. It was why he had chosen that particular last name for himself, and also why he had joined White's several years before on a flying visit to London, in the main because his friend Catarina Loss had bet him that he could not do it.

Edmund swung around one of the black cast-iron lamps set before the door. The leaping flame behind the glass was dim compared to his eyes.

"This used to be a place where highwaymen drank hot chocolate," Magnus told Edmund carelessly as they walked inside. "The hot chocolate was very good. Being a highwayman is chilly work."

"Did you ever ask someone to stand and deliver?"

"I'll just say this," said Magnus. "I look dashing in a tasteful mask and a large hat."

Edmund laughed again—he had an easy and delighted laugh, like a child. His gaze was roving all over the room, from the ceiling—constructed to look as if they stood in a vast stone barrel—to the chandelier dripping glittering jewels like a duchess; to the green baize-covered tables that clustered on the right side of the room, where men were playing cards and losing fortunes.

Edmund's quality of bright wonder and surprise made him seem younger than he was; it lent a fragile air to his beauty. Magnus did not wonder why he, one of the Nephilim, was not warier of a Downworlder. He doubted Edmund Herondale was wary of anything in life. He was eager to be entertained, ready to be thrilled, essentially trusting of the world.

Edmund pointed to where two men stood, one making an entry in a large book with a defiant flourish of his pen.

"What's afoot there?"

"I presume they are recording a wager. There is a betting book here in White's that is quite celebrated. All sorts of bets are taken—whether a gentleman could manage to ravish a lady in a balloon a thousand feet off the ground, whether a man could live underwater for a day."

Magnus found them a pair of chairs near a fire, and made a gesture indicating that he and his companion were sorely in need of a drink. Their thirst was supplied the next instant. There were advantages to a truly excellent gentlemen's club.

"Do you think one could?" Edmund inquired. "Not live underwater; I know mundanes cannot. The other thing."

"My experiences in a balloon with a lady were not very pleasant," Magnus said, wincing at the memory. Queen Marie Antoinette had been an exciting but not comfortable traveling companion. "I would be disinclined to indulge in carnal delights in a balloon with a lady or a gentleman. No matter how delightful they were."

Edmund Herondale did not seem in the least surprised by the mention of a gentleman in Magnus's romantic speculations.

"It would be a lady in the balloon for me," he said.

"Ah," said Magnus, who had suspected as much.

"But I am always flattered to be admired," said Edmund, with an engaging grin. "And I am always admired."

He said it with that easy smile and another golden flutter of eyelashes, in the same way he had wound Amalia Morgenstern around his finger. It was clear he knew he was outrageous, and he expected people to like it. Magnus suspected they all did.

"Ah, well," Magnus said, giving up the matter gracefully. "Any particular lady?"

"I am not perfectly certain I believe in marriage. Why have just one bonbon when you can have the box?"

Magnus raised his eyebrows and took a swallow of his excellent brandy. The young man had a way with words and the naïve delight of someone who had never had his heart broken.

"No one's ever really hurt you, have they?" said Magnus, who saw no point in beating about the bush.

Edmund looked alarmed. "Why, are you about to?"

"With all those whips on your person? Hardly. I merely meant that you seem like someone who has never had his heart broken."

"I lost my parents as a child," said Edmund candidly. "But rare is the Shadowhunter with an intact family. I was taken in by the Fairchilds and raised in the Institute. Its halls have ever been my home. And if you mean love, then no, my heart has never been broken. Nor do I foresee that it will be."

"Don't you believe in love?"

"Love, marriage, the whole business is extremely overrated. For instance, this chap I know called Benedict Lightwood recently got leg-shackled, and the affair is hideous—"

"Your friends moving forward into a different era of their lives can be difficult," Magnus said sympathetically.

Edmund made a face. "Benedict is not my friend. It's the poor young lady I feel sorry for. The man is peculiar in his habits, if you see what I'm trying to say."

"I don't," Magnus said flatly.

"Bit of a deviant, is what I'm getting at."

Magnus regarded him with a cold air.

"Bad News Benedict, we call him," said Edmund. "Mostly due to his habit of consorting with demons. The more tentacles, the better, if you catch my meaning."

"Oh," Magnus said, enlightened. "I know who you mean. I have a friend from whom he bought some most unusual woodcuts. Also a couple of engravings. Said friend is simply an honest tradesman, and I have never bought anything from him myself, mind you."

"Also Benedict Lightworm. And Bestial Benedict," Edmund continued bitterly. "But he sneaks about while the rest of us get up to honest larks, and the Clave all think that he's superlatively well behaved. Poor Barbara. I'm afraid she acted hastily because of her broken heart."

Magnus leaned back in his chair. "And who broke her heart, might I ask?" he asked, amused.

"Ladies' hearts are like bits of china on a mantelpiece. There are so many of them, and it is so easy to break them without noticing." Edmund shrugged, a little rueful but mostly amused, and then a man in an unfortunate waistcoat walked into his armchair.

"I beg your pardon," said the gentleman. "I believe I am somewhat foxed!"

"I am prepared to charitably believe you were drunk when you got dressed," Magnus said under his breath.

"Eh?" said the man. "The name's Alvanley. You ain't one of those Indian nabobs, are you?"

Though he never much felt like explaining his origins to white-skinned Europeans who didn't care to know the difference between Shanghai and Rangoon, given the troubles in India, it was not actually a good idea for Magnus to be taken for Indian. He sighed and disclaimed, made his introduction and his bow.

"Herondale," said Edmund, bowing too. Edmund's golden assurance and open smile did their work.

"New to the club?" Alvanley asked, suddenly benevolent. "Well, well. It's a celebration. May I offer you both another drink?"

Alvanley's friends, some at the card table and some milling about, raised a discreet cheer. Queen Victoria had, so the happy report went, risen safe from childbed, and both mother and daughter were doing admirably.

"Drink to the health of our new Princess Beatrice, and to the queen!"

"Doesn't the poor woman have nine children?" asked Magnus. "By the ninth I would think she would be too exhausted to think of a new name, and certainly too fatigued to rule a country. I will drink to her health by all means."

Edmund was very ready to be plied with more drinks, though at one point he slipped up and referred to the queen as Vanessa rather than Victoria.

"Ahahaha," said Magnus. "He is on the ran-tan, and no mistake!"

Edmund was flushed with drink and almost immediately got absorbed in a card game. Magnus joined in playing Macao as well, but he found himself observing the Shadowhunter with some concern. People who blithely believed that the world owed them good luck could be dangerous at the gaming table. Add to that the fact that Edmund clearly craved excitement, and his kind of temperament was the very one most suited for disaster at play. There was something unsettling about the glitter of the boy's eyes suddenly, changed by the light of the club's wax candles, from being like a sky to being like a sea an instant before a storm.

Edmund, Magnus decided, put him in mind of nothing so

much as a boat—a shining beautiful thing, buffeted by the whims of the water and winds. Only time would tell if he would find anchor and harbor, or if all that beauty and charm would be reduced to a wreck.

All imaginings aside, there was no need for Magnus to play nursemaid to Shadowhunters. Edmund was a man full-grown and able to care for himself. It was Magnus who grew bored in the end, and coaxed Edmund out of White's for a sobering walk in the night air.

They had not wandered far from St. James's Street when Magnus paused in his retelling of a certain incident in Peru because he felt Edmund come to attention next to him, every line of that angelic athlete's body suddenly tensed. He brought to mind forcibly a pointer dog hearing an animal in the undergrowth.

Magnus followed the line of Edmund's sight until he saw what the Shadowhunter was seeing: a man in a bowler hat, his hand set firmly on a carriage door, having what appeared to be an altercation with the occupants of the carriage.

It was shockingly uncivil, and but a moment later it became worse. The man had hold of a woman's arm, Magnus saw. She was dressed plainly, as befit an abigail or lady's maid. The man tried to wrench her from the carriage by main force.

He would have succeeded but for the interference of the other occupant of the carriage, a small dark lady, this one in a gown that rustled like silk as her voice rang out like thunder.

"Unhand her, you wretch!" said the lady, and she belabored the man about the head with her bonnet.

The man started at the unexpected onslaught and let go of

the woman, but turned his attention to the lady and grasped the hand holding the bonnet instead. The woman gave a shout that seemed more outrage than terror, and struck him in the nose. The man's face turned slightly at the blow, and Magnus and Edmund were both able to see his eyes.

There was no mistaking the void behind those brilliant poison-green eyes. *Demon,* Magnus thought. A demon, and a hungry one, to be trying to abduct women from carriages in a London street.

A demon, and a very unlucky one, to do so in front of a Shadowhunter.

It did occur to Magnus that Shadowhunters generally hunted in groups, and that Edmund Herondale was inebriated.

"Very well," Magnus said. "Let us pause for a moment and consider— Oh, you have already run off. Splendid."

He found himself addressing Edmund's coat, wrenched off and left in a heap upon the cobblestones, and his hat, spinning gently beside it.

Edmund jumped and somersaulted in midair, vaulting neatly onto the roof of the carriage. As he did so, he drew weapons from the concealing folds of his garments: the two whips he had spoken of before, arcs of sizzling light against the night sky. He wielded them with cutting precision, their light waking golden fire in his tousled hair and casting a glow on his carved features, and by that light Magnus saw his face change from a laughing boy's to the stern countenance of an angel.

One whip curled around the demon's waist like a gentleman's hand around a lady's waist during a waltz. The other wrapped as tight as wire about his throat. Edmund twisted one hand, and the demon spun, crashing to the ground.

"You heard the lady," said Edmund. "Unhand her."

The demon, his teeth suddenly much more numerous than before, snarled and lunged for the carriage. Magnus raised his hand and made the carriage door fly shut and the carriage jolt forward a few paces, despite the fact that the carriage driver was missing—presumed eaten—and despite the Shadowhunter who was still standing atop it.

Edmund did not lose his balance. As surefooted as a cat, he simply leaped down to the ground and struck the Eidolon demon a blow across the face with his whip, sending him flying backward again. Edmund landed a foot upon the demon's throat, and Magnus saw the creature begin to writhe, its outlines blurring into a changing shape.

He heard the creak of a carriage door being opened and saw the lady who had punched the demon essaying to emerge from relative safety to the demon-haunted street.

"Ma'am," Magnus said, advancing. "I must counsel you not to exit the carriage while a demon-slaying is in progress."

She looked him full in the face. She had large dark blue eyes, the color of the sky immediately before night turned it black, and the hair slipping from her elaborate coiffure was black, as if night had come with no stars. Though her beautiful eyes were very wide, she did not look frightened, and the hand that had struck the demon was still clenched in a fist.

Magnus made a silent vow to come to London far more often in the future. He was meeting the most delightful people.

"We must render assistance to that young man," said the lady, in a lilting musical accent.

Magnus glanced over to Edmund, who was at present being thrown against a wall and who was bleeding rather profusely, but grinning and sliding a dagger from his boot with one hand as he choked the demon with the other.

"Do not be alarmed, dear lady. He has the matter well in hand," he said as Edmund slid the dagger home. "So to speak."

The demon gurgled and thrashed in its death throes. Magnus made the decision to ignore the furor behind him, and made the two women a superb bow. It did not seem to console the maidservant, who shrank into the shadowed recesses of the carriage and attempted to crawl into a pocket handkerchief, face foremost.

The lady of the shining ebony hair and pansy eyes let go her hold on the carriage door and gave Magnus her hand instead. Her hand was small, soft, and warm; she was not even trembling.

"I am Magnus Bane," said Magnus. "Call on me for aid at any time of mortal danger, or if in urgent need of an escort to a flower show."

"Linette Owens," said the lady, and dimpled. She had delicious dimples. "I heard the capital held many dangers, but this seems excessive."

"I am aware that all this must seem very strange and frightening to you."

"Is that man an evil faerie?" Miss Owens inquired. She met Magnus's startled look with her own steady gaze. "I am from Wales," she said. "We still believe in the old ways and the fey folk there."

She tipped her head back to scrutinize Magnus. Her crown of midnight-colored plaits seemed like it had to be too massive for such a small head, on such a slender neck.

"Your eyes . . . ," she said slowly. "I believe you must be a good faerie, sir. What your companion is, I cannot tell."

Magnus glanced over his shoulder at his companion, who he had almost forgotten was there. The demon was darkness and dust at Edmund's feet, and with his foe well and truly vanquished, Edmund had turned his attention to the carriage. Magnus observed the spark of Edmund's golden charm kindle at the sight of Linette, blooming from candle to sun in an instant.

"What am I?" he asked. "I am Edmund Herondale, and, my lady, I am always and forever at your service. If you will have me."

He smiled, and the smile was slow and devastating. In the dark narrow street long past midnight, his eyes were high summer.

"I do not mean to seem indelicate or ungrateful," said Linette Owens, "but are you a dangerous lunatic?"

Edmund blinked.

"I fear I must point out that you are walking the streets armed to the teeth. Did you expect to do battle with a monstrous creature this night?"

"Not 'expect' exactly," said Edmund.

"Then are you an assassin?" asked Linette. "Are you an overzealous soldier?"

"Madam," said Edmund. "I am a Shadowhunter."

"I am not familiar with the word. Can you do magic?" Linette asked, and placed her hand on Magnus's sleeve. "This gentleman can do magic."

She bestowed an approving smile on Magnus. Magnus was extremely gratified.

"Honored to be of assistance, Miss Owens," he murmured.

Edmund looked as if he had been struck about the face with a fish.

"Of course—of course I can't do magic!" he managed to splutter out, sounding in true Shadowhunter fashion appalled by the very idea.

"Oh, well," said Linette, clearly rather disappointed. "That is not your fault. We all make do with what we have. I am indebted to you, sir, for saving me and my friend from an unspeakable fate."

Edmund preened, and in his pleasure spoke incautiously. "Think nothing of it. It would be my honor to escort you to your home, Miss Owens. The streets about Mall Pall can be very treacherous for women at night."

There was a silence.

"Do you mean Pall Mall?" Linette asked, and smiled slightly. "I am not the one overset by strong liquor. Should you like me to escort you home instead, Mr. Herondale?"

Edmund Herondale was left at a loss for words. Magnus suspected it was a novel experience, and one that would probably be good for him.

Miss Owens turned slightly from Edmund back to Magnus.

"My abigail, Angharad, and I were traveling from my estate in Wales," she explained. "We are to spend the London season with a distant relative of mine. We have had a long and tiring journey, and I wished to believe that we might reach London before nightfall. It was very stupid and reckless of me, and it has caused Angharad great distress. Your aid was invaluable."

Magnus could discern a great deal more from what Linette Owens had told him than what the lady had actually said. She had referred not to her papa's estate but to her own, in a casual manner, as one accustomed to ownership. That combined with the costly material of her dress and a certain something about her bearing confirmed it for Magnus—the lady was an heiress, and not simply the heiress of a fortune but of an estate. The way she spoke of Wales made Magnus think the lady would not wish to have her lands cared for by some steward at a remove. Society would think it a scandal and a shame for an estate to be in the hands of a woman, especially one so young and so pretty. Society would expect her to contract a marriage so that her husband could administer the estate, take possession of both the land and the lady.

She must have come to London because she'd found the suitors available in Wales not to her taste, and was on a quest to find a husband to take back to Wales with her.

She had come to London in search of love.

Magnus could sympathize with that. He was aware that love was not always part of the bargain in high-society marriages, but Linette Owens seemed to have a mind of her own. He thought it likely she had a purpose—the right marriage, to the right man—and that she would accomplish it.

"Welcome to London," Magnus told her.

Linette dropped a small curtsy in the open carriage. Her eyes traveled over Magnus's shoulder and softened. Magnus looked around, and Edmund was standing there, one whip curled around his wrist as if he were comforting himself with it. Magnus had to admit it was a feat to look so gloriously handsome and yet so woebegone.

Linette visibly yielded to a charitable impulse and stepped out of the carriage. She made her way across the cobblestones and stood before the forlorn young Shadowhunter.

"I am sorry if I was uncivil, or if I in any way implied I thought you were a . . . *twpsyn*," said Linette, tactfully not translating the word.

She put her hand out, and Edmund offered his, palm up and whip still curled around his shirt-sleeved wrist. There was a sudden hungry openness to his face; the moment had a sudden weight. Linette hesitated and then placed her hand in his.

"I am very much obliged to you for saving me and Angharad from a dreadful fate. Truly I am," said Linette. "Again, I apologize if I was ungracious."

"I will give you leave to be as ungracious as you choose," Edmund said. "If I can see you again."

He looked down at her, not making play with his eyelashes. His face was naked and open.

The moment turned. Edmund's serious, humble honesty did what eyelashes and swagger had not, and made Linette Owens hesitate.

"You can pay a call at 26 Eaton Square, at Lady Caroline Harcourt's," she said. "If you still wish to in the morning."

She drew her hand away, and after a single uncertain instant, Edmund let her.

Linette touched Magnus's arm before she ascended into the carriage. She was just as pretty and amiable as before, but something in her manner had changed. "Please come pay a call on me as well, if you care to, Mr. Bane."

"Sounds delightful."

He took her hand and helped her into the carriage, giving her away in one light graceful movement.

"Oh, and Mr. Herondale," said Miss Owens, putting her

lovely laughing head through the carriage window. "Please leave your whips at home."

Magnus made a small shooing gesture, minuscule cerulean sparks dancing between his fingers. The carriage set off driverless in the dark, down the London streets.

It was some time before Magnus attended another meeting about the proposed Accords, in the main because there had been disagreements about the choice of venue. Magnus himself had voted that they meet somewhere other than the section of the Institute that had been built off sacrosanct ground. He felt that the place had the air of the servants' quarters. Mainly because Amalia Morgenstern had mentioned that the area used to be the Fairchilds' servants' quarters.

The Shadowhunters had resisted the idea of frequenting any low den of Downworlders (direct quote from Granville Fairchild), and the suggestion of staying outdoors and going to the park was vetoed because it was felt that the dignity of a conclave would be much impaired if some oblivious mundanes had a picnic in their midst.

Magnus did not believe a word of it.

After weeks of wrangling, their group finally capitulated and trailed dispiritedly back to the London Institute. The only bright spot was a literal bright spot—Camille was wearing an extremely fascinating red hat, and dainty red lace gloves.

"You look foolish and frivolous," said de Quincey under his breath as the Shadowhunters found their places around the table in the large dim room.

"De Quincey is quite right," said Magnus. "You look foolish, frivolous, and fabulous."

Camille preened, and Magnus found it delightful and sympathetic, the way a small compliment could please a woman who had been beautiful for centuries.

"Exactly the effect I was attempting to produce," said Camille. "Shall I tell you a secret?"

"Pray do." Magnus leaned in toward her, and she inclined toward him.

"I wore it for you," Camille whispered.

The dim, stately room, its walls cloaked in tapestries emblazoned with swords, stars, and the runes the Nephilim wore on their own skin, brightened suddenly. All of London seemed to brighten.

Magnus had been alive hundreds of years himself, and yet the simplest things could turn a day into a jewel, and a succession of days into a glittering chain that went on and on. Here was the simplest thing: a pretty girl liked him, and the day shone.

Ralf Scott's thin pale face turned paler still, and was set in lines of pain now, but Magnus did not know the boy and was not bound to care overmuch for his broken heart. If the lady preferred Magnus, Magnus was not inclined to argue with her.

"How pleased we are to receive you all here again," said Granville Fairchild, as stern as ever. He folded his hands before him on the table. "At long last."

"How pleased we are that we could come to an agreement," said Magnus. "At long last."

"I believe Roderick Morgenstern has prepared a few words," said Fairchild. His face was set, and his deep voice rang hollow. There was a slight suggestion of a kitten crying all alone in a large cave.

"I believe I have heard enough from Shadowhunters," said Ralf Scott. "We have already heard the terms of the Nephilim for the preservation of peace between our kind and yours—"

"The list of our requirements was by no means complete," interrupted a man called Silas Pangborn.

"Indeed it was not," said the woman at his side, as stern and beautiful as one of the Nephilim's statues. Pangborn had introduced her as "Eloisa Ravenscar, my *parabatai*" with the same proprietary air as he might have said "my wife."

Evidently, they stood united against Downworlders.

"We have terms of our own," said Ralf Scott.

There was utter silence from the Shadowhunters. From their faces, Magnus did not think they were preparing themselves to listen attentively. Instead they seemed stunned by Downworlder impudence.

Ralf persisted, despite the utter lack of encouragement for him to do so. The boy was valiant even in a lost cause, Magnus thought, and despite himself he felt a little pang.

"We will want guarantees that no Downworlder whose hands are clean of mundane blood will be slaughtered. We want a law that states that any Shadowhunter who does strike down an innocent Downworlder will be punished." Ralf bore the outbreak of protest, and shouted it down. "You people live by laws! They are all you understand!"

"Yes, our laws, passed down to us by the Angel!" thundered Fairchild.

"Not rules that demon scum try to impose on us," sneered Starkweather.

"Is it too much to ask, to have laws to defend us as well as laws to defend the mundanes and the Nephilim?" Ralf demanded.

"My parents were slain by Shadowhunters because of a terrible misunderstanding, because my parents were in the wrong place at the wrong time and presumed guilty because they were werewolves. I am raising my young brother alone. I want my people to be protected, to be strong, and not to be driven into corners until they either become killers or are killed!"

Magnus looked over to Camille, to share the spark of sympathy and indignation for Ralf Scott, so terribly young and terribly hurt and terribly in love with her. Camille's face was untouched, more like a porcelain doll's face than a person's, her skin porcelain that could not redden or pale, her eyes cold glass.

He felt a qualm and dismissed it out of hand. It was a vampire's face, that was all—no reflection of how she actually felt. There were many who could not read anything but evil in Magnus's own eyes.

"What a terrible shame," said Starkweather. "I would have thought you might have more siblings to share the burden. You people generally have litters, do you not?"

Ralf Scott jumped up and hit the table with an open palm. His fingers grew claws and scored the surface of the table.

"I think we need scones!" exclaimed Amalia Morgenstern.

"How dare you?" bellowed Granville Fairchild.

"That table is mahogany!" cried Roderick Morgenstern, looking appalled.

"Good Lord, you people are stupid," said Ralf darkly. "Many, many things are made out of mahogany."

"I would very much like a scone," said Arabella the mermaid. "Also possibly some cucumber sandwiches."

"I like egg and cress," contributed Rachel Branwell.

"I will not stand to be so insulted!" said a Shadowhunter called Waybread, or some such thing.

"You will not be insulted, and yet you will insist on murdering us," Camille remarked, her cool voice cutting the air. Magnus felt almost unbearably proud of her, and Ralf threw her a passionately grateful look. "It seems hardly fair."

"Do you know that, last time, they threw away the plates that our very touch had profaned, once we were gone?" Magnus asked softly. "We can come to an agreement only if we begin at a position of some mutual respect."

Starkweather barked a laugh. Magnus actually did not hate Starkweather; at least he was no hypocrite. No matter how foul, Magnus did appreciate honesty.

"Then we won't come to an agreement."

"I fear I must agree," Magnus murmured. He pressed a hand over his heart and his new peacock-blue waistcoat. "I strive to find some respect in my heart for you, but alas! It seems an impossible quest."

"Damned insolent magical libertine!"

Magnus inclined his head. "Just so."

When the refreshments tray arrived, the pause in hurling insults in order to consume scones was so excruciatingly awkward that Magnus excused himself under the pretext that he had to use the conveniences.

There were only a few chambers in the Institute into which Downworlders were permitted to venture. Magnus had simply intended to creep off into a shadowed corner, and he was rather displeased to find that the first shadowed corner he came upon was occupied.

There was an armchair and a small table. Slumped on the tabletop that depicted filigree gold angels was a seated man, cradling a small box in his hands. Magnus recognized the shining hair and broad shoulders immediately.

"Mr. Herondale?" he inquired.

Edmund started badly. For a moment Magnus thought he might fall from his chair, but Shadowhunter grace saved him. He stared at Magnus with blurred, wounded surprise, like a child slapped from sleep. Magnus doubted he had been doing much sleeping; his face was marked with sleepless nights.

"Had a night of it, did we?" Magnus asked, a little more gently.

"I had a few glasses of wine with the duck a l'orange," Edmund said, with a pallid smile that vanished as soon as it was born. "I shall never eat duck again. I cannot believe I used to like duck. The duck betrayed me." He was silent, then admitted, "Perhaps more than a few glasses. I have not seen you in Eaton Square."

Magnus wondered why on earth Edmund had thought he would, and then he recalled. It was the beautiful young Welsh girl's address.

"You went to Eaton Square?"

Edmund looked at him as if Magnus were dull-witted.

"Pardon me," said Magnus. "I simply find it hard to imagine one of the mundanes' glorious invisible protectors paying a social call."

This time Edmund's grin was the old one, brilliant and engaging, even though it did not last. "Well, they did ask me for a card, and I had not the faintest idea what they meant by that. I was turned away with vast contempt by her butler."

"I take it you did not give the matter up there."

"No indeed," said Edmund. "I simply lay in wait, and after a mere few days had the opportunity to follow Li—Miss Owens, and caught up with her riding in Rotten Row. I have seen her every day since then."

"'Follow' her? I wonder that the lady did not alert a constable."

The glow returned to Edmund's face, rendering him in gold and blue and pearl again. "Linette says I am fortunate she did not." He added, a little shyly, "We are engaged to be married."

That was news indeed. The Nephilim generally married among themselves, an aristocracy based on their belief in their own sanctity. Any prospective mundane bride or bridegroom would be expected to drink from the Mortal Cup and be transformed through dangerous alchemy into one of the Angel's own. It was not a transformation that all survived.

"Congratulations," said Magnus, and he kept his concerns locked in his own bosom. "I presume Miss Owens will soon Ascend?"

Edmund took a deep breath. "No," he said. "She will not."

"Oh," said Magnus, understanding at last.

Edmund looked down at the box he held in his hands. It was a simple wooden affair, with the symbol for infinity drawn upon the side in what looked like burned match. "This is a Pyxis," he said. "It holds within it the spirit of the first demon I ever slew. I was fourteen years old, and it was the day when I knew what I was born to do, what I was born to be—a Shadowhunter."

Magnus looked at Edmund's bowed head, his scarred warrior's hands clenched on the small box, and could not help the sympathy kindling within him.

Edmund spoke, in a confessional stream to his own soul

and to the only person he knew who might listen and not think Edmund's love was blasphemy. "Linette thinks it her duty and her calling to care for the people on her estate. She does not wish to be a Shadowhunter. And I—I would not wish it, or ask it of her. Men and women perish in attempts to Ascend. She is brave and beautiful and unwavering, and if the Law says she is not worthy exactly as she is, then the Law is a lie. I cannot believe the unfairness of it, that I have found the one woman in all the world whom I could love, and what does the Law say to this feeling that I know is sacred? In order to be with her, either I am meant to ask my dearest love to risk her life, a life that is worth more to me than my own. Or I am meant to cut away the other part of my soul—burn away my life's purpose and all the gifts the Angel gave me."

Magnus remembered how Edmund had looked in that gorgeous leap to attack the demon, how his whole body had changed from restless energy to absolute purpose when he saw a demon: when he threw himself into the fray with the simple, natural joy of one who was doing what he was made for.

"Did you ever want to be anything else?"

"No," said Edmund. He stood and put a hand against the wall and raked the other hand through his hair, an angel brought to his knees, wild and bewildered by pain.

"But what of your dim view of marriage?" Magnus demanded. "What of having only one bonbon when you could have the box?"

"I was very stupid," Edmund said, almost violently. "I thought of love as a game. It is not a game. It is more serious than death. Without Linette, I might as well be dead."

"You speak of giving up your Shadowhunter nature," said

Magnus softly. "One can give up many things for love, but one should not give up oneself."

"Is that so, Bane?" Edmund whirled on him. "I was born to be a warrior, and I was born to be with her. Tell me how to reconcile the two, because I cannot!"

Magnus made no answer. He was looking at Edmund and remembering when he had drunkenly thought of the Shadowhunter as a lovely ship, that might sail straight out to sea or wreck itself upon the rocks. He could see the rocks now, dark and jagged on the horizon. He saw Edmund's future without Shadowhunting, how he would yearn for the danger and the risk. How he would find it at the gaming tables. How fragile he would always be once his sense of purpose was gone.

And then there was Linette, who had fallen in love with a golden Shadowhunter, an avenging angel. What would she think of him when he was just another Welsh farmer, all his glory stripped away?

Yet love was not something to be thrown aside lightly. It came so rarely, only a few times in a mortal life. Sometimes it came but once. Magnus could not say Edmund Herondale was wrong to seize love when he had found it.

He could think Nephilim Law was wrong for making him choose.

Edmund exhaled. He looked drained. "I beg your pardon, Bane," he said. "I am simply being a child, screaming and kicking against fate, and it is time to stop being a stupid boy. Why struggle against a choice that is already made? If I were asked to choose between sacrificing my life or sacrificing Linette's every day for the rest of eternity, I would sacrifice my own every time."

Magnus looked away, so as not to see the wreckage. "I wish you luck," he said. "Luck and love."

Edmund made a small bow. "I bid you good day. I think we will not meet again."

He walked away, into the inner reaches of the Institute. A few feet away, he wavered and paused, light from one of the narrow church windows turning his hair rich gold, and Magnus thought he would turn. But Edmund Herondale never looked back.

Magnus returned with a heavy heart to the room where the Shadowhunters and Downworlders were still fighting a war of words. Neither side seemed inclined to give way. Magnus was inclined to give the matter up as hopeless.

Through the stained-glass windows the curtains of night began to show the signs of drawing down to reveal the day, and the vampires had to leave.

"It seems to me," said Camille, drawing on her scarlet gloves, "that another meeting will prove just as futile as these have been."

"If Downworlders continue to be insolent wretches," said Starkweather.

"If Shadowhunters continue to be sanctimonious murderers," snapped Scott. Magnus could not quite look at his face, not after Edmund Herondale's. He did not want to watch as another boy's dreams died.

"Enough!" said Granville Fairchild. "Madam, do not ask me to believe that you have never harmed a human soul. I am not a fool. And what kills Shadowhunters have made, they have made in the cause of justice and in the defense of the helpless."

Camille smiled a slow, sweet smile. "If you believe that," she murmured, "then you are a fool."

Cue another dreary, wearying burst of outrage from the assembled Shadowhunters. It warmed Magnus to see Camille defending the boy. She was fond of Ralf Scott, he thought. Perhaps more than fond. Magnus might hope that she would choose him, but he found he could not begrudge Scott her affection. He offered her his arm as they left the room, and she took it. They went out into the street together.

And there on the very doorstep of the Institute, the demons descended. Achaieral demons, their teeth razors and their wide wings scorched-black leather like the aprons of blacksmiths. They blanketed the night, blotting out the moon and wiping away the stars, and Camille shuddered at Magnus's side, her fangs out. At the sign of Camille's fear, Ralf Scott lunged at the enemy, transforming as he went, and brought one down in a bloody tangle onto the cobbles.

The Shadowhunters rushed out too, weapons sliding out of sheaths and garments alike. Amalia Morgenstern, it emerged, had been hiding a small tasteful axe under her hoop skirt. Roderick Morgenstern ran out into the street and stabbed the demon Ralf Scott was wrestling with.

From the small cart that contained her aquarium, Arabella gave a scream of real fear, and ducked down to the bottom of her woefully inadequate tank.

"To me, Josiah!" thundered Fairchild, and Josiah Waybread—no, Magnus thought it was Wayland, actually—joined him. They ranged themselves in front of Arabella's cart and stood to defend her, letting no demon past the bright line of their blades.

Silas Pangborn and Eloisa Ravenscar moved to the street,

fighting back-to-back, their weapons bright blurs in their hands and their movements in perfect synchronization, as if the pair of them had melded into a single fierce creature. De Quincey followed and fought with them.

The presence at Magnus's side was gone suddenly. Camille left him and went running to help Ralf Scott. One demon leaped onto her from behind and seized her up in its bladelike talons. Ralf howled despair and grief. Magnus blasted the demon out of the sky. Camille went tumbling onto the ground, and Magnus knelt and gathered her, shaking, into his arms. He was amazed to see the gleam of tears in her green eyes, was amazed at how fragile she felt.

"I beg your pardon. I am not generally so easily overset. A mundane fortune-teller once told me that death would come to me as a surprise," Camille said, her voice trembling. "A foolish superstition, is it not? Yet I always wish to be warned. I fear nothing, if only I am told that danger is coming."

"I would be entirely overset myself, if my ensemble had been spoiled by demons who know nothing of fashion," said Magnus, and Camille laughed.

Her eyes looked like grass under the dew, and she was brave and beautiful and would fight for their kind and yet rest against him. It was in that moment that Magnus felt as if he had stopped searching for love.

Magnus looked up from Camille's enchanting face to see that the Shadowhunters and Downworlders were, for a wonder, not arguing. Instead they were all observing one another, standing in the suddenly-quiet street with the bodies of their foes around them, vanquished because they had stood together. There was a certain wonder in the air, as if the Nephilim could not see the Downworlders as demonic when they had fought alongside them against true demons. The Shadowhunters were warriors; the bonds of war meant a great deal to them.

Magnus was no warrior, but he remembered how the Shadowhunters had moved to protect a mermaid and a werewolf. That meant something to him, too. Perhaps there was something to be salvaged here this night. Perhaps they could make this wild idea of the Accords work after all.

Then he felt Camille move in his arms, and saw where she was looking. She was gazing at Ralf Scott, and he was looking back at her. There was a world of hurt in his eyes.

The boy climbed to his feet, and vented his ire on the Shadowhunters.

"You people did this," he raged. "You want us all dead. You lured us here—"

"Are you *mad?*" Fairchild demanded. "We are Nephilim. If we wanted you dead, you would be dead. We do not require demons to do our killing for us, and we certainly do not wish for them to befoul our very doorstep. My daughter lives here. I would not put her in danger for anything you care to name, and certainly not for Downworlders."

Magnus had to admit he had a point.

"It is you people who brought that filth to us!" Starkweather bellowed.

Magnus opened his mouth to argue, and then he recalled how excessively vehement the queen of the faeries had been when she argued against an agreement with Shadowhunters, and yet how strangely curious she had been about the details thereof, such as the time and place of their meetings. He closed his mouth.

Fairchild gave Magnus a condemning glance, as if the Shadowhunter could read the guilt of all Downworlders on his countenance. "If what Starkweather says is true, you have lost any opportunity to forge an agreement between our people."

It was done, then, and Magnus saw the rage pass from Ralf Scott's face as he visibly gave up his struggle. Ralf looked up at Fairchild with clear eyes, and spoke in a calm, ringing voice.

"You will not give us aid? Very well. We do not need it. Werewolves will take care of their own. I will see it done."

The werewolf boy evaded de Quincey's detaining hand and paid no heed to Fairchild's sharp reply. The only one he paid attention to was Camille. He looked at her for a moment. Camille lifted her hand, then dropped it, and Ralf whirled and walked away from both Shadowhunters and his fellow Downworlders. Magnus saw him square his thin shoulders as he went, a boy accepting a heavy burden and accepting that he had lost what he loved best. Magnus was reminded of Edmund Herondale.

Magnus did not see Edmund Herondale again, but he heard him once more.

The Shadowhunters decided that Magnus and Camille were the most reasonable among the Downworlders that they had assembled. Given that the other choices were intemperate werewolves and Alexei de Quincey, Magnus could not feel himself flattered by the preference.

The Nephilim asked Magnus and Camille to come for a private meeting, to exchange information so that they could continue to correspond, independent of Ralf Scott. Implicit in their request was the promise that the Shadowhunters might offer their protection if Magnus and Camille needed it at some future time. In exchange, of course, for magic or Downworlder information.

Magnus went to the meeting to see Camille, and for no other reason. He told himself that he was not thinking at all of that fight against the demons, and how they had been united.

When he stepped into the Institute, however, he was pulled up short by the sounds. The noises came from the depths of the building, and they were the rattling, tormented sounds of someone being flayed alive. They sounded like the screams of a soul in Hell, or a soul being ripped from Heaven.

"What is that?" Magnus asked.

There were only a few Shadowhunters present at this unofficial meeting, instead of the mass of Clave representatives. Only Granville Fairchild, Silas Pangborn, and Josiah Wayland were in attendance. The three Shadowhunters stood in the small hall, cries of agony reverberating from the tapestry-covered walls and the domed ceiling, and all three Nephilim appeared entirely indifferent.

"A young Shadowhunter by the name of Edmund Herondale has disgraced his family name and forsaken his calling so that he might fling himself into the arms of a mundane chit," Josiah Wayland answered, with no sign of emotion. "He is being stripped of his Marks."

"And being stripped of your Marks," Magnus said slowly. "It is like that?"

"It is being remade, into a baser thing," said Granville Fairchild, his voice cold, though his face was pale. "It is against the will of the Angel. Of course it hurts."

There was a shuddering scream of agony to underlie his words. He did not turn his head.

Magnus felt cold with horror. "You're barbarians."

"Do you want to rush to his aid?" inquired Wayland. "If you try, every one of us will move to strike you down. Do not dare to question our motives or our way of life. You speak of that which is higher and nobler than you can possibly understand."

Magnus heard another scream, and this one broke off into desperate sobbing. The warlock thought of the bright boy he had spent one night at a club with, his face radiant and untouched by pain. This was the price Shadowhunters set on love.

Magnus started forward, but the Shadowhunters drew together with bared blades and stern faces. An angel with a flaming sword, proclaiming that Magnus should not pass, could not have expressed more conviction of his own righteousness. He heard the echoes of his stepfather's voice in his mind: *devil's child, Satan's get, born to be damned, forsaken by God.*

The long lonely cry of a suffering boy he could not help chilled Magnus through to the bone, like cold water seeping through to find a grave. Sometimes he thought they were all forsaken, every soul on this earth.

Even the Nephilim.

"There is nothing to be done, Magnus. Come away," said Camille's voice in his ear in an undertone. Her hand was small but held Magnus's arm in a firm grip. She was strong, stronger than Magnus was, perhaps in all ways. "Fairchild raised the boy from a child, I believe, and yet he is throwing him away like refuse into the street. The Nephilim have no pity."

Magnus allowed her to draw him away, into the street and away from the Institute. He was impressed that she was still so calm. Camille had fortitude, Magnus thought. He wished she could teach him the trick of being less foolish, and less easily hurt.

"I hear you are leaving us, Mr. Bane," Camille said. "I shall be sorry to see you go. De Quincey hosts the most famous parties, and I hear you are quite the life and soul of any party you attend."

"I am sorry to go, indeed," said Magnus.

"If I might ask why?" said Camille, her lovely face upturned, her green eyes glittering. "I had rather thought that London had caught your fancy, and that you might stay."

Her invitation was almost irresistible. But Magnus was no Shadowhunter. He could have pity on someone who was suffering, and young.

"That young werewolf, Ralf Scott," Magnus said, abandoning pretense. "He is in love with you. And it seemed to me you looked at him with some interest as well."

"And if that is true?" Camille asked, laughing. "You do not strike me as the sort of man to step aside and renounce a claim for the benefit of another!"

"Ah, but I am not a man. Am I? I have years, and so do you," he added, and that was glorious too, the idea of loving someone and not fearing they would soon be lost. "But werewolves are not immortals. They age and die. The Scott boy has but one chance for your love, where I—I might go and return, and find you here again."

She pouted prettily. "I might forget you."

He bent to her ear. "If you do, I shall have to recall myself forcibly to your attention." His hands spanned her waist, the silk of her dress smooth under the pads of his fingertips. He could feel the swell and rise of her under his touch. His lips brushed her skin, and he felt her jump and shudder. He whispered, "Love the boy. Give him his happiness. And when I return, I shall devote an age to admiring you."

"An entire age?"

"Perhaps," said Magnus, teasing. "How does Marvell's poem go?

"An hundred years should go to praise
Thine eyes and on thy forehead gaze;
Two hundred to adore each breast,
But thirty thousand to the rest;
An age at least to every part,
And the last age should show your heart. . . ."

Camille's eyebrows had lifted at the reference to her bosom, but her eyes were sparkling. "And how do you know that I have a heart?"

Magnus raised his own eyebrows, conceding the point. "I have heard it said that love is faith."

"Whether your faith is justified," Camille said, "time will tell."

"Before time tells us anything more," Magnus said, "I humbly beg of you to accept a small token of my regard."

He reached inside his coat, which was made of blue superfine fabric and which he hoped Camille found dashing, and produced the necklace. The ruby glinted in the light of a nearby streetlamp, its heart the rich color of blood.

"It is a pretty thing," said Magnus.

"Very pretty." She sounded amused at the understatement.

"Not worthy of your beauty, of course, but what could be? There is one small thing besides prettiness to recommend it. There is a spell on the jewel, to warn you when demons are near."

Camille's eyes went very wide. She was an intelligent

woman, and Magnus saw she knew the full value of the jewel and of the spell.

Magnus had sold the house in Grosvenor Square, and what else had he to do with the proceeds? He could think of nothing more valuable than purchasing a guarantee that would keep Camille safe, and cause her to remember him kindly.

"I will think of you when I am far away," Magnus promised, fastening the pendant about her white throat. "I would like to think of you fearless."

Camille's hand fluttered, a white dove, to the sparkling heart of the necklace and away again. She looked up into Magnus's eyes.

"In all justice, I must give you a token to remember me by," she said, smiling.

"Oh, well," said Magnus as she drew close. His hand settled on the small silk circle of her waist. Before his lips met hers, he murmured, "If it is in the cause of justice."

Camille kissed him. Magnus spared a thought to making the streetlamp burn more brightly, and the flame within the iron and glass case filled the whole street with soft blue light. He held her and the promise of possible love, and in that warm instant all the narrow streets of London seemed to expand, and he could even think kindly of Shadowhunters, and one more than the rest.

He spared a moment to hope that Edmund Herondale would find comfort in the arms of his beautiful mundane love, that he would live a life that made all he had lost and all he had suffered seem worthwhile.

Magnus's ship would sail that night. He left Camille so that she might search out Ralf Scott, and he boarded his steamship, a glorious iron-hulled thing called the *Persia* that had been made with the latest of mundane inventiveness. His interest in the ship and his thoughts of an adventure to come made him regret his departure less, but even so, he stood at the rail as the ship departed into night waters. He looked his last on the city he was leaving behind.

Years later Magnus would return to London and Camille Belcourt's side, and find it not all that he had dreamed. Years later another desperate Herondale boy with blue, blue eyes would come to his door, shaking with the cold of the rain and his own wretchedness, and this one Magnus would be able to help.

Magnus knew none of that then. He only stood on the deck of the ship and watched London and all its light and shadows slide away out of sight.

The Midnight Heir

By Cassandra Clare and Sarah Reese Brennan

A loud explosion caused him to look up. There was a boy standing in the middle of the room, a cocked silver pistol in his hand. He was surrounded by broken glass, having just shot off one arm of the chandelier.

—The Midnight Heir

BANG

It took Magnus nearly twenty minutes to notice the boy shooting out all the lights in the room, but to be fair, he had been distracted by the décor.

It had been nearly a quarter century since Magnus had been in London. He had missed the place. Certainly New York had an energy at the turn of the century that no other city could match. Magnus loved being in a carriage rattling into the dazzling lights of Longacre Square, pulling up outside the Olympia Theatre's elaborate French Renaissance facade, or rubbing elbows with a dozen different kinds of people at the hot dog festival in Greenwich Village. He enjoyed traveling on the elevated railways, squealing brakes and all, and he was much looking forward to traveling through the vast underground systems they were building below the very heart of the city. He had seen the construction of the great station at Columbus Circle just before he had left, and hoped to return to find it finished at last.

But London was London, wearing its history in layers, with every age contained in the new age. Magnus had history here too. Magnus had loved people here, and hated them. There had been one woman whom he had both loved and hated, and he had fled London to escape that memory. He sometimes wondered if he had been wrong to leave, if he should have endured the bad memories for the sake of the good, and suffered, and stayed.

Magnus slouched down in the tufted velvet chair—shabby at the arms, worn by decades of sleeves rubbing away the fabric—and gazed around the room. There was a gentility to English places that America, in all her brash youthfulness, could not match. Glimmering chandeliers dripped from the ceiling—cut glass, of course, not crystal, but it shed a pretty light—and electric sconces lined the walls. Magnus still found electricity rather thrilling, though it was duller than witchlight.

Groups of gentlemen sat at tables, playing rounds of faro and piquet. Ladies who were no better than they should be, whose dresses were too tight and too bright and too all the things Magnus liked most, lounged on velvet-covered benches along the walls. Gentlemen who had done well at the tables approached them, flushed with victory and pound notes; those whom Lady Luck had not smiled on drew on their coats at the door and slunk off silently into the night, bereft of money and companionship.

It was all very dramatic, which Magnus enjoyed. He had not yet grown tired of the pageantry of ordinary life and ordinary people, despite the passage of time and the fact that people were all very much the same in the end.

A loud explosion caused him to look up. There was a boy standing in the middle of the room, a cocked silver pistol in his hand. He was surrounded by broken glass, having just shot off one arm of the chandelier.

Magnus was overwhelmed with the feeling the French called déjà vu, the feeling that *I have been here before*. He had, of course, been in London before, twenty-five years past.

This boy's face was a face to recall the past. This *was* a face from the past, one of the most beautiful faces Magnus could ever recall seeing. It was a face so finely cut that it cast the shabbiness of this place into stark relief—a beauty that burned so fiercely that it put the glare of the electric lights to shame. The boy's skin was so white and clear that it seemed to have a light shining behind it. The lines of his cheekbones, his jaw, and his throat—exposed by a linen shirt open at the collar—were so clean and perfect that he almost would have looked like a statue were it not for the much disheveled and slightly curling hair falling into his face, as black as midnight against his lucent pallor.

The years drew Magnus back again, the fog and gaslight of a London more than twenty years lost rising to claim Magnus. He found his lips shaping a name: Will. Will Herondale.

Magnus stepped forward instinctively, the movement feeling as if it were not of his own volition.

The boy's eyes went to him, and a shock passed through Magnus. They were not Will's eyes, the eyes Magnus remembered being as *blue as a night sky in Hell*, eyes Magnus had seen both despairing and tender.

This boy had shining golden eyes, like a crystal glass filled brimful with crisp white wine and held up to catch the light of a blazing sun. If his skin was luminous, his eyes were radiant. Magnus could not imagine these eyes as tender. The boy was very, very lovely, but his was a beauty like that Helen of Troy might have had once, disaster written in every line. The light of his beauty made Magnus think of cities burning.

Fog and gaslight receded into memory. His momentary lapse into foolish nostalgia was over. This was not Will. That broken, beautiful boy would be a man now, and this boy was a stranger.

Still, Magnus did not think that such a great resemblance could be a coincidence. He made his way toward the boy with little effort, as the other denizens of the gaming hell seemed, perhaps understandably, reluctant to approach him. The boy was standing alone as though the broken glass all around him were a shining sea and he were an island.

"Not precisely a Shadowhunter weapon," Magnus murmured. "Is it?"

Those golden eyes narrowed into bright slits, and the long-fingered hand not holding the pistol went to the boy's sleeve, where Magnus presumed his nearest blade was concealed. His hands were not quite steady.

"Peace," Magnus added. "I mean you no harm. I am a warlock the Whitelaws of New York will vouch for as being quite—well, mostly—harmless."

There was a long pause that felt somewhat dangerous. The boy's eyes were like stars, shining but giving no clue to his feelings. Magnus was generally good at reading people, but he found it difficult to predict what this boy might do.

Magnus was truly surprised by what the boy said next.

"I know who you are." His voice was not like his face; it had gentleness to it.

Magnus managed to hide his surprise and raised his eyebrows in silent inquiry. He had not lived three hundred years without learning not to rise to every bait offered.

"You are Magnus Bane."

Magnus hesitated, then inclined his head. "And you are?"

"I," the boy announced, "am James Herondale."

"You know," Magnus murmured, "I rather thought you might be called something like that. I am delighted to hear that I am famous."

"You're my father's warlock friend. He would always speak of you to my sister and me whenever other Shadowhunters spoke slightingly of Downworlders in our presence. He would say he knew a warlock who was a better friend, and more worth trusting, than many a Nephilim warrior."

The boy's lips curled as he said it, and he spoke mockingly but with more contempt than amusement behind the mockery, as if his father had been a fool to tell him this, and James himself was a fool to repeat it.

Magnus found himself in no mood for cynicism.

They had parted well, he and Will, but he knew Shadowhunters. The Nephilim were swift to judge and condemn a Downworlder for ill deeds, acting as if every sin were graven in stone for all time, proving that Magnus's people were evil by nature. Shadowhunters' conviction of their own angelic virtue and righteousness made it easy for them to let a warlock's good deeds slip their minds, as if they were written in water.

He had not expected to see or hear of Will Herondale on this journey, but if Magnus had thought of it, he would have been unsurprised to be all but forgotten, a petty player in a boy's tragedy. Being remembered, and remembered so kindly, touched him more than he would have thought possible.

The boy's star-shining, burning-city eyes traveled across Magnus's face and saw too much.

"I would not set any great store by it. My father trusts a great many people," James Herondale said, and laughed. It was quite clear suddenly that he was extremely drunk. Not that Magnus had imagined he was firing at chandeliers while stone-cold sober. "Trust. It is like placing a blade in someone's hand and setting the very point against your own heart."

"I have not asked you to trust me," Magnus pointed out mildly. "We have just met."

"Oh, I'll trust you," the boy told him carelessly. "It hardly matters. We are all betrayed sooner or later—all betrayed, or traitors."

"I see that a flair for the dramatic runs in the blood," Magnus said under his breath. It was a different kind of dramatics, though. Will had made an exhibition of vice in private, to drive away those nearest and dearest to him. James was making a public spectacle.

Perhaps he loved vice for vice's own sake.

"What?" James asked.

"Nothing," said Magnus. "I was merely wondering what the chandelier had done to offend you."

James looked up at the ruined chandelier, and down at the shards of glass at his feet, as if he were noticing them only now.

"I was bet," he said, "twenty pounds that I would not shoot out all the lights of the chandelier."

"And who bet you?" said Magnus, not divulging a hint of what he thought—that anyone who bet a drunk seventeen-year-old boy that he could wave around a deadly weapon with impunity ought to be in gaol.

"That fellow there," James announced, pointing.

Magnus looked in the general direction James was gesturing toward, and spied a familiar face at the faro table.

"The green one?" Magnus inquired. Coaxing drunken Shadowhunters into making fools of themselves was a favorite occupation among the Downworlders, and this performance had been a tremendous success. Ragnor Fell, the High Warlock of London, shrugged, and Magnus sighed inwardly. Perhaps gaol would be a bit extreme, though Magnus still felt his emerald friend could use taking down a peg or two.

"Is he *really* green?" James asked, not seeming to care overmuch. "I thought that was the absinthe."

Then James Herondale, son of William Herondale and Theresa Gray, the two Shadowhunters who had been the closest of their kind to friends that Magnus had ever known—though Tessa had not been quite a Shadowhunter, or not entirely—turned his back on Magnus, set his sights on a woman serving drinks to a table surrounded by werewolves, and shot her down. She collapsed on the floor with a cry, and all the gamblers sprang from their tables, cards flying and drinks spilling.

James laughed, and the laugh was clear and bright, and it was then that Magnus began to be truly alarmed. Will's voice would have shaken, betraying that his cruelty had been part of his playacting, but his son's laugh was that of someone genuinely delighted by the chaos erupting all around him.

Magnus's hand shot out and grasped the boy's wrist, the hum and light of magic crackling along his fingers like a promise. "That's enough."

"Be easy," James said, still laughing. "I am a very good shot, and Peg the tavern maid is famous for her wooden leg. I think that is why they call her Peg. Her real name, I believe, is Ermentrude."

"And I suppose Ragnor Fell bet you twenty pounds that you couldn't shoot her without managing to draw blood? How very clever of you both."

James drew his hand back from Magnus's, shaking his head. His black locks fell around a face so like his father's that it prompted an indrawn breath from Magnus. "My father told me you acted as a sort of protector to him, but I do not need your protection, warlock."

"I rather disagree with that."

"I have taken a great many bets tonight," James Herondale informed him. "I must perform all the terrible deeds I have promised. For am I not a man of my word? I want to preserve my honor. And I want another drink!"

"What an excellent idea," Magnus said. "I have heard alcohol only improves a man's aim. The night is young. Imagine how many barmaids you can shoot before dawn."

"A warlock as dull as a scholar," said James, narrowing his amber eyes. "Who would have thought such a thing existed?"

"Magnus has not always been so dull," said Ragnor, appearing at James's shoulder with a glass of wine in hand. He gave it to the boy, who took it and downed it in a distressingly practiced manner. "There was a time, in Peru, with a boat full of pirates—"

James wiped his mouth on his sleeve and set down his glass. "I should love to sit and listen to old men reminiscing about their lives, but I have a pressing appointment to do something that is actually interesting. Another time, chaps."

He turned upon his heel and left. Magnus made to follow him.

"Let the Nephilim control their brat, if they can," Ragnor said, always happy to see chaos but not be involved in it. "Come have a drink with me."

"Another night," Magnus promised.

"Still such a soft touch, Magnus," Ragnor called after him. "Nothing you like better than a lost soul or a bad idea."

Magnus wanted to argue with that, but it was difficult when he was already forsaking warmth and the promise of a drink and a few rounds of cards, and running out into the cold after a deranged Shadowhunter.

Said deranged Shadowhunter turned on him, as if the narrow cobbled street were a cage and he some wild, hungry animal held there too long.

"I wouldn't follow me," James warned. "I am in no mood for company. Especially the company of a prim magical chaperone who does not know how to enjoy himself."

"I know perfectly well how to enjoy myself," remarked Magnus, amused, and he made a small gesture so that for an instant all the iron streetlamps lining the street rained down varicolored sparks of light. For an instant he thought he saw a light that was softer and less like burning in James Herondale's golden eyes, the beginnings of a childlike smile of delight.

The next moment, it was quenched. James's eyes were as bright as the jewels in a dragon's hoard, and no more alive or joyful. He shook his head, black locks flying in the night air, where the magic lights were fading.

"But you do not wish to enjoy yourself, do you, James Herondale?" Magnus asked. "Not really. You want to go to the devil."

"Perhaps I think I will enjoy going to the devil," said James Herondale, and his eyes burned like the fires of Hell, enticing, and promising unimaginable suffering. "Though I see no need to take anyone else with me."

No sooner had he spoken than he vanished, to all appearances softly and silently stolen away by the night air, with no one but the winking stars, the glaring streetlamps, and Magnus as witnesses.

Magnus knew magic when he saw it. He spun, and at the same moment heard the click of a decided footstep against a cobblestone. He turned to face a policeman walking his beat, truncheon swinging at his side, and a look of suspicion on his stolid face as he surveyed Magnus.

It was not Magnus the man had to watch out for.

Magnus saw the buttons on the man's uniform cease their gleaming, even though he was under a streetlamp. Magnus was able to discern a shadow falling where there was nothing to cast it, a surge of dark within the greater darkness of the night.

The policeman gave a shout of surprise as his helmet was whisked away by unseen hands. He stumbled forward, hands fumbling blindly in the air to retrieve what was long gone.

Magnus gave him a consoling smile. "Cheer up," he said. "You can find far more flattering headgear at any shop in Bond Street."

The man fainted. Magnus considered pausing to help him, but there was being a soft touch, and then there was being ridiculous enough to not pursue a most enticing mystery. A Shadowhunter who could turn into a shadow? Magnus turned and bolted after the bobbing policeman's helmet, held aloft only by a taunting darkness.

They ran down street after street, Magnus and the darkness,

until the Thames barred their path. Magnus heard the sound of its rushing swiftness rather than saw it, the dark waters at one with the night.

What he did see was white fingers suddenly clenched on the brim of the policeman's helmet, the turn of James Herondale's head, darkness replaced with the tilt of his slowly appearing grin. Magnus saw a shadow coalescing once more into flesh.

So the boy had inherited something from his mother as well as his father, then. Tessa's father had been a fallen angel, one of the kings of demons. The boy's lambent golden eyes seemed to Magnus like his own eyes suddenly, a token of infernal blood.

James saw Magnus looking, and winked before he hurled the helmet up into the air. It flew for a moment like a strange bird, spinning gently around in the air, then hit the water. The darkness was disrupted by a silver splash.

"A Shadowhunter who knows magic tricks," Magnus observed. "How novel."

A Shadowhunter who attacked the mundanes it was his mandate to protect—how delighted the Clave would be by that.

"We are but dust and shadows, as the saying goes," said James. "Of course, the saying does not add, 'Some of us also turn into shadows occasionally, when the mood takes us.' I suppose nobody predicted that I would come to pass. It's true that I have been told I am somewhat unpredictable."

"May I ask who bet you that you could steal a policeman's helmet, and why?"

"Foolish question. Never ask about the last bet, Bane," James advised him, and reached casually to his belt, where his gun was slung, and then he drew it in one fluid, easy motion. "You should be worrying about the next one."

"There isn't any chance," Magnus asked, without much hope, "that you are rather a nice fellow who believes he is cursed and must make himself seem unlovable to spare those around him from a terrible fate? Because I have heard that happens sometimes."

James seemed amused by the question. He smiled, and as he smiled, his waving black locks blended with the night, and the glow of his skin and his eyes grew as distant as the light of the stars until they became so pale, they diffused. He was nothing but a shadow among shadows again. He was an infuriating Cheshire cat of a boy, nothing left of him but the impression of his smile.

"My father was cursed," James said from the darkness. "Whereas I? I'm damned."

The London Institute was exactly as Magnus remembered it, tall and white and imposing, its tower cutting a white line against the dark sky. Shadowhunter Institutes were built as monuments to withstand the ravages of demons and time. When the doors opened, Magnus beheld again the massive stone entryway and the two flights of stairs.

A woman with wildly curling red hair, whom Magnus was sure he should remember but didn't, answered the door, her face creased with sleep and crossness. "What d'you want, warlock?" she demanded.

Magnus shifted the burden in his arms. The boy was tall, and Magnus had had a long night besides. Annoyance made his tone rather sharp as he answered:

"I want you to go tell Will Herondale that I have brought his whelp home."

The woman's eyes widened. She gave an impressed sort of whistle and vanished abruptly. A handful of moments later Magnus saw a white figure come softly down one of the staircases.

Tessa was like the Institute: hardly changed at all. She had the same smooth youthful face that she had worn twenty-five years before. Magnus thought she must have stopped aging no more than three or four years after he had last seen her. Her hair was in a long brown plait, hanging over one shoulder, and she was holding a witchlight in one hand and had a small sphere of light shining in her palm in the other.

"Been taking magic lessons, have we, Tessa?" Magnus asked.

"Magnus!" Tessa exclaimed, and her grave face lit with a welcoming smile that sent a pang of sweetness through Magnus. "But they said— Oh, no. Oh, where did you find Jamie?"

She reached the bottom of the steps, went over to Magnus, and cradled the boy's damp head in her hand in an almost absentminded gesture of affection. In that gesture Magnus saw how she had changed, saw the ingrained habit of motherhood, love for someone she had created and whom she cherished.

No other warlock would ever have a child of their own blood. Only Tessa could have that experience.

Magnus turned his head away from Tessa at the sound of a new footfall on the stairs.

The memory of Will the boy was so fresh that it was something of a shock to see Will himself now, older, broader of shoulder, but still with the same tousled black hair and laughing blue eyes. He looked just as handsome as he had ever been—more so perhaps, since he seemed so much happier. Magnus saw more marks of laughter than of time on his face, and found himself smiling. It was true what Will had said, he realized. They were friends.

Recognition crossed Will's face, and with it pleasure, but almost instantly he saw the burden Magnus carried, and worry erased all else.

"Magnus," he said. "What on earth happened to James?"

"What happened?" Magnus asked musingly. "Well, let me see. He stole a bicycle and rode it, not using his hands at any point, through Trafalgar Square. He attempted to climb Nelson's Column and fight with Nelson. Then I lost him for a brief period of time, and by the time I caught up with him, he had wandered into Hyde Park, waded into the Serpentine, spread his arms wide, and was shouting, 'Ducks, embrace me as your king!'"

"Dear God," said Will. "He must have been vilely drunk. Tessa, I can bear it no longer. He is taking awful risks with his life and rejecting all the principles I hold most dear. If he continues making an exhibition of himself throughout London, he will be called to Idris and kept there away from the mundanes. Does he not realize that?"

Magnus shrugged. "He also made inappropriate amorous advances to a startled grandmotherly sort selling flowers, an Irish wolfhound, an innocent hat stand in a dwelling he broke into, and myself. I will add that I do not believe his admiration of my person, dazzling though I am, to be sincere. He told me I was a beautiful, sparkling lady. Then he abruptly collapsed, naturally in the path of an oncoming train from Dover, and I decided it was well past time to take him home and place him in the bosom of his family. If you had rather I put him in an orphanage, I fully understand."

Will was shaking his head, shadows in his blue eyes now. "Bridget," he shouted, and Magnus thought, *Oh, yes, that was the maid's name*. "Call for the Silent Brothers," Will finished.

"You mean call for Jem," Tessa said, dropping her voice, and she and Will shared a look—what Magnus could describe only as a *married* look, the look of two people who understood each other completely and yet found each other adorable all the same.

It was quite sickening.

He cleared his throat. "Still a Silent Brother, then, is he?"

Will gave Magnus a withering look. "It does tend to be a permanent state. Here, give me my son."

Magnus let Will take James from his arms, which were left lighter if more damp, and Magnus followed Will's and Tessa's lead up the stairs. Inside the Institute it was clear they had been redecorating. Charlotte's dark drawing room now held several comfortable-looking sofas, and the walls were covered in light damask. Tall shelves were lined with books, volumes with the gilt rubbed off their spines and, Magnus was sure, the pages much thumbed. It appeared both Tessa and Will remained great readers.

Will deposited James onto one of the sofas. Tessa rushed to find a blanket as Magnus turned toward the door, only to find his hand caught in Will's grasp.

"It was very good of you to bring Jamie home," Will said. "But you were always so good to me and mine. I was little more than a boy then, and not as grateful or as gracious as I should have been."

"You were well enough, Will," said Magnus. "And I see you have grown to be better. Also, you are not bald, and neither have you grown fat. All that dashing about and fighting evil you people do is at least useful for keeping a trim figure in middle age."

Will laughed. "It's very good to see you, too." He hesitated. "About Jamie . . ."

Magnus tensed. He had not wanted to distress Will and Tessa too much. He had not told them that James had fallen when he was in the Serpentine, and made very little effort to rescue himself from drowning. He had not seemed to want to be taken from the cold depths of the water: had fought Magnus as he dragged him out, then laid his pale cheek against the dank earth of the riverbank and hid his face in his arms.

For a moment Magnus had thought he was crying, but as he stooped down to check on the boy, he found he was barely conscious. With his cruel golden eyes closed, he once again reminded Magnus of the lost boy Will had been. Magnus touched his damp hair gently and said "James," in as kind a voice as he could.

The boy's pale hands were splayed against the dark earth. The glimmer of the Herondale ring shone against his skin, and the edge of something metallic shone under his sleeve as well. His eyes were shut, the black lashes ink-dark crescents against the lines of his cheekbones. Sparkling drops of water were caught in the curling ends of those lashes, which made him look unhappy in a way he did not when awake.

"*Grace*," James had whispered in his sleep, and was silent.

Magnus had not been angry: he had found himself wishing for a benevolent grace many times himself. He bent and gathered the boy up in his arms. His head lolled against Magnus's shoulder. In sleep James had looked peaceful and innocent, and wholly human.

"This just isn't like him," Will was saying now as Tessa drew a blanket up over the boy, tucking him in firmly.

Magnus raised an eyebrow. "He's *your* son."

"What are you trying to imply?" Will demanded, and for a moment Magnus saw his eyes flash, and saw the boy with messy black hair and glaring blue eyes standing in his drawing room, furious at the whole world and at no part of it more than himself.

"It isn't like him," Tessa agreed. "He's always been so quiet, so studious. Lucie was the impetuous one, but they are both kind, good-hearted children. At parties Jamie could most often be found curled up in a corner with his Latin, or laughing at a private joke with his *parabatai*. He always kept Matthew out of trouble as well as himself. He was the only one who could make that indolent boy attend to his studies," she remarked, with a slight smile that betokened she was fond of her son's *parabatai*, no matter what his faults. "Now he is out at all hours, doing the most disgraceful things, and he will not listen to reason. He will not listen to anybody. I understand what you mean about Will, but Will was lonely and wretched in the days when he behaved badly. James has been wrapped in love all his life."

"Betrayed!" Will muttered. "Cruelly maligned by my friend and now by my own cherished wife, scorned, my name blackened—"

"I see you are still fond of histrionics, Will," said Magnus. "As well as still handsome."

They had grown up. Neither of them looked startled at all. Tessa raised her eyebrows, and Magnus saw something of her son in her then. They both had the same expressive, arched brows, giving their faces a look of both inquiry and amusement, though in James's face the amusement was bitter.

"Do stop flirting with my husband," said Tessa.

"I shall not," Magnus declared, "but I will pause briefly so that I may catch up on your news. I have not heard from you since you sent word the baby had arrived and both he and his lovely mother were thriving."

Will looked surprised. "But we sent you several letters in care of the Morgensterns, who were going to visit the Whitelaws at the New York Institute. It was you who proved to be a shocking correspondent."

"Ah," said Magnus. He himself was not even slightly surprised. This was typical behavior from Shadowhunters. "The Morgensterns must have forgotten to deliver them. How careless."

Tessa, he saw, did not look too surprised either. She was both warlock and Shadowhunter, and yet not quite either. The Shadowhunters believed that Shadowhunter blood trumped all else, but Magnus could well believe that many of the Nephilim might be unkind to a woman who could do magic and whom the years did not touch.

He doubted any of them dared be unkind in front of Will, though.

"We will be more careful about whom we entrust with our letters in future," Tessa said decisively. "We have been out of touch for far too long. How fortunate that you are here in London, both for us and for Jamie. What brings you here, business or pleasure?"

"I wish it were the business of pleasure," Magnus told her. "But no, it is very dull. A Shadowhunter I believe you know sent for me—Tatiana Blackthorn? The lady used to be a Lightwood, did she not?" Magnus turned to Will. "And your sister Cecily married her brother. Gilbert. Gaston. I have a shocking memory for Lightwoods."

"I begged Cecily not to throw herself away on a Lightworm," Will muttered.

"Will!" said Tessa. "Cecily and Gabriel are very happy together."

Will threw himself dramatically into an armchair, touching his son's wrist as he passed by, with a light, careful caress that spoke volumes.

"At least you must admit, Tess, that Tatiana is as mad as a mouse trapped in a teapot. She refuses to speak to any of us, and that includes her brothers, because she says we had a hand in her father's death. Actually, she says we pitilessly slew him. Everybody tries to point out that at the time of the pitiless slaying her father was a giant worm who had eaten her husband and followed up his meal with a palate-cleansing servant sorbet, but she insists on lurking about the manor house and sulking with all the curtains drawn."

"She has lost a great deal. She lost her child," Tessa said. "And she did speak to us that once, in Idris." She stroked back her son's hair, her face troubled. Will looked to James and fell silent.

"Mrs. Blackthorn has come from Idris to her family manor in England specifically so I might visit her, and she sent me a message through the usual Downworlder channels promising me a princely sum if I would come and cast a few spells to increase the attractions of her young ward," Magnus said, attempting to strike a lighter note. "I gather she wishes to marry her off."

Tatiana would not be the first Shadowhunter to seek a

warlock's spells to make her life easier and more pleasant. She was, however, the Shadowhunter offering the best price.

"Did she?" Will asked. "It's not as if the girl looks like a toad in a bonnet."

Tessa laughed and stifled the laugh against her hand, and Will grinned, looking pleased with himself, as he always had when he'd managed to amuse Tessa.

"I suppose I should not be casting aspersions on anybody else's children, since my son is all about in his wits. He shoots things, you know."

"I did know that he shoots things," Magnus said tactfully. "Yes."

Will sighed. "The Angel grant me patience so I do not strangle him, and wisdom so I can talk some sense into his great fat head."

"I do wonder where he gets it from," said Magnus pointedly.

"It is not the same," said Tessa. "When Will was Jamie's age, he tried to drive everyone he loved away. Jamie is as loving as ever to us, to Lucie, to Matthew, his *parabatai*. It is himself he wishes to destroy."

"And yet there is no reason for it," Will said, striking the arm of his chair with his clenched fist. "I know my son, and he would not behave this way unless he felt he had no other choice. Unless he was trying to achieve a goal, or punish himself in some way, because he felt he had done some wrong—"

You called for me? I am here.

Magnus looked up to see Brother Zachariah standing in the doorway. He was a slender outline, the hood of his robe down, baring his face. The Silent Brothers rarely bared their faces, knowing how most Shadowhunters reacted to the scars and disfigurement of their skin. It was a sign of trust that Jem showed himself to Will and Tessa in this way.

Jem was still Jem—like Tessa, he had not aged. The Silent Brothers were not immortal but aged incredibly slowly. The powerful runes that gave them knowledge and allowed them to speak with their minds also slowed their bodies' aging, turning the Brothers to living statues. Jem's hands were pale and slender under the cuffs of his robe, still musician's hands after all this time. His face seemed carved out of marble, his eyes shuttered crescents, the dark runes of the Brothers standing out on his high cheekbones. His hair waved around his temples, darkness shot with silver.

A great sadness welled up in Magnus at the sight of him. It was human to age and die, and Jem stood outside that humanity now, outside the light that burned so brightly and so briefly. It was cold outside that light and fire. No one had greater cause to know that cold than Magnus did.

On seeing Magnus, Jem inclined his head. *Magnus Bane. I did not know you would be here.*

"I—" Magnus began, but Will was already on his feet, striding across the room to Jem. He had lit up at the sight of him, and Magnus could feel Jem's attention move from himself to Will, and catch there. Those two boys had been so different, yet at times they had seemed so wholly one that it was strange for Magnus to see Will changed as all humans changed, while Jem was set apart, to see that both had gone somewhere the other could not follow. He imagined it must be even stranger for them.

And yet. There was still about them what had always reminded Magnus of an old legend he'd heard of the red thread of fate: that an invisible scarlet thread bound certain people, and however tangled it became, it could not and would not break.

The Silent Brothers moved the way one imagined a statue would move if it could. Jem had moved the same way coming in, but as Will neared him, Jem took a step toward his former *parabatai*, and the step was swift, eager, and human, as if being close to the people whom he loved made him feel made of flesh and racing blood once more.

"You're here," said Will, and implicit in the words was the sense that Will's contentment was complete. Now Jem was there, all was right with the world.

"I knew you would come," said Tessa, rising from her son's side to go after her husband, toward Jem. Magnus saw Brother Zachariah's face glow at the sound of her voice, runes and pallor no longer mattering. He was a boy again for an instant, his life just beginning, his heart full of hope and love.

How they loved each another, these three, how they had suffered for each another, and yet how much joy they clearly took from simply being in the same room. Magnus had loved before, many times, but he did not ever recall feeling the peace that radiated out from these three only from being in the others' presence. He had craved peace sometimes, like a man wandering for centuries in the desert never seeing water and having to live with the want of it.

Tessa, Will, and their lost Jem stood together in a tight knot. Magnus knew that for a few moments nothing existed in the world but the three of them.

He looked at the sofa where James Herondale lay, and saw that he was awake, his gold eyes like watchful flames teaching the candles to burn brightly. James was the young one, the boy with his whole life ahead of him, but there was no hope or joy in his face. Tessa, Will, and Jem looked natural being together, but even in this room with those who loved him better than life, James looked utterly alone. There was something desperate and desolate about his face. He tried to lean up on one elbow, and collapsed back against the cushions of the sofa, his black head tipped back as if it were too heavy for him to bear. A Herondale ring glittered on his finger, a silver bracelet on his wrist.

Tessa, Will, and Jem were murmuring together, Will's hand on Jem's arm. Magnus had never seen anyone touch a Silent Brother like that, in simple friendship. It made him ache inside, and he saw that hollow ache reflected on the face of the boy on the sofa.

Obeying an impetuous impulse, Magnus crossed the room and knelt down by the couch, close to Will's son, who looked at him with tired golden eyes. "You see them," James said. "The way they all love one another. I used to think everyone loved that way. The way it is in fairy tales. I used to think that love was giving and generous and good."

"And now?" Magnus asked.

The boy turned his face away. Magnus found himself facing the back of James's head, seeing his mop of black hair so like his father's, and the edge of his *parabatai* rune just under his collar. It must be on his back, Magnus thought, above the blade of his shoulder, where an angel's wing would be.

"James," said Magnus in a low, hurried voice. "Once your father had a terrible secret that he thought he could not tell to a soul in the world, and he told me. I can see that there is something gnawing at you, something you are keeping hidden. If there is anything you want to tell me, now or at any time, you have my word that I will keep your secrets, and that I will help you if I can."

James shifted to look at Magnus. In his face Magnus thought he caught a glimpse of softening, as if the boy were releasing his relentless grip on whatever was tormenting him. "I am not like my father," he said. "Do not mistake my despair for nobility in disguise, for it is not that. I suffer for myself, not for anyone else."

"But *why* do you suffer?" Magnus said in frustration. "Your mother was correct when she said you have been loved all your life. If you would just let me help you—"

The boy's expression shut like a door. He turned his face away from Magnus again, and his eyes closed, the light falling on the fringe of his eyelashes.

"I gave my word I would never tell," he said. "And there is not a living soul on this earth who can help me."

"James," Magnus said, honestly surprised by the despair in the boy's tone, and the alarm in Magnus's voice caught the attention of the others in the room. Tessa and Will looked away from Jem and to their son, the boy who bore Jem's name, and as one they all moved over to where he lay, Will and Tessa hand in hand.

Brother Zachariah bent over the back of the sofa and touched James's hair tenderly with those musician's fingers.

"Hello, Uncle Brother Zachariah," James said without opening his eyes. "I would say that I'm sorry to bother you, but I'm sure this is the most excitement you've had all year. Not so lively in the City of Bones, now is it?"

"James!" Will snapped. "Don't talk to Jem like that."

As if I am not used to badly behaved Herondales, Brother Zachariah said, in the way Jem had always tried to make peace between Will and the world.

"I suppose the difference is that Father always cared what you thought about him," said James. "And I don't. But don't take it personally, Uncle Jem. I do not care what anybody thinks."

And yet he made a habit of making an exhibition of himself, as Will had put it, and Magnus had no doubt it was deliberate. He must care what someone thought. He must be doing all this for a purpose. *But what purpose could it be?* Magnus wondered.

"James, this is so unlike you," Tessa said worriedly. "You have always cared. Always been kind. What is troubling you?"

"Perhaps nothing is troubling me. Perhaps I have simply realized I was rather boring before. Don't you think I was boring? All that studying, and the Latin." He shuddered. "Horrible."

There is nothing boring about caring, or about an open, loving heart, said Jem.

"So say all of you," replied James. "And it is easy to see why, the three of you, falling over yourself to love one another—each more than the other. And it *is* kind of you to trouble yourselves about me." His breath caught a little, and then he smiled, but it was a smile of great sadness. "I wish I did not trouble you so."

Tessa and Will exchanged looks of despair. The room was thick with worry and parental concerns. Magnus was beginning to feel bowed under by the weight of humanity.

"Well," he announced. "As educational and occasionally damp as this evening has been, I do not wish to intrude on a family reunion, and I really do not wish to experience any family drama, as I find with Shadowhunters that it tends to be extensive. I must be on my way."

"But you could stay here," Tessa offered. "Be our guest. We would be delighted to have you."

"A warlock in the hallowed chambers of a Shadowhunter Institute?" Magnus shuddered. "Only think."

Tessa gave him a sharp look. "Magnus—"

"Besides, I have an appointment," Magnus said. "One I should not be late for."

Will looked up with a frown. "At this time of night?"

"I have a peculiar occupation, and keep peculiar hours," said Magnus. "I seem to recall you coming to me for assistance quite a few times at odd hours of the night." He inclined his head. "Will. Tessa. Jem. Good evening."

Tessa moved to his side. "I will show you out."

"Good-bye, whoever you are," said James sleepily, closing his eyes. "I cannot recall your name."

"Don't mind him," Tessa said in a low voice as she moved with Magnus toward the exit. She paused in the doorway for a moment, looking back at her son and the two men who stood with him. Will and Jem were shoulder to shoulder, and from across the room it was impossible to miss Jem's slighter frame, the fact that he had not aged, as Will had. Though, there was in Will's voice all the eagerness of a boy when he said, in answer to a question Magnus did not hear, "Why, yes, of course you can play it before you go. It is in the music room as always, kept ever the same for you."

"His violin?" Magnus murmured. "I did not think the Silent Brothers cared for music."

Tessa sighed softly and moved out into the corridor, Magnus beside her. "Will does not see a Silent Brother when he looks at James," she said. "He sees only Jem."

"Is it ever difficult?" he asked.

"Is what difficult?"

"Sharing your husband's heart so entirely with someone else," he said.

"If it were different, it would not be Will's heart," Tessa said. "He knows he shares my heart with Jem as well. I would have it no other way—and he would have it no other way with me."

So much a part of one another that there was no way to be untangled, even now, and no wish to be so. Magnus wanted to ask if Tessa was ever afraid of what would happen to her when Will was gone, when their bond was finally severed, but he did not. It would with luck be a long time until Tessa's first death, a long time before she entirely realized the burden of being immortal and yet loving that which was not.

"Very beautiful," Magnus said instead. "Well, I wish you all the best with your little hellion."

"We shall see you again before you leave London, of course," said Tessa in that tone of hers she had had even as a girl, that brooked no contradiction.

"Indeed," Magnus said. He hesitated. "And, Tessa, if you ever need me—and I hope if you do, it will be many long, happy years from now—send me a message, and I will be with you at once."

They both knew what he meant.

"I will," said Tessa, and she gave him her hand. Hers was small and soft, but her grip was surprisingly strong.

"Believe me, dear lady," Magnus told her with an assumption of lightness. He released her hand and bowed with a flourish. "Call me and I come!"

As Magnus turned to walk away from the church, he heard

the sound of violin music carried to him on the cloudy London air, and remembered another night, a night of ghosts and snow and Christmas music, and Will standing on the steps of the Institute, watching Magnus as he went. Now it was Tessa who stood at the door with her hand lifted in farewell until Magnus was at the gate with its ominous lettered message: WE ARE DUST AND SHADOWS. He looked back and saw her slight pale figure at the Institute threshold and thought again, *Yes, perhaps I was wrong to leave London.*

It was not the first time Magnus had made his way from London to Chiswick to visit Lightwood House. Benedict Lightwood's home had often been thrown open to Downworlders who'd been amenable to his idea of a good time.

It had been a grand manor once, the stone brilliant white and adorned with Greek statuary and too many pillars to count. The Lightwoods were proud and ostentatious people, and their home, in all its neoclassical glory, had reflected that.

Magnus knew what had become of all that pride. The patriarch, Benedict Lightwood, had contracted a disease from consorting with demons and had transformed into a murderous monster that his own sons had been forced to slay, with the assistance of a host of other Shadowhunters. Their manor had been taken away by the Clave as punishment, their monies confiscated, and their family had become a laughingstock, a byword for sin and a betrayal of all that the Shadowhunters held dear.

Magnus had little time for the Shadowhunters' overweening arrogance, and usually enjoyed seeing them taken down a peg, but even he had rarely seen a family fall so far so terribly fast. Gabriel and Gideon, Benedict's two sons, had managed to claw their way back to respectability through good behavior and the graces of the Consul, Charlotte Branwell. Their sister, however, was another matter entirely.

How she had managed to get Lightwood House back into her clutches, Magnus did not know. *As mad as a mouse trapped in a teapot,* Will had said of her, and knowing of the family's disgraced state, Magnus hardly expected the grandeur of Benedict's time. Doubtless the place would be shabby now, dusty with time, only a few servants left to keep it up and in order—

The carriage Magnus had hired came to a stop. "The place looks abandoned," opined the driver, casting a doubtful eye over at the iron gates, which looked rusted shut and bound with vines.

"Or haunted," Magnus suggested brightly.

"Well, I can't get in. Them gates won't open," said the driver gruffly. "You'll have to get out and walk, if you're that determined."

Magnus was. His curiosity was alight now, and he approached the gates like a cat, ready to scale them if need be.

A tweak of magic, a bit of an opening spell, and the gates burst wide with a shower of rusted metal flakes, onto a long, dark overgrown drive that led up to a ghostly manor house in the distance, glimmering like a tombstone under the full moon.

Magnus closed the gates and went forward, listening to the sound of night birds in the trees overhead, the rustle of leaves in the night wind. A forest of blackened tangles loomed all about him, the remains of the famous Lightwood gardens. Those gardens had been lovely once. Magnus distantly recalled overhearing Benedict Lightwood drunkenly saying that they had been his dead wife's joy.

Now the high hedges of the Italian garden had formed a maze, a twisted one from which there was clearly no escape. They had killed the monster Benedict Lightwood had become in these gardens, Magnus remembered hearing, and the black ichor had seeped from the monster's veins into the earth in a dark unstoppable flood.

Magnus felt a scratch against one hand and looked down to see a rosebush that had survived but gone wild. It took him a moment to identify the plant, for though the shape of the blooms was familiar, the color was not. The roses were as black as the blood of the dead serpent.

He plucked one. The flower crumbled in his palm as if it were made of ash, as if it had already been dead.

Magnus passed on toward the house.

The corruption that had claimed the roses had not spared the manor. What had once been a smooth white facade was now gray with years, streaked with the black of dirt and the green of rot. The shining pillars were twined about with dying vines, and the balconies, which Magnus remembered as like the hollows of alabaster goblets, were now filled with the dark snarls of thorns and the debris of years.

The door knocker had been an image of a shining golden lion with a ring held in its mouth. Now the ring lay rotted on the steps, and the gray lion's mouth hung open and empty in a hungry snarl. Magnus knocked briskly on the door. He heard the sound echo through the inside of the house as if all were the heavy silence of a tomb therein and ever would be, as if any noise was a disturbance.

The conviction that everyone in this house must be dead had gained such a hold on Magnus that it was a shock when the woman who had summoned him here opened the door.

It was, of course, rather odd for a lady to be opening her own front door, but from the look of the place, Magnus assumed the entire staff of servants had been given the decade off.

Magnus had a dim recollection of seeing Tatiana Lightwood at one of her father's parties: a glimpse of a perfectly ordinary girl with wide green eyes, behind a hastily closing door.

Even after seeing the house and the grounds, he was not prepared for Tatiana Blackthorn.

Her eyes were still very green. Her stern mouth was bracketed with lines of bitter disappointment and grave pain. She looked like a woman in her sixties, not her forties. She was wearing a gown of a fashion decades past—it hung from her wasted shoulders and fluttered around her body like a shroud. The fabric bore dark brown stains, but in patches it was a faded pastel bordering on white, while other spots remained what Magnus thought must have been its original fuchsia.

She should have looked ridiculous. She was wearing a silly bright pink dress for a younger woman, someone who was almost a girl, in love with her husband and going on a visit to her papa.

She did not look ridiculous. Her stern face forbade pity. She, like the house, was awe-inspiring in her ruin.

"Bane," Tatiana said, and held the door open wide enough that Magnus could pass through. She said no word of welcome.

She shut the door behind Magnus, the sound as final as the closing of a tomb. Magnus paused in the hall, waiting for the woman behind him, and as he waited, he heard another footstep above their heads, a sign there was someone else alive in the house.

Down the wide curving staircase toward them came a girl. Magnus had always found mortals to be beautiful, and had seen many mortals whom anybody would have described as beautiful.

This was extraordinary beauty, beauty unlike the beauty of most mortals.

In the stained and filthy ruin the house had become, she shone like a pearl. Her hair was the color of a pearl too, palest ivory with a sheen of gold on it, and her skin was the luminous pink and white of a seashell. Her lashes were thick and dark, veiling eyes of deep unearthly gray.

Magnus drew in a breath. Tatiana heard him and looked over, smiling a triumphant smile. "She's glorious, isn't she? My ward. My Grace."

Grace.

The realization struck Magnus like a blow. Of course James Herondale had not been calling out for something as inchoate and distant as a benediction, the soul's yearning for divine mercy and understanding. His desperation had been centered on something far more flesh-and-blood than that.

But why is it a secret? Why can no one help him? Magnus struggled to keep his face a blank as the girl moved toward him and offered her hand.

"How do you do," she murmured.

Magnus stared down at her. Her face was a porcelain cup, upturned; her eyes held promises. The combination of beauty, innocence, and the promise of sin was staggering. "Magnus Bane," she said, in a breathy, soft voice. Magnus couldn't help staring at her. Everything about her was so perfectly constructed to appeal. She was beautiful, yes, but it was more than that. She seemed shy, yet all her attention was focused on Magnus, as if he were the most fascinating thing she had ever seen. There was no man who did not want to see himself reflected like that in a beautiful girl's eyes. And if the neckline of her dress was a shade low, it did not seem scandalous, for her gray eyes were full of an innocence that said that she did not know of desire, not yet, but there was a lushness to the curve of her lip, a dark light in her eyes that said that under the right hands she would be a pupil who yielded the most exquisite result. . . .

Magnus took a step back from her as if she were a poisonous snake. She did not look hurt, or angry, or even startled. She turned a look on Tatiana, a sort of curious inquiry. "Mama?" she said. "What is wrong?"

Tatiana curled her lip. "This one is not like others," she said. "I mean, he likes girls well enough, and boys as well, I hear, but his taste does not run to Shadowhunters. And he is not mortal. He has been alive a long time. One cannot expect him to have the normal—reactions."

Magnus could well imagine what the normal reactions would be—the reactions of a boy like James Herondale, sheltered and taught that love was gentle, love was kind, that one should love with all one's heart and give away all one's soul. Magnus could imagine the normal reactions to this girl, a girl whose every gesture, every expression, every line, cried, *Love her, love her, love her.*

But Magnus was not that boy. He reminded himself of his manners, and bowed.

"Charmed," he said. "Or whatever effect would please you best, I'm sure."

Grace regarded him with cool interest. Her reactions were muted, Magnus thought, or rather, carefully gauged. She seemed a creature made to attract everyone and express nothing real, though it would take a master observer, like Magnus, to know it.

She reminded Magnus suddenly not of any mortal but of the vampire Camille, who had been his latest and most regrettable real love.

Magnus had spent years imagining there was fire behind Camille's ice, that there were hopes and dreams and love waiting for him. What he had loved in Camille had been nothing but illusion. Magnus had acted like a child, fancying there were shapes and stories to be made of the clouds in the sky.

He turned away from the sight of Grace in her trim white-and-blue dress, like a vision of Heaven in the gray hell of this house, and looked to Tatiana. Her eyes were narrowed with contempt.

"Come, warlock," she said. "I believe we have business to discuss."

Magnus followed Tatiana and Grace up the stairs and down a long corridor that was almost pitch black. Magnus heard the crack and crunch of broken glass beneath his feet, and in the dim, hardly-there light he saw something scuttling away from his approach. He hoped it was something as harmless as a rat, but something about its movements suggested a shape far more grotesque.

"Do not try to open any doors or drawers while you are here, Bane." Tatiana's voice floated back to him. "My father left behind many guardians to protect what is ours."

She opened the door, and Magnus beheld the room within.

There were an upturned desk and heavy curtains sagging in the windows like bodies from a gibbet, and on the wooden floor were splinters and streaks of blood, the marks of a long-ago struggle nobody had cleaned up.

There were many picture frames hanging askew or with the glass broken. A great many of them seemed to contain nautical adventures—Magnus had been put off the sea by his ill-fated attempt to live a piratical life for a day—but even the pictures that were whole were clouded with gray. The painted ships appeared to be sinking in seas of dust.

There was only one portrait that was whole and clean. It was an oil painting, with no glass covering it, but there was not a speck of dust on its surface. It was the only clean thing, besides Grace, in the entire house.

The portrait was of a boy, about seventeen years old. He was sitting in a chair, his head resting against the back as if he did not have the strength to support it on his own. He was terribly thin and as white as salt. His eyes were a deep, still green, like a woodland pool hidden under the overhanging leaves of a tree, never exposed to sun or wind. He had dark hair falling, as fine-spun and straight as silk, across his brow, and his long fingers were curled over the arms of the chair, almost clinging to it, and the desperate clutch of those hands told a silent story of pain.

Magnus had seen portraits like this before, the last images of the lost. He could tell even across the years how much effort it had cost the boy to sit for that portrait, for the comfort of loved ones who would live after he was gone.

His pallid face had the distant look of one who had already taken too many steps along the path to death for him to be recalled. Magnus thought of James Herondale, burning up with too much light, too much love, too much, too much—while the boy in the portrait was as lovely as a dying poet, with the fragile beauty of a candle about to gutter out.

On the ragged wallpaper that might once have been green and that had mutated to a grayish-green color, like a sea flooded with waste, were words written in the same dark brown as the stains on Tatiana's dress. Magnus had to admit to himself what that color was: blood that had been spilled years since and yet never washed clean.

The wallpaper was hanging off the walls in tatters. Magnus could make out only a word here and there on the remaining pieces: PITY, REGRET, INFERNAL.

The last sentence in the series was still legible. It read, MAY GOD HAVE MERCY ON OUR SOULS. Beneath this, written not in blood but cut through the wallpaper into the wall by what Magnus suspected was a different hand, were the words, GOD HAS NO MERCY AND NOR WILL I.

Tatiana sank into an armchair, its upholstery worn and stained by the years, and Grace knelt at her adoptive mother's side on the grimy floor. She knelt daintily, delicately, her skirts billowing around her like the petals of a flower. Magnus supposed that it must have been a habit with her to come to rest in filth, and rise from it to all outward appearance radiantly pure.

"To business, then, madam," said Magnus, and he added silently to himself, *To leaving this house as soon as possible.* "Tell me exactly why you have need of my fabulous and unsurpassed powers, and what you would have me do."

"You can already see, I trust," said Tatiana, "that my Grace is in no need of spells to enhance her natural charms."

Magnus looked at Grace, who was gazing at her hands linked in her lap. Perhaps she was already using spells. Perhaps she was simply beautiful. Magic or nature, they were much the same thing to Magnus.

"I'm sure she is already an enchantress in her own right."

Grace said nothing, only glanced up at him from under her lashes. It was a demurely devastating look.

"I want something else from you, warlock. I want you," Tatiana said, slowly and distinctly, "to go out into the world and kill me five Shadowhunters. I will tell you how it is to be done, and I will pay you most handsomely."

Magnus was so astonished, he honestly believed he must have heard her incorrectly. "Shadowhunters?" he repeated. "Kill?"

"Is my request so very strange? I have no love for the Shadowhunters."

"But, my dear madam, you *are* a Shadowhunter."

Tatiana Blackthorn folded her hands in her lap. "I am no such thing."

Magnus stared at her for a long moment. "Ah," he said. "I beg your pardon. Uh, would it be terribly uncivil of me to inquire what you do believe yourself to be? Do you think that you are a lamp shade?"

"I do not find your levity amusing."

Magnus's tone was hushed as he said, "I beg your pardon again. Do you believe yourself to be a pianoforte?"

"Hold your tongue, warlock, and do not talk of matters about which you know *nothing*." Tatiana's hands were clenched suddenly, curled as tight as claws in the skirt of her once-bright dress. The note of real agony in her voice was enough to silence

Magnus, but she continued. "A Shadowhunter is a warrior. A Shadowhunter is born and trained to be a hand of God upon this earth, wiping it free of evil. That is what our legends say. That is what my father taught me, but my father taught me other things too. He decreed that I would not be trained as a Shadowhunter. He told me that was not my place, that my place in life was to be the dutiful daughter of a warrior, and in time the helpmeet of a noble warrior and the mother of warriors who would carry on the glory of the Shadowhunters for another generation."

Tatiana made a sweeping gesture to the words on the walls, the stains on the floor.

"Such glory," she said, and laughed bitterly. "My father and my family were disgraced, and my husband was torn apart in front of my eyes—torn apart. I had one child, my beautiful boy, my Jesse, but he could not be trained to be a warrior. He was always so weak, so sickly. I begged them not to put the runes on him—I was certain that would kill him—but the Shadowhunters held me back and held him down as they burned the Marks into his flesh. He screamed and screamed. We all thought he would die then, but he did not. He held on for me, for his mama, but their cruelty damned him. Each year he grew sicker and weaker until it was too late. He was sixteen when they told me he could not live."

Her hands moved restlessly as she spoke, from her gesture at the walls to plucking at her gown dyed with old, old blood. She touched her arms as if they still hurt where she had been held back by the Shadowhunters, and she toyed with a large ornate locket that hung around her neck. She opened and closed it, the tarnished metal gleaming between her fingers, and Magnus thought he saw a glimpse of a ghastly portrait. Her son again?

He looked toward the picture on the wall, the pale young face, and calculated how old a child of Rupert Blackthorn's must have been when the man had died twenty-five years before. If Jesse Blackthorn had died when he was sixteen then the boy must have been dead for nine years, but perhaps a mother's mourning never ended.

"I am aware that you have suffered greatly, Mrs. Blackthorn," said Magnus, as gently as he was able. "But instead of some plot of vengeance through the senseless slaughter of Shadowhunters, consider that there are many Shadowhunters who desire nothing more than to help you, and to ease your pain."

"Indeed? Of whom do you speak? William Herondale"—and in Tatiana's mouth hatred dripped from every syllable of Will's name—"sneered at me because all I did was scream as my beloved died, but tell me, what else could I have done? What else had I ever been taught to do?" Tatiana's eyes were huge and poison-green, eyes with enough pain in them to eat away at a world and devour a soul. "Can you tell me, warlock? Could William Herondale tell me? Can anyone tell me what I should have done, when I did everything I was ever asked to do? My husband is dead, my father is dead, my brothers are lost, my home was stolen, and the Nephilim had no power to save my son. I was everything I was ever asked to be, and as my reward my life was burned to ash. Do not speak to me of easing my pain. My pain is all that I have left. Do not speak to me of being a Shadowhunter. I am not one of them. I refuse to be."

"Very well, madam. You have made your anti-Shadowhunter position amply clear," said Magnus. "What I do not know is why you think I will help you get what you want."

Magnus was many things, but he had never been a fool. The death of a few Shadowhunters was not an aim in itself. If that were all she wanted, she would not have needed to go to Magnus.

The only reason she could have to go to a warlock was if she wanted to use those deaths, to alchemize Shadowhunter lives into magic for a spell. It would be the darkest of dark spells, and the fact that Tatiana knew of it told Magnus this was not the first time she had turned to dark magic.

What Tatiana Blackthorn, whose pain had eaten away at her like a wolf inside her breast, wanted from dark magic, Magnus did not know. He did not want to know what she had done with power in the past, and he certainly did not want her to have power that could be cataclysmic now.

Tatiana frowned a little puzzled frown that made her look like Benedict Lightwood's spoiled and cosseted daughter again. "For money, of course."

"You imagine I would kill five people, and leave untold power in your hands," said Magnus, "for money?"

Tatiana waved a hand. "Oh, don't try to drive the price up by aping your betters and pretending that you have any morals or tender feelings, demon spawn. Name a higher sum and be done with it. The hours of the night are precious to me, and I wish to waste no further time on one such as you."

It was the casualness with which she spoke that was so chilling. Mad though Tatiana might have been, here she was not raving or bitter. She was simply working from the facts as Shadowhunters knew them: that a Downworlder must be so entirely corrupt that she did not even dream he had a heart.

Of course, of course, the vast majority of the Shadowhunters thought of him as something less than human, and as far below the children of the Angel as apes were below men. He might sometimes be useful, but he was a creature to be despised, used but then discarded, his touch avoided because it was unclean.

He had been very useful to Will Herondale, after all. Will had not come to him searching for a friend but a convenient source of magic. Even the best Shadowhunters were not so different from the rest.

"Let me say to you what I said once, in an entirely different context, to Catherine the Great," Magnus declared. "My dear lady, you cannot afford me, and also, please leave that horse alone. Good night."

He made a bow and then made his way, with some speed, out of the room. As the door shut with a snap, he heard Tatiana's voice snapping to match it: "Go after him!"

He was not surprised to hear soft footsteps pattering after him down the stairs. Magnus turned from the front door and met Grace's eyes.

Her footfalls were as light as a child's, but she did not look like a child. In that porcelain-pure face her eyes were gray hollows, deep alluring lakes with sirens in their depths. She met Magnus's eyes with a level gaze, and Magnus was reminded once again of Camille.

It was remarkable that a girl who looked no more than sixteen could rival a centuries-old vampire for self-possession. She had not had time to freeze past caring. *There must*, Magnus thought, *be something behind all this ice.*

"You will not return upstairs, I see," Grace said. "You want no part of Mama's plan."

It was not a question, and she did not sound shocked or curious. It did not seem unthinkable to her, then, that Magnus might have scruples. Perhaps the girl had qualms of conscience herself, but she was shut up here in this dark house with a madwoman, nothing but bitterness poured into her ears from dusk to daybreak. Little wonder if she was different from other girls.

Magnus felt regret suddenly for the way he had shuddered back from Grace. She was not much more than a child, after all, and nobody knew better than he what it was like to be judged and shunned. He reached out to touch her arm. "Do you have somewhere else to go?" Magnus asked her.

"Somewhere else?" said Grace. "We reside mainly in Idris."

"What I mean is, would she let you leave? Do you need help?"

Grace moved with such speed that it was as if she were a bolt of lightning wrapped in muslin, the long gleaming blade flying from her skirts to her hand. She held the glittering point against Magnus's chest, over his heart.

Here was a Shadowhunter, Magnus thought. Tatiana had learned something from the mistakes of her father. She'd had the girl trained.

"I am no prisoner here."

"No?" Magnus asked. "Then what are you?"

Grace's awful, awe-inspiring eyes narrowed. They were glittering like the steel, and were, Magnus was sure, no less deadly. "I am my mother's blade."

Shadowhunters often died young, and left children behind to be raised by others. That was nothing unusual. It was natural that such a ward, taken into a Shadowhunter's home, would think of and speak to their guardian as a parent. Magnus had thought nothing of it. Yet now it occurred to him that a child might be so grateful to be taken in that her loyalty would be fierce, that a girl raised by Tatiana Blackthorn might not wish for rescue. She might wish for nothing more than the fulfillment of her mother's dark plans.

"Are you threatening me?" Magnus said softly.

"If you do not intend to help us," she said, "then leave this house. Dawn is coming."

"I am not a vampire," Magnus said. "I shall not disappear with the light."

"You will if I kill you before the sun comes up," said Grace. "Who would miss one warlock?"

And she smiled, a wild smile that reminded him again of Camille. That potent blend of beauty and cruelty. He had fallen victim to it himself. He could only imagine again, with growing horror, what the effect would have been on James Herondale, a gentle boy who had been reared to believe that love, too, was gentle. James had given his heart to this girl, Magnus thought, and Magnus knew well enough from Edmund and Will what it meant when a Herondale gave his heart away. It was not a gift that could be returned.

Tessa, Will, and Jem had raised James in love, and had surrounded him with love and the goodness it could produce. But they had given him no armor against the evil. They had wrapped his heart in silks and velvet, and then he had given it to Grace Blackthorn, and she had spun for it a cage of razor wire and broken glass, burned it to bits, and blown away the remains, another layer of ashes in this place of beautiful horrors.

Magnus waved a hand behind his back, then stepped away from Grace's blade, away through the magically open door.

"You will tell no one of what my mother asked of you tonight," said Grace. "Or I will ensure your destruction."

"I believe you think you could," Magnus breathed. She was terrible and brilliant, like the light shining off the edge of a razor. "Oh, and by the way? I suspect that if James Herondale had known I was coming here, he would have sent his regards."

Grace lowered her sword, nothing more. Its point rested gently on the ground. Her hand did not shake, and her lashes screened her eyes. "What do I care for James Herondale?" she asked.

"I thought you might. After all, a blade does not get to choose where it is pointed."

Grace looked up. Her eyes were still, deep pools, entirely unruffled.

"A blade does not care," she told him.

Magnus turned and made his way past tangles of black roses and undergrowth down toward the rusted gates. He looked back at the manor only once, saw the wreck of what had been grand and gracious, and saw a curtain fluttering in a window high above, and the suggestion of a face. He wondered who was watching him go.

He could warn Downworlders to steer clear of Tatiana and her endeavors. No matter what the price offered, no Downworlder would fail to listen to a warning against one of the Nephilim. Tatiana would raise no dark magic.

Magnus could do that much, but he did not see a way to help James Herondale. Grace and Tatiana might have cast a spell on him, Magnus supposed. He would not put it past either of them, but he could not see why they would. What possible role could James Herondale have to play in whatever dark plot they were hatching? More likely the boy had simply fallen prey to her charms. Love was love; there was no spell to cure a broken heart that did not also destroy that heart's capacity for love forever.

And there was no reason for Magnus to tell Will and Tessa what he had learned. James's feelings for Grace were his secret to keep. Magnus had told the boy he would never betray his secrets; he had sworn it. He had never betrayed Will's confidence, and he would not betray James's now. What good would it do Will and Tessa, to know the name of their son's pain and still have no remedy for it?

He thought once more of Camille, and how it had hurt him to learn the truth about her, how he had struggled like a man crawling over knives not to know it, and finally, with even greater pain, had been forced to accept it.

Magnus did not take such suffering lightly, but even mortals did not die of broken hearts. No matter how cruel Grace had been, he told himself, James would heal. Even though he was a Herondale.

He opened the gates with his hands, thorns scratching his flesh, and he remembered again his first sight of Grace and the feeling he'd had of being faced with a predator. She was very different from Tessa, who had always steadied and anchored Will, softened his eyes into humor and his lips to gentleness.

It would be ironic, Magnus thought, terribly and cruelly ironic, for one Herondale to be saved by love, and another Herondale damned by it.

He tried to shake off both the memory of Tessa and Will and the echo of Tatiana's condemning words. He had promised Tessa that he would return, but now he found all he wanted to do was escape. He did not want to care what Shadowhunters thought of him. He did not want to care what would become of them or their children.

He had offered help to three Shadowhunters this night. One of them had replied that he was beyond help, one had asked him to commit murder, and one had pointed a blade at him.

His relationship of mutual distant tolerance with the Whitelaws of the New York Institute seemed suddenly alluring. He was part of Downworld New York, and would have it no other way. He was glad he had left London. He discovered in himself a pang for New York and its brighter lights, and fewer broken hearts.

"Where to?" asked the driver.

Magnus thought of the ship from Southampton to New York, of standing on the deck of the boat, letting the sea air wash him clean of the musty air of London. He said, "I believe I am going home."

The Rise of the Hotel Dumort

By Cassandra Clare and Maureen Johnson

The arrow made a kind of singing noise as it cut through the air. It entered Aldous's chest like a knife sliding easily into an apple. Aldous sat upright for a moment, looking at it; then he slumped to the side, dead.

Magnus watched his blood hit the granite.

—The Rise of the Hotel Dumort

SHUNK
STAY OR GO. DECIDE NOW, AS I AM GOING TO OPEN THE POR–
RUN!
KRAK
BRRRM

Late September 1929

Magnus spotted the little vamp vampire right away. She was winding her way through the crowd, pausing for a moment for a quick shimmy by the band. She had perfectly bobbed hair, shiny black with a straight bang, just like Louise Brooks. She wore an electric-blue dress with delicate, dripping beadwork that skimmed her knees.

In most ways, she looked exactly like a normal customer at Magnus's speakeasy, and she easily blended in with the three or four dozen people who packed onto his small dance floor. But there was something *separate* about her, something dreamy and strange. The music was fast, but she danced at a sultry middle pace. Her skin was stark white, but not the dusty white from cosmetic powder. And as she did her lonely little snake dance right in front of the saxophone player, she turned herself and made direct eye contact with Magnus. When she did so, two little half fangs appeared against a bright red lip. Realizing they were out, she giggled and clapped a hand to her mouth. A moment later, they had retracted.

Meanwhile, Alfie, who was by now clinging to the bar for support, forged on with a story.

"I tole him . . . Magnus, you listenin'?"

"Of course, Alfie," Magnus said. Alfie was a very handsome and entertaining regular with excellent taste in suits and a love of strong cocktails. He told very good stories and smiled very good smiles. He was a banker or something. Stockbroker maybe. Everyone had something to do with money these days.

". . . I tole him, you can't take a boat up to your hotel room. And he said, ''Course I can. I'm a *captain*!' I said, I said to him, I said—"

"One moment, Alfie. Something I need to attend to."

"I'm just gettin' to the bes' part. . . ."

"Just one moment," Magnus said again, patting his friend's arm. "I'll be right back."

Alfie followed the track of Magnus's gaze and arrived at the girl.

"Now that's a tasty tomato," he said, nodding. "But I didn't think that was your taste."

"My tastes are universal," Magnus replied with a smile.

"Well, getta wiggle on. She won't be here all night. I'll watcha bar for you." Alfie slapped the bar. "You can trust me."

Magnus nodded to Max, his excellent bartender, and Max

immediately made another South Side for Alfie. "To keep your whistle wet while I'm gone."

"Ver' kind," Alfie said, nodding. "You're an egg, Dry."

Magnus called his bar Mr. Dry's. America was technically now all "dry," alcohol being illegal everywhere. But the truth was, most places were "wet"—awash with the stuff. New York especially. Everyone in New York drank, and the fact that they now did so illegally only made it better. The speakeasy, as far as Magnus was concerned, was one of mankind's greatest achievements. Intimate, celebratory, illegal without being immoral—a frisson of danger without any real peril.

Mr. Dry's was not a large place—speakeasies rarely were. By nature, they were secret. His was concealed behind the facade of a wig store on West 25th Street. To get in, you needed to say the password to his very efficient doorman, who viewed the prospective guest through a small slit panel in a reinforced door in the back wall of the shop. Once inside, you squeezed through a narrow hallway and entered Magnus's proud domain—ten tables and a marble bar (imported from Paris) backed by a mahogany display of every elusive bottle of things exotic Magnus had been able to get his hands on.

Most of the space went to his stage and dance floor. It pulsated under the pounding of dancing feet. In the morning, it would be cleaned and waxed, and the scuff marks of a thousand blows of dance shoes would be wiped away. He gently slipped through the dancers, most so intense and inebriated that they were unaware he was there. He enjoyed the soft (and occasionally not so soft) pummeling of flying limbs and kicking heels. He enjoyed feeling the body heat and being carried by the movement and the surge of the dancers as they more or less became one solid, pulsating mass.

The little vampire was young—no more than sixteen—and she only came up to Magnus's chest height. He leaned down and spoke into her ear.

"Perhaps I can buy you a drink?" he said. "A private one? In the back?"

The tips of the fangs popped out again when she smiled.

Magnus already felt somewhat reassured—the half-fanged smile probably wasn't from hunger. Drunkenness could cause fangs to poke out a bit. But vampires, like mundanes, often sought after salty foods and amorous encounters when inebriated.

"This way," he said, pushing back a curtain and revealing a short hallway leading to a single door. Right behind the main club, Magnus had constructed a small and intensely private room with a zinc bar. This room was lined in large stained-glass panels, illuminated from behind with electric lights, portraying Dionysus, the Greek god of wine. This was where he kept the very best and the very worst of his stock, and this was where he conducted his most private business.

"I don't believe we've met before," he said as she plopped happily onto a bar stool and spun around.

"Oh, I know who *you* are. You're Magnus Bane."

She had one of those New York accents that Magnus was still getting used to, even though he had been here for several months. It was brassy and big, like a blinking neon sign. Her kid-leather dancing shoes had scuffed toes, and there was a mud stain halfway up the base of the heel, plus flecks of other substances that Magnus didn't want to know anything about. These were shoes for dancing *and* shoes for hunting.

"And what may I call you?"

"Call me Dolly," she said.

Magnus pulled a bottle of cold champagne out of the large tub of ice that contained at least sixty identical bottles.

"I like this place," Dolly said. "It's got class."

"I'm glad you think so."

"Lotsa places are classy," Dolly said, reaching into a jar on the bar and helping herself to some maraschino cherries, plucking them up with her long (and probably dirty) fingernails. "But they're fake classy, you know? This seems real classy. You got good wine. Like that stuff."

She indicated the cut-rate champagne Magnus was holding and pouring into a glass for her. The bottle, like the others in the tub, was certainly nice, but they'd all been filled with fizzed-up cheap wine and cunningly recorked. Vampires could drink quite a lot and could be expensive to have around, and he felt certain she would not be able to tell the difference. He was right. She drained half the glass in the first sip and held it out for a top-up.

"Well, Dolly," Magnus said, refilling her glass, "I certainly don't care what you get up to on the street or anywhere else, but I do like my clientele. I consider it a matter of good service to make sure vampires don't eat them under my roof."

"I didn't come here to eat," she said. "We go down to the Bowery for that. I was told to come down here and ask about you."

The shoes did bear out the Bowery story. Those downtown streets could be filthy.

"Oh? And who is so kind as to inquire about little me?"

"Nobody," the girl said.

"Nobody," Magnus said, "is one of my favorite names."

This caused the vampire girl to giggle and spin on her stool. She drained off the glass and held it out for more. Magnus refilled it once again.

"My friend . . ."

"Nobody."

"Nobody, yeah. I just met h—this person, but this person is one of mine, ya know?"

"A vampire."

"Right. Anyways, they want to tell you something," she said. "They said you gotta get out of New York."

"Oh really? And why is that?"

In reply, she giggled and half slid, half fell from the stool and broke into a shuffling and drunken private Charleston to the music that came pounding through the wall.

"See," she said, as she did her little dance, "things are about to get dangerous. Something about the mundie money and how it's an omen. See, it's all going to break, or something. All the money. And when it does, it means that the world is going to end. . . ."

Magnus sighed internally.

The New York Downworld was one of the most ridiculous places he had ever been, which was partly the reason he now spent his time serving illegal alcohol to mundanes. And still, he couldn't avoid this nonsense. People came to bars to talk, and so did Downworlders. The werewolves were paranoid. The vampires were gossips. Everyone had a story. Something was always *about to happen*, something big. It was just part of the mood of the time. The mundanes were making absurd amounts of money on Wall Street and spending it on fripperies and moving pictures and booze. These were things Magnus could respect. But the Downworld dealt in half-baked omens and pointless rivalries. Clans were fighting one another for control of small, inconsequential patches of ground. The fey kept to themselves as ever, occasionally snatching the stray human from outside the Central Park Casino and luring them down to their world with the promise of a party they would never forget.

At least a pretty flapper vampire talking nonsense was better than a slobbering drunk werewolf. Magnus nodded as if listening and mentally counted the bottles of brandy and rum in the storage shelves below the bar.

"These mundies, see, they're trying to raise a demon. . . ."

"Mundanes do that all too frequently," Magnus said, moving a misplaced bottle of gold rum that had been put in with the spiced. "Right now, they also enjoy sitting on the top of flagpoles and walking on the wings of airborne biplanes. This is the age of stupid hobbies."

"Well, these mundies mean business."

"They always mean business, Dolly," Magnus said. "It always ends messily. I've seen enough mundanes splattered on walls to last me—"

Suddenly a bell on the wall started ringing feverishly. This was followed by a loud, deep call from the main room.

"RAID!"

This was followed by a lot of screaming.

"Excuse me a moment," Magnus said. He set the bottle of cheap champagne on the bar and indicated that Dolly should help herself, as he was sure she would even without permission. He went back through into the main bar, where an atmosphere of general madness had taken over. The band didn't pack up, but they had stopped playing. Some people were gulping back drinks, others running for the door, still others crying and panicking.

"Ladies and gentlemen!" he called. "Please simply set your drinks on the tables. All will be well. Remain seated."

Magnus had enough regulars now that there was somewhat of an established routine. These people were sitting down and cheerfully lighting cigarettes, barely turning to look at the axes that were already picking their way through the door.

"Lights!" Magnus called dramatically.

At once, the bar staff turned off all the lights and the speakeasy was thrown into darkness, save for the glowing orange tips of cigarettes.

"Now, please, everyone," Magnus said, over the yells of police and the banging of the axe and the splintering of the wood. "If we could all count to three together. One!"

They joined in nervously for "two" and "three." There was a flash of blue, then a final crack as the door came down and the police tumbled inside. Then all at once, the lights came up again. But the speakeasy was gone. All the patrons found in front of them were porcelain teapots and cups of tea. The jazz band had been replaced by a string quartet, who immediately began playing soothing music. The bottles behind the bar were gone, replaced by a well-stocked bookshelf. Even the décor had changed—the walls were lined with bookshelves and velvet draperies, all concealing the bar and the stock of alcohol.

"Gentlemen!" Magnus threw open his arms. "Welcome to our tea and book circle. We were just about to discuss tonight's book, *Jude the Obscure*. You're just in time! I may have to ask you to pay for the door, but I understand the impulse. One simply mustn't be late to the discussion!"

The crowd began to fall about laughing. They waggled their teacups at the police and waved copies of the books.

Magnus tried to vary this routine every time. Once, when the lights came back up, he had transformed the bar into an apiary, with buzzing beehives all around the room. Another time it became a prayer circle, with many of the guests wearing the garb of nuns and ministers.

Usually, this confused the police so much that the raids were brief and relatively nonviolent. But each time, he sensed their frustration growing. Tonight the group was led by McMantry, as crooked a cop as Magnus had ever met. Magnus had refused to pay him off on principle, and now he was coming down on Mr. Dry's Bar. They had come prepared this time. Every officer had a tool—at least a dozen axes, just as many sledgehammers, crowbars, and even a shovel or two.

"Take them all," McMantry said. "Everyone goes in the wagon. And then take this joint apart."

Magnus waggled his fingers behind his back to conceal the blue light that webbed between them. At once, four panels fell away from the walls, revealing hallways and escape routes. His customers ran for them. They would come out in four different locations, some blocks away. Just a bit of gentle, protective magic. No one deserved to go to jail for having a cocktail. A few officers tried to follow, only to find the passages were suddenly blind.

Magnus let the heavy glamour drop, and the speakeasy regained its normal appearance. This stunned the police long enough to allow him to slip behind a nearby curtain and glamour himself invisible. He walked right out of the bar, past the officers. He paused only for a moment to watch them pull back the curtain and study the wall behind, looking for the way to access the escape hatch they assumed had to be there.

Back out on the street, it was a thick September night. New York often stayed hot this time of year, and New York humidity had its own special quality. The air was viscous, full of the murk of the East River and the Hudson and the sea and the swamp, full of smoke and ash, full of the smell of every kind of cooking food, and the raw smell of gas.

He walked down to one of the exit points, where an excited cluster of customers stood laughing and talking about what had just happened. This group was made up of some of his favorite regulars, including the handsome Alfie.

"Come on!" Magnus said. "I think we should continue this at my place, don't you?"

A dozen people agreed that this was an excellent idea. Magnus hailed a taxi, and some of the others did the same. Soon there was a merry little chain of taxis ready to go. Just as one more person was squeezing into the backseat with Magnus, Dolly leaned in the window and spoke into his ear.

"Hey, Magnus!" she said. "Don't forget. Watch the money!"

Magnus gave her a polite, *yes, whatever* nod, and she giggled and tripped off. She was such a tiny thing. Very pretty indeed. And very drunk. She would probably go off to the Bowery now and eat her fill on the city's less fortunate.

Then the train of taxis began to move, and the entire party (which, from a glance out the back window, looked to have expanded by another dozen) made its way uptown to the Plaza Hotel.

* * *

When Magnus woke the next morning, the first thing he noticed was the fact that it was much, much, much too bright. Someone really needed to get rid of the sun.

Magnus quickly worked out that the excessive brightness was due to the fact that all the curtains seemed to be missing from the bedroom of his suite. He then noted the four fully dressed (*sigh*) people sleeping around him on the bed, all oblivious to the sunlight and dead to the world.

The third thing he noticed, perhaps the most puzzling, was the pile of car tires at the foot of the bed.

It took Magnus a few moments and a number of strange contortions to get over the sleepers and out of his bed. There were easily twenty more sleeping and passed-out people all over the living room. The curtains were also missing from the windows of this room, but he could see where they'd all gone. People were using them as blankets and improvised tenting. Alfie alone was awake, sitting on the sofa and looking out at the sunny day miserably.

"Magnus," he groaned. "Kill me, won't you?"

"Why, that's *illegal*!" Magnus replied. "And you know how I feel about breaking the law. And who are all these people? There weren't this many when I fell asleep."

Alfie shrugged, indicating that the universe was mysterious and nothing would ever be fully understood.

"I mean it," Alfie said. "If you don't want to use that voodoo whatever, just hit me on the head with something. You gotta kill me."

"I'll get you a bracer," Magnus said. "Iced tomato juice and Tabasco, sliced grapefruits, and a plate of scrambled eggs, that's what we need. I'll have room service send up two dozen of each."

He stumbled over a few people to the phone, only to find that he had actually reached for a large, decorative cigarette dispenser. It was possible he was not quite at his best either.

"And coffee," he added, setting this down and picking up the telephone receiver with tremendous dignity. "I will order some of that as well."

Magnus placed the order with room service, who had by now stopped questioning Mr. Bane's unusual needs for things like twenty-four plates of scrambled eggs and "enough coffee to fill one of your larger bathtubs." He joined Alfie on the sofa and watched a few of his new guests turn and groan in their slumber.

"I gotta stop this," Alfie said. "I can't go on like this."

Alfie was clearly one of those people who turned maudlin after a good night out. Somehow, this only made him more attractive.

"It's just a hangover, Alfie."

"It's more than that. See, there's this girl. . . ."

"Ah," Magnus said, nodding. "You know, the quickest way to mend a broken heart is to get right back on the wagon. . . ."

"Not for me," Alfie said. "She was the only one. I make good money. I got everything I want. But I lost her. See . . ."

Oh no. A story. This was perhaps too maudlin and too much for the early hour, but handsome and heartbroken young men could occasionally be indulged. Magnus tried to look attentive. It was hard to do so over the glare of the sun and his desire to go back to sleep, but he tried. Alfie recounted a story about a girl named Louisa, something about a party, and some confusion over a letter, and there was something about a dog and possibly a speedboat. It was either a speedboat or a mountain cabin. Those things are hard to mix up, but it really was *much too early* for this. Anyway, there was definitely a dog and a letter, and it all ended in disaster and Alfie coming to Magnus's bar every night to drink away his sorrows. As the story lurched to its conclusion, Magnus saw the first of the sleepers on his floor start to show signs of life. Alfie did too, and he leaned in to speak to Magnus more privately.

"Listen, Magnus," Alfie said. "I know you can . . . do things."

This sounded promising.

"I mean . . ." Alfie struggled for a moment. "You can do things that aren't natural. . . ."

This sounded very promising *indeed*, at least at first. However, Alfie's saucer-eyed expression indicated that this was not an amorous inquiry.

"What do you mean?" Magnus asked.

"I mean . . ." Alfie lowered his voice further. "You do . . . those things you do. They're . . . they're magic. I mean, they have to be. I don't believe in the stuff, but . . ."

Magnus had maintained the premise that he was nothing but a showman. It was a premise that made sense, and most people were happy to accept it. But Alfie—an otherwise down-to-earth mundie—appeared to have seen through it.

Which was attractive. And worrying.

"What exactly are you asking me, Alfie?"

"I want her back, Magnus. There has to be a way."

"Alfie . . ."

"Or help me forget. I bet you could do that."

"Alfie . . ." Magnus didn't really want to lie, but this was not a discussion he was going to get into. Not now, and not here. Yet it seemed like he needed to say *something*.

"Memories are important," he said.

"But it *hurts*, Magnus. Thinking about her makes me ache."

Magnus didn't really want this kind of thing this early in the morning—this talk of aching memories and wanting to forget. This conversation needed to end, now.

"I need a quick splash in the bath to restore myself. Let room service in, won't you? You'll feel better once you eat something."

Magnus patted Alfie on the shoulder and made his way to the bathroom. He had to eject two more sleepers from the bathtub and the bathroom floor in order to engage in his ablutions. By the time he emerged, room service had produced six rolling tables laden with pitchers of tomato juice and all the eggs and grapefruit and coffee needed to make the morning bright again. Some of the near dead sleeping around the suite had risen and were now noisily eating and drinking and comparing notes to see who was feeling the worst.

"Did you get our presents, Magnus?" one of the men said.

"I did, thank you. I'd been needing some spare tires."

"We got them off a police car. To get them back for ruining your place."

"Very kind of you. Speaking of, I suppose I should go check on what's left of my establishment. The police didn't look happy last night."

No one paid much attention when he left. They continued to eat and drink and talk and laugh over their suffering, and occasionally run to the bathroom to be ill. It was this way more or less every night and every morning. Strangers appeared in his hotel room, always a wreck after the previous night. In the morning, they stuck themselves back together again. They rubbed at raccoon-eyed faces full of smeared makeup, looked for lost hats and feathers and beads and phone numbers and shoes and hours. It wasn't a bad life. It wouldn't last, but nothing ever did.

They would all be like Alfie in the end, crying on his sofa at dawn and regretting it all. Which was why Magnus stayed away from those kinds of problems. Keep moving. Keep dancing.

Magnus whistled as he closed the door to his suite, and he doffed his hat to a very disapproving-looking older lady in the hall who heard the ruckus inside. By the time he had taken the elevator down to the lobby, he was in a good enough mood to tip the elevator operator five dollars.

Magnus's good mood lasted only a few minutes. This taxi ride was considerably less merry than the last one. The sun was being obstinately bright, the taxi choked and sputtered, and the streets were more full of traffic than usual—six cars across, all honking at once, all blowing noxious fumes through the window. Every police car he saw reminded him of the indignities he had suffered last night.

When he reached 25th Street, the full extent of the destruction was immediately made clear. The door to the wig shop was broken and had been replaced (not very carefully) with a wooden board and a chain. Magnus opened this with a quick shot of blue light from his fingers and pulled the wood away. The wig shop had sustained fairly serious damage—displays overturned, wigs all over the floor in a shallow wash of beer and wine, looking like strange sea life. The hidden door had been ripped completely off its hinges and was thrown across the room. He sloshed his way through the tight hallway, which had about three inches of mixed and souring alcohol pooled on the recessed floor. The head of this stream came trickling down the three steps that led up to the bar. This door was completely gone, reduced to splinters. Beyond that, Magnus saw only destruction—shattered glass, broken tables, piles of debris. Even the innocent chandelier had been beaten down from its perch and lay in pieces on what was left of the dance floor.

But this was not the worst of it. Sitting in the wreckage on one of three unbroken chairs was Aldous Nix, the High Warlock of Manhattan.

"Magnus," he said. "Finally. I've been waiting for an hour."

Aldous was old—even by warlock standards. He predated the calendar. Based on his recollections of things, the general consensus was that he was probably just under two thousand years old. He had the appearance of a man maybe in his late fifties, with a fine white beard and a neatly trimmed head of white hair. His mark was his clawed hands and feet. The feet were disguised by specially made boots, the hands by the fact that he almost always kept one pocketed and the other wrapped around the silver ball handle of a long black cane.

That Aldous sat there in the middle of the wreckage was a sort of accusation.

"What have I done to deserve this honor?" Magnus said, carefully stepping onto the mess on the floor. "Or have you always wanted to see a deconstructed bar? It is something of a spectacle."

Aldous knocked a bit of broken bottle away with his cane.

"There's better business to be done, Magnus. Do you really

want to spend your time selling illegal liquor to mundanes?"

"Yes."

"Bane . . ."

"*Aldous* . . . ," Magnus said. "I've been involved in so many problems and battles. There's nothing wrong with wanting to live simply for a while and avoid trouble."

Aldous waved his hand at the wreckage.

"This isn't trouble," Magnus said. "Not real trouble."

"But it's also not a serious endeavor."

"There's nothing wrong with wanting to enjoy life a little. We have forever. Should we really spend all of it working?"

It was a stupid question to ask. Aldous probably would spend all of eternity working.

"Magnus, you can't have failed to notice that things are changing. Things are afoot. The Great Mundane War . . ."

"They always get into wars," Magnus said, picking up the bases of a dozen shattered wineglasses and setting them in a row.

"Not like that. Not so global. And they are approaching magic. They make light and sound. They communicate over distances. It doesn't worry you?"

"No," Magnus said. "It doesn't."

"So you don't see it coming?"

"Aldous, I've had a long night. What are you talking about?"

"It comes, Magnus." Aldous's voice was suddenly very deep. "You can feel it all around. It's coming, and everything will break apart."

"*What's* coming?"

"The break, and the fall. The mundanes put their faith in their paper money, and when that turns to ash, the world will turn upside down."

Being a warlock certainly didn't preclude you from going a little funny in the head. In fact, being a warlock could easily *make* you go a little funny in the head. When the true weight of eternity really settled on you—usually in the middle of the night when you were alone—the weight could be unbearable. The knowledge that all would die and you would live on and on, into some vast unknown future populated by who knew what, that everything would always keep falling away and you would go on and on . . .

Aldous had been thinking about it. He had the look.

"Have a drink, Aldous," Magnus said compassionately. "I keep a few special bottles hidden in a safe under the floor in the back. I have a Château Lafite Rothschild from 1818 that I've been saving for a sunny day."

"You think that's the solution to everything, don't you, Bane? Drinking and dancing and making love . . . but I tell you this, something is coming, and we'd be fools to ignore it."

"When have I *ever* claimed not to be a fool?"

"Magnus!" Aldous stood suddenly and slammed the tip of his walking stick down, sending a flood of purple bolts crackling along the wreckage of the floor. Even when he was talking crazy, Aldous was a powerful warlock. Stick around for two thousand years—you're bound to pick up a thing or two.

"When you decide to be serious, come and find me. But don't wait too long. I have a new residence, at the Hotel Dumont, on 116th Street."

Magnus was left in the dripping remains of his bar. One Downworlder coming in and talking a load of nonsense about omens and disaster was to be ignored. But having that followed by a visit from Aldous, who seemed to be saying much the same thing . . .

. . . unless those two rumors were one and the same, and they had both originated with Aldous, who was not sounding like the voice of complete reason.

That made sense, actually. The High Warlock of Manhattan gets a little strange, starts talking about doom and mundane money and disaster . . . someone would pick that story up and carry it along, and like all stories, it would find its way to Magnus.

Magnus tapped his fingers on the cracked marble of his once-pristine bar. Time, he had noticed, moved more quickly these days. Aldous wasn't completely wrong about that. Time was like water, sometimes glacial and slow (the 1720s . . . *never again*), sometimes a still pond, sometimes a gentle brook, and then a rushing river. And sometimes time was like vapor, vanishing even as you passed through it, draping everything in mist, refracting the light. That had been the 1920s.

Even in fast times like these, Magnus could not instantly reopen his bar. He had to keep up some pretense of normalcy. A few days, maybe a week. Maybe he would even clean it up the mundie way, by hiring people to come with buckets and wood and nails. Maybe he would even do it himself. It would probably do him good.

So Magnus rolled up his sleeves and set to work, collecting broken glass, throwing broken chairs and tables into a pile. He got a mop and pushed along puddles of mixed booze and dirt and splinters. After a few hours of this, he grew tired and bored and snapped his fingers, setting the whole place to rights.

Aldous's words still preyed on his mind. Something should

be done. Someone should be told. Someone more responsible and interested than him should take over this concern. Which, of course, meant only one group of people.

Shadowhunters would not come to speakeasies. They respected the mundane law against alcohol (always so tedious with their "The law is hard but it is the law"). This meant that Magnus had to take a trip to the Upper East Side, to the Institute.

The grandeur of the Institute never failed to impress him—the way it towered high and mighty above everything else, timeless and unmoving in its Gothic disapproval of all that was modern and changeable. Downworlders could not normally enter the Institute through the main door—the Sanctuary was their entrance. But Magnus was no ordinary Downworlder, and his connection to the Shadowhunters was long and well-known.

This didn't mean that he got a warm reception. The housekeeper, Edith, said nothing as she admitted him except, "Wait here." He was left in the foyer, where he eyed the fusty decorations with a critical eye. The Shadowhunters did love their burgundy wallpaper and their rose-shaped lamps and their heavy furnishings. Time would never move quickly here.

"Come on," Edith said, returning.

Magnus followed her down the hall to a reception room, where Edgar Greymark, the head of the Institute, stood in front of a bookstand.

"Edgar," Magnus said, nodding. "I see you've bowed to the pressure and installed a telephone."

Magnus pointed to a telephone sitting on a small table in a dark corner, as if it was being punished for existing.

"It's a dammed nuisance. Have you heard the noise it

makes? But you can speak to the other Institutes easily and get ice delivered, so . . ."

He let the book he was reading close heavily.

"What brings you to see us, Magnus?" he said. "I understand you've been running a drinking establishment. Is that correct?"

"Quite correct," Magnus said with a smile. "Though it currently might be more useful as a pile of kindling."

Edgar didn't ask for an explanation of that remark, and Magnus didn't offer one.

"You are aware that the sale of liquor is currently against the law," Edgar went on, "but I suppose that's why you enjoy it."

"Everyone should have a hobby or two," Magnus said. "Mine just happen to include illegal trade, drinking, and carousing. I've heard of worse."

"We tend not to have time for hobbies."

Shadowhunters. Always better than you.

"I'm here because I've heard things in this drinking establishment of mine, things about the Downworld that you might want to know about."

Magnus recounted everything he could think of—everything Aldous had said, including his odd demeanor. Edgar listened, his expression never changing.

"You're basing this on the ramblings of Aldous Nix?" he said, when Magnus had finished. "Everyone knows Aldous isn't himself these days."

"I've lived longer than you," Magnus said. "My experience is wide, and I've learned to trust my instincts."

"We do not act on instinct," Edgar said. "Either you have information, or you do not."

"Considering our long history, Edgar, I think that perhaps you should act on what I am saying."

"What would you have us do?"

Magnus resented having to spell everything out. He had come to the Shadowhunters with information. It wasn't up to him to explain precisely how they should interpret it.

"Speak to him, perhaps?" Magnus said. "Do what you do best—keep an eye out."

"We are always watchful, Magnus." There was a slight edge of sarcasm to Edgar's tone that Magnus really did not appreciate. "We will bear all of this in mind. Thank you for coming to see us. Edith will show you out."

He rang a bell, and the sour-faced Edith appeared in an instant to take the Downworlder out of her house.

Before going to the Institute, Magnus had been resolved to do nothing. Just pass on the information and get on with his endless life. But Edgar's dismissal of his concerns motivated him. Aldous said the Hotel Dumont was on 116th Street, which wasn't far at all. That was just up in Italian Harlem, perhaps a twenty-minute walk away. Magnus set his course northward. New York was a place that changed very abruptly from neighborhood to neighborhood. The Upper East Side was moneyed and dignified to the point of pain. But as he went up, the houses got smaller, the driving more aggressive, and the horse carts more frequent. Above 100th Street, the children got more boisterous, playing stickball in the street and chasing one another as mothers shouted through windows.

The feeling on these streets was altogether more pleasant. There was more of a family atmosphere, with good smells coming from the windows. And it was nice to see a neighborhood where not everyone had white skin. Harlem was the center of black culture and the best music in the entire world. It was the hottest, most cutting-edge place to be.

Which, he supposed, was why someone had plopped down this grand monstrosity of a hotel. The Dumont didn't quite fit in with the brownstones and the shops and restaurants, but the Dumont didn't look like the kind of place that cared if its neighbors liked it or not. It sat back a bit, on a small side street that may very well have been custom-made for it. It had a great colonnaded front with dozens of sash windows, all with drawn curtains. A pair of heavy metal doors were firmly closed.

Magnus sat in the soda fountain across the street and decided to watch and wait. What he was waiting for, he wasn't sure. Something. Anything. He wasn't really sure that anything would happen at all, but he was now set on his course. The first hour or so was deadly dull. He read a newspaper to kill time. He ate a sardine sandwich and had some coffee. He used his power to retrieve a lost ball for some kids across the street, who had no idea he was doing so. He was almost ready to give up when a parade of extremely expensive automobiles began to roll up to the front of the hotel. It was like seeing a showing of the grandest cars in the world—a Rolls-Royce, a Packard, a few Pierce-Arrows, an Isotta Fraschini, three Mercedes-Benzes, and a Duesenberg—all polished to such a high degree that Magnus could hardly see them in the dazzling glow of the sunset. He blinked his watering eyes and observed driver after driver opening doors and releasing the cars' passengers.

These were most certainly wealthy people. The rich bought wonderful clothes you recognized. The *richest* had their people go to Paris and buy the entire new collection that no one outside of the fashion house had seen. These people belonged to the latter group. They were all, Magnus noted, between forty and sixty years of age. The men were all bearded and hatted, the women not quite young or free enough for the petal-pink Chanels and the ethereal chiffon Vionnets they had acquired. They all walked quickly into the hotel, without conversing or stopping to admire the sunset. They looked sufficiently self-important and grim to suggest that they could probably have come together to try to raise a demon. (People who tried to raise demons always looked like that.) But what troubled Magnus the most was that they were clearly seeking Aldous's help in this. Aldous had powers and knowledge that Magnus couldn't even begin to guess at.

And so Magnus waited. About an hour passed. The chauffeurs brought the cars around in a row, and one by one, the group got into them and rolled back into the New York night. There were no demons. Nothing. Magnus left his stool and began walking back down to the Plaza, trying to make sense of it all.

Maybe it had all been nothing. Aldous took a dim view of mundanes. Perhaps he was simply playing with this group of supposedly important people. There were worse amusements than toying with a bunch of deluded and stupid millionaires, taking their money and telling them you were going to do magic for them. You could make a fortune in no time at all and make your way to the French Riviera and not lift a finger again for ten years. Maybe twenty.

But Aldous was not the kind of warlock who played those games, and ten or twenty years—those weren't even measures of time he counted.

Maybe Aldous had simply gotten weird. It happened. Magnus wondered if, hundreds of years from now, the same thing would happen to him. Maybe he would also hole himself up in a hotel and spend time with some rich people, doing who knew what. Was that really so different from what he was doing now? Hadn't he spent the morning clearing garbage from his mundane bar?

It was time to go home.

October 1929

Magnus had lost interest in his bar somewhat. His planned closure of a few days stretched into a week, then two, then three. With Mr. Dry's temporarily closed, a few of Magnus's regulars found themselves with nowhere to go. So, of course, they simply came to Magnus's hotel room every night. First it was just one or two, but within a week there was a constant stream of people. This included the hotel management, who politely suggested that Mr. Bane "might like to take his friends and associates elsewhere." Magnus replied, equally politely, that these were not friends or associates. Usually they were strangers. This did not make the management very happy.

And this wasn't entirely true, either. Alfie was there from the start, and now had taken up permanent residence on Magnus's sofa. He had grown only more morose as time wore on. He went off to wherever he worked during the day, came back drunk, and stayed that way. Then he stopped going to work.

"It's getting bad, Magnus," he said one afternoon, waking from a whiskey-induced stupor.

"I'm sure it is," Magnus said, not looking up from his copy of *War and Peace*.

"I mean it."

"I'm sure you do."

"Magnus!"

Magnus lifted his head wearily.

"It's getting bad. It can't last. It's already starting to crumble. See?"

He rattled a newspaper in Magnus's direction.

"Alfie, you need to be a bit more specific. Unless you are talking about that newspaper, which seems fine."

"I mean"—Alfie pulled himself up and looked over the back of the sofa—"that the entire financial structure of the United States could fall down at any second. Everybody said it could happen and I never believed them, but now it seems like it could really happen."

"These things do."

"How can you not care?"

"Practice," Magnus said, looking back to his book and turning the page.

"I don't know." Alfie slid down a bit. "Maybe you're right. Maybe it will all be fine. It has to be, right?"

Magnus didn't bother to point out that that wasn't what he had said. Alfie seemed appeased, and that was good enough. But now Magnus had lost the flow of what he was reading and no longer felt like continuing. These visitors were getting annoying.

After a few days, Magnus was completely tired of the company, but he was not inclined to throw them out. That would have been unseemly. He simply took a second suite on a different floor and stopped coming home. His guests seemed aware of this, but no one minded as long as the door to Magnus's old suite was open and no one cut off the room service account.

Magnus tried to fill the time with ordinary pursuits—reading, walks in Central Park, a talking picture or a show, some shopping. The heat broke, and a mellow October settled over the city. One day he hired a boat and spent the day drifting around Manhattan, looking at the skeletons of the many new skyscrapers and wondering what actually would happen if it all fell apart, and wondering how much he currently cared. He had seen governments and economies fall before. But these people . . . they made big things and had a long way to fall.

So he opened some champagne.

He noticed that many people spent their days huddled around the stock tickers that graced every club and hotel, many restaurants, even some bars and barbershops. It amazed Magnus how these silly little clockworks under glass could fascinate some people. People gathered around them, sitting hour after hour, just watching the machine spit out a long tongue of paper full of symbols. Someone would catch the paper as it unscrolled and read the magic it contained.

The twenty-fourth of October brought the first scare, with the market tumbling and regaining a bit of footing. Everyone had an uneasy weekend; then the next week came, and everything got much worse. Then came Tuesday the twenty-ninth, and it all came down, just like everyone had apparently predicted, yet never really believed would happen. Magnus couldn't avoid the shock wave, not even in the peace of his room at the Plaza. The telephone began to ring. There were voices in the hall, even a scream or two. He went down to the lobby, where a full-on panic was in progress, people running out with their suitcases, every telephone cabinet occupied, a man crying in the corner.

Out on the street it was worse. A group of people outside were in fevered conversation.

"They're jumping out of buildings downtown," one man said. "I heard it. My friend works down there, and he says they're just opening the windows and throwing themselves out."

"So it's really happening?" another man said, grabbing his hat off his head and holding it over his heart, as if for protection.

"Happening? It's happened! The banks are starting to board up the doors!"

Magnus decided it was probably best to go back upstairs, lock the door, and get out a good bottle of wine.

He did get upstairs, and he did get into his room, but the moment he arrived, one of the recent strangers from his other room appeared in the doorway.

"Magnus," he said, his breath reeking of booze, "you gotta come. Alfie's trying to jump out the window."

"Well, that craze took hold fast," Magnus said with a sigh. "Where?"

"In your old room."

There was no time for Magnus to inquire how long they had known about his new room. He followed the man as he stagger-ran through the halls of the Plaza. They took the back stairs up three floors to the old suite, where the door was hanging open and several people were gathered around the door to Magnus's old bedroom.

"He's locked himself in there and put something against the door," one of the men said. "We looked out of this window and saw him on the ledge."

"All of you, get out," Magnus said. "Now."

When they were gone, Magnus extended his hand and sent the bedroom door flying open. The bedroom window, once the source of a beautiful view of Central Park and too much sunlight, now framed the crouching figure of Alfie. He was perched on the thin concrete lip just outside, nervously smoking a cigarette.

"Don't come any closer, Magnus!" he said.

"I don't plan on it," Magnus said, sitting on the bed. "But could you share your cigarettes? This is my room you plan on defenestrating from, after all."

This puzzled Alfie for a moment, but he carefully reached into his pocket, produced a pack of cigarettes, and threw them inside.

"So," Magnus said, picking them up off the floor and pulling one from the pack, "before you go, why don't you tell me what this is all about?"

He snapped his fingers and the cigarette caught flame. This was entirely for Alfie's benefit, and definitely caught his attention.

"You . . . you know what this is about . . . what did you just do?"

"I lit a cigarette."

"I mean, what did you just *do*?"

"Oh, that." Magnus crossed his legs and sat back a bit. "Well, I think you've guessed by now, Alfie, that I'm not like the other children."

Alfie squat-bounced on his heels for a moment, considering this. His gaze was clear, and Magnus thought this was probably the first time in weeks that he had been completely sober.

"So it's true," he said.

"So it's true."

"So, what are you?"

"What I am is someone who doesn't want you to jump out of the window. The rest are details."

"Give me one good reason not to jump," Alfie said. "Everything is gone. Louisa. Everything I owned, everything I made."

"Nothing is permanent," Magnus said. "I know this from experience. But you can get new things. You can meet new people. You can go on."

"Not when I remember what I had," Alfie said. "So if you are . . . whatever you are, you can do something, can't you?"

Magnus drew on the cigarette for a moment in thought.

"Come inside, Alfie," he finally said. "And I will help you."

The actual process of altering memory was tricky. The mind is a complex web, and memory is important to learning. Pull the wrong memory and you might make someone who forgets that fire burns. But memories can be softened, or shortened. A talented warlock—and Magnus was nothing if not talented—can embroider the past into something quite different in shape and tone.

But it was not easy work.

Why Magnus was doing this for no money for a mundane who had been freeloading off him for weeks was unclear. Maybe it was because this day was a day of great suffering, and this was the part of the suffering Magnus could end.

An hour later Alfie walked out of his suite not quite remembering a girl named Louisa, who was a bus fare collector or something. Perhaps a librarian in his hometown? He couldn't have told you why he even had thought of her name. He also had no clear recollection of his brief fortune.

It was tiring, and when it was done, Magnus leaned against the sill of the window and looked over the darkening city, over the great expanse of Central Park.

That was when he noticed the strange light in the sky, right over the uptown area. It was a cone-shaped light, smaller toward the skyline and widening into the clouds, and it had a faintly greenish cast.

It was right over the Hotel Dumont.

There was no getting a cab. Every cab in the city was taken, and they were all speeding. Everybody was going somewhere, trying to ditch stocks or sell something, or they were just moving in total panic, zigzagging the city in a frenzy. So Magnus ran up the east side of the park, all the way to 116th Street. The Hotel Dumont looked exactly the same as it had when Magnus had last seen it. All the curtains were still drawn, the doors still closed. It was cold, quiet, and unwelcoming. But when Magnus tried the front door, he found it unlocked.

The first odd thing was that the hotel seemed to be completely vacant. There was no one at the desk, no one in the lobby, no one anywhere. It was certainly a magnificent setting, with a graceful and gilded grand staircase. And it was all very plush and padded. A rich red-and-gold carpet covered the floor, and the windows were covered with heavy drapes that stretched from floor to ceiling. It was cool, shaded, muffled, and disturbingly quiet. Magnus looked up and around, right up to the frescoed ceiling with its fat-faced cherubs pointing at one another and gleefully swinging on vine swings in gardens.

Just to the left, there was a wide archway flanked by pillars covered in a floral pattern. This clearly led to one of the hotel's grander rooms and seemed as likely a place as any to look. Magnus opened this door. It led to a ballroom—an utterly magnificent one—with a white marble floor and a lacing of gilded balconies all around the room, broken by gilded mirrors that reflected the room back on itself over and over.

They also reflected the pile of human bodies scattered at the far end of the floor, around what appeared to be a highly polished granite slab. That these were the same people Magnus had seen getting out of the many expensive cars, he was fairly certain. There were some faces left, some bits of fine clothing scattered around the room in strips and ribbons, sometimes still attached to a loose arm or torso. The floor on that end of the room was entirely blackish-red, the blood having spread and pooled evenly over the marble like a fine glaze.

"By the Angel . . ."

Magnus turned and found Edgar Greymark standing behind him, in full Shadowhunter battle black, his seraph blade drawn.

"Good of you to come," Magnus said. The remark was meant to be sarcastic but came out flat. It *was* good of them to come. Whatever was happening, help would be required.

"Did you think we would just ignore your warning?" Edgar asked.

Magnus decided not to reply to that. They probably had ignored his warning and, like him, seen the light in the sky.

"Who are these people?" Edgar asked.

"I believe these are some mundanes who came here to see Aldous."

"And where is Aldous?"

"I haven't seen him. I've only arrived myself."

Edgar raised his hand, and a half-dozen more Shadowhunters appeared and went to the bodies and examined them.

"Looks like a Behemoth attack to me," one girl said as she examined a pile of blood and fleshy bits and some shredded crepe de chine. "Messy. Disorganized. And these are probably double rows of teeth marks, but it's hard to tell. . . ."

Behind them, there was a massive bang, and they all turned as a young man yelled and dropped something to the ground, which smoked and hissed.

"My Sensor exploded," he growled.

"I think we can assume some very serious demonic activity," Edgar said. "Search the hotel. Find Aldous Nix and bring him here."

The Shadowhunters ran off, and Edgar and Magnus remained with the pile of bodies.

"Do you have any idea what might be happening here?" Edgar asked.

"I told you all I knew," Magnus said. "I came because I saw something in the sky. I found this."

"What is Aldous capable of?"

"Aldous is two thousand years old. He's capable of *anything*."

"Aldous Nix is two thousand years old?"

"So I've heard. He doesn't invite me to his birthday parties."

"He seemed a bit dotty to me, but I never thought . . . well, it doesn't matter what I thought. We clearly have several demons in the area. That's our first concern. And Nix . . ."

"Is here," said a voice.

Aldous stepped out from behind one of the heavy wall hangings. He leaned heavily on his cane, walking slowly to the granite slab, where he sat. Edgar raised his weapon a bit, but Magnus steadied his arm.

"What happened here, Aldous?" Magnus asked.

"It was merely a test," Aldous said. "For the benefit of my sponsors, who have kindly engaged this entire hotel to allow me to do my work in peace."

"Your sponsors," Magnus said. "These people here, on the floor, in pieces."

"What is this work?" Edgar asked.

"The work? Ah. Now that is an interesting subject. But not for your ears. I will speak to him." He pointed to Magnus. "The rest of you can go and keep busy. You Shadowhunters always keep busy. There must be ten demons out there. I didn't make note of them all, but as the girl said, they looked to be mostly Behemoths. Nasty things. Go kill them."

Edgar Greymark was not the kind of man who liked to be dismissed, but Magnus gave him a look and tried to encourage him to back away.

"Yes," Edgar growled. "We do have some work. But do not leave, Nix. We will be back to discuss this."

Magnus nodded, and Edgar left the ballroom, shutting the doors loudly behind him. Aldous regarded his gnarled hands for a moment before speaking.

"Magnus, we don't belong here. We never have belonged here. I've lived in this world longer than anyone I know, and that is the only truth I can rely on. I'm sure you've come to that conclusion as well."

"Not exactly," Magnus said. He stepped a bit closer but avoided the great sea of blood and bodies that lay between them.

"Not exactly?"

"I sometimes feel a bit out of place, but I very much consider myself of this world. Where else would I be from?"

"You may have been born here, but you originate in another dimension."

"You mean the Void?"

"I mean that exactly. I intend to go where I do belong. I want to go to the only place I feel I can truly call my home. I want to go to Pandemonium. I was opening up a Portal to allow me to get there."

"And these people?"

"These people believed they ran the world. They believed that their money entitled them to control. They heard about me, they came to me seeking a way to gain that control without war, without force. And I told them that I would expose them to a power they never knew possible if they gave me what I needed. So they gave me this hotel. I've been working here for some months, preparing the way. This entire building is now a latticework of spells and enchantments. The walls are spun with electrum and demon metal. It is a channel now. It will be the perfect and strongest Portal."

"And they came here . . ."

"For a demonstration. I did tell them there were risks. Perhaps I wasn't clear enough. I thought I was. . . ."

He smiled a bit at this.

"They were monsters, Magnus. They could not be allowed

to live. Stupid mundanes, thinking they could rule their world by harnessing *our* power? No. They died quickly."

"And, I would imagine, in great pain and terror."

"Perhaps. But their sufferings have ended. And now, so have mine. Come with me."

"Come with you? To Pandemonium? To the *Void*? And here I thought that my invitation to summer in New Jersey was the worst I had ever received."

"This isn't the time for jokes, Bane."

"Aldous," Magnus said, "you are talking about going to the demon realm. You do not come back from there. And you know what horrors you would face."

"We don't know what it's like. We don't know anything. I wish to know. My final wish is for knowledge of that most mysterious place, my true home. The final step to finish the spell," he said, pulling up on the balled head of his cane and revealing a knife. "A few drops of warlock blood. Just a bit will do. A slice across the palm."

Aldous looked at the knife thoughtfully, then at Magnus.

"If you stay here, the Portal will open, and you will come with me. If you do not wish to come, leave now."

"Aldous, you can't—"

"I most certainly can, and I'm about to. Make your choice, Magnus. Stay or go, but if you go, go now."

What was now extremely clear to Magnus was that Aldous was insane. You did not plan trips to the Void if you were compos mentis. Going to the Void was an act greater and more terrible than suicide—it was sending yourself to Hell. But it was also very, very hard to talk to people who had gone insane. Alfie could be talked off the window with reason. It would not be so easy with Aldous. Physical force was just as difficult an approach. Any move Magnus made here would likely be predicted and met with equal or greater strength.

"Aldous . . ."

"You stay then? You come with me?"

"No. I just—I—"

"You worry for me," Aldous said. "You think I don't know what I'm doing."

"I wouldn't put it like that, exactly. . . ."

"I have considered this for a long time, Magnus. I know what I am doing. So please. Stay or go. Decide now, as I am going to open the Por—"

The arrow made a kind of singing noise as it cut through the air. It entered Aldous's chest like a knife sliding easily into an apple. Aldous sat upright for a moment, looking at it; then he slumped to the side, dead.

Magnus watched his blood hit the granite.

"RUN," he yelled.

The young Shadowhunter was still proudly looking at his work, how perfectly he had hit his mark. He didn't notice the web of cracks spreading from the altar and across the floor, splintering the white marble into hundreds and thousands of pieces with a sound like breaking ice.

Magnus ran. He ran in a way he wasn't aware he could run, and when he reached the Shadowhunter, he grabbed him and dragged him along. They had just reached the door and jumped out when one great belch of fire exploded into the foyer, filling the room with fire from floor to ceiling. Just as quickly, the fire was suctioned back into the ballroom. The doors of the hotel pulled themselves shut. The very building shook as if an enormous vacuum had appeared just over it and was sucking it up.

"What's happening?" said the Shadowhunter.

"He's opened some kind of channel to the Void," Magnus said, staggering to his feet.

"What?"

Magnus shook his head. There was no time to explain.

"Was everyone out of the building?" he asked.

"I'm not sure. The demons were both inside and out. We caught a half dozen of them in the street, but . . ."

The building shuddered and seemed to stretch just an inch or two, as if it was being pulled upward.

"Get back from here," Magnus said. "I have no idea what happens next, but it looks like this whole thing could . . . just get back!"

In all his years, in all his studies, Magnus had never encountered anything that had prepared him for this—a building turned into a perfect Portal, a warlock who wanted to go home to the Void, using his own blood as a key. This was not in the lesson books. This would require guesswork. And a lot of luck. And probably some stupidity.

If he was wrong at any point, which he likely would be, he would be sucked into the Void. Into Hell itself. Which was where the stupidity came in.

Magnus pulled open the door. The Shadowhunter behind him cried out, but Magnus just yelled for him to stay back.

This is a terrible idea, Magnus thought as he found himself in the lobby again. *This may be the worst idea I've ever had.*

The fire that had blasted into the heart of the building had scorched every surface, blackening the ceiling, destroying the furnishings, exposing the floor under the carpet, and charring the great staircase. The doors to the ballroom, however, were completely unharmed.

Magnus stepped back inside the ballroom carefully.

Still not sucked into the Void, he thought. *Good. Definitely good.*

The bodies were now smoldering skeletons, and the white marble floor was completely fractured. The blood had evaporated and left a dark stain. The granite slab, however, was fine. It was also levitating, about six feet from the ground, bathed in the faint green light Magnus had seen earlier. Aldous was nowhere to be seen.

What are you?

The voice came from nowhere. It was in the room. It was outside. It was in Magnus's head.

"A warlock," Magnus answered. "And what are you?"

We are many.

"Please don't say you are legion. Someone's taken that."

Do you make mirth from the mundane scriptures, warlock?

"Just breaking the ice," Magnus said to himself.

Ice?

"Where is Aldous?" Magnus said, more loudly.

He is with us. Now you will come with us. Come to the altar.

"I think I'll pass," Magnus said. "I've got a place here I like a lot."

This was interesting. It didn't seem that the demons could come out. If they could, they would have. This was what demons did. But a connection had been opened. A one-way connection, but still a connection.

Magnus stepped just a tiny bit closer, trying to look for any markings on the floor, anything to tell him how large the Portal was. There was nothing.

Warlock, do you not tire of your life?

"That's a very philosophical question for a nameless and faceless voice from a Void," Magnus replied.

Do you not tire of eternity? Do you not wish to end your suffering?

"By leaping into the Void? Not really."

You are like us. You have our blood. You are one of us. Come and be welcome. Come and be with your own.

Blood . . .

If warlock blood opened the Portal . . . well, warlock blood might be able to close it.

. . . or not.

It was as good a guess as any.

"Why would you want that?" Magnus asked. "Pandemonium has to be a pretty crowded place, considering you're always trying to leave it."

Would you not know your father?

"My father?"

Yes, warlock. Your father. Would you not know him?

"My father never took much interest in me," Magnus said.

Would you not know your father, even if you spoke to him?

Magnus stopped on that one.

"No," he said. "I don't suppose I would. Unless you are trying to tell me that what I am hearing now is the voice of my father."

You hear your own blood, warlock.

Magnus regarded the levitating slab, the destruction, the remains of the bodies. He also became dimly aware of a presence behind him. Some of the Shadowhunters had come inside and were looking at the slab, but seemed to hear nothing.

"Magnus?" one of them asked.

"Keep back," Magnus replied.

Why do you protect them? They would not protect you.

Magnus went to the closest Shadowhunter, grabbed a blade, and cut himself.

"You." He pointed to the Shadowhunter who had shot Aldous. "Give me an arrow. Now."

The arrow was handed over, and Magnus tipped it in his blood. Then he rubbed some more blood down the shaft for good measure. He didn't need the bow. He directed the arrow at the slab with all his might, casting every Portal-closing spell he knew.

It felt like he was locked in place, his entire body concrete, time stretched and slow. Magnus was no longer certain where, or maybe even what, he was, only that he was still spell-casting, only that the altar remained, and the voices in his mind were yelling. Hundreds of voices. Thousands of them.

Magnus . . .

Magnus, come to me. . . .

Magnus, come. . . .

But Magnus held on. And then the slab fell to the ground, breaking into countless pieces.

There was a figure leaning against Magnus's hotel door when he returned home that night.

"You got the message then, huh?" Dolly said. "About the mundie money? Guess it all went bust, huh?"

"It does appear to have all gone bust," Magnus said.

"I didn't think you believed me."

Magnus leaned against the opposite wall and sighed heavily. There was no noise from any of the rooms on the hall, except for some distant, muffled yelling at the far end. He got the feeling that many people were probably leaving the hotel now that they had no money to pay the bill, or they were sitting behind their doors in stunned silence. And yet they had no idea that the crash was really the least of their worries, and the real danger had been averted. They would never know. They never did.

"You look tired," Dolly said. "Like you need a pick-me-up."

"I just closed a Portal to the Void. I need sleep. About three days' worth."

Dolly let out a low whistle.

"My friend said you're a hot potato. She wasn't joking, huh?"

"She?"

Dolly slapped a hand over her mouth, nicking her nose with her long, lacquered nails.

"Oops!"

"Who sent you?" Magnus asked.

Dolly lowered her hand and flashed a smile.

"A good friend of yours."

"I'm not sure I have any good friends."

"Oh, you do." Dolly swung her tiny beaded purse in a loop. "You do. See ya around, Magnus."

She made her way down the hall with a swinging step, turning around every once in a while to look back at him. Magnus slid down the wall a few inches, feeling the exhaustion hanging over his entire body. But with one massive effort, he pulled himself up and hurried after Dolly. He watched from around the corner as she got into an elevator, and he immediately pushed the button for the next one. This elevator was quite full of grim-looking people, visibly shattered by the day's news. So what he was going to do next was very unfortunate for them.

Magnus flicked his fingers and took over the control of the elevator from the operator, sending it on a very fast, somewhat uncontrolled descent. He'd tipped the operator very well the other day, so he felt he had a pass to take over if he liked. He had no such pass for the other passengers, who all started screaming as the elevator dropped floor after floor.

He made it to the lobby before Dolly, pushing past the still-traumatized (and several praying) people in his elevator. He ducked through the lobby, staying off to the side, behind columns and potted palms and groups of people. He slipped inside a telephone cabinet and watched Dolly pass by, her heels clicking lightly on the marble floor. He followed her, as quietly and inconspicuously as possible, to the front door, glamouring himself to slip past the doorman. There was a car just outside, a massive red Pierce-Arrow, with silver curtains over the windows of the passenger area, concealing the inhabitant's face. The door, however, was open. A driver stood by, at attention. Through the opening, Magnus could see a foot and an ankle, both very handsome, and a little silver shoe, and a bit of stockinged leg. Dolly bounced over to the car and leaned into the open door. They had a conversation Magnus couldn't hear, and then Dolly proceeded to climb inside the car, giving all the people in front of the Plaza a nice look at her rear end. Then the passenger leaned forward to speak to the driver, and Magnus caught her face in profile. There was no mistaking the face.

It was Camille.

Saving Raphael Santiago

By Cassandra Clare and Sarah Rees Brennan

He uncoiled, as swift as a snake, and sprang.

It was only because Magnus had seen where the vampire was looking and because he knew how Raphael felt, the exact exquisitely cold feeling of being an outcast, so alone that he barely seemed to exist, that he moved fast enough.

—Saving Raphael Santiago

THEY'RE ALL DEAD
AND I AM DEAD TOO.
GRAB

It was a violent heat wave in the late summer of 1953. The sun was viciously pummeling the pavement, which seemed to have become flatter than usual in submission, and some Bowery boys were opening a fire hydrant to make a fountain in the street and gain a few minutes of relief.

It was the sun getting to him, Magnus thought later, that had filled him with the desire to be a private eye. That and the Raymond Chandler novel he had just completed.

Still, there was a problem with the plan. On the covers of books and in films, most detectives looked like they were dressed up in Sunday suits for a small-town jamboree. Magnus wished to wash away the stain of his newly adopted profession and dress in a way that was both suitable to the profession, pleasing to the eye, and on the cutting edge of fashion.

He ditched the trench coat and added some green velvet cuffs to his gray suit jacket, along with a curly-brimmed bowler hat.

The heat was so awful that he had to take off his jacket as soon as he set foot out of doors, but it was the thought that counted, and besides, he was wearing emerald-green suspenders.

Becoming a detective wasn't really a decision based wholly on his wardrobe. He was a warlock, and people—well, not everyone thought of them as people—often came to him for magical solutions to their problems, which he gave them, for a fee. Word had spread throughout New York that Magnus was the warlock who would get you out of a jam. There was a Sanctuary, too, up in Brooklyn, if you needed to hide, but the witch who ran it didn't solve your problems. Magnus solved problems. So why not get paid for it?

Magnus had not thought that simply deciding to become a private eye would cause a case to land in his lap the moment he painted the words MAGNUS BANE, PRIVATE DETECTIVE onto his window in bold black letters. But as if someone had whispered his private conviction into Fate's ear, a case arrived.

Magnus arrived back at his apartment building after getting an ice-cream cone, and when he saw her, he was glad that he'd finished it. She was clearly one of those mundanes who knew enough about the Shadow World to come to Magnus for magic.

He tipped his hat to her and said, "Can I help you, ma'am?"

She wasn't a blonde to make a bishop kick a hole through a stained-glass window. She was a small dark woman and though she was not beautiful, she had a bright, intelligent charm about her, powerful enough so that if she wanted any windows smashed, Magnus would see what he could do. She was wearing a slightly worn but still very becoming plaid dress, belted at her small waist. She looked to be in her late thirties, the same age as Magnus's current lady companion, and under black curling hair she had a small heart-shaped face, and eyebrows so thin that they gave her a challenging air that made her both more attractive and more intimidating.

She shook his hand, her hand small but her grip firm. "I am Guadalupe Santiago," she said. "You are a—" She waved her hand. "I do not know the word for it precisely. A sorcerer, a magic maker."

"You can say 'warlock,' if you like," said Magnus. "It doesn't matter. What you mean is, someone with the power to help you."

"Yes," said Guadalupe. "Yes, that's what I meant. I need you to help me. I need you to save my son."

Magnus ushered her in. He thought he understood the situation now that she had mentioned help for a relative. People would often come to him for healing, not as often as they came to Catarina Loss but often enough. He would much rather heal a young mundane boy than one of the haughty Shadowhunters who came to him so often, even if there was less money in it for him.

"Tell me about your son," he said.

"Raphael," said Guadalupe. "His name is Raphael."

"Tell me about Raphael," said Magnus. "How long has he been sick?"

"He is not sick," said Guadalupe. "I fear he may be dead." Her voice was firm, as if she were not voicing what must assuredly be the most horrible fear of every parent.

Magnus frowned. "I don't know what people have told you, but I can't help with that."

Guadalupe held up a hand. "This is not about ordinary sickness or anything that anyone in my world can cure," she told him. "This is about your world, and how it has touched mine. This is about the monsters from whom God has turned his face away, those who watch in the darkness and prey on innocents."

She took a turn about his living room, her plaid skirt belling about her brown legs.

"*Los vampiros*," she whispered.

"Oh God, not the bloody vampires again," said Magnus. "No pun intended."

The dread words spoken, Guadalupe regained her courage and proceeded with her tale. "We have all heard whispers of such creatures," she said. "Then there were more than whispers. There was one of the monsters, creeping around our neighborhood. Taking little girls and boys. One of my Raphael's friends, his small brother was taken and found almost on his own doorstep, his little body drained of blood. We prayed, we mothers all prayed, every family prayed, that the scourge would be lifted. But my Raphael, he had started hanging around with a crowd of boys who were a little older than him. Good boys, you understand, from good families, but a little—rough, wanting a little too much to show that they were men before they truly were men at all, if you know what I mean?"

Magnus had stopped making jokes. A vampire hunting children for sport—a vampire who had the taste for it and no inclination to stop—was no joke. He met Guadalupe's eyes with a level, serious gaze, to show that he understood.

"They formed a gang," said Guadalupe. "Not one of the street gangs, but—well, it was to protect our streets from the monster, they said. They tracked him to his lair once, and they were all talking about how they knew where he was, how they could go get him. I should have— I was not paying attention to the boys' talk. I was afraid for my younger boys, and it all seemed like a game. But then Raphael, and all his friends . . . they disappeared, a few nights ago. They'd stayed out all night before, but this—this is too long. Raphael would never make me worry like this. I want you to find out where the vampire is, and I want you to go after my son. If Raphael is alive, I want you to save him."

If a vampire had already killed human children, a gang of teenagers coming after him would seem like bonbons delivered to his door. This woman's son was dead.

Magnus bowed his head. "I will try to find out what happened to him."

"No," said the woman.

Magnus found himself looking up, arrested by her voice.

"You don't know my Raphael," she said. "But I do. He is with older boys, but he is not the tagalong. They all listen to him. He is only fifteen, but he is as strong and as quick and as clever as a grown man. If only one of them has survived, he will be that one. Do not go looking for his body. Go and save Raphael."

"You have my word," Magnus promised her, and meant it.

He was in a hurry to leave. Before he visited the Hotel Dumont, the place which had been abandoned by mortals and haunted by vampires since the 1920s, the place where Raphael and his friends had gone, he had other inquiries to make. Other Downworlders would know about a vampire who was breaking the Law that flagrantly, even if they had been hoping the vampires would work it out among themselves, even if the other Downworlders had not yet decided to go to the Shadowhunters.

Guadalupe grasped Magnus's hand before he went, though, and her fingers clung to him. Her challenging look had turned beseeching. Magnus had the feeling she would never have begged for herself, but she was willing to beg for her boy.

"I gave him a cross to wear around his throat," she said. "The padre at Saint Cecilia's gave it to me with his own hands, and I gave it to Raphael. It is small and made of gold; you will know him by it." She took a shaking breath. "I gave him a cross."

"Then you gave him a chance," said Magnus.

Go to faeries for gossip about vampires, to werewolves for gossip about faeries, and do not gossip about werewolves, because they try to bite your face off: that was Magnus's motto.

He happened to know a faerie who worked in Lou Walters's Latin Quarter nightclub, on the seedier and nakeder side of Times Square. Magnus had gone to see Mae West here a time or two and had spotted a chorus girl with a glamour that covered up her faerie wings and pale amethyst skin. He and Aeval had been friendly ever since—as friendly as you could be when both you and the dame were in it only for information.

She was sitting on the steps, already in costume. There was a great deal of delicate lilac flesh on display.

"I'm here to see a faerie about a vampire," he said in a low voice, and she laughed.

Magnus couldn't laugh back. He had the feeling that he would not be able to shake off the memory of Guadalupe's face or her hold on his arm anytime soon. "I'm looking for a boy. Human. Taken by one of the Spanish Harlem clan, most likely."

Aeval shrugged, one graceful fluid motion. "You know vampires. Could be any one of them."

Magnus hesitated, and then added, "The word is, this vampire likes them very young."

"In that case . . ." Aeval fluttered her wings. Even the most hardened Downworlders didn't like the thought of preying on children. "I might have heard something about a Louis Karnstein."

Magnus motioned for her to go on, leaning in and tipping back his hat so she could speak into his ear.

"He was living in Hungary until very recently. He's old and powerful, which is why the Lady Camille has welcomed him. And he has a particular fondness for children. He thinks their blood is the purest and sweetest, as young flesh is the tenderest. He was chased out of Hungary by mundanes who found his lair . . . who found all the children in it."

Save Raphael, Magnus thought. It seemed a more and more impossible mission.

Aeval looked at him, her huge oval eyes betraying a faint flicker of worry. When the fey were worried, it was time to panic.

"Get it done, warlock," she said. "You know what the Shadowhunters will do if they find out about someone like that. If Karnstein is up to his old tricks in our city, it will be the worse for us all. The Nephilim will kill every vampire they see. It will be seraph blades first and questions later for everybody."

Magnus did not like to go near the Hotel Dumont if he could help it. It was decrepit and unsettling, it held bad memories, and it also occasionally held his evil former lady love.

But today it seemed like the hotel was his inescapable destination.

The sun was scalding in the sky, but it would not be for

long. If Magnus had vampires to fight, he wanted to do it when they were at their weakest.

The Hotel Dumont was still beautiful, but barely so, Magnus thought as he walked inside. It was being buried by time, thick clusters of spiderwebs forming curtains on every arch. Ever since the twenties the vampires had considered it their private property and had hung around there. Magnus had never asked how Camille and the vampires had been involved in the tragedy of the 1920s, or what right they felt they now had to the building. Possibly the vampires simply enjoyed the allure of a place that was both decadent and abandoned. Nobody else came near it. The mundanes whispered that it was haunted.

Magnus had not let go of the hope that mundanes would come back, claim and restore it, and chase the vampires away. It would annoy Camille so much.

A young vampire hurried toward Magnus across the foyer, the colors of her red-and-green cheongsam and her henna-dyed hair vivid in the gray gloom.

"You are not welcome here, warlock!" she said.

"Am I not? Oh dear, what a social faux pas. I do apologize. Before I go, may I ask one thing? What can you tell me about Louis Karnstein?" Magnus asked conversationally. "And the children he has been bringing into the hotel and murdering?"

The girl shrank back as if Magnus had brandished a cross in her face.

"He's a guest here," she said, low. "And the Lady Camille said we were to show him every honor. We didn't know."

"No?" Magnus asked, and disbelief colored his voice like a drop of blood in water.

The vampires of New York were careful, of course. There was a minimum of human bloodshed, and any "accidents" were covered up fast, under the nose of Shadowhunters as they were. Magnus could easily believe, however, that if Camille had reason to please a guest, she would let him get away with murder. She would do it as easily as she would have the guest plied with luxurious surroundings: silver, velvet, and human lives.

And Magnus did not believe for a second that once Louis Karnstein had brought the succulent morsels home, carrying all the blame but willing to share some of the blood, that they had not feasted. He looked at the delicate girl and wondered how many people she had killed.

"Would you rather," he said very gently, "that I go away and come back with the Nephilim?"

The Nephilim—the bogeyman for monsters, and all those who could be monsters. Magnus was sure this girl could be a monster if she wanted. He knew that he could be a monster himself.

He knew something else. He did not intend to leave a young boy in the monsters' lair.

The girl's eyes widened. "You're Magnus Bane," she said.

"Yes," Magnus said. It was sometimes good to be recognized.

"The bodies are upstairs. In the blue room. He likes to play with them . . . after." She shuddered and stepped out of his way, disappearing back into the shadows.

Magnus squared his shoulders. He assumed the conversation had been overheard, since no challenge was offered to him and no other vampires arrived as he made his way up the curving staircase, the gold and scarlet of it lost under a carpet of gray but the shape intact. He went higher and higher to the apartments, where he knew that the vampire clan of New York would entertain their valued guests.

He found the blue room easily enough: it was one of the largest and had probably been the most grand of the hotel's apartments. If this had still been a hotel in any normal sense of the word, the guest in these quarters would have had to pay substantial damages. A hole had been staved in the high ceiling. The arched ceiling had been painted baby blue, robin's egg blue, the delicate blue that artists imagined the summer sky to be.

The true summer sky showed through the hole in the roof, a blazing unforgiving white, as relentless as the hunger that drove Karnstein, burning as brightly as a torch wielded by someone going to face a monster.

Magnus saw dust all over the floor, dust that he did not think was simply an indication of the accumulation of time. He saw dust, and he saw bodies: humped-up, tossed aside like rag dolls, sprawled like crushed spiders upon the ground and against the walls. There was no grace in death.

There were the bodies of teenage boys, the ones who had come in an eager fearless bevy to hunt the predator who was stalking their streets, who had innocently thought good would triumph. And there were other bodies, the older bodies of younger children. The children that Louis Karnstein had seized off Raphael Santiago's streets, and killed, and kept.

There was no saving these children, Magnus thought. There was nothing in this room but blood and death, and the echo of fear, the loss of all possibility of redemption.

Louis Karnstein was mad, then. It happened sometimes, with age and distance from humanity. Magnus had seen it happen with a fellow warlock thirty years before.

Magnus hoped if he ever went mad like that himself, so mad that he poisoned the very air around him and hurt everyone he came into contact with, that there would be someone who loved him enough to stop him. To kill him, if it came to that.

Arterial spray and bloody handprints decorated the dingy blue walls, and on the floor there were dark pools. There was human and vampire blood: vampire blood a deeper red, a red that stayed red even when it dried, red forever and always. Magnus edged around the spots, but in one pool of human blood he saw something glittering, submerged almost past hope but with a stubborn shine that caught his eye.

Magnus stooped and plucked the shining thing out of that dark pool. It was a cross, small and golden, and he thought that he could return this to Guadalupe at least. He put it in his pocket.

Magnus took a step forward, and then another step. He was not sure the floor would hold him, he told himself, but he knew that was only an excuse. He did not want to step out amid all that death.

But suddenly he knew that he had to.

He had to because at the farthest corner of the room, in the deepest shadows, he heard ugly, greedy sucking sounds. He saw a boy in the arms of a vampire.

Magnus lifted his hand, and the force of his magic flung the vampire through the air into one of the blood-streaked walls. Magnus heard a crack and saw the vampire slump to the ground. He would not stay down long.

Magnus ran across the room, stumbling over the bodies and sliding on the blood, to fall to his knees beside the boy, to gather him into his arms. He was young, fifteen or sixteen, and he was dying.

Magnus could not magic blood into a body, especially not one already shutting down from the lack of it. He cradled the boy's lolling dark head in one hand, watched his fluttering eyelids, and waited to see if there might be a moment in which the boy could focus. In which Magnus could tell him good-bye.

The boy never looked at him and never spoke. He clutched at Magnus's hand. Magnus thought he was reaching out by reflex, as a baby might, but Magnus held on and tried to give the boy what comfort he could.

The boy breathed once, twice, three times, and then his grip went slack.

"Did you know his name?" Magnus demanded roughly of the vampire who had killed him. "Was it Raphael?"

He did not know why he asked. He did not want to know that the boy Guadalupe had sent him to find had just died in his arms, that the last member of that gallant, doomed mission to save innocents had almost survived long enough—but not quite. He could not forget the imploring look on Guadalupe Santiago's face.

He looked over at the vampire, who had not moved to attack. He was sitting down, slumped against the wall where Magnus had thrown him.

"Raphael," the vampire answered slowly. "You came here looking for Raphael?" He gave a short, sharp, almost incredulous laugh.

"Why is that funny?" Magnus demanded. A dark fury was rising in his chest. It had been a long time since he had killed a vampire, but he was willing to do it again.

"Because I am Raphael Santiago," said the boy.

Magnus stared at the vampire boy—at Raphael. He had his

knees pulled up to his chest, his arms wrapped around them. Under his head of loose curls was a delicate heart-shaped face like his mother's, big dark eyes that would have enchanted women—or men—when he was grown, and a soft, childish mouth stained with blood. Blood masked the lower half of his face, and Magnus could see the white gleam of teeth against Raphael's lower lip, like diamonds in the darkness. He was the only thing moving in that whole room full of terrible stillness. He was shaking, fine tremors running all along his thin frame, shaking so hard that Magnus could see it, so hard that it looked violent, the teeth-rattling chill of someone so cold, they were about to slip into stillness and death. It was as hot as the mundanes imagined Hell to be in this room full of death, but the boy shook as though he were so cold, he could never be warm again.

Magnus stood up, moved carefully around dust and the dead until he was close to the vampire boy, and then said gently, "Raphael?"

Raphael lifted his face to the sound of Magnus's voice. He had seen many other vampires with skin as white as salt. Raphael's skin was still brown, but it did not have the warm tone of his mother's skin. It was not the flesh of a living boy any longer.

There was no saving Raphael.

His hands were covered in dirt and blood, as though he had crawled out of his grave very recently. His face was streaked with grave dirt too. He had black hair, a soft-looking curly mass of it that his mother must have loved to run her fingers through, that she must have stroked when he had nightmares and called for her, touched with light fingers when he was sleeping in his bed and she did not want to wake him, hair that she might have kept a baby curl of. That hair was full of grave dust.

There were red tear tracks on his face, shining darkly. There was blood on his neck, but Magnus knew the wound had closed over.

"Where's Louis Karnstein?" Magnus asked.

When Raphael spoke, this time in low, soft Spanish, he said, "The vampire thought I would help him with the others if he turned me into one of his own kind." He laughed suddenly, a bright, mad sound. "But I did not," he added. "No. He wasn't expecting that. He's dead. He turned to ashes and they blew away on the wind." He gestured toward the hole in the roof.

Magnus was startled into silence. It was extremely unusual for a new vampire to rise and overcome the hunger enough to think, or do anything else besides feed. Magnus wondered if Raphael had killed more than one of his friends.

He would not ask, and not only because it would have been cruel to ask. Even if Raphael had killed and then turned on his master and overcome Karnstein, he had to have a will of iron.

"They're all dead," said Raphael, seeming to master himself. His voice was clear suddenly. His dark eyes were clear too as he stared at Magnus, and then he deliberately turned away from Magnus, dismissing him as unimportant.

Raphael, Magnus saw with an ever-growing sense of unease, was looking at that blazingly bright hole in the ceiling, the one he had gestured to when he said that Karnstein had turned to ashes.

"They're all dead," Raphael repeated slowly. "And I am dead too."

He uncoiled, as swift as a snake, and sprang.

It was only because Magnus had seen where the vampire was looking and because he knew how Raphael felt, the exact exquisitely cold feeling of being an outcast, so alone that he barely seemed to exist, that he moved fast enough.

Raphael sprang for the spot of lethal light on the floor, and Magnus sprang at Raphael. He knocked the boy to the floor just before he reached the sunlight.

Raphael gave an incoherent scream like a bird of prey, a vicious cry that was nothing but rage and hunger, that echoed in Magnus's head and made his flesh creep. Raphael thrashed and crawled for the sun, and when Magnus would not let him go, Raphael used every bit of his fledgling vampire strength to struggle free, clawing and twisting. He had no hesitation, no remorse, and none of the usual vampire fledgling's discomfort with his new power. He tried to bite Magnus's throat out. He tried to tear him limb from limb. Magnus had to use magic to fasten his limbs to the floor, and even with Raphael's whole body pinned, Magnus had to evade his snapping fangs and only just managed it.

"Let me go!" shouted the boy at last, his voice breaking.

"Hush, hush," Magnus whispered. "Your mother sent me, Raphael. Be still. Your mother sent me to find you." He drew the gold cross he had found from his pocket and held it gleaming in front of Raphael's face. "She gave me this, and she told me to save you."

Raphael flinched away from the cross, and Magnus put it away hastily, but not before the boy stopped fighting and began to sob, sobs that racked his whole body, as if he could wrench himself, his hated new self, apart from the inside out if he shook and raged enough.

"Are you stupid?" he gasped out. "You *can't* save me. Nobody can do that."

Magnus could taste his despair as if it were blood. Magnus believed him. He held on to the boy, newborn in grave dirt and blood, and he wished that he had found him dead.

The sobbing had rendered Raphael worn enough that he was docile. Magnus brought him to his own home because he had not the faintest idea what else to do with him.

Raphael sat, a small tragic bundle on Magnus's sofa.

Magnus would have felt painfully sorry for him, but he had stopped in a phone booth on his way home to ring up Etta at the small jazz club where she was singing tonight, to tell her not to come around to his place for a while because he had a baby vampire to deal with.

"A baby vampire, huh?" Etta had asked, laughing, the same way a wife might laugh at her husband who always brings home the strangest items from a local antiques market. "I don't know any exterminator in the city you could call to deal with that."

Magnus had smiled. "I can deal with it myself. Trust me."

"Oh, I usually do," Etta had said. "Though my mama tried to teach me better judgment."

Magnus had been on the phone gabbing with Etta for only a couple of minutes, but when he'd gotten out, it had been to find Raphael crouched on the pavement. He'd hissed, fangs white and needle-sharp in the night, like a cat protective of his prey when Magnus had approached. The man in his arms, the crisp white collar of his shirt dyed crimson, had been already unconscious; Magnus wrenched him away from the hissing vampire and propped him in an alley, hoping he'd think he'd been mugged.

When he came back to the sidewalk, Raphael was still sitting there, hands curled into claws and pressed to his chest. There was still a trace of blood on his mouth. Magnus felt despair hollow his heart. Here was not simply a suffering child. Here was a monster with the face of a Caravaggio angel.

"You should have let me die," Raphael said in a small, hollow voice.

"I couldn't."

"Why not?"

"Because I promised your mother I would bring you home," said Magnus.

Raphael went still at the mention of his mother, as he had back at the hotel. Magnus could see his face in the glow of the streetlights. He had the blankly hurt look of a child who had been slapped: pain and bewilderment and no way to handle either of those feelings.

"And do you think she would want me home?" Raphael asked. "L-like *this?*"

His voice trembled, and his lower lip, still stained with a man's blood, wobbled. He swiped a vicious hand across his face, and Magnus saw it again: the way he pulled himself together in an instant, the stern control he exerted over himself.

"Look at me," he said. "Tell me she would invite me in."

Magnus could not tell him that. He remembered how Guadalupe had talked about monsters, those who walked in the darkness and preyed on innocents. He thought of how she might react—the woman who had given her son a cross—to a son with blood on his hands. He remembered his stepfather forcing him to repeat prayers until once-holy words tasted bitter in his mouth, remembered his mother and how she had not been able to touch him once she'd known, and how his stepfather had held him down under the surface of the water. Yet they had loved him once, and he had loved them.

Love did not overcome everything. Love did not always endure. All you had could be taken away, love could be the last thing you had, and then love could be taken too.

Magnus knew, though, how love could be a last hope and a star to steer by. Light that went out had still shone once.

Magnus could not promise Raphael his mother's love, but since Raphael still loved his mother, Magnus wanted to help him and thought he might know how.

He prowled forward, over his own rug, and saw Raphael's dark eyes flash, startled, at his sudden purposeful movement.

"What if she never had to know?"

Raphael blinked slowly, almost reptilian in his hesitation. "What do you mean?" he asked warily.

Magnus reached into his pocket and produced the glittering thing inside it, held cupped in the palm of his hand.

"What if you came to her door," Magnus asked, "wearing the cross that she gave you?"

He dropped the cross, and reflexively Raphael caught it in his open hand. The cross hit Raphael's palm, and he saw Raphael wince, saw the wince become a shudder that ran all through his thin body and made his face go tight with pain.

"All right, Raphael," Magnus said gently.

Raphael opened his eyes and glared at Magnus, which was not what Magnus had been expecting. The smell of burning flesh filled Magnus's room. He was going to have to invest in some potpourri.

"Well done, Raphael," Magnus said. "Bravely done. You can put it down now."

Raphael held Magnus's gaze, and very slowly he closed his fingers over the cross. Tiny wisps of smoke filtered out through the spaces between his fingers.

"Well done?" echoed the vampire boy. "Bravely done? I'm just getting started."

He sat there on Magnus's sofa, his whole body an arch of pain, and he held on to his mother's cross. He did not let go.

Magnus reassessed the situation.

"A good start," Magnus told him in a condescending tone. "But it's going to take a lot more than that."

Raphael's eyes narrowed, but he did not respond.

"Of course," Magnus added casually, "maybe you can't do it. It's going to be a lot of work, and you're just a kid."

"I know it's going to be a lot of work," Raphael told him, biting off the end of every word. "I have only you to help me, and you're not terribly impressive."

It dawned on Magnus that Raphael's question in the vampires' hotel—*Are you stupid?*—had been not only an expression of despair but also an expression of Raphael's personality.

He was soon to learn that it was also Raphael's favorite question.

In the nights that followed, Raphael acquired a good deal of horribly monochrome clothing, chased off several of Magnus's clients with caustic and unkind remarks, devoted his unlife to rattling Magnus's cage, and remained sternly unimpressed by any magic Magnus displayed. Magnus warned him about Shadowhunters, the Angel's children who would try to chase him down if he broke any of their Laws, and told him about all that there was to offer and all the people he could meet. The whole of Downworld was laid out before him, faeries and werewolves and enchantment, and the only thing Raphael seemed interested in was how long he could hold the cross for, how much longer he could hold it for each night.

Etta's verdict was that nothing razzed that kid's berries.

Etta and Raphael were distant with each other. Raphael was openly and insultingly surprised that Magnus had a lady friend, and Etta, though she knew of Downworld, was wary around all Downworlders but Magnus. Chiefly Raphael stayed out of the way when Etta came by.

They had met at a club fifteen years before, Etta and Magnus. He had convinced her to dance with him, and she said she had been in love by the end of the song. He told her he had been in love before the beginning.

It was their tradition that when Etta came in after a late night during which Magnus had not been able to join her—and Magnus was missing many nights, because of Raphael—Etta would kick off her high heels, feet aching from a long night, but keep her fancy beaded dress on, and they would dance together, murmuring bebop into each other's ears and competing as to which tune they would dance to the longest.

The first time Etta encountered Raphael, she was a little quiet afterward.

"He was made a vampire only a few days ago," she said eventually, when they were dancing. "That's what you said. Before that he was just a boy."

"If it helps, I have a suspicion that he was a menace."

Etta did not laugh. "I always thought of vampires as so old," she said. "I never thought about how people can become them. I guess it makes sense. I mean—Raphael, the poor kid, he's too young. But I can see how people might want to stay young forever. The same way you do."

Etta had been talking about age more and more in the last few months. She had not mentioned the men who came to hear her sing at clubs, who wanted to take her away and have children with her. She had not had to.

Magnus understood, could read the signs like a sailor knew which clouds in the sky would bring a storm. He had been left before, for many reasons, and this one was not unusual.

Immortality was something you paid for, and those you loved paid for, over and over again. There had been a precious few who had stayed with Magnus until death had parted them, but come death or a new stage of their lives where they felt he could not follow, they were all parted from him by something.

He could not blame Etta.

"Would you want it?" Magnus asked at last, after a long time swaying together. He did not make the offer, but he thought it, that he could have it arranged. There were ways. Ways one might pay a terrible price for. Ways his father knew of, and Magnus hated his father. But if she could stay with him always—

There was another silence. All Magnus heard was the click of his shoes, and the soft shuffle of her bare feet, on his wooden floors.

"No," said Etta, her cheek pressed against his shoulder. "No. If I could have it all my own way, I'd want a little more time with you. But I wouldn't stop the clock for it."

Strange and painful reminders came to Magnus every now and then, when he had become accustomed to Raphael as the always irritated and irritating housemate who had been wished upon him. He would be surprised with a reminder of what he already knew: that Raphael's clock had been stopped, that his human life had been viciously wrenched away from him.

Magnus was constructing a new hairstyle with the aid of Brylcreem and a dash of magic when Raphael came up behind him and surprised him. Raphael often did that, since he had the silent tread of his vampire kind. Magnus suspected that he did it on purpose, but since Raphael never cracked a smile, it was hard to tell.

"You're very frivolous," Raphael remarked disapprovingly, staring at Magnus's hair.

"And you're very fifteen," Magnus shot back.

Raphael usually had a retort for whatever Magnus threw at him, but instead of a reply Magnus received a long silence. When Magnus looked up from his mirror, he saw that Raphael had moved over to the window and was looking out onto the night.

"I would be sixteen by now," said Raphael, voice as distant and cold as the light of the moon. "If I had lived."

Magnus remembered the day when he had realized that he was no longer aging, looking in a mirror that seemed colder than all other mirrors had before, as if he had been viewing his reflection in a shard of ice. As if the mirror had been responsible for holding his image so utterly frozen and so utterly distant.

He wondered how different it was to be a vampire, to know down to the precise day, the hour, the minute when you stopped belonging to the common warm and changing course of humanity. When you stood still, and the world whirled on and never missed you.

He did not ask.

"You people," said Raphael, which was how he referred to warlocks, because he was quite the charmer. "You stop aging randomly, don't you? You're born like a human is born, and you're always what you are, but you age like a human does, until you don't anymore."

Magnus wondered if Raphael had read those same thoughts on Magnus's face.

"That's right."

"Do you think your people have souls?" Raphael asked. He was still staring out the window.

Magnus had known people who thought he did not. He believed he did, but that did not mean he had never doubted.

"Doesn't matter," Raphael continued before Magnus could answer. His voice was flat. "Either way I envy you."

"Why so?"

The moonlight poured in on Raphael, bleaching his face so he looked like a marble statue of a saint who had died young.

"Either you still have your souls," said Raphael, "or you never had them, and you do not know what it is to wander the world damned, exiled, and missing them forever."

Magnus put his hairbrush down. "All Downworlders have souls," he said. "It's what makes us different from demons."

Raphael sneered. "That is a Nephilim belief."

"So what?" Magnus said. "Sometimes they're right."

Raphael said something unkind in Spanish. "They think they are such saviors, the *cazadores de sombras*," he said. "The Shadowhunters. Yet they have never come to save me."

Magnus looked at the boy silently. He had never been able to argue against his stepfather's convictions regarding what

God wanted or God judged. He did not know how to convince Raphael that he might still have a soul.

"I see you're trying to distract me from the real point here," Magnus said instead. "You had a birthday—a perfect excuse for me to throw one of my famous parties—and you didn't even tell me about it?"

Raphael stared at him silently, then turned and walked away.

Magnus had often thought of getting a pet, but he had never considered acquiring a sullen teenage vampire. Once Raphael was gone, he thought, he was getting a cat. And he would always throw his cat a birthday party.

It was soon afterward that Raphael wore a cross around his neck, all night, without crying out or exhibiting any visible signs of discomfort. At the end of the night, when he removed it, there was a faint mark against his chest, as of a long-healed burn, but that was all.

"So that's it," Magnus said. "That's great. You're done! Let's go visit your mother."

He had sent her a message telling her not to worry and not to visit, that he was using all the magic he could to save Raphael and could not be disturbed, but he knew it would not keep her away forever.

Raphael's expression was blank as he fiddled with the chain in one hand, his only sign of uncertainty. "No," he said. "How many times are you going to underestimate me? I'm not done. I'm not even close."

He explained to Magnus what he wanted to do next.

"You are doing a good deal to help me," Raphael said the

next night as they approached the graveyard. His voice was almost clinical.

Magnus thought but did not say, *Yes, because there were times when I was as desperate as you, and as miserable, and as convinced that I had no soul.* People had helped him when he'd needed it, because he had needed it and for no other reason. He remembered the Silent Brothers coming for him in Madrid, and teaching him that there was still a way to live.

"You don't need to be grateful," Magnus said instead. "I'm not doing it for you."

Raphael shrugged, a fluid easy gesture. "All right, then."

"I mean, you could be grateful occasionally," Magnus said. "You could tidy up the apartment once in a while."

Raphael considered this. "No, I don't think I will."

"I think your mother should have beaten you," said Magnus. "Frequently."

"My father hit me once, back in Zacatecas," Raphael said casually.

Raphael had not mentioned a father before, and Guadalupe had not mentioned a husband, though Magnus knew there were several brothers.

"He did?" Magnus tried to make his voice both neutral and encouraging, in case Raphael wanted to confide in him.

Raphael, not the confiding type, looked amused. "He didn't hit me twice."

It was a small graveyard, secluded and far away in Queens, hemmed in by tall and dark buildings, one warehouse and one abandoned Victorian home. Magnus had arranged for the area to be sprinkled with holy water, blessed, and made sacred. Churches were hallowed ground but graveyards not so. All vampires had to be buried somewhere, and had to rise.

It would not provide a barrier like the Institute of the Shadowhunters, but it would be hard enough for Raphael to rest his foot on the ground.

It was another test. Raphael had promised not to do more than touch his foot to the ground.

Raphael had promised.

When Raphael lifted his chin, like a horse taking a bit between its teeth, and charged right onto the holy ground, running and burning and screaming, Magnus wondered how he could ever have believed him.

"Raphael!" he shouted, and ran after him, into the darkness and onto the sacred earth.

Raphael sprang onto a gravestone, landed balanced on it. His curly hair was blown back from his thin face, his body arched, his fingers clawed against the marble edge. His teeth were bared from vicious tip to gum, and his eyes were black and lifeless. He looked like a revenant, a nightmare rearing up from a grave. Less human, with less of a soul, than any savage beast.

He leaped. Not at Magnus but at the perimeter of the graveyard. He came out on the other side.

Magnus chased after him. Raphael was swaying, leaning against the low stone wall as if he could barely stay on his feet. The skin on his arms was visibly bubbling. He looked as if he wanted to claw off the rest of his skin in agony but did not have the strength.

"Well, you did it," Magnus remarked. "By which I mean you almost gave me a heart attack. Don't stop now. The night is young. What are you going to do to upset me next?"

Raphael glanced up at him and grinned. It was not a nice expression.

"I am going to do the same thing again."

Magnus supposed he had asked for that.

When Raphael had run through the holy ground again not once but ten times, he leaned against the wall looking worn and spent, and while he was too weak to run, he leaned against the wall and murmured to himself, choking at first and then getting the word out, the name of God.

He choked up blood as he said it, coughed, and kept murmuring. "*Dios.*"

Magnus bore the sight of him, too weak to stand and still hurting himself, as long as he could.

"Raphael, don't you think you've done enough?"

Predictably, Raphael glared at him. "No."

"You have forever to learn how to do this and how to control yourself. You have—"

"But *they don't*!" Raphael burst out. "*Dios*, do you understand nothing? The only thing I have left is the hope of seeing them, of not breaking my mother's heart. I need to convince her. I need to do it perfectly, and I need to do it soon, while she still hopes that I am alive."

He had spoken "*Dios*" almost without flinching that time.

"You're being very good."

"It is no longer possible for me to be good," Raphael said, his voice steely. "If I were still good and brave, I would do what my mother would want if she knew the truth. I would walk out into the sun and end my own life. But I am a selfish, wicked, heartless beast, and I do not want to burn in the fires of Hell yet. I want to go see my m-mother, and I will. I will. I will!"

Magnus nodded. "What if God could help you?" he asked gently.

It was as close as he could get to saying, *What if everything you believe is wrong and you could still be loved and still be forgiven?*

Raphael shook his head stubbornly.

"I am one of the Night Children. I am no longer a child of His, no longer under His watchful eye. God will not help me," Raphael said, his voice thick, speaking through a mouthful of blood. He spat the blood out again. "And God will not stop me."

Magnus did not argue with him again. Raphael was still so young in so many ways, and his whole world had shattered around him. All he had left to make sense of the world were his beliefs, and he would cling to them even if his very beliefs told him that he was hopelessly lost, damned, and dead already.

Magnus did not even know if it would be right to try to take those beliefs away.

That night when Magnus was sleeping, he woke and heard the low, fervent murmur of Raphael's voice. Magnus had heard people praying many times and recognized the sound. He heard the names, unfamiliar names, and wondered if they had been Raphael's friends. Then he heard the name Guadalupe, the name of Raphael's mother, and he knew the other names had to be the names of Raphael's brothers.

As mortals called on God, on angels and saints, as they chanted while telling their rosary, Raphael was pronouncing the only names that were sacred to him and would not burn his tongue to utter. Raphael was calling on his family.

There were many drawbacks to having Raphael as a roommate that did not concern Raphael's conviction that he was a damned lost soul, or even the fact that Raphael used up so much soap in the shower (even though he never sweated and hardly needed to shower so often) and never did the washing up. When Magnus pointed this out, Raphael responded that he never ate food and was therefore not creating any washing up, which was just like Raphael.

One more drawback became apparent the day that Ragnor Fell, High Warlock of London and perpetual enormous green thorn in Magnus's side, came by to pay an unexpected visit.

"Ragnor, this is a welcome surprise," said Magnus, flinging the door open wide.

"I was paid by some Nephilim to make the trip," said Ragnor. "They wished for a spell."

"And my waiting list was too long." Magnus nodded sadly. "I am in great demand."

"And you constantly give the Shadowhunters lip, so they all dislike you, save a few wayward rebellious souls," said Ragnor. "How many times have I told you, Magnus? Behave professionally in a professional setting. Which means no being rude to Nephilim, and also no getting attached to Nephilim."

"I never get attached to Nephilim!" Magnus protested.

Ragnor coughed, and in the midst of the cough said something that sounded like "blerondale."

"Well," said Magnus. "Hardly ever."

"No getting attached to the Nephilim," Ragnor repeated sternly. "Speak respectfully to your clients and give them the service they wish for as well as the magic. And save incivility for your friends. Talking of which, I have not seen you in this age, and you look even more of a horror than you usually do."

"That's a filthy lie," said Magnus.

He knew he looked extremely sharp. He was wearing an amazing brocade tie.

"Who is at the door?" Raphael's imperious voice drifted from the bathroom, and the rest of Raphael came with it, dressed in a towel but looking just as critical as ever. "I told you that you have to start keeping regular business hours, Bane."

Ragnor squinted over at Raphael. Raphael looked balefully back at Ragnor. There was a certain tension in the air.

"Oh, Magnus," said Ragnor, and he covered his eyes with one large green hand. "Oh no, no."

"What?" said Magnus, puzzled.

Ragnor abruptly lowered his hand. "No, you're right, of course. I'm being silly. He's a vampire. He only looks fourteen. How old are you? I bet you're older than either of us, ha-ha."

Raphael looked at Ragnor as if he were mad. Magnus found it quite refreshing to have someone else looked at that way for a change.

"I'd be sixteen by now," he said slowly.

"Oh, Magnus!" Ragnor wailed. "That's disgusting! How could you? Have you lost your mind?"

"What?" Magnus asked again.

"We agreed eighteen was the cutoff age," said Ragnor. "You, I, and Catarina made a vow."

"A v— Oh, wait. You think I'm dating Raphael?" Magnus asked. "Raphael? That's ridiculous. That's—"

"That's the most revolting idea I've ever heard."

Raphael's voice rang out to the ceiling. Probably people in the street could hear him.

"That's a little strong," said Magnus. "And, frankly, hurtful."

"And if I did wish to indulge in unnatural pursuits—and let

me be clear, I certainly do not," Raphael continued scornfully, "as if I would choose *him*. Him! He dresses like a maniac, acts like a fool, and makes worse jokes than the man people throw rotten eggs at outside the Dew Drop every Saturday."

Ragnor began to laugh.

"Better men than you have begged for a chance to win all this," Magnus muttered. "They have fought duels in my honor. One man fought a duel *for* my honor, but that was a little embarrassing since it is long gone."

"Do you know he spends hours in the bathroom sometimes?" Raphael announced mercilessly. "He wastes actual magic on his hair. On his hair!"

"I love this kid," said Ragnor.

Of course he did. Raphael was filled with grave despair about the world in general, was eager to insult Magnus in particular, and had a tongue as sharp as his teeth. Raphael was obviously Ragnor's soul mate.

"Take him," Magnus suggested. "Take him far, far away."

Instead Ragnor took a chair, and Raphael got dressed and joined him at the table.

"Let me tell you another thing about Bane," Raphael began.

"I'm going out," Magnus announced. "I'd describe what I'm going to do when I go out, but I find it hard to believe that either of you would understand the concept of 'enjoying a good time with a group of entertaining companions.' I do not intend to return until you people are done insulting your charming host."

"So you're moving out and giving me the apartment?" Raphael asked. "I accept."

"Someday that smart mouth is going to get you into a lot

of trouble," Magnus called darkly over his shoulder.

"Look who's talking," said Ragnor.

"Hello?" said Raphael, as laconic as usual. "Damned soul."

Worst roommate ever.

Ragnor stayed for thirteen days. They were the longest thirteen days of Magnus's life. Every time Magnus tried to have a little fun, there they were, the short one and the green one, shaking their heads in tandem and then saying snotty things. On one occasion Magnus turned his head very quickly and saw them exchanging a fist bump.

"Write to me," Ragnor said to Raphael when he was leaving. "Or call me on your telephone if you want. I know the youths like that."

"It was great to meet you, Ragnor," said Raphael. "I was beginning to think all warlocks were completely useless."

It was not long after Ragnor left that Magnus tried to recall the last time Raphael had drunk blood. Magnus had always avoided thinking about how Camille got her meals, even when he'd loved her, and he did not want to see Raphael kill again. But he saw Raphael's skin tone change, saw the strained look about his mouth, and thought about getting this far and having Raphael shrivel up out of sheer despair.

"Raphael, I don't know quite how to put this, but are you eating right?" Magnus asked. "Until recently you were a growing boy."

"*El hambre agudiza el ingenio*," said Raphael.

Hunger sharpens the wit.

"Good proverb," said Magnus. "However, like most proverbs, it sounds wise and yet does not actually clarify anything."

"Do you think I would permit myself to be around my mother—around my small brothers—if I were not sure beyond a shadow of a doubt that I could control myself?" Raphael said. "I want to know that if I were trapped in a room with one of them, if I had not tasted blood in days, I could control myself."

Raphael almost killed another man that night, in front of Magnus's eyes. He proved his point.

Magnus did not have to worry about Raphael starving himself out of pity, or mercy, or any softer feeling for the rest of humanity. Raphael did not consider himself a part of humanity anymore and thought he could commit any sin in the world because he was already damned. He had simply been abstaining from drinking blood to prove to himself that he could, to test his own limits, and to exercise the absolute self-control that he was determined to achieve.

The next night Raphael ran over sacred ground and then calmly drank blood from a tramp sleeping on the street who might never wake up, despite the healing spell Magnus whispered over him. They were walking through the night, Raphael calculating out loud how much longer it would take him to become as strong as he needed to be.

"I think you're fairly strong," said Magnus. "And you have quite a lot of self-control. Look how you sternly repress all the hero worship you are longing to show me that you feel."

"It is sometimes an exercise of real self-control not to laugh in your face," Raphael said gravely. "That much is true."

It was then that Raphael stiffened, and when Magnus made an inquiring sound, Raphael hushed him sharply. Magnus looked down at Raphael's dark eyes and followed the direction in which they were fixed. He didn't know what Raphael was casting an eyeball at, but he figured it was no harm to follow him when Raphael moved.

There was an alley stretching behind an abandoned Automat. In the shadows there was a rustling that could have been rats in garbage, but as they drew closer, Magnus could hear what had attracted Raphael: the sound of giggling, and the sound of sucking, and the whimpers of pain.

He was not sure what Raphael was doing, but he had no plans to abandon him now. Magnus clicked his fingers, and there was light—radiating from his hand, filling the alleyway with brightness, and falling onto the faces of the four vampires in front of him, and their victim.

"What do you people think you're doing?" Raphael demanded.

"What does it look like?" said the only girl of the group. Magnus recognized her as the lone brave soul who had accosted him at the Hotel Dumont. "We're drinking blood. What, are you new?"

"Is that what you were doing?" Raphael asked in a voice of exaggerated surprise. "So sorry. That must have escaped my attention, since I was preoccupied with how incredibly stupid you were all being."

"Stupid?" echoed the girl. "Do you mean 'wrong'? Are you lecturing us on—"

Raphael clicked his fingers impatiently at her. "Do I mean 'wrong'?" he said. "We're all dead and damned already. What would 'wrong' even mean to beings like us?"

The girl tilted her head and looked thoughtful.

"I mean *stupid*," said Raphael. "Not that I consider hunting down a slow-witted child honorable, mind you. Consider this: you kill her, you bring the Shadowhunters down on all of us. I don't know about you people, but I do not wish for the Nephilim to come and cut my life short with a blade because someone was a little too peckish and a lot dumb."

"So you're saying, 'Oh, spare her life,'" sneered one of the boys, though the girl elbowed him.

"But even if you don't kill her," Raphael continued relentlessly, as if nobody had interrupted him at all, "well, then, you've already drunk from her, under uncontrolled and frenzied conditions that would make it easy for her to accidentally taste some of your blood. Which will leave her with a compulsion to follow you about. Do this to enough victims and you'll either be snowed under with subjugates—and frankly they are not the best conversationalists—or you'll make them into more vampires. Which, mathematically speaking, eventually leaves you with a blood supply problem because there are no humans left. Humans can waste resources knowing that at least they will not be around to deal with the consequences, but you chumps don't even have that excuse. *Goodness me*, you nosebleeds are going to think when a seraph blade cuts your head off or you stare around at a bleak landscape while starving to death, *if only I'd been a smart cookie and listened to Raphael when I had the chance.*"

"Is he serious?" another vampire asked, sounding awed.

"Almost invariably," Magnus said. "It's what makes him such tedious company."

"Is that your name? Raphael?" asked the vampire girl. She was smiling, her black eyes dancing.

"Yes," said Raphael irritably, immune to flirtation the same way he was immune to all things that were fun. "What is the point of being immortal if you do nothing with it but be irresponsible and unacceptably stupid? What's your name?"

The vampire girl's smile spread, showing her fangs sparkling behind her lipsticked mouth. "Lily."

"Here lies Lily," said Raphael. "Killed by vampire hunters because she was murdering people and then not even having the intelligence to cover her tracks."

"What, now you're telling us to be afraid of mundanes?" another vampire said, laughing, this one a man with silver at his temples. "Those are old stories told to frighten the youngest of us. I assume you're pretty young yourself, but—"

Raphael smiled, fangs bared, though his expression had nothing to do with humor. "I am rather young," he said. "And when I was alive, I was a vampire hunter. I killed Louis Karnstein."

"You're a vampire vampire hunter?" asked Lily.

Raphael swore in Spanish. "No, of course I'm not a vampire vampire hunter," he said. "Exactly what kind of treacherous weasel would I be then? Additionally, what a stupid thing to be. I would instantly be killed by all the other vampires, who would come together over a common threat. At least I hope they would. Maybe they would all be too stupid. I am someone who talks sense," Raphael informed them all severely, "and there is *very little* job competition."

The vampire with graying hair was almost pouting. "Lady Camille lets us do what we want."

Raphael was not a fool. He was not going to insult the leader of the vampire clan in his own city.

"Lady Camille clearly has enough to do without running around after you idiots, and she assumes you have more sense than you have. Let me give you something to think about it, if you are capable of thinking."

Lily sidled over to Magnus, her eyes still on Raphael.

"I like him," she said. "He's kind of boss, even though he's such an oddball. You know what I mean?"

"Sorry. I went deaf with sheer amazement that anyone could like Raphael."

"And he isn't afraid of anything," Lily continued, grinning. "He's talking to Derek like a schoolteacher talking to a naughty child, and I personally have seen Derek rip people's heads off and drink from the stem."

They both looked at Raphael, who was giving a speech. The other vampires were cowering away slightly.

"You are already dead. Do you wish to be crushed out of existence completely?" Raphael asked. "Once we leave this world, all we have to look forward to is torment in the eternal fires of Hell. Do you want your damned existence to count for nothing?"

"I think I need a drink," Magnus murmured. "Does anyone else want a drink?"

Every vampire who was not Raphael silently raised their hand. Raphael looked accusing and judgmental, but Magnus believed his face was stuck that way.

"Very well. I'm prepared to share," said Magnus, taking his gold-embossed flask out from its specially designed place on his gold-embossed belt. "But I'm warning you, I'm all out of blood of the innocent. This is Scotch."

After the other vampires were drunk, Raphael and Magnus sent the mundane girl on her way, a little dizzy from lack of blood but otherwise fine. Magnus was not surprised when Raphael performed the *encanto* on her perfectly. He supposed

Raphael had been practicing that, too. Or possibly it just came extremely naturally to Raphael to impose his will on others.

"Nothing happened. You will go tuck yourself up in your bed and remember nothing. Do not go wandering in these areas at night. You will meet unsavory men and bloodsucking fiends," Raphael told the girl, his eyes on hers, unwavering. "And go to church."

"Do you think your calling might be telling everyone in the world what to do?" Magnus asked as they were walking home.

Raphael regarded him sourly. He had such a sweet face, Magnus thought—the face of an innocent angel, and the soul of the crankiest person in the entire world.

"You should never wear that hat again."

"My point exactly," said Magnus.

The Santiagos' house was in Harlem, on 129th Street and Lenox Avenue.

"You don't have to wait around for me," Raphael told Magnus as they walked. "I was thinking that after this, however it ends up, I will go to Lady Camille Belcourt and live with the vampires. They could use me there, and I could use—something to do. I'm . . . sorry if that offends you."

Magnus thought about Camille, and all that he suspected about her, remembered the horror of the twenties and that he still did not know quite how she had been involved in that.

But Raphael could not stay as Magnus's guest, a temporary guest in Downworld with nowhere to belong to, nothing to anchor him in the shadows and keep him away from the sun.

"Oh no, Raphael, please don't leave me," Magnus said in a monotone. "Where would I be without the light of your sweet smile? If you go, I will throw myself upon the ground and weep."

"Will you?" asked Raphael, raising one thin eyebrow. "Because if you do, I will stay and watch the show."

"Get out," Magnus told him. "Out! I want you out. I'm going to throw a party when you leave, and you know you hate those. Along with fashion, and music, and fun as a concept. I will never blame you for going and doing what suits you best. I want you to have a purpose. I want you to have something to live for, even if you don't think you're alive."

There was a brief pause.

"Well, excellent," said Raphael. "Because I was going anyway. I am sick of Brooklyn."

"You are an insufferable brat," Magnus informed him, and Raphael smiled one of his rare, shockingly sweet smiles.

His smile faded quickly as they approached his old neighborhood. Magnus could see that Raphael was fighting back panic. Magnus remembered his stepfather's and his mother's faces. He knew how it felt when family turned away from you.

He would rather have the sun taken away from him, as it had already been for Raphael, than have love taken away. He found himself praying, as he seldom had in years, like the man who had raised him used to, like Raphael did, that Raphael would not have to bear both being taken.

They approached the door of the house, a stoop with weathered green latticework. Raphael stared at it with mingled longing and fear, as a sinner might stare at the gates of Heaven.

It was up to Magnus to knock on the door, and wait for the answer.

When Guadalupe Santiago answered the door and saw her son, the time for prayer was over.

Magnus could see her whole heart in her eyes as she looked at Raphael. She had not moved, had not flung herself upon him. She was staring at him, at his angel's face and dusky curls, at his slight frame and flushed cheeks—he had fed before he came, so that he would look more alive—and more than anything else, at the gold chain gleaming around his neck. Was it the cross? He could see her wondering. Was it her gift, meant to keep him safe?

Raphael's eyes were shining. It was the one thing they had not planned for, Magnus realized in sudden horror. The one thing they had not practiced—preventing Raphael from weeping. If he shed tears in front of his mother, those tears would be blood, and the whole game would be over.

Magnus started talking as fast as he could.

"I found him for you, as you asked," he said. "But when I reached him, he was very close to death, so I had to give him some of my own power, make him like me." Magnus caught Guadalupe's eyes, though that was difficult since her entire attention was on her son. "A magic maker," he said, as she'd said to him once. "An immortal sorcerer."

She thought vampires were monsters, but she had come to Magnus for help. She could trust a warlock. She could believe a warlock was not damned.

Guadalupe's whole body was tense, but she gave a tiny nod. She recognized the words, Magnus knew, and she wanted to believe. She wanted so badly to believe what they were saying that she could not quite bring herself to trust them.

She looked older than she had a few months ago, worn by the time her son had been gone. She looked older but no less fierce, and she stood with her arm blocking the doorway, children peering in around her but protected by her body.

But she did not shut the door. She listened to the story, and she gave her absolute attention to Raphael, her eyes tracing the familiar lines of his face whenever he spoke.

"All this time I have been in training so I could come home to you and make you proud. Mother," Raphael said, "I assure you, I beg you will believe me. I still have a soul."

Guadalupe's eyes were still fixed on the thin, glittering chain around his neck. Raphael's shaking fingers pulled the cross free from his shirt. The cross danced as it dangled from his hand, gold and shining, the brightest thing in all the night-time city.

"You wore it," Guadalupe whispered. "I was so afraid that you would not listen to your mother."

"Of course I did," said Raphael, his voice trembling. But he did not cry, not Raphael of the iron will. "I wore it, and it kept me safe. It saved me. You saved me."

Guadalupe's whole body changed then, from enforced stillness to movement, and Magnus realized that more than one person in this conversation had been exercising iron self-control. He knew where Raphael got it from.

She stepped over the threshold and held out her arms. Raphael ran into them, gone from Magnus's side more quickly than a human could move, and clasped one arm tight around her neck. He was shaking in her arms, shaking all over as she stroked his hair.

"Raphael," she murmured into his black curls. First Magnus and Raphael had not been able to stop talking, and now it seemed she could not. "Raphael, *mijo*, Raphael, my Raphael."

At first Magnus knew in the jumble of words of love and

comfort only that she was inviting Raphael in, that they were safe, that they had succeeded, that Raphael could have his family and his family would never have to know. All the words she said were both endearments and statements, love and laying claim: my son, my boy, my child.

The other boys crowded up around Raphael, given their mother's blessing, and Raphael touched them with gentle hands, touched the little ones' hair, tugging with affection that looked careless, though it was so very careful, and shoved the older boys in rough but never too rough greeting.

Playing his role as Raphael's benefactor and teacher, Magnus hugged Raphael too. As prickly as he was, Raphael did not invite embraces. Magnus had not been so close to him since the day he'd fought to stop Raphael from going into the sun. Raphael's back felt thin under Magnus's hands—fragile, though he was not.

"I owe you, warlock," Raphael said, a cool whisper against Magnus's ear. "I promise you I won't forget."

"Don't be ridiculous," said Magnus, and then because he could get away with it, when he drew back, he ruffled Raphael's curly hair.

The indignant look on Raphael's face was hilarious.

"I will leave you to be alone with your family," Magnus told him, and he went.

Before he did, though, he paused and created a few blue sparks from his fingers that formed tiny play houses and stars, that made magic something fun that the children did not fear. He told them all that Raphael was not quite as accomplished or fabulously talented as he himself was, and would not be able to perform such tiny miracles for years. He made a flourishing bow that had the little ones laughing and Raphael rolling his eyes.

Magnus did leave, walking slowly. The winter was coming but was not quite there yet, and he was happy to simply walk and enjoy the little things in life, the crisp winter air, the few stray golden leaves still curling under his feet, the bare trees above him waiting to be reborn in glory. He was going home to an apartment that he suspected would feel slightly too empty, but soon he would invite Etta over, and she would dance with him and fill the rooms with love and laughter, as she would fill his life with love and laughter, for a little while yet before she left him.

He heard steps thundering after him and thought it was Raphael for a moment, the masquerade in ruins around them suddenly, when they'd thought they were victorious.

But it was not Raphael. Magnus did not see Raphael again for several months, and by then Raphael was Camille's second-in-command, calmly ordering around vampires hundreds of years older than himself as only Raphael could. Raphael spoke to Magnus then as one important Downworlder to another, with perfect professionalism, but Magnus knew Raphael had not forgotten anything. Relations had always been strained between Magnus and the vampires of New York, Camille's clan, but suddenly they were less strained. New York vampires came to his parties, though Raphael did not, and came to him for magical aid, though Raphael never would again.

The footsteps chasing Magnus's in the cool winter night were not Raphael's but Guadalupe's. She was panting from how hard she had been running, her dark hair slipping free of its pins, forming a cloud about her face. She almost ran into him before she could stop herself.

"Wait," she said. "I haven't paid you."

Her hands were shaking, spilling over with bills. Magnus closed her fingers around the money and closed his hands around hers.

"Take it," she urged him. "Take it. You earned it; you earned more. You brought him back to me, my oldest boy, the sweetest of them all, my dear heart, my brave boy. You saved him."

She was still shaking as Magnus held her hands, so Magnus rested his forehead against hers. He held her close enough to kiss, close enough to whisper the most important secrets in the world, and he spoke to her as he would have wanted some good angel to speak to his family, to his own shivering young soul, long ago and in a land far away.

"No," he murmured. "No, I didn't. You know him better than anyone else ever has or ever will. You made him, you taught him to be all he is, and you know him down to his bones. You know how strong he is. You know how much he loves you. If I gave you anything, give me your faith now. Teach one thing to all your children. I have never told you anything more true than this. Believe this, if you believe nothing else. Raphael saved himself."

The Fall of the Hotel Dumort

By Cassandra Clare and Maureen Johnson

Her silver-blond hair was long and down, looking wild. She patted the end of the bed. This was not the greeting he'd been expecting. This was not the Camille he remembered, or even the one he had seen in passing.

—The Fall of the Hotel Dumort

MAGNUS! MAGNUS! MAGNUS! COME HERE! COME! SIT DOWN!

July 1977

"What do *you* do?" the woman asked.

"This and that," Magnus said.

"Are you in fashion? You look like you're in fashion."

"No," he said. "I *am* fashion."

It was a bit of a twee remark, but it seemed to delight his seat companion on the plane. The comment had been a bit of a test, actually. Everything seemed to delight his companion—the seat back in front of her, her nails, her glass, her own hair, everyone else's hair, the barf bag . . .

The plane had been in the air for only an hour, but Magnus's companion had gotten up to use the restroom four times. Each time she'd emerged moments later, furiously rubbing her nose and visibly twitching. Now she was leaning over him, her winged blond hair dipping into his champagne glass, her neck reeking of Eau de Guerlain. The faint trace of white powder still clung to her nose.

He could have done this trip in seconds by stepping through a Portal, but there was something pleasant about aircraft. They were charming, intimate, and slow. You got to meet people. Magnus liked meeting people.

"But your *outfit*?" she said. "What *is* it?"

Magnus looked down at his red-plaid-and-black-vinyl oversize suit with a shredded T-shirt underneath. It was au courant for the London punk set, but New York wasn't quite there yet.

"I do PR," the woman said, apparently forgetting the question. "For discos and clubs. The best clubs. Here. Here."

She dug around in her massive purse—and stopped for a moment when she found her cigarettes. She shoved one of these between her lips, lit it, and continued digging until she produced a small tortoiseshell card case. She popped this open and picked out one card, which read: *ELECTRICA*.

"Come," she said, tapping the card with a long, red nail. "Come. It's just opening. It's going to be smash-ing. *Soooo* much better than Studio 54. Oh. Excuse me a second. You want?"

She showed him a small vial in the palm of her hand.

"No, thank you."

And then she was fumbling out of the seat again, her purse bumping into Magnus's face as she went back to the bathroom.

The mundanes had gotten very interested in drugs again. They went through these phases. Now it was cocaine. He hadn't seen this much of the stuff since the turn of the century, when they'd been putting it in everything—tonics and potions and even Coca-Cola. He thought for a while that they'd put this drug behind them, but it was back again, in full force.

Drugs had never interested Magnus. A good wine, absolutely, but he steered clear of potions and powders and pills. You didn't take drugs and do magic. Also, people who did drugs were boring. Hopelessly, relentlessly boring. Drugs made them either too slow or too fast, and mostly they talked about drugs. And then they either quit—a gruesome process—or they died. There was never a step in between.

Like all mundane phases, this too would pass. Hopefully soon. He closed his eyes and decided to sleep his way across the Atlantic. London was behind him. Now it was time to go home.

Stepping outside at JFK, Magnus got his first reminder of why he'd summarily left New York two summers before. New York was *too damn hot* in the summer. It was just touching a hundred degrees, and the smell of jet fuel and exhaust fumes mixed with the swampy gasses that hung around this far tip of the city. The smell, he knew, would only get worse.

With a sigh he joined a taxi line.

The cab was as comfortable as any metal box in the sun, and his sweating driver added to the general perfume in the air.

"Where to, buddy?" he asked, taking in Magnus's outfit.

"Corner of Christopher and Sixth Avenue."

The cabbie grunted and hit the meter, and then they pulled out into traffic. The smoke from the driver's cigar streamed back directly into Magnus's face. He lifted a finger and redirected it out the window.

The road from JFK to Manhattan was a strange one, weaving through family neighborhoods, and desolate stretches, and past sprawling graveyards. It was an age-old tradition. Keep the dead out of the city—but not too far. London, where he had just been, was ringed with old graveyards. And Pompeii, which he'd visited a few months back, had an entire avenue of the dead, tombs leading right up to the city wall. Past all of the New York neighborhoods and graveyards, at the end of the crowded expressway, shimmering in the distance—there was Manhattan—its spires and peaks just lighting up for the night. From death to life.

He hadn't meant to be away from the city for so long. He had just been going to take the briefest trip to Monte Carlo . . . but then, these things can go on. A week in Monte Carlo turns into two on the Riviera, which turns into a month in Paris, and two months in Tuscany, and then you end up on a boat headed for Greece, and then you wind up back in Paris again for the season, and then you go to Rome for a bit, and London . . .

And sometimes you accidentally go for two years. It happens.

"Where you from?" the cabbie asked, eyeing Magnus in the rearview mirror.

"Oh, around. Here mostly."

"You're from here? You been away? You look like you been away."

"For a while."

"You hear about these murders?"

"Haven't read a paper in a while," Magnus said.

"Some loony-tune. Calls himself Son of Sam. They called him the forty-four-caliber killer too. Goes around shooting couples on lovers' lanes, you know? Sick bastard. Real sick. Police haven't caught him. They don't do nothing. Sick bastard. City's full of them. You shouldn'ta come back."

New York cabdrivers—always little rays of sunshine.

Magnus got out on the tree-lined corner of Sixth Avenue and Christopher Street, in the heart of the West Village. Even at nightfall the heat was stifling. Still, it seemed to encourage a party atmosphere in the neighborhood. The Village had been an interesting place before he'd left. It seemed that in his absence things had taken on a whole new level of festivity. Costumed men walked down the street. The outdoor cafés were swarming. There was a carnival atmosphere that Magnus found instantly inviting.

Magnus's apartment was a walk-up, on the third story of one of the brick houses that lined the street. He let himself in and sprang lightly up the steps, full of high spirits. His spirits fell when he reached his landing. The first thing he noticed, right by his door, was a strong and bad smell—something rotten, mixed with something like skunk, mixed with other things he had no desire to identify. Magnus did not live in a stinky apartment. His apartment smelled of clean floors, flowers, and incense. He put the key into the lock, and when he tried to push the door open, it stuck. He had to shove it hard to get it to open. The reason was immediately clear—there were boxes of empty wine bottles on the other side. And, much to his surprise, the television was on. Four vampires were crashed on his sofa, blankly watching cartoons.

He knew they were vampires at once. The draining of the color behind the skin, the languid pose. Also, these vampires hadn't even bothered to wipe the blood from the corners of their mouths. All of them had dried bits of the stuff around their faces. There was a record spinning on the player. It had reached the end and was stuck on the blank end strip, hissing gently in disapproval.

Only one of the vampires even turned to look at him.

"Who are you?" she asked.

"Magnus Bane. I live here."

"Oh."

She turned back to the cartoon.

When Magnus had left two years before, he'd left his apartment in the care of a housekeeper, Mrs. Milligan. He'd sent money every month for the bills and the cleaning. Clearly she had paid the bills. The electricity was still on. But she hadn't cleaned, and Mrs. Milligan probably hadn't invited these four vampires to come and stay and generally trash the place. Everywhere Magnus looked there were signs of destruction and decay. One of the kitchen chairs had been broken and was in pieces on the floor. The others were piled with magazines and newspapers. There were overflowing ashtrays, and makeshift ashtrays, and then just trails of ash and plates full of cigarette butts. The living room curtains were cockeyed and torn. Everything was askew, and some things were simply missing. Magnus had many lovely pieces of art that he'd collected over the years. He looked for a favorite piece of Sevres porcelain that he'd kept on a table in the hall. That, of course, was gone. As was the table.

"I don't want to be rude," Magnus said, unhappily eyeing a pile of stinking garbage on the corner of one of his best Persian carpets, "but may I ask why you're in my house?"

This got a bleary look.

"We live here," said the girl at the end, the spunky one who could actually turn her head.

"No," Magnus said. "I think I just explained that I live here."

"You weren't here. So we lived here."

"Well, I'm back. So you're going to need to make other arrangements."

No response.

"Let me be more clear," he said, standing in front of the television. Blue light crackled between his fingers. "If you're here, you may know who I am. You may know what I'm capable of. Perhaps you'd like me to summon up someone to help you out? Or perhaps I could open a Portal and send you to the far side of the Bronx? Ohio? Mongolia? Where would you like to be dropped?"

The vampires on the sofa said nothing for a minute or two. Then they managed to look at one another. There was a grunt, a second grunt, and then they pulled themselves up from the sofa with tremendous difficulty.

"Don't worry about your things," Magnus said. "I'll send them along. To the Dumont?"

The vampires had long ago claimed the doomed old Hotel Dumont. It was the general address of all New York vampires.

Magnus looked at them more closely. He had never quite seen vampires like these. They appeared to be—sick? Vampires didn't really get sick. They got hungry, but they didn't get sick. And these vampires had eaten. The evidence was all over their faces. Also, they were twitching a bit.

Considering the state of the place, he didn't feel like worrying over their health.

"Come on," one of them said. They shuffled out onto the landing and then down the stairs. Magnus shut the door firmly and, with a swoop of his hand, moved a marble-topped dry sink to block the door from the inside. At least that had been too heavy and sturdy to break or remove, but it was full of old dirty clothes that seemed to be covering up something he instinctively knew he never wanted to see.

The smell was terrible. That had to go first. One crack of blue hit the air, and the funk was replaced with the light smell of night-blooming jasmine. He took the record off the record player. The vampires had left behind a pile of albums. He had a look through this and picked out the new Fleetwood Mac album that everyone was playing. He liked them. There was a light magical sound to the music. Magnus swept his hand through the air again, and slowly the apartment began to right itself. As a thank-you, he sent the garbage and the various disgusting little piles over to the Dumont. He had promised to send them their things, after all.

Despite the magic he used on his window air-conditioning unit, despite the cleaning, despite everything he had done—the apartment still felt sticky and dirty and unpleasant. Magnus slept poorly. He gave up at around six in the morning and went out in search of coffee and breakfast. He was still on London time anyway.

Out on the street some people were clearly just coming home for the night. There was a woman hopping along in one high heel and one bare foot. There were three people covered in glitter and sweat, all wearing flopping feather boas, emerging from a cab by his corner. Magnus settled down in the corner booth of a diner across the street. It was the only thing open. It was surprisingly full. Again, most of the people seemed to be at the end of their day, not the start, and were gobbling pancakes to soak up the alcohol in their stomachs.

Magnus had purchased a paper by the cash register. The

cabbie hadn't been lying—the news in New York was bad. He'd left a troubled city and returned to a broken one. The city was broke. Half the buildings in the Bronx had burned down. Trash piled up on the streets because there was no money for collection. Muggings, murders, robbery . . . and yes, someone calling himself the Son of Sam and claiming to be an agent of Satan was running around with a gun and shooting people at random.

"I thought that was you," said a voice. "Magnus. Where you been, man?"

A young man slid into the other side of the booth. He wore jeans, a leather vest with no shirt, and a gold cross on a chain around his neck. Magnus smiled and folded his paper away.

"Greg!"

Gregory Jensen was an extremely handsome young werewolf with shoulder-length blond hair. Blond was not Magnus's favorite hair color, but Greg certainly carried his well. Magnus had had a bit of a crush on Greg for a while, a crush he'd eventually let go of when he'd met Greg's wife, Consuela. Werewolf love was intense. You didn't get near it.

"I'm telling you"—Greg pulled the ashtray from under the table's jukebox and lit up a cigarette—"things have been messed up recently. I mean, *messed up*."

"Messed up how?"

"The vampires, man." Greg took a long drag. "There's something wrong with them."

"I found a few in my apartment last night when I got home," Magnus said. "They didn't seem right. They were disgusting, for a start. And they looked sick."

"They are sick. They're feeding like crazy. It's getting bad, man. It's getting bad. I'm telling you . . ."

He leaned in and lowered his voice.

"Shadowhunters are going to be *all over us* if the vampires don't get it under control. Right now I'm not sure the Shadowhunters know what's going on. The murder rate in the city is so high, maybe they can't tell. But it won't be long before they figure it out."

Magnus leaned back in his seat.

"Camille usually keeps things under control."

Greg gave a heavy shrug. "I can only tell you that the vamps started coming around to all the clubs and discos. They love that stuff. But then they just started attacking people all the time. In the clubs, on the streets. The NYPD thinks the attacks are weird muggings, so it's been kept quiet so far. But when the Shadowhunters find out, they're going to come down on us. They're getting trigger-happy. Any excuse."

"The Accords prohibit—"

"The Accords my ass. I'm telling you, it won't be long before they start ignoring the Accords. And the vampires are so in violation that anything can happen. I'm telling you, it's all so *messed up*."

A plate of pancakes was deposited in front of Magnus, and he and Greg stopped speaking for a moment. Greg stubbed out his barely smoked cigarette.

"I gotta go," he said. "I was out patrolling to see if anyone had been attacked, and I saw you through the window. Wanted to say hi. It's nice to see you back."

Magnus dropped five dollars onto the table and pushed the pancakes away.

"I'll come with you. I want to see this for myself."

* * *

The temperature had shot up in the hour or so he'd been in the diner. This amplified the pong of the overflowing trash—spilling out of metal trash cans (which only cooked it and intensified the scent), bags of it piled up on the curbs. Trash just thrown down onto the street itself. Magnus stepped over the hamburger wrappers and cans and newspapers.

"Two basic areas to patrol," Greg said, lighting up a new cigarette. "This area and midtown west. We go street by street. I'm working west from here. There are a lot of clubs over by the river, in the Meatpacking District."

"It's quite warm."

"This heat, man. I guess it could be the heat making them freak out. It gets to everyone."

Greg pulled off his vest. There were certainly worse things than taking a walk with a handsome, shirtless man on a summer morning. Now that it was more of a civilized hour, people were out. Gay couples walking hand in hand, in the open, during the day. That was fairly new. Even as the city seemed to be falling apart, something good was happening.

"Has Lincoln spoken to Camille?" Magnus asked.

Max Lincoln was the head of the werewolves. Everyone just called him by his last name, which fit with his tall and gaunt frame and bearded face—and because, like the more famous Lincoln, he was a famously calm and resolute leader.

"They don't talk," Greg said. "Not anymore. Camille comes down here for the clubs, and that's it. You know what she's like."

Magnus knew all too well. Camille had always been a bit aloof, at least to strangers and acquaintances. She had the air of royalty. The private Camille was a different beast entirely.

"What about Raphael Santiago?" Magnus asked.

"He's gone."

"Gone?"

"Rumor is that he's been sent away. I heard that from one of the fey. They claim to have overheard it from some vamps walking through Central Park. He must have known about what was happening and had some words with Camille. Now he's just gone."

This didn't bode well.

They walked through the Village, past the shops and cafés, up toward the Meatpacking District, with its cobbled streets and disused warehouses. Many of these were now clubs. There was a desolate feel here in the morning—just the remains of the abandoned parties and the river slugging along below. Even the river seemed to resent the heat. They checked everywhere—in the alleys, next to the trash. They looked under vans and trucks.

"Nothing," Greg said as they peered into and poked the last pile of trash in the last alley. "Guess it was a quiet night. Time to check in. It's late.

This required a quick walk in the ever-increasing heat. Greg couldn't pay for a cab and refused to allow Magnus to do so, so Magnus unhappily joined in the jog all the way down to Canal Street. The werewolves' den was concealed behind the facade of a takeout-only restaurant in Chinatown. One werewolf stood behind the counter, under the menu and the stock photos of various Chinese dishes. She looked Magnus over. When Greg nodded, she let them pass through a beaded curtain to the back.

There was no kitchen behind the back wall. Instead there was a door that led to a much larger facility—the old Second Precinct police station. (The cells came in handy during the full moon.) Magnus followed Greg down the dimly lit hallway to the main room of the station, which was already full. The pack had gathered, and Lincoln stood at the head of the room, listening to a report and nodding gravely. When he saw Magnus, he raised a hand in greeting.

"All right," Lincoln said. "Looks like everyone is here. And we have a guest. Many of you know Magnus Bane. He's a warlock, as you see, and a friend to this pack."

This was accepted at once, and there were nods and greetings all around. Magnus leaned against a file cabinet near the back to watch the proceedings.

"Greg," Lincoln said, "you're the last in. Anything?"

"Nope. My patch was clean."

"Good. But unfortunately, there was an incident. Elliot? Want to explain?"

Another werewolf stepped forward.

"We found a body," he said. "In midtown, near Le Jardin. Definitely a vampire attack. Clear marking on the neck. We slit the throat so the puncture marks were hidden."

There was a general groan around the room.

"That will keep the words 'vampire killer' out of the papers for a while," Lincoln said. "But clearly things have gotten worse, and now someone is dead."

Magnus heard various remarks in low voices about vampires, and some in louder voices. All of the remarks contained profanity.

"Okay." Lincoln put his hands up and silenced the general sounds of dismay. "Magnus, what do you think about this?"

"I don't know," Magnus said. "I only just got back."

"Ever seen anything like this? Mass, random attacks?"

All heads turned in his direction. He steadied himself against the file cabinet. He wasn't quite ready to give a presentation on the ways of vampires at this hour of the morning.

"I've seen bad behavior," Magnus said. "It really depends. I've been in places where there was no police force and no Shadowhunters nearby, so sometimes it can get out of hand. But I've never seen anything like it here, or in any developed area. *Especially* not near an Institute."

"We need to take care of this," a voice called out.

Various voices of assent echoed around the room.

"Let's talk outside," Lincoln said to Magnus.

He nodded at the door, and the werewolves parted so that Magnus could pass. Lincoln and Magnus got some burned coffee at the corner deli and sat on a stoop in front of an acupuncturist's shop.

"Something's wrong with them," Lincoln said. "Whatever it is, it hit fast, and it hit hard. If we have diseased vampires around causing this kind of bloodshed . . . eventually we'll have to act, Magnus. We can't let it go on. We can't let murders happen, and we can't run the risk of bringing the Shadowhunters down here. We can't have problems like that starting up again. It will end badly for all of us."

Magnus examined the crack in the step below. "Have you contacted the Praetor Lupus?" he asked.

"Of course. But we can't identify who is doing this. It doesn't seem like the work of one rogue fledgling. This is multiple attacks in multiple locations. The only luck for us is that all of the victims have been on various substances, so they can't articulate what happened to them. If one of them says vampire, the police will think it's because they're high. But eventually the story will take shape. The press will get wind of it, and the Shadowhunters will get wind of it, and the whole thing will escalate rapidly."

Lincoln was right. If this went on, the werewolves would be well within their rights to act. And then there would be blood.

"You know Camille," Lincoln said. "You could talk to her."

"I *knew* Camille. You probably know her better than I do at this point."

"I don't know how to talk to Camille. She's a difficult person to communicate with. I would have spoken to her already if I knew how. And our relationship isn't quite the same as the relationship you had."

"We don't really get along," Magnus said. "We haven't spoken for several decades."

"But everyone knows that you two were . . ."

"*That* was a long time ago. A hundred years ago, Lincoln."

"For you two does that kind of time even matter?"

"What would you want me to say to her? It's hard to walk in after that long a time and just say, 'Stop attacking people. Also, how have you been since the turn of the century?'"

"If there's something wrong, maybe you could help them. If they're just overfeeding, then they need to know that we're prepared to act. And if you care for her, which I think you do, she deserves this warning. It would be for the good of us all."

He put his hand on Magnus's shoulder.

"Please," Lincoln said. "It's possible we can still fix this. Because if this goes on, we'll all suffer."

Magnus had many exes. They were strewn throughout history. Most of them were memories, long dead. Some were now very old. Etta, one of his last loves, was now in a nursing home and no longer recognized him. It had become too painful to visit her.

Camille Belcourt was different. She'd come into Magnus's life under the light of a gas lamp, looking regal. That had been in London, and it had been a different world. Their romance had happened in fog. It had happened in carriages bumping along cobbled streets, on settees covered in damson-colored silk. They'd loved in the time of the clockwork creatures, before the mundane wars. There seemed to be more time then, time to fill, time to spend. And they'd filled it. And they'd spent it.

They had parted badly. When you love someone that intensely and they do not love you in the same way, it is impossible to part well.

Camille had arrived in New York at the end of the 1920s, just as the Crash had been happening and everything had been falling apart. She had a great sense of drama, and a good nose for places that were in crisis and in need of a guiding hand. In no time at all she'd become the head of the vampires. She had a place inside the famous Eldorado building on the Upper West Side. Magnus knew where she was, and she knew where Magnus was. But neither of them contacted the other. They had passed each other, purely by accident, at various clubs and events over the years. They'd exchanged only a quick nod. That relationship was over. It was a live wire, not to be touched. It was the one temptation in life Magnus knew to leave alone.

And yet here he was, just twenty-four hours back in New York, stepping into the Eldorado. This was one of New York's great art deco apartment buildings. It sat right on the west side of Central Park, overlooking the reservoir. It was notable for its two matching square towers jutting up like horns. The Eldorado was the home of the old money, the celebrities, the people who simply *had*. The uniformed doorman was trained not to take notice of anyone's attire or mien as long as they looked like they had come to the building for a legitimate reason. For the occasion Magnus had decided to skip his new look. There would be no punk here—no vinyl or fishnet. Tonight was a Halston suit, black, with wide satin lapels. This passed the test, and he got a nod and a light smile. Camille lived on the twenty-eighth floor of the north tower, a silent oak-paneled and brass-railed elevator ride up into some of the most expensive real estate in Manhattan.

The towers made for some very small, very intimate floors. Some had only one or two inhabitants. There were two in this case. Camille lived in 28C. Magnus could hear music seeping out from under the door. There was a strong smell of smoke and the leftover perfume of whoever had just passed this way. Despite the fact that there was activity inside, it took about three minutes of knocking before someone answered.

He was surprised to find that he recognized this person at once. It was a face from long ago. At the time the woman had had a little black bob and had worn a flapper dress. She'd been young then, and while she had retained the basic youth (vampires didn't really age), she looked world-worn. Now her hair was bleached blond and formed into heavy, long curls. She wore a skin-tight gold dress that skimmed her knees, and a cigarette dangled from the side of her mouth.

"Well, well, well. It's everyone's favorite warlock! I haven't seen you since you were running that speakeasy. It's been a long time."

"It has," Magnus said. "Daisy?"

"Dolly." She pushed the door open wider. "Look who it is, everyone!"

The room was full of vampires, all of whom were dressed extremely well. Magnus had to give them that. The men wore the white suits that were so popular this season. The women all had fantastic disco dresses, mostly in white or gold. The mix of hair spray, cigarette smoke, incense, and colognes and perfumes took his breath away for a moment.

Aside from the strong smells, there was a tension in the air that had no real basis. Magnus was no stranger to vampires, yet this group was *uptight*, looking to one another. Shifting around. Waiting for something.

There was no invitation to enter.

"Is Camille in?" Magnus finally asked.

Dolly cocked a hip against the door.

"What brings you here tonight, Magnus?"

"I've just gotten back from an extended vacation. It just felt right to pay a visit."

"Did it?"

In the background someone turned down the record player until the music was barely audible.

"Someone go talk to Camille," Dolly said without turning around. She remained where she was, blocking the doorway with her tiny body. She closed the door a bit to reduce the space she had to fill. She continued smiling up at Magnus in a way that was a bit unnerving.

"Just a minute," she said.

In the background someone moved into the hallway.

"What's this?" Dolly said, plucking something from

Magnus's pocket. "Electrica? I've never heard of this club."

"It's new. They claim to be better than Studio 54. I've never been to either, so I don't know. Someone gave me the passes."

Magnus had stuck the passes into his pocket as he'd been walking out the door. After all, he had gone to the effort of dressing up. Should this errand end as badly as he thought it would, it would be nice to have somewhere to go afterward.

Dolly twisted the passes into a fan and waved it lightly in front of her face.

"Take them," Magnus said. It was evident that Dolly had already taken them and was not giving them back, so it seemed polite to make it official.

The vampire emerged from the hallway and conferred with some others on the sofa and around the room. Then a different vampire came over to the door. Dolly stepped behind the door for a moment, closing it farther. Magnus heard a mumbling. Then the door opened again, wide enough to admit him.

"It's your lucky night," she said. "This way."

The white wall-to-wall carpet was so shaggy and thick that Dolly wobbled on her high heels as she traversed it. The carpet had stains all over it—spilled drinks, ash, and puddles of things he supposed were blood. The white sofas and chairs were in similar condition. The many large plants and potted palms and fronds were all dry and sagging. Several pictures on the walls were askew. There were bottles and empty glasses with dried-up wine at the bottom everywhere. It was the same kind of disarray Magnus had found in his apartment.

More disturbing was the silence from all the vampires in the room who watched him being led along by Dolly to the hallway. And then there was the sofa full of unmoving humans—subjugates, no doubt, all dazed and slumped, their mouths hanging open, the bruises and wounds on their necks and arms and hands looking quite ugly. The glass table in front of them had a fine coating of white powder and a few razor blades. The only noise was the muted music and a low rumble of thunder outside.

"This way," Dolly said, taking Magnus by the sleeve.

The hall was dark, and there were clothes and shoes all over the floor. Muffled noises came from the three doors along the hall. Dolly walked right to the end, to a double door. She rapped on this once and pushed it open.

"Go ahead," she said, still smiling her weird little smile.

In stark contrast to the whiteness of everything in the living room, this room was the dark side of the apartment. The carpet was an indigo black, like a nighttime sea. The walls were covered in deep silver wallpaper. The lamp shades were all covered by gold and silver shawls and throws. The tables were all mirrored, reflecting the view back and forth again. And in the middle of it all was a massive black lacquer bed with black sheets and a heavy gold cover. And on it was Camille, in a peach silk kimono.

And a hundred years seemed to vanish. Magnus felt himself unable to speak for a moment. It might as well have been London again, the whole twentieth century rolled up into a ball and tossed aside.

But then the present moment came crashing back when Camille began an ungainly crawl in his direction, slipping on the satin sheets.

"Magnus! Magnus! Magnus! Come here! Come! Sit down!"

Her silver-blond hair was long and down, looking wild. She patted the end of the bed. This was not the greeting he'd been expecting. This was not the Camille he remembered, or even the one he had seen in passing.

As he made to step over what he thought was a lump of clothing, he realized there was a human on the floor, facedown. He bent down and gently reached into the mass of long black hair to turn the person's face upward. It was a woman, and there was still some warmth in her, and a faint pulse beating in her neck.

"That's Sarah," Camille said, flopping onto the bed and hanging her head off the end to watch.

"You've been feeding from her," Magnus said. "Is she a willing donor?"

"Oh, she loves it. Now, Magnus . . . You look marvelous, by the way. Is that Halston? . . . We're just about to go out. And *you* are coming with us."

She slid from the bed and tripped her way into a massive closet. Magnus heard hangers being scraped along rails. Magnus examined the girl on the floor again. She had punctures all over her neck—and now she was smiling weakly at Magnus and pushing back her hair, offering him a bite.

"I'm not a vampire," he said, resting her head gently on the floor again. "And you should get out of here. Do you want my help?"

The girl made a sound that was just between a laugh and a whimper.

"Which one of these?" Camille said as she came stumbling back out of the closet, holding two almost identical black evening dresses.

"This girl is weak," he said. "Camille, you've taken too much blood from her. She needs a hospital."

"She's fine. Leave her alone. Help me pick a dress."

Everything about this exchange was wrong. This was not how the reunion should have gone. It should have been coy; it should have had many strange pauses and moments of double meaning. Instead Camille was acting like she'd just seen Magnus yesterday. Like they were simply friends. It was enough of an entry to allow him to get to the point.

"I'm here because there's a problem, Camille. Your vampires are killing people and leaving bodies on the street. They're overfeeding."

"Oh, Magnus." Camille shook her head. "I may be in charge, but I don't control them. You have to allow for a certain amount of freedom."

"This includes killing mundanes and leaving their bodies out on the sidewalk?"

Camille was no longer listening. She had dropped the dresses onto the bed and was picking though a pile of earrings. Meanwhile Sarah was attempting to crawl in Camille's direction. Without even looking at her, Camille set a mirror full of white powder down on the floor. Sarah went right for it and began sniffing it up.

And then Magnus understood.

While human drugs didn't quite work on Downworlders, there was no telling what would happen when that drug was run through a human circulatory system *and then ingested* through the human blood.

It all made sense. The disarray. The confused behavior. The frenzied feeding in the clubs. The fact that they all looked so ill, that their personalities seemed to have changed. He'd seen this a thousand times in mundanes.

Camille was looking at him now, her gaze unwavering.

"Come out with us tonight, Magnus," she cooed. "You are a man who knows a good time. I am a woman who provides a good time. Come out with us."

"Camille, you have to stop. You have to know how dangerous this is."

"It's not going to kill me, Magnus. That's quite impossible. And you don't understand how it *feels*."

"The drug can't kill you, but other things can. If you continue like this, you know there are people out there who can't let you go on murdering mundanes. Someone will act."

"Let them try," she said. "I could take on ten Shadowhunters once I've had some of this."

"It may not be—"

Camille dropped to the floor before he could finish and buried her face into Sarah's neck. Sarah flailed once and groaned, then became silent and motionless. He heard the sickening sound of the drinking, the sucking. Camille lifted her head, blood all around her mouth, running down her chin.

"Are you coming or not?" she said. "I would simply love to take you to Studio 54. You've never had a night out like one of our nights out."

Magnus had to force himself to keep looking at her like this.

"Let me help you. A few hours, a few days—I could get this out of your system."

Camille dragged the back of her hand across her mouth, smearing the blood onto her cheek.

"If you're not coming along, then stay out of our way. Consider this a polite warning, Magnus. Dolly!"

Dolly was already at the door. "Think you're done here," she said.

Magnus watched Camille sink her teeth into Sarah again.

"Yes," he said. "I think I am."

Outside, a downpour was in progress. The doorman held an umbrella over Magnus's head and hailed him a cab. The incongruity of the civility downstairs and what he'd seen upstairs was . . .

It wasn't to be thought about. Magnus got into the cab, gave his destination, and closed his eyes. The rain drummed onto the cab. It felt like the rain was beating directly onto his brain.

Magnus wasn't surprised to find Lincoln sitting on the steps by his door. Wearily he waved him inside.

"Well?" Lincoln said.

"It's not good," Magnus replied, pulling off his wet jacket. "It's the drugs. They're feeding on the blood of people who are taking drugs. It must be escalating their need and lowering their impulse control."

"You're right," Lincoln said. "That isn't good. I thought it might have something to do with the drugs, but I thought they were immune to things like addiction."

Magnus poured them each a glass of wine, and they sat and listened to the rain for a moment.

"Can you help her?" Lincoln asked.

"If she lets me. But you can't cure an addict who doesn't want to be cured."

"No," Lincoln said. "I've seen that myself with our own. But you understand . . . we can't let this behavior continue."

"I know you can't."

Lincoln finished his wine and set the glass down gently.

"I'm sorry, Magnus. I really am. But if it happens again, you need to leave it to us."

Magnus nodded. Lincoln gave him a squeeze on the shoulder, then let himself out.

For the next several days Magnus kept to himself. The weather was brutal, flicking between heat and storm. He tried to forget about the scene in Camille's apartment, and the best way to forget was to keep busy. He hadn't really kept up with his work for the last two years. There were clients to call. There were spells to study and translations to do. Books to read. The apartment needed redecorating. There were new restaurants and new bars and new people. . . .

Every time he stopped, he flashed back to the sight of Camille squatting on the carpet, the girl limp in her arms, the mirror full of drugs, Camille's face covered in blood. The mess. The stink. The horror. The blank looks.

When you lost someone to addiction—and he had lost many—you lost something very precious. You watched them fall. You waited for them to hit the bottom. It was a terrible wait. He would have nothing to do with it. What happened now was not his problem. He had no doubt that Lincoln and the werewolves would take care of things, and the less he knew the better.

It kept him awake at night. That, and the thunder.

Sleeping alone was Hell, so he decided not to sleep alone.

He still woke up.

It was the night of July thirteenth—lucky thirteen. The thunderstorm outside was incredibly loud, louder than the air conditioner, louder than the radio. Magnus was just finishing up a translation and was about to go out to dinner, when the lights flickered. The radio faded in and out. Then everything went very bright as power surged through the wires. Then . . .

Out. Air conditioner, lights, radio, everything. Magnus flicked his hand absently and lit a candle on his desk. Power outages were not uncommon. It was a moment before he realized that things had grown very quiet and very dark indeed, and there were voices shouting outside. He went to the window and opened it.

Everything was dark. The streetlights. Every building. Everything except the headlights of the cars. He took the candle and carefully walked down the two flights to the street and joined the excited masses of people. The rain had stopped—it was just thunder grumbling in the background.

New York . . . was off. Everything was off. There was no skyline. There was no glow of the Empire State Building. It was utterly, utterly dark. And one word was being yelled from window to window, from street to car to doorway . . .

"BLACKOUT."

The parties started almost at once. It was the ice cream shop on the corner that kicked it off, selling anything they had for a dime a cone, and then just giving away the ice cream to anyone who came by with a bowl or a cup. Then the bars started passing around cocktails in paper cups to passersby. Everyone poured out onto the streets. People propped battery-powered radios in the windows, so there was a mix of music and news reports. The outage had been caused by a lightning strike. All of New York was down. It would be hours—days?—before service was restored.

Magnus returned to his apartment, got a bottle of champagne from his refrigerator, and returned to his front stoop to drink it, sharing it with a few people who walked past. It was too hot to stay inside, and the outside was far too interesting to miss. People started dancing on the sidewalk, and he joined in for a while. He accepted a martini from a nice young man with a beautiful smile.

Then there was a hissing. People gathered around one of the radios, one playing news. Magnus and his new friend, who was named David, joined them.

"*. . . fires throughout the five boroughs. More than a hundred fires have been reported in the last hour. And we have multiple reports of lootings. Gunfire is being exchanged. Please—if you are out tonight, use extreme caution. Though all police have been called in to duty, there are not enough officers to . . .*"

Another radio a few yards away, on a different station, gave a similar report.

"*. . . hundreds of stores have been broken into. There are reports of total breakdowns in some areas. You are strongly advised to stay indoors. If you cannot get home, seek shelter in a . . .*"

In the short silence, Magnus could hear sirens in the distance. The Village was a tight community, so it celebrated. But clearly this was not the case all over the city.

"Magnus!"

Magnus turned to find Greg breaking through the group. He pulled Magnus away from the crowd, into a quiet space between two parked cars.

"I thought that was you," he said. "It's all happening. They've gone nuts. The blackout. . . . The vampires are going crazy at this club. I can't even explain it. It's on Tenth Ave and down a block. No cabs in this blackout. You have to run."

Now that Magnus was trying to get somewhere, he realized the pure madness of the blacked-out streets. Since there were no traffic lights, normal people were trying to guide traffic. Cars were either frozen in place or moving far too fast. Some were parked and turned inward, their headlights being used to illuminate stores and restaurants. Everyone was out—the Village had poured out of every building, and there was no room anywhere. Magnus and Greg had to weave through the people, through the cars, tripping in the dark.

The crowds thinned somewhat the closer they got to the river. The club was in one of the old meatpacking warehouses. The brick industrial facade had been painted silver, and the word ELECTRICA, along with a lightning bolt, was above the old service doors. Two werewolves stood by these, holding flashlights, and Lincoln waited off to the side. He was deep in conversation with Consuela, who was his second-in-command. When they saw Magnus, Consuela stepped aside to a waiting van, and Lincoln came over.

"This is what we feared," Lincoln said. "We waited too long."

The werewolves guarding the entrance parted, and Lincoln pushed open the doors. Inside the club it was entirely pitch black, save for the beams from the werewolves' flashlights. There was a strong smell of spilled, mixed liquor and something unpleasantly tangy and sharp.

Magnus raised his hands. The neon lights around the room buzzed and glowed. The overhead work lights—unflattering fluorescents—sputtered on. And the disco ball crept to life, slowly spinning, sending a thousand points of colored reflected light around the room. The dance floor, made of large squares of colored plastic, was also illuminated from below.

Which made the scene all the more terrible.

There were four bodies, three women and one man. All looked like they had been running for various points of exit. Their skin was the color of ash, marked everywhere with greenish-purple bruises and dozens of marks, and garishly lit by the red, yellow, and blue lights below them. There was very little blood. Just a few small puddles here and there. Not nearly as much blood as there should have been.

One of the dead women, Magnus noticed, had familiar long blond hair. He'd last seen her on the plane, handing him the passes . . .

Magnus had to turn away quickly.

"They were all drained," Lincoln said. "The club hadn't opened for the night yet. They were having trouble with their sound system even before the power went out, so the only people here were the employees. Two there. . . ."

He pointed to the raised DJ platform with its piles of turntables and speakers. Some werewolves were up there examining the scene.

"Two behind the bar," he continued. "Another one ran and hid in the bathroom, but the door was broken down. And these four. Nine total."

Magnus sat down on one of the nearby chairs and put his head in his hands for a moment to gather himself. No matter how long you lived, you never got used to seeing terrible things. Lincoln gave him a moment to collect himself.

"This is my fault. When I went to see Camille, one of them took the passes to this place from my pocket."

Lincoln pulled over a chair and sat next to Magnus.

"That doesn't make it your fault. I asked you to speak to Camille. If Camille came here because of you . . . it doesn't put the blame on either of us, Magnus. But you can see now, it can't go on."

"What do you plan on doing?" Magnus said.

"There are fires tonight. All over the city. We take this opportunity. We burn this place down. I think it would spare the victims' families for them to think their loved ones died in a fire, rather than . . ."

He indicated the terrible scene just behind them.

"You're right," Magnus said. "No good could come of anyone seeing their loved one like that."

"No. And no good would come of the police seeing this. It would send the city into a complete panic, and the Shadowhunters would be forced to come down here. We keep this quiet. We deal with it."

"And the vampires?"

"We're going to go and get them, and lock them in here while it burns. We have permission from the Praetor Lupus. The entire clan is to be treated as infected, but we'll try to be judicious. The first one we'll be getting, though, is Camille."

Magnus exhaled slowly.

"Magnus," Lincoln said, "what else can we do? She's the clan leader. We need this to end now."

"Give me an hour," Magnus said. "One hour. If I can get them off the streets in an hour—"

"There's already a group headed up to Camille's apartment. Another will go to the Hotel Dumont."

"How long ago did they leave?"

"About a half hour."

"Then I'm going now." Magnus stood. "I have to try to do something."

"Magnus," Lincoln said, "if you stand in the way, the pack will remove you from the situation. Do you understand that?"

Magnus nodded.

"I'll come up when we're done here," Lincoln said. "I'll go to the Dumont. That's where they'll end up anyway."

A Portal was required. Given the situation on the streets, there was every chance that the werewolves hadn't gotten to Camille's apartment yet—if that was even where she was. He would just need to get to her. But before he could even start to draw the runes, he heard a voice in the dark.

"You're here."

Magnus turned on his heel and threw up a hand to illuminate the alley.

Camille was moving toward him, unsteady. She wore a long, black dress—rather, it was a dress that was now colored black from the sheer quantity of blood on it. It was still wet and heavy, and it stuck to her legs as she made her way forward.

"Magnus . . ."

Her voice was thick. Smears of blood covered Camille's face, her arms, her silver-blond hair. She held one hand against a wall for support as she moved toward him in a series of heavy, toddler-like steps.

Magnus approached her slowly. As soon as he got close enough, she gave up the effort of standing and fell forward. He caught her halfway to the ground.

"I knew you'd come," she said.

"What have you done, Camille?"

"I was looking for you. . . . Dolly said you were . . . you were here."

Magnus gently lowered her to the ground.

"Camille . . . do you know what's happened? Do you know what you did?"

The smell coming from her was nauseating. Magnus breathed sharply through his nose to steady himself. Camille's eyes were rolling back into her head. He gave her a shake.

"You need to listen to me," he said. "Try to stay awake. You need to summon all of them."

"I don't know where they are. . . . They're everywhere. It's so *dark*. It's our night, Magnus. For my little ones. For us."

"You must have grave dirt," Magnus said.

This got a loose nod.

"Okay. We get the grave dirt. You use it to summon them. Where is the grave dirt?"

"In the vault."

"And where is the vault?"

"Green-Wood . . . Cemetery. Brooklyn . . ."

Magnus stood and began to draw the runes. When he was finished and the Portal began to open, he picked Camille up from the ground and held on to her tightly.

"Think of it now," he said. "Get it clearly in your mind. The vault."

Considering Camille's state, this was a risky proposition. Holding her closer, feeling the blood on her clothing seep through his shirt . . . Magnus stepped through.

There were trees here. Trees and a bit of moonlight cutting through the cloudy night sky. Absolutely no people, no voices. Just the distant rumble of the stuck traffic. And hundreds of white slabs jutting up from the ground.

Magnus and Camille were standing in front of a mausoleum that resembled a folly—the front piece of a tiny colonnaded temple. It was built directly into the side of a low hill.

Magnus looked down and saw that Camille had found the strength to wrap her slender arms around him. She was shuddering a bit.

"Camille?"

She tipped her head upward. She was crying. Camille did not cry. Even under these circumstances, Magnus was moved. He still wanted to console her, wanted to take the time to tell her everything would be all right. But all he could say was, "Do you have the key?"

She shook her head. There hadn't been much chance of that. Magnus put his hand on the lock securing the wide metal doors, closed his eyes, and concentrated until he felt the light click under his fingertips.

The vault was about eight-foot square and was made of concrete. The walls were lined with wooden shelves, floor to ceiling. And those shelves were filled with small glass vials of earth. The vials varied quite a bit—some were thick green, or yellow blown glass with visible bubbles. There were thinner bottles, some extremely small bottles, a few tiny brown bottles. The oldest ones were stopped up with corks. Some had glass stoppers. The newest had screw-on caps. The age was also seen in the layers of dust, the grime, the amount of webbing running between them. In the back, you wouldn't have been able to lift some of the bottles from the shelves, so thick was the accumulated residue. There was a history of New York vampirism here that would probably have interested many, that was probably worth studying. . . .

Magnus put out his hands, and with one great blast of blue light, all the vials burst at once. There was a great cough of dirt and glass powder.

"Where will they go?" he asked Camille.

"The Dumont."

"Of course," Magnus said. "Them and everyone else. We're going there, and you're going to do as I say. We need to make this right, Camille. You have to try. Do you understand?"

She nodded once.

This time Magnus was in control of the Portal. They emerged on 116th Street, in the middle of what appeared to be a full-scale riot. There were fires here. The echoes of screams and breaking glass went from one end of the street to the other. No one took any notice of the fact that Magnus and Camille were suddenly in their midst. It was too dark, and far too crazy. The heat was much worse in this area, and Magnus felt his entire body dripping with sweat.

There were two vans parked directly in front of the Dumont, and an unmistakable crowd of werewolves was already gathered. They had baseball bats and chains. That was all that was visible. There were undoubtedly some containers of holy water. There was already plenty of fire around.

Magnus pulled Camille down behind the cover of a parked Cadillac that had already had all its windows smashed. He reached around inside and popped open the door.

"Get in," he said to Camille. "And stay down. They're after you. Let me go and talk to them."

Even as Magnus was making his way around the car, Camille found the strength to crawl across the glass-strewn front seat and was falling out through the driver's side door. When Magnus tried to get her back inside, she pushed him away.

"Get out of the way, Magnus. It's me they want."

"They'll *kill* you, Camille."

But she had been seen. The werewolves crossed the street, bats at the ready. Camille held up a hand. Several vampires had just arrived in front of the hotel. Several others had already fought, and several others were lying, still, on the sidewalk. A few more were being restrained.

"Go inside the hotel," she ordered.

"Camille—they'll burn us," one said. "*Look* at them. Look at what's happening."

Camille looked to Magnus, and he understood. She was leaving this to him.

"Get inside," she said again. "That is not a request."

One by one over the course of the next hours, every vampire in New York—no matter what condition they were in—appeared on the steps of the Dumont. Camille, leaning against the doors for support, ordered them inside. They passed through the phalanx of werewolves with their bats and chains, looking wary. It was almost dawn when the last groups appeared.

Lincoln arrived at the same time.

"Some are missing," Camille said as he got out of his car.

"Some are dead," Lincoln replied. "You have Magnus to thank that more aren't dead."

Camille nodded once, then went inside the hotel and shut the doors.

"And now?" Lincoln said.

"You can't cure them without their consent—but you can dry them out. They stay locked in there until they are clean," Magnus said.

"And if this doesn't work?"

Magnus looked at the broken-down facade of the Dumont. Someone, he noticed, had changed the *n* to an *r*. Dumort. Hotel of the dead.

"Let's see what happens," Magnus said.

For three days, Magnus kept the wards on the Dumont. He went by several times a day. Werewolves patrolled the perimeter all hours, making sure no one got out. On the third day, just after sunset, Magnus released the ward on the front door and went inside, and sealed it again behind him.

Clearly there had been an organizing principle at work inside the hotel. The vampires who had not been affected by the drug were littered throughout the lobby and on the balconies and steps. They were mostly sleeping. The werewolves now permitted them to rise and leave.

With Lincoln and his aides by his side, Magnus retraced the steps he had taken almost fifty years before, to the ballroom of the Dumont. Once again the doors were sealed—this time with a chain.

"Get the cutters from the van," Lincoln said.

There was a truly terrible smell coming from under the door.

Please, Magnus thought. *Be empty*.

Of course the ballroom would not be empty. It was a silly wish that all the events of the last three days simply hadn't happened. Because in the end nothing is worse than seeing the fall of one you loved. It was somehow worse than losing a love. It made everything seem questionable. It made the past bitter and confused.

The werewolf returned with the bolt cutters, and the chain

was snapped, and landed on the floor with a hollow clank. A few of the unaffected vampires had remained behind to watch, and they were gathered at the werewolves' backs.

Magnus pushed the door open.

The white marble floor of the ballroom was splintered. Had that really been fifty years ago, right here, where Aldous had opened the Portal to the Void?

The vampires were scattered in every part of the room, maybe thirty in all. These were the sick, and they were all in a profound state of suffering. The smell alone was enough to gag anyone. And the werewolves lifted their hands to their faces to block it out.

The vampires made no move and gave no greeting. Only a few lifted their faces to see what was happening. Magnus stepped over them, looking at each one. He found Dolly near the center of the room, not moving. He found Camille sprawled behind one of the long curtains that hung at the far end of the ballroom. Like the others, she was surrounded by a number of foul pools of regurgitated blood.

Her eyes were open.

"I want to walk," she said. "Help me, Magnus. Help me walk a bit. I need to look strong."

There was a steadiness to her voice, despite the fact that she was too weak to get up on her own. Magnus bent down and lifted her to her feet, then supported her as she walked, with as much dignity as she could, over the slumped bodies of her clan. He sealed the doors again when they had left.

"Up," she said. "Around. I need to walk. Upstairs."

He could feel the strain as she took each step. Sometimes he was mostly carrying her.

"Do you remember?" she said. "Old Aldous opening the Portal here . . . remember? I had to warn you about what he was doing."

"I remember."

"Even the mundanes knew to stay away from the place and let it rot. I hate that some of my little ones live in rotten places, but it's dark. It's safe."

It was too difficult to talk and walk, so she fell silent again and leaned against Magnus's chest. When they reached the top floor, they stood against the rail and looked down at the wreckage of the hotel lobby.

"It never really went away for us, did it?" she said. "There's really never been another—not like you. Is it the same for you?"

"Camille . . ."

"I know we can't go back. I know. Just tell me there's never been another like me."

In truth there had been many others. And while Camille was certainly in a class by herself, there had been much love—at least on Magnus's part. Yet there was a hundred years of pain in that question, and Magnus had to wonder if maybe he had not been so alone in his feeling.

"No," Magnus said. "There's never been another like you."

She seemed to gain some strength from that.

"It was never meant to happen," she said. "There was a club downtown where some of the mundanes enjoyed getting bitten. They had the drugs in their system. They are quite powerful, these substances. It just took hold. I was given some of the infected blood to drink as a gift. I didn't know what I was drinking—I only knew what effect it had. I didn't know we were capable of addiction. We didn't know."

Magnus looked at the char on the ceiling. Old wounds. Nothing ever *really* went away.

"I will . . . I will make the command," she said. "What happened here will never happen again. You have my word."

"It's not me you have to tell."

"Tell the Praetor," she replied. "Tell the Shadowhunters if you must. It will not happen again. I'll forfeit my life before I allow it."

"It's probably best you speak to Lincoln."

"Then I will speak to him."

The mantle of dignity had returned to her shoulders. Despite all that had happened, she was still Camille Belcourt.

"You should leave now," she said. "This isn't for you anymore."

Magnus wavered for a moment. Something—some part of him wanted to remain. But he found that he was already walking down the steps.

"Magnus," Camille called.

He turned.

"Thank you for lying to me. You have always been kind. I never have been. That was why we couldn't be, wasn't it?"

Without replying, Magnus turned and continued down the stairs. Raphael Santiago passed him on the way up.

"I am sorry," Raphael said.

"Where have you been?"

"When I saw what was happening, I tried to stop them. Camille attempted to make me drink some of the blood. She wanted everyone in her inner circle to participate. She was sick. I have seen such things before and knew how they would end. So I went away. I returned when a vial of my grave soil was broken."

"I never saw you enter the hotel," Magnus said.

"I entered through a broken basement window. I thought it was best to remain hidden for a while. I have been caring for the sick. It has been very unpleasant, but . . ."

He looked up, past Magnus's shoulder, in Camille's direction.

"I must go now. We have much to do here. Go, Magnus. There's nothing for you here."

Raphael had always been able to read Magnus a little too well.

Magnus made his decision when he was in the cab going home. Once he got inside his apartment, he prepared without hesitation, gathering everything he would need. He would need to be very specific. He would write it all down.

Then he called Catarina. He drank some wine while he waited for her to arrive.

Catarina was perhaps Magnus's truest and closest friend, aside from Ragnor (and that relationship was often in a state of flux). Catarina was the only one who'd gotten any letters or calls while he'd been on his two-year trip. He hadn't, however, actually told her he was home.

"Really?" she said when he opened the door. "*Two years*, and then you come back and don't even call for two weeks? And then it's, 'Come over, I need you'? You didn't even *tell* me you were home, Magnus."

"I'm home," he said, giving what he considered to be his most winning smile. The smiling took a bit of effort, but hopefully it looked genuine.

"Don't even try that face with me. I am not one of your

conquests, Magnus. I am your friend. We are supposed to get pizza, not do the nasty."

"The nasty? But I—"

"Don't." She held up a warning finger. "I mean it. I almost didn't come. But you sounded so pathetic on the phone that I had to."

Magnus examined her rainbow T-shirt and pair of red overalls. Both of these stood out strongly against her blue skin. The contrast hurt Magnus's eyes. He decided not to comment on her attire. The red overalls were very popular. It was just that most people weren't blue. Most people did not *live* the rainbow.

"Why are you looking at me like that? Seriously, Magnus—"

"Let me explain," he said. "Then yell at me if you want."

So he explained. And she listened. Catarina was a nurse, and a good listener.

"Memory spells," she said, shaking her head. "Not really my thing. I'm a healer. You're the one who handles all this kind of stuff. If I do it wrong . . ."

"You won't."

"I might."

"I trust you. Here."

He handed Catarina the folded piece of paper. On it was a list of every time he'd seen Camille in New York. Every time in the entire twentieth century. These were the things that had to go.

"You know, there's a reason we can remember," she said more softly.

"That's much easier when your life has an expiration date."

"It may be more important for us."

"I loved her," he said. "I can't take what I saw."

"Magnus . . ."

"Either you do this or I attempt to do it on myself."

Catarina sighed and nodded. She examined the paper for several moments, then took hold of Magnus's temples very gently.

"You remember you're lucky to have me, right?" she said.

"Always."

Five minutes later Magnus was puzzled to find Catarina sitting beside him on the sofa.

"Catarina? What—"

"You were sleeping," she said. "You left the door open. I let myself in. You have to lock your door. This city is nuts. You may be a warlock, but that doesn't mean you won't get your stereo stolen."

"I usually lock it," Magnus said, rubbing his eyes. "I didn't even realize I fell asleep. How did you know I was—"

"You called me and said you were home and wanted to go out for pizza."

"I did? What time is it?"

"Time for pizza," she replied.

"I called you?"

"Uh-huh." She stood and put out a hand to help him up. "And you've been back for two weeks and just called me tonight, so you're in trouble. You sounded sorry on the phone but not sorry enough. More groveling will be needed."

"I know. I'm sorry. I was . . ."

Magnus struggled for the words. What had he been doing the last couple of weeks? Working. Calling clients. Dancing with handsome strangers. Something else too, but he couldn't quite think of it. It didn't matter.

"Pizza," she said again, pulling him to his feet.

"Pizza. Sure. Sounds good."

"Hey," she said as he was locking the door. "Have you heard anything about Camille recently?"

"*Camille?* I haven't seen her in at least . . . eighty years? Something like that? Why are you asking about Camille?"

"No reason," she said. "Her name just popped into my mind. By the way, you're buying."

What to Buy the Shadowhunter Who Has Everything (And Who You're Not Officially Dating Anyway)

By Cassandra Clare and Sarah Rees Brennan

"Is Alec your lover?" asked Elyaas the tentacle demon.

Magnus stared. He was not ready for anyone to say "lover" to him with an oozing note of slime beneath the word. He felt he would never be ready.

–What to Buy the Shadowhunter Who Has Everything (And Who You're Not Officially Dating Anyway)

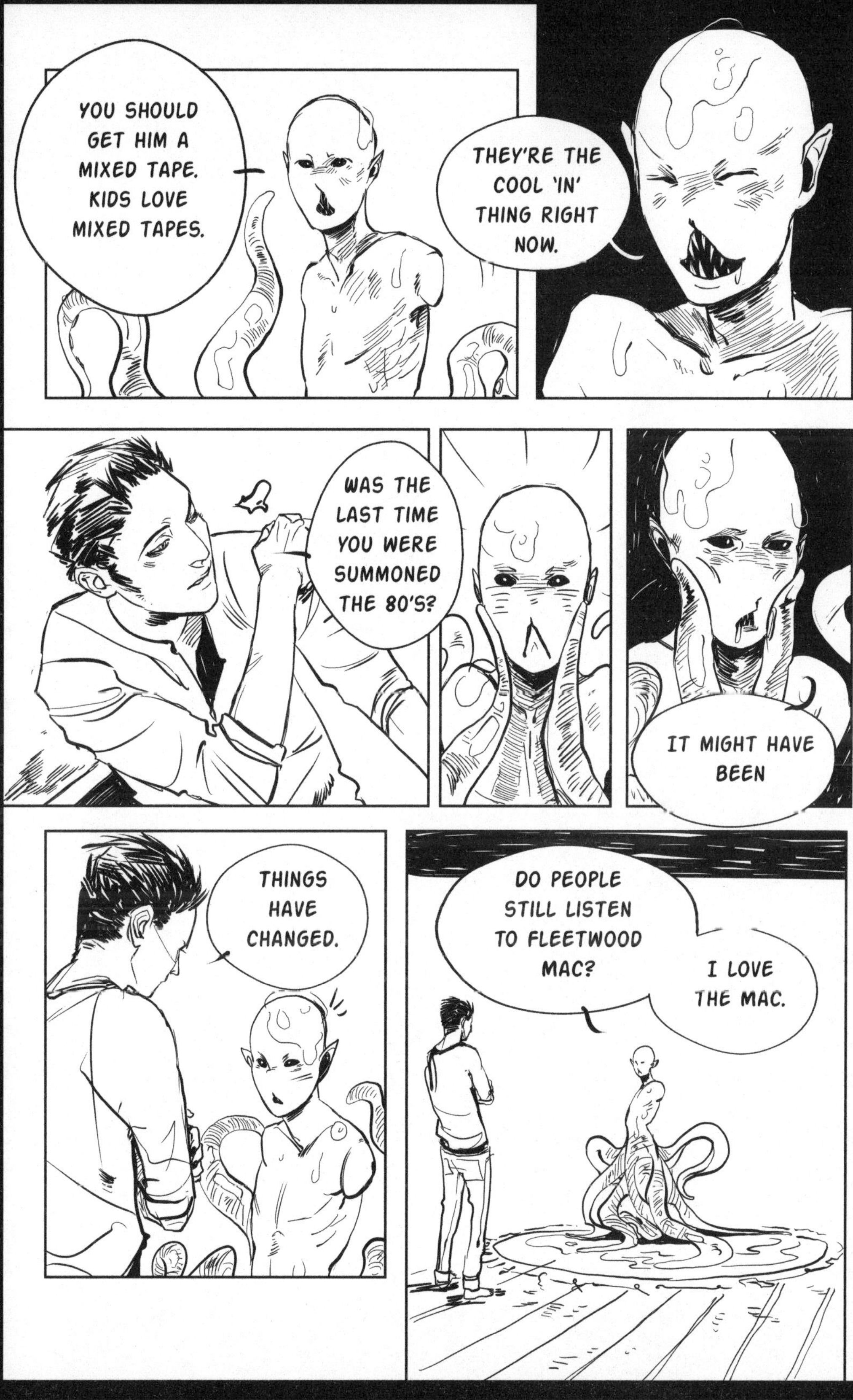

YOU SHOULD GET HIM A MIXED TAPE. KIDS LOVE MIXED TAPES.
THEY'RE THE COOL 'IN' THING RIGHT NOW.
WAS THE LAST TIME YOU WERE SUMMONED THE 80'S?
IT MIGHT HAVE BEEN
THINGS HAVE CHANGED.
DO PEOPLE STILL LISTEN TO FLEETWOOD MAC?
I LOVE THE MAC.

Magnus woke up with the slow golden light of midday fil-tering through his window, and his cat sleeping on his head.

Chairman Meow sometimes expressed his affection in this unfortunate way. Magnus gently but very firmly disentangled the cat from his hair, tiny claws doing even more damage as the Chairman was dislodged with a long sad cry of feline discomfort.

Then the cat jumped onto the pillow, apparently fully recovered from his ordeal, and leaped from the bed. He hit the floor with a soft thump and dashed with a rallying cry to the food bowl.

Magnus rolled over in bed so that he was lying across the mattress sideways. The window overlooking his bed was stained glass. Diamonds of gold and green drifted over his sheets, resting warmly against his bare skin. He lifted his head from the pillow he was clutching and then realized what he was doing: searching the air for a trace of the smell of coffee.

It had happened a few times in the last several weeks, Magnus stumbling out into the kitchen toward the rich scent of coffee, pulling on a robe from his wide and varied selection, and finding Alec there. Magnus had bought a coffeemaker because Alec had consistently seemed mildly distressed by Magnus's magicking-slash-slightly-stealing cups of coffee and tea from The Mudd Truck. The machine was extra bother, but Magnus was glad he had bought it. Alec had to know the coffeemaker was for him and his delicate moral sensibilities, and Alec seemed to feel a sense of comfort around the machine that he felt about nothing else, making coffee without asking if he could, bringing Magnus a cup when he was working. Everywhere else in Magnus's loft Alec was still careful, touching things as if he had no right to them, as if he were a guest.

And of course he was a guest. It was only that Magnus had an irrational desire for Alec to feel at home in his loft, as if that would mean something, as if that would give Magnus a claim on Alec or indicate that Alec wanted a claim on him. Magnus supposed that was it. He badly wanted Alec to want to be here, and to be happy when he was here.

He could not kidnap the Lightwoods' eldest born and keep him as a decoration about the house, however. Alec had fallen asleep twice—on the sofa, not the bed. Once after a long slow night of kissing; and once when Alec had come over for a brief coffee, clearly exhausted after a long day of demon-hunting, and he had slid into unconsciousness almost instantly. Magnus had also taken to leaving his front door open, since nobody was going to rob the High Warlock of Brooklyn, and Alec would sometimes come by in the early mornings.

Every time Alec had dropped by—or in the mornings after Alec had fallen asleep there—Magnus had woken to the sounds and smells of Alec's making him coffee, even though Alec knew that Magnus could magic coffee out of the air. Alec had done it only a few times, had been there for only a handful of mornings. It was not something Magnus should be getting used to.

Of course Alec wasn't here today, because it was his birthday, and he was going to be with his family. And Magnus wasn't exactly the kind of boyfriend you could bring to family outings. In fact, speaking of family outings, the Lightwoods didn't even know Alec had a boyfriend—much less one that was also a warlock—and Magnus had no idea if they ever would. It wasn't something he pushed Alec about. He could tell by Alec's carefulness that it was too early.

There was no reason for Magnus to slide out of bed, amble out through the living space into the kitchen space, and picture Alec kneeling at the counter, making coffee and wearing an ugly sweater, his face intent on the simple task. Alec was even conscientious about coffee. *And he wears truly awful sweaters,* Magnus thought, and was dismayed when the thought brought with it a rush of affection.

It was not the Lightwoods' fault. They obviously provided Alec's sister, Isabelle, and Jace Wayland with plenty of money to dress themselves in flattering outfits. Magnus suspected that Alec's mother bought his clothes, or Alec bought them himself on the basis of pure practicality—*Oh, look, how nice; gray won't show the ichor too much*—and then he wore the ugly functional clothes on and on without even seeming to notice that age was fraying them, or wear and tear causing holes.

Against his will, Magnus found a smile curving his lips as he rummaged around for his big blue coffee cup that said BETTER THAN GANDALF across the front in sparkly letters. He was besotted; he was officially revolted by himself.

He might have been besotted, but he had other things to think of besides Alec today. A mundane company had hired him to summon up a cecaelia demon. For the amount of money they were paying, and considering that cecaelia demons were lesser demons who could scarcely cause all that much fuss, Magnus had agreed to not ask questions. He sipped his coffee and contemplated his demon-summoning outfit for the day. Demon summoning was not something Magnus did often, on account of it being technically extremely illegal. Magnus did not have enormous respect for the Law, but if he was breaking it he wanted to look good doing it.

His thoughts were interrupted by the sound of the buzzer. He had not left his door open for Alec today, and he raised his eyebrows at the sound. Ms. Connor was twenty minutes early.

Magnus deeply disliked people who were early to business meetings. It was just as bad as being late, since it put everyone out, and even worse, people who were early always acted terribly superior about their bad timekeeping skills. They acted as though it were morally more righteous to get up early than to stay up late, even if you got the same amount of work done in the exact same amount of time. Magnus found it to be one of the great injustices of life.

It was possible that he was a bit cranky about not getting to finish his coffee before he had to deal with work.

He buzzed in the company representative. Ms. Connor

turned out to be a woman in her midthirties whose looks bore out her Irish name. She had thick red hair done up in a twist, and the kind of impenetrable white skin that Magnus was prepared to bet never tanned. She was wearing a boxy but expensive-looking blue suit, and she looked extremely askance at Magnus's outfit.

This was Magnus's home, she had arrived early, and Magnus felt entirely within his rights to be dressed in nothing but black silk pajama bottoms decorated with a pattern of tigers and flamingos dancing. He did realize that the pants were sliding down his hips a fraction, and pulled them up. He saw Ms. Connor's disapproving gaze slip down his bare chest and fasten on the smooth brown skin where a belly button should have been. Devil's mark, his stepfather had called it, but he'd said the same thing about Magnus's eyes. Magnus was long past caring whether mundanes judged him.

"Caroline Connor," said the woman. She did not offer a hand. "CFO and vice president of marketing for Sigblad Enterprises."

"Magnus Bane," said Magnus. "High Warlock of Brooklyn and Scrabble champion."

"You come highly recommended. I have heard you are an extremely powerful wizard."

"Warlock," said Magnus, "actually."

"I expected you to be . . ."

She paused like someone hovering over a selection of chocolates, all of which she was extremely doubtful about. Magnus wondered which she would choose, which marker of a trustworthy magic user she had been imagining or hoping for—elderly, bearded, white. Magnus had encountered many people in the market for a sage. He had very little time for it.

Still, he had to admit that this was perhaps not the most professional he had ever been.

"Did you expect me to be, perhaps," he suggested gently, "wearing a shirt?"

Ms. Connor lifted her shoulders in a slight shrug.

"Everybody told me that you make eccentric fashion choices, and I'm sure that's a very fashionable hairstyle," she said. "But frankly, it looks like a cat has been sleeping on your head."

Magnus offered Caroline Connor a coffee, which she declined. All she would accept was a glass of water. Magnus was becoming more and more suspicious of her.

When Magnus emerged from his room wearing maroon leather pants and a glittering cowl-neck sweater, which had come with a jaunty little matching scarf, Caroline looked at him with a cool distance that suggested she did not find it to be a huge improvement on his pajama pants. Magnus had already accepted the fact that there would never be an eternal friendship between them, and did not find himself heartbroken.

"So, Caroline," he said.

"I prefer 'Ms. Connor,'" said Ms. Connor, perched on the very edge of Magnus's gold velvet sofa. She was looking around at the furniture as disapprovingly as she had looked at Magnus's bare chest, as if she thought that a few interesting prints and a lamp with bells were somewhat equivalent to Roman orgies.

"Ms. Connor," Magnus amended easily. The customer was always right, and that would be Magnus's policy until the job was completed, at which point he would decline to ever be employed by this company again.

She produced a file from her briefcase, a contract in a dark green binder, which she passed over to Magnus to flip through. Magnus had signed two other contracts in the past week, one graven into a tree trunk in the depths of a German forest under the light of a new moon, and one in his own blood. Mundanes were so quaint.

Magnus scanned through it. Summon minor demon, mysterious purpose, obscene sums of money. Check, check, and check. He signed it with a flourish and handed it back.

"Well," said Ms. Connor, folding her hands in her lap. "I would like to see the demon now, if you please."

"It takes a little while to set up the pentagram and the summoning circle," Magnus said. "You might want to get comfortable."

Ms. Connor looked startled and displeased. "I have a lunch meeting," she noted. "Is there no way to expedite the process?"

"Er, no. This is dark magic, Ms. Connor," said Magnus. "It is not quite the same as ordering a pizza."

Ms. Connor's mouth flattened like a piece of paper being folded in half. "Would it be possible for me to come back in a few hours?"

Magnus's conviction that people who arrived early to meetings had no respect for other people's time was being confirmed. On the other hand, he did not really wish for this woman to remain in his house for any longer than necessary.

"Off you go," Magnus said, keeping his voice urbane and charming. "When you return, there will be a cecaelia demon in place for you to do with as you wish."

"Casa Bane," Magnus muttered as Ms. Connor left, his voice not quite low enough to be sure she wouldn't hear him.

"Hot- and cold-running demons, at your service."

He didn't have time to sit around being annoyed. There was work to be done. Magnus set about arranging his circle of black candles. Inside the circle he scratched a pentagram, using a rowan stick freshly cut by faerie hands. The whole process took a couple of hours before he was ready to begin his chant.

"*Iam tibi impero et praecipio, maligne spiritus!* I summon you, by the power of bell, book, and candle. I summon you from the airy void, from the darkest depths. I summon you, Elyaas who swims in the midnight seas of eternally drowning souls, Elyaas who lurks in the shadows that surround Pandemonium, Elyaas who bathes in tears and plays with the bones of lost sailors."

Magnus drawled the words, tapping his nails on his cup and examining his chipped green nail polish. He took pride in his work, but this was not his favorite part of his job, not his favorite client, and not the day for it.

The golden wood of his floor began to smoke, and the smoke rising had the smell of sulfur. But the smoke rose in sullen wisps. Magnus felt a resistance as he pulled the demon dimension closer to him, like a fisherman drawing on a line and getting a fish who put up a fight.

It was too early in the afternoon for this. Magnus spoke in a louder voice, feeling the power rise in him as he spoke, as if his blood were catching on fire and sending sparks from the center of his being out into the space between worlds.

"As the destroyer of Marbas, I summon you. I summon you as the demon's child who can make your seas dry to desert. I summon you by my own power, and by the power of my blood, and you know who my father is, Elyaas. You will not, you dare not, disobey."

The smoke rose higher and higher, became a veil, and beyond the veil for an instant Magnus glimpsed another world. Then the smoke became too thick to see through. Magnus had to wait until it dwindled and coalesced into a shape—not quite the shape of a man.

Magnus had summoned many disgusting demons in his life. The amphisbaena demon had the wings and the trunk of a vast chicken. Mundane stories claimed it had the head and tail of a snake, but that was not in fact true. Amphisbaena demons were covered in tentacles, with one very large tentacle containing an eye, and a mouth with snapping fangs. Magnus could see how the confusion had arisen.

The amphisbaena demons were the worst, but cecaelia demons were not Magnus's favorites either. They were not aesthetically pleasing, and they left slime all over the floor.

Elyaas's shape was more blob than anything else. His head was something like a man's, but with his green eyes set close together in the center of his face, and a triangular slit serving as both nose and mouth. He had no arms. His torso was abruptly truncated, and his lower parts resembled those of a squid, the tentacles thick and short. And from head to stubby tentacles, he was coated in greenish-black slime, as if he had arisen from a fetid swamp and was sweating out putrefaction from every pore.

"Who summons Elyaas?" he asked in a voice that sounded like a normal, rather jolly, man's voice, with the slight suggestion that it was being heard underwater. It was possible that this was simply because he had a mouthful of slime. Magnus saw the demon's tongue—like a human's but green and ending in a thick point—flicker between his sharp slime-stained teeth as he spoke.

"I do," said Magnus. "But I rather believe we covered that when I was summoning you and you proved recalcitrant."

He spoke cheerfully, but the blue-white flame of the candles responded to his mood and contracted, forming a cage of light around Elyaas that made him yelp. His slime had no effect upon their fire whatsoever.

"Oh, come on!" Elyaas grumbled. "Don't be like that! I was on my way. I was held up by some personal business."

Magnus rolled his eyes. "What were you doing, demon?"

Elyaas looked shifty, insofar as you could tell under the slime. "I had a thing. So how have you been, Magnus?"

"What?" Magnus asked.

"You know, since the last time you summoned me. How have you been keeping?"

"What?" Magnus asked again.

"You don't remember me?" said the tentacle demon.

"I summon a lot of demons," Magnus said weakly.

There was a long pause. Magnus stared into the bottom of his coffee cup and desperately willed more coffee to appear. This was something a lot of mundanes did too, but Magnus had one up on those suckers. His mug did slowly fill again, until it was brimming with rich dark liquid. He sipped and looked at Elyaas, who was shifting uncomfortably from tentacle to tentacle.

"Well," said Elyaas. "This is awkward."

"It's nothing personal," said Magnus.

"Maybe if I jogged your memory," Elyaas suggested helpfully. "You summoned me when you were searching for a demon who cursed a Shadowhunter? Bill Herondale?"

"Will Herondale," said Magnus.

Elyaas snapped his tentacles as if they were fingers. "I knew it was something like that."

"You know," Magnus said, enlightened, "I think I do remember. I'm sorry about that. I realized right away that you weren't the demon I was looking for. You looked kind of blue in one of the drawings, but obviously you are not blue, and I was wasting your time. You were pretty understanding about it."

"Think nothing of it." Elyaas waved a tentacle. "These things happen. And I can look blue. You know, in the right light."

"Lighting's important, it's true," said Magnus.

"So whatever happened with Bill Herondale and that curse a blue demon put on him?" The cecaelia demon's interest seemed genuine.

"*Will* Herondale," Magnus said again. "It's actually rather a long story."

"You know, sometimes we demons pretend we're cursing people and we don't really do it," said Elyaas chattily. "Like, just for kicks? It's kind of a thing with us. Did you know that?"

"You could have mentioned it a century or two ago," Magnus observed frostily.

Elyaas shook his head, smiling a slime-bedecked smile. "The old pretend-to-curse. It's a classic. Very funny." He appeared to notice Magnus's unimpressed expression for the first time. "Not from your perspective, of course."

"It wasn't funny for Bill Herondale!" said Magnus. "Oh, damn it. Now you've got me doing it."

Magnus's phone buzzed on the counter where he had left it. Magnus made a dive for it, and was delighted when he saw that it was Catarina. He had been expecting her call.

Then he realized the demon was looking at him curiously.

"Sorry," Magnus said. "Mind if I take this?"

Elyaas waved a tentacle. "Oh no, go right ahead."

Magnus pressed the answer button on the phone and walked toward the window, away from the demon and the sulfur fumes.

"Hello, Catarina!" said Magnus. "I am so pleased that you finally called me back."

He might have laid a slight pointed emphasis on the "finally."

"I only did because you said it was urgent," said his friend Catarina, who was a nurse first and a warlock second. Magnus did not think she'd had a date in fifteen years. Before that she'd had a fiancé whom she had kept meaning to marry, but she'd never found the time, and eventually he'd died of old age, still hoping that one day she would set a date.

"It is urgent," said Magnus. "You know that I've been, ah, spending time with one of the Nephilim at the New York Institute."

"A Lightwood, right?" Catarina asked.

"Alexander Lightwood," said Magnus, and he was mildly horrified to hear how his own voice softened on the name.

"I wouldn't have thought you'd have time, with all the other things going on."

It was true. The night when Magnus had met Alec, he had just wanted to throw a party, have some fun, act the part of a warlock filled with joie de vivre until he could feel it. He remembered how in the past, every few years, he used to feel a restless craving for love, and would start to search for the possibility of love in beautiful strangers. Somehow this time around it hadn't happened. He had spent the eighties in a strange cloud of misery, thinking of Camille, the vampire he had loved more than a century before. He had not loved anyone, not really loved them and had them love him back, since Etta in the fifties. Etta had been dead for years and years, and had left him before she'd died. Since then there had been affairs, of course, lovers who'd let him down or whom he'd let down, faces he now barely remembered, glimpses of brightness that had flickered and gone out even as he'd approached.

He hadn't stopped wanting love. He had simply, somehow, stopped looking.

He wondered if you could be exhausted without knowing it, if hope could be lost not all at once but could slip away gradually, day by day, and vanish before you ever realized.

Then Clary Fray had appeared at his party, the girl whose mother had been hiding Clary's Shadowhunter heritage from her all her life. Clary had been brought to Magnus so that he could ensorcel her memory and cloud her sight, over and over again as she'd been growing up, and Magnus had done it. It was not a terribly kind thing to do to a girl, but her mother had been so afraid for her, and it had not felt like Magnus's place to refuse. Yet Magnus had not been able to stop himself from taking a personal interest. Seeing a child grow up, year after year, had been new to him, as had feeling the weight of her memories in his hands. He had started to feel a little responsible, had wanted to know what would become of her and had begun to want the best for her.

Magnus had been interested in Clary, the little redheaded scrap who had grown into a—slightly bigger little redheaded scrap, but had not thought he would be terribly interested in the companions she had found for herself. Not the nondescript mundane boy; not golden-eyed Jace Wayland, who reminded Magnus of too much of a past that he would rather forget; and certainly not either of the Lightwood siblings, the dark boy and girl whose parents Magnus had good reason to dislike.

It made no sense that his eyes had been drawn to Alec, over and over again. Alec had hung to the back of their little group, had made no effort to attract the eye. He had striking coloring, the rare combination of black hair and blue eyes that had always been Magnus's favorite, and Magnus supposed that was why he had looked in Alec's direction at first. Strange to see the coloring that had so distinguished Will and his sister, so many miles and years gone by, and on someone with an entirely different last name . . .

Then Alec had smiled at one of Magnus's jokes, and the smile had lit a lamp in his solemn face, making his blue eyes brilliant, and briefly taking Magnus's breath away. And when Magnus's attention had been held, he'd seen a flicker of returned interest in Alec's eyes, a mixture of guilt, intrigue, and pleasure at Magnus's attention. Shadowhunters were old-fashioned about such matters, which was to say bigoted and hidebound, as they were about everything. Magnus had been approached by male Shadowhunters before, of course, but always in a hole-and-corner way, always as if they were doing Magnus some huge favor and as if Magnus's touch, though desired, might sully them. (Magnus had always turned them down.) It had been a shock to see such feelings open and innocent on a beautiful boy's face.

When Magnus had winked at Alec and told him to call him, it had been a reckless impulse, little more than a whim. He had certainly not expected the Shadowhunter on his doorstep a few days later, asking for a date. Nor had he expected the date to go so spectacularly bizarrely, or expected to like Alec quite so much afterward.

"Alec took me by surprise," said Magnus to Catarina at last, which was a massive understatement and so true that it felt like revealing too much.

"Well, it seems like a mad idea to me, but those usually work out for you," said Catarina. "What's the problem?"

That was the million-dollar question. Magnus resolved to sound casual about it. This was not something that he should be worrying about as much as he was, and he wanted advice but did not want to let anyone, not even Catarina, see how much it mattered.

"I'm glad you asked. Here's the thing," said Magnus. "It's Alec's birthday today. He's eighteen. And I'd like to get him a present, because the celebration of one's birth is a traditional time for the giving of gifts, and it indicates your affection for them. But—and at this point I'd like to say that I wish you had returned my call sooner—I don't really have any idea what to get him, and I would appreciate some advice. The thing is, he doesn't really seem to care about material goods, including clothes, which I don't understand, though I find it strangely charming. He is impossible to buy for. The only new things I ever see him with are weapons, and nunchakus are not a romantic gift. Also, I wondered if you thought that getting a present at all might make me seem too keen and chase him off. I've been seeing him for only a little while, and his parents don't even know he likes boys, let alone likes degenerate warlocks, and so I want to be subtle. Maybe getting a gift at all would be a mistake. It's possible that he will think I am being too intense.

And as you know, Catarina, I am not intense. I am laissez-faire. I am a jaded sophisticate. I don't want him to get the wrong idea about me or think the present means more than it should. Maybe just a token gift. What do you think?"

Magnus took a deep breath. That had come out a little less cool, calm, well-reasoned, and sophisticated than he had been hoping for.

"Magnus," said Catarina, "I have lives to save."

Then she hung up on him.

Magnus stared at the phone in disbelief. He would never have thought Catarina would do this to him. It seemed like wanton cruelty. He had not sounded that bad on the telephone.

"Is Alec your lover?" asked Elyaas the tentacle demon.

Magnus stared. He was not ready for anyone to say "lover" to him with an oozing note of slime beneath the word. He felt he would never be ready.

"You should get him a mixed tape," said Elyaas. "Kids love mixed tapes. They're the cool 'in' thing right now."

"Was the last time you were summoned the eighties?" Magnus asked.

"It might have been," Elyaas said defensively.

"Things have changed."

"Do people still listen to Fleetwood Mac?" asked the tentacle demon. There was a plaintive note in his voice. "I love the Mac."

Magnus ignored the demon, who had softly begun to sing a slimy song to himself. Magnus was contemplating his own dark fate. He had to accept it. There was no way around it. There was no one else he could turn to.

He was going to have to call Ragnor Fell and ask for advice about his love life.

* * *

Ragnor was spending a lot of time lately in Idris, the Shadowhunters' city of glass, where phones, television, and the Internet did not work, and where Magnus imagined the Angel's chosen ones had to resort to pornographic woodcuts when they wanted to unwind after a long day's demon-hunting. Ragnor had used his magic to install a single telephone, but he could not be expected to hang around it all the livelong day. So Magnus was deeply thankful when Ragnor's phone actually rang and the warlock actually picked up.

"Ragnor, thank goodness," he said.

"What is it?" asked Ragnor. "Is it Valentine? I'm in London, and Tessa's in the Amazon and there's no way to contact her. All right. Let me wrap this up fast. You call Catarina, and I will be with you in—"

"Ah," said Magnus. "There's no need for that. Though thank you for your immediate leaping to my rescue, my sweet emerald prince."

There was a pause. Then Ragnor said, in a much less intent and much more grumpy voice, "Why are you bothering me, then?"

"Well, I'd like some advice," said Magnus. "So I turned to you, as one of my oldest and dearest friends, as a fellow warlock and a trusted comrade, as the former High Warlock of London in whom I have implicit confidence."

"Flattery from you makes me nervous," said Ragnor. "It means you want something. Doubtless something awful. I am not becoming a pirate with you again, Magnus. I don't care how much you pay me."

"I wasn't going to suggest it. My question for you is of a

more . . . personal nature. Don't hang up. Catarina was already extremely unsympathetic."

There was a long silence. Magnus fiddled with his window catch, gazing out at the line of warehouses-turned-apartments. Lace curtains were fluttering in a summer breeze in an open window across the street. He tried to ignore the reflection of the demon in his own window.

"Wait," said Ragnor, and he started to snigger. "Is this about your Nephilim *boyfriend?*"

"Our relationship is as yet undefined," said Magnus with dignity. Then he clutched the phone and hissed, "And how do you know private details about my personal life with Alexander?"

"Ooooh, *Alexander*," Ragnor said in a singsong voice. "I know all about it. Raphael called and told me."

"Raphael Santiago," said Magnus, thinking darkly of the current leader of the New York vampire clan, "has a black ungrateful heart, and one day he will be punished for this treachery."

"Raphael calls me every month," said Ragnor. "Raphael knows that it is important to preserve good relations and maintain regular communication between the different Downworlder factions. I might add, Raphael always remembers important occasions in my life."

"I forgot your birthday one time sixty years ago!" said Magnus. "You need to let that go."

"It was fifty-eight years ago, for the record. And Raphael knows we need to maintain a united front against the Nephilim and not, for instance, sneak around with their underage sons," Ragnor continued.

"Alec is eighteen!"

"Whatever," said Ragnor. "Raphael would never date a Shadowhunter."

"Of course, why would he, when you two are in loooove?" Magnus asked. "'Oooh, Raphael is always so professional.' 'Oooh, Raphael brought up the most interesting points in that meeting you forgot to attend.' 'Oooh, Raphael and I are planning a June wedding.' Besides, Raphael would never date a Shadowhunter because Raphael has a policy of never doing anything that is awesome."

"Stamina runes are not the only things that matter in life," said Ragnor.

"So says someone who is wasting his life," Magnus told him. "And anyway, it's not like . . . Alec is . . ."

"If you tell me about your gooey feelings for one of the Nephilim, I will go double green and be sick," said Ragnor. "I'm warning you now."

Double green sounded interesting, but Magnus did not have time to waste. "Fine. Just advise me on this one practical matter," said Magnus. "Should I buy him a birthday present, and if so, what should it be?"

"I just remembered that I have some very important business to attend to," said Ragnor.

"No," said Magnus. "Wait. Don't do this. I trusted you!"

"I'm sorry, Magnus, but you're breaking up."

"Maybe a cashmere sweater? What do you think about a sweater?"

"Oops, tunnel," said Ragnor, and a dial tone echoed in Magnus's ear.

Magnus did not know why all of his immortal friends had

to be so callous and horrible. Ragnor's important business was probably getting together to write a burn book with Raphael. Magnus could see them now, sharing a bench and scribbling happily away about Magnus's stupid hair.

Magnus was drawn from this dark private vision by the actual dark vision currently happening in his loft. Elyaas was generating more and more slime. It was steadily filling the pentagram. The cecaelia demon was wallowing in the stuff.

"I think you should buy him a scented candle," Elyaas proposed, his voice stickier by the minute. He waved his tentacles enthusiastically to illustrate his point. "They come in many exciting scents, like bilberry and orange blossom. It will bring him serenity and he'll think about you when he goes to sleep. Everybody likes scented candles."

"I need you to shut up," said Magnus. "I have to think."

He threw himself onto his sofa. Magnus should have expected that Raphael, filthy traitor and total priss that he was, would have reported back to Ragnor.

Magnus remembered the night when he took Alec to Taki's. Usually they went to places frequented by mundanes. The haunts of Downworld, crawling with faeries, werewolves, warlocks, and vampires who might pass on word to his parents, clearly made Alec nervous. Magnus did not think Alec understood how much Downworld preferred to keep apart from Shadowhunter business.

The café was bustling, and the center of attention was a peri and a werewolf having some kind of territorial dispute. Nobody paid Alec and Magnus any attention at all, except Kaelie, the little blond waitress, who had smiled when they'd come in and who'd been very attentive.

"Do you know her?" asked Magnus.

"A little," said Alec. "She's part nixie. She likes Jace."

She wasn't the only one who liked Jace, Magnus knew that. He didn't see what all the fuss was about, personally. Other than the fact that Jace had a face like an angel's and abs for days.

Magnus started to tell Alec a story about a nixie nightclub he'd been to once. Alec was laughing, and then Raphael Santiago came in the door of the café with his most faithful vampire followers, Lily and Elliott. Raphael spotted Magnus and Alec, and then his thin arched eyebrows hit his hairline.

"Nope, nope, nope, and also no," Raphael said, and he actually took several steps back toward the door. "Turn around, everybody. I do not wish to know this. I refuse to be aware of this."

"One of the Nephilim," said Lily, bad girl that she was, and she drummed on the table of their booth with shining blue fingernails. "My, my."

"Hi?" said Alec.

"Wait a minute," said Raphael. "Are you Alexander Lightwood?"

Alec looked more panicked by the minute. "Yes?" he said, as if he were uncertain on the subject. Magnus thought he might be considering changing his name to Horace Whipplepool and fleeing the country.

"Aren't you twelve?" Raphael demanded. "I distinctly recall you being twelve."

"Uh, that was a while ago," said Alec.

He looked even more freaked out. Magnus supposed it must have been unsettling to be accused of being twelve by someone who looked like a boy of fifteen.

Magnus might have found the situation funny at another

time, but he looked at Alec. Alec's shoulders were tense.

He knew Alec well enough by now to know what he was feeling, the conflicting impulses that warred in him. He was conscientious, the kind of person who believed that the others around him were so much more important than he was, who already believed that he was letting everybody down. And he was honest, the kind of person who was naturally open about all he felt and all he wanted. Alec's virtues had made a trap for him: these two good qualities had collided painfully. He felt he could not be honest without disappointing everybody he loved. It was a hideous conundrum for him. It was as if the world had been designed to make him unhappy.

"Leave him alone," Magnus said, and reached for Alec's hand over the table. For a moment Alec's fingers relaxed under Magnus's, began to curl around them, holding his hand back. Then he glanced at the vampires and snatched his hand away.

Magnus had known a lot of men and women over the years who'd been afraid of who they were and what they wanted. He had loved many of them, and had hurt for them all. He had loved the times in the mundane world when people had had to be a little less afraid. He loved this time in the world, when he could reach out in a public place and take Alec's hand.

It did not make Magnus feel any more kindly toward the Shadowhunters to see one of their Angel-touched warriors made afraid by something like this. If they had to believe they were so much better than everyone else, they should at least be able to make their own children feel good about who they were.

Elliott leaned against Alec's seat, shaking his head so his thin dreadlocks whipped about his face. "What would your parents think?" he asked with mock solemnity.

It was funny to the vampires. But it wasn't funny to Alec.

"Elliott," said Magnus. "You're boring. And I don't want to hear that you've been telling any tedious tales around the place. Do you understand me?"

He played with a teaspoon, blue sparks traveling from his fingers to the spoon and back again. Elliott's eyes said that Magnus would not be able to kill him with a spoon. Magnus's eyes invited Elliott to test him.

Raphael ran out of patience, which admittedly was like a desert running out of water.

"*Dios*," snapped Raphael, and the other two vampires flinched. "I am not interested in your sordid encounters or constantly deranged life choices, and I am certainly not interested in prying into the affairs of Nephilim. I meant what I said. I don't want to know about this. And I won't know about this. This never happened. I saw nothing. Let's go."

So now Raphael had gone running off to report to Ragnor. That was vampires for you: always going for the jugular, both literally and metaphorically. They were messing up his love life as well as being inconsiderate party guests who had got blood in Magnus's stereo system at his last party and turned Clary's idiot friend Stanley into a rat, which was just bad manners. Magnus was never inviting any vampires to his parties ever again. It was going to be all werewolves and faeries all the time, even if it was hell getting fur and faerie dust out of the sofa.

Magnus and Alec sat in brief silence after the vampires departed, and then something else happened. The fight between the peri and the werewolf got out of hand. The werewolf's face changed, snarling, and the peri turned the table upside down. A crash rang out.

Magnus started slightly at the sound, and Alec acted. He leaped to his feet, palming a throwing knife with one hand, his other hand going to a weapon in his belt. He moved faster than any other being in the room—werewolf, vampire, or faerie—could have moved.

And he moved automatically in front of the booth where Magnus was sitting, placed his body between Magnus and the threat without even thinking about it. Magnus had seen how Alec acted with his fellow Shadowhunters, with his sister and his *parabatai*, closer than a brother. He guarded their backs, watched out for them, behaved at all times as if their lives were more precious than his own.

Magnus was the High Warlock of Brooklyn, and for centuries had been powerful beyond the dreams of not only mundanes but most of Downworld. Magnus certainly did not need protection, and nobody had ever even thought to offer it, certainly not a Shadowhunter. The best one could hope for from Shadowhunters, if you were a Downworlder, was to be left alone. Nobody had tried to protect him, that he could remember, since he was very young. He had never wanted anybody to do so, not since he'd been a child who'd had to run to the cold mercy of the Silent Brothers' sanctuary. That had been long ago in a country far away, and Magnus had never wanted to be so weak ever again. Yet seeing Alec spring to defend him caused Magnus to feel a pang in the center of his chest, at once sweet and painful.

And the customers in Taki's café shrank back from Alec, from angelic power revealed in a sudden blaze of fury. In that moment nobody doubted that he could lay waste to them all.

The peri and the werewolf slunk to opposite corners of the

café, and then hastily made their retreat from the building. Alec subsided into the booth opposite Magnus, and sent him an embarrassed smile.

It was strange and startling and terribly endearing, like Alec himself.

Magnus then dragged Alec outside, pushed him up against the brick wall of Taki's under the sparking upside-down sign, and kissed him. Alec's blue eyes that had blazed with angelic fury were tender suddenly, and darker with passion. Magnus felt Alec's strong lithe body strain against Magnus's, felt his gentle hands slide up Magnus's back. Alec kissed him back with shattering enthusiasm, and Magnus thought, *Yes, this one, this one fits, after all the stumbling around and searching, and here it is.*

"What was that for?" Alec asked a long time later, eyes shining.

Alec was young. Magnus had never been old, had never known how the world reacted to you when you were old, and had not been allowed to be really young for long either. Being immortal meant being apart from such concerns. All the mortals Magnus had loved had seemed younger and older than him, both at once. But Magnus was keenly aware that this was Alec's first time dating, doing anything at all. He had been Alec's first kiss. Magnus wanted to be good to him, not burden him with the weight of feelings that Alec might not return.

"Nothing," Magnus lied.

Thinking about that night at Taki's, Magnus realized what the perfect present for Alec would be. He also realized that he had no idea how to give it to him.

In the only piece of luck in a terrible day filled with slime and cruel friends, at that very moment the buzzer rang.

Magnus crossed the floor in three easy strides and boomed into the intercom: "WHO DARES DISTURB THE HIGH WARLOCK AT WORK?"

There was a pause.

"Seriously, if you are Jehovah's Witnesses . . ."

"Ah, no," said a girl's voice, light, self-confident, and with the slight, odd inflection of Idris. "This is Isabelle Lightwood. Mind if I come up?"

"Not at all," said Magnus, and he pressed the button to let her in.

Isabelle Lightwood walked straight for the coffee machine and got herself a cup without asking if she could have any. She was that kind of girl, Magnus thought, the kind who took what she wanted and assumed you would be delighted that she'd taken a fancy to it. She studiously ignored Elyaas as she went: she had taken one look at him when she'd come into Magnus's apartment and apparently decided that asking questions about the presence of the tentacle demon would be impolite and probably boring.

She looked like Alec, had his high cheekbones, porcelain-pale skin, and black hair, though she wore hers long and carefully styled. Her eyes were different, though, glossy and black, like lacquered ebony: both beautiful and indestructible. She seemed as if she could be as cold as her mother, as if she might be as prone to corruption as so many of her ancestors had been. Magnus had known a lot of Lightwoods, and he had not been terribly impressed by most of them. Not until one.

Isabelle hopped up onto the counter, stretching out her long legs. She was wearing tailored jeans and boots with spike heels, and a deep red silk tank top that matched the ruby necklace at her throat, which Magnus had bought for the price of a London town house more than a hundred years before. Magnus rather liked seeing her wear it. It felt like watching Will's niece, brash, laughing, cheroot-smoking Anna Lightwood—one of the few Lightwoods he had liked—wearing it a hundred years before. It charmed him, made him feel as if he had mattered in that space of time, to those people. He wondered how horrified the Lightwoods would be if they knew that the necklace had once been a dissolute warlock's love gift to a murderous vampire.

Probably not as horrified as they would be if they learned Magnus was dating their son.

He met Isabelle's bold black eyes, and thought that she might not be horrified to learn where her necklace had come from. He thought she might get a bit of a kick out of it. Maybe someday he would tell her.

"So it's Alec's birthday today," Isabelle announced.

"I'm aware," said Magnus.

He said nothing more. He didn't know what Alec had told Isabelle, knew how painfully Alec loved her and wanted to shield her, not to let her down, as he wanted not to let any of them down and passionately feared he would. Secrecy did not sit well with Magnus, who had winked at Alec the first night he'd met him, when Alec had been simply a deliriously good-looking boy glancing at Magnus with shy interest. But it was all more complicated now, when he knew how Alec could be hurt, when Magnus knew how much it would matter to him if Alec were hurt.

"I know you two are . . . seeing each other," said Isabelle, picking her words carefully but still meeting Magnus's eyes dead-on. "I don't care. I mean, it doesn't matter to me. At all."

She flung the words defiantly at Magnus. There was no need to be defiant with him, but he understood why she was, understood that she must have practiced the defiant words that she might have to say to her parents one day, if she stood by her brother.

She would stand by him. She loved her brother, then.

"That's good to know," said Magnus.

He had known Isabelle Lightwood was beautiful, and had thought she seemed strong, and funny—had known that she was someone he would not mind having a drink with or having at a party. He had not known that there were depths of loyalty and love in her.

He was not adept at reading Shadowhunter hearts, behind their smooth angelically arrogant facades. He thought that might be why Alec had surprised him so much, had wrong-footed him so that Magnus had stumbled into feelings he had not planned to have. Alec had no facade at all.

Isabelle nodded, as if she understood what Magnus was telling her. "I thought—it seemed important to tell someone that, on his birthday," she said. "I can't tell anyone else, even though I would. It's not like my parents or the Clave would listen to me." Isabelle curled her lip as she spoke of both her parents and the Clave. Magnus was liking her more and more. "He can't tell anyone. And you won't tell anyone, right?"

"It is not my secret to tell," said Magnus.

He might not enjoy sneaking around, but he would not tell anybody's secret. Least of all would he risk causing Alec pain or fear.

"You really like him, right?" Isabelle asked. "My brother?"

"Oh, did you mean Alec?" Magnus retorted. "I thought you meant my cat."

Isabelle laughed and kicked at one of Magnus's cabinet doors with one spike heel, careless and radiant. "Come on, though," she said. "You do."

"Are we going to talk about boys?" Magnus inquired. "I didn't realize, and I am honestly not prepared. Can't you come over another time, when I'm in my jammies? We could do homemade facials and braid each other's hair, and then and only then will I tell you that I think your brother is totally dreamy."

Isabelle looked pleased, if a little mystified. "Most people go for Jace. Or me," she added blithely.

Alec had said as much to Magnus once, seeming stunned that Magnus might hope to see him instead of Jace.

Magnus was not planning on talking about why he preferred Alec. The heart had its reasons, and they were seldom all that reasonable. You might as well have asked why Clary hadn't created a hilarious love triangle by getting a crush on Alec, since he was—in Magnus's admittedly biased opinion—extremely handsome, and had been consistently sullen in her direction, which some girls liked. You liked the people you liked.

For all that, Magnus had many reasons. Nephilim were guarded, Nephilim were arrogant, Nephilim were to be avoided. Even the Shadowhunters Magnus had met and liked had been, every one, a trouble sundae with dark secret cherries on top.

Alec was not like any Shadowhunter Magnus had met before.

"May I see your whip?" asked Magnus.

Isabelle blinked, but to do her justice, she did not demur.

She un-looped the electrum whip and tangled its silvery-gold length around her hands for a moment, like a child playing cat's cradle.

Magnus took the whip carefully, laid across his palms like a snake, and he carried it to his closet door, which he opened. He drew out a special potion, one that he had paid an exorbitant price for and that he had been saving for something special. Shadowhunters had their runes to protect them. Warlocks had magic. Magnus had always liked his magic better than theirs. Only a Shadowhunter could bear runes, but he could give magic to anyone. He tipped the potion—faerie dust and blood taken in one of the old rituals, hematite and hellebore and more besides—onto the whip.

In the last extremity this weapon will not fail you; in the darkest hour this weapon will bring your enemy low.

Magnus carried the whip back to Isabelle when he was done.

"What did you do to it?" Isabelle asked.

"I gave it a little extra kick," said Magnus.

Isabelle regarded him with narrowed eyes. "And why would you do that?"

"Why did you come to tell me that you knew about me and Alec?" asked Magnus. "It's his birthday. That means the people who care about him want to give him what he wishes for most. In your case, acceptance. In mine, I know that the most important thing to him in the world is that you be safe."

Isabelle nodded, and their eyes met. Magnus had said far too much, and he worried that Isabelle could see more.

She launched herself off the counter, toward Magnus's small alabaster-topped coffee table, and scrawled on his notepad. "Here's my number."

"May I ask why you're giving it to me?"

"Well, wow, Magnus. I knew you were hundreds of years old and all, but I hoped you were keeping up with modern technology." Isabelle held out her phone to illustrate her point, and waggled it about. "So that you can call me, or text me. If you ever need Shadowhunter help."

"Me need Shadowhunter help?" Magnus inquired, incredulous. "Over the—you're right, hundreds of years—let me tell you that I've found it is almost invariably the other way around. I presume you'll be wanting my number in return, and I'm also prepared to bet, based on nothing more than a passing acquaintance with your circle of friends, that you are going to get into trouble and need my expert magical assistance rather a lot."

"Yeah, maybe," said Isabelle with a rakish grin. "I've been known to be a troublemaker. But I didn't give you my number because I want magical help, and okay, I understand that the High Warlock of Brooklyn probably doesn't need an assist from a bunch of underage Nephilim. I was thinking that, if you're going to be important to my brother, we should be able to get in touch. And I was thinking that you might want to have it if—if you need to contact me about Alec. Or if I need to contact you."

Magnus understood what the girl meant. His number was easy enough to get—the Institute had it—but in giving him her own, Isabelle was offering the free exchange of information about Alec's safety. The Nephilim led dangerous lives, chasing after demons, stalking the Downworld for lawbreakers, their rune-Marked, angel-swift bodies the last line of defense for the mundane world. The second time Magnus had ever seen Alec, he had been dying of demon poison.

Alec could die at any time, in any of the battles to come. Isabelle would be the only one of the Shadowhunters who knew for sure that there was anything between Magnus and Alec. She would be the only one who knew that if Alec died, Magnus would be someone who needed to be told.

"All right," he said slowly. "Thank you, Isabelle."

Isabelle winked. "No need to thank me. I'll be driving you mad before long."

"I'll be expecting it," said Magnus as she clattered out on her high, weaponized heels. He admired anyone who made beauty and utility work together.

"By the way, that demon is dripping slime all over your floor," said Isabelle, poking her head back around the door.

"Hi," said Elyaas, and he waved a tentacle at her.

Isabelle regarded him with disdain, then raised an eyebrow in Magnus's direction. "Just thought I'd point it out," she said, and closed the door.

"I don't underssssstand the point of your present," said Elyaas. "He isn't even going to know about it? You should have just gone with flowers. Red rossssses are very romantic. Or perhaps tulips if you think that roses say you just want him for sssssex."

Magnus lay upon his golden sofa and contemplated the ceiling. The sun was low in the sky, a flash of golden paint inscribed with a careless hand over the New York skyline. The demon's shape had become more and more gelatinous as the day had progressed, until he seemed like nothing more than a lurking pile of slime. Possibly Caroline Connor would never come back. Possibly Elyaas was going to live with Magnus now. Magnus had always thought Raphael Santiago was the worst possible roommate he could ever have. Possibly he was about to be proven wrong.

He wished, with a profundity of longing that surprised him, that Alec were here.

Magnus remembered a town in Peru whose Quechua name meant "quiet place." He recalled even more vividly being obscenely drunk and unhappy over his heartbreak of that time, and the maudlin thoughts that had recurred to him over the years, like an unwanted guest slipping in through his doors: that there was no peace for such as he, no quiet place, and there never would be.

Except he found himself remembering lying in bed with Alec—all of their clothes on, lounging on the bed on a lazy afternoon, Alec laughing, head thrown back, the marks Magnus had left on his throat very plain to see.

Time was something that moved in fits and starts for Magnus, dissipating like mist or dragging like chains, but when Alec was here, Magnus's time seemed to fall into an easy rhythm with Alec's, like two heartbeats falling into sync. He felt anchored by Alec, and his whole self felt restless and mutinous when Alec was not there, because he knew how different it would be when Alec *was* there, how the tumultuous world would quiet at the sound of Alec's voice.

It was part of the dichotomy of Alec that had caught Magnus unaware and left him fascinated—that Alec seemed old for his age, serious and responsible, and yet that he approached the world with a tender wonder that made all things new. Alec was a warrior who brought Magnus peace.

Magnus lay on the sofa and admitted it to himself. He knew why he had been acting demented and pestering his friends over a birthday present. He knew why, on an ordinary unpleasant workday, his every thought had been punctuated with a thought of Alec, with insistent longing for him. This was love, new and bright and terrifying.

He had been through a hundred heartbreaks, but he found himself afraid when he thought of Alexander Lightwood breaking his heart. He did not know how this boy with the messy black hair and the worried blue eyes, with his steady hands and his rare sweet smile that was less rare in Magnus's presence, had acquired such power over him. Alec hadn't tried to get it, had never seemed to realize that he had it or tried to do anything with it.

Maybe he didn't want it. Perhaps Magnus was being a fool, as he had been so many times before. He was Alec's first experience, not a boyfriend. Alec was still nursing his first crush, on his best friend, and Magnus was a cautious experimentation, a step away from the safety that golden and much-beloved Jace represented. Jace, who looked like an angel: Jace, who, like an angel, like God himself, would never love Alec back.

Magnus might simply be a walk on the wild side, a rebellion by one of Idris's most careful sons before Alec retreated back into secrecy, circumspection. Magnus remembered Camille, who had never taken him seriously, who had never loved him at all. How much more likely was a Shadowhunter to feel that way?

His gloomy thoughts were interrupted by the sound of the buzzer.

Caroline Connor offered no explanation for her lateness. Indeed, she breezed by Magnus as if he were the doorman, and began immediately to explain her problem to the demon.

"I am part of Pandemonium Enterprises, which caters to a certain subsection of the wealthy."

"Those who have used their money and influence to purchase knowledge of the Shadow World," said Magnus. "I'm aware of your organization. It's been around quite a long time."

Ms. Conner inclined her head. "My particular area is in providing entertainment for our customers in a nautical environment. While there are other cruises in New York Harbor, we provide our customers with a gourmet meal served on a yacht with a view of the more magical denizens of the city—nixies, kelpies, mermaids, various and sundry water sprites. We make it a very exclusive experience."

"Sounds classy," gurgled Elyaas.

"However, we do not want to make it a very exclusive experience in which rebellious mermaids drag our wealthy customers to the bottom of the river," said Ms. Connor. "Unfortunately some of the mermaids do not like being stared at, and this has been occurring. I simply want you to use your infernal powers to dispatch this threat to my company's economic growth."

"Wait a second. You want to *curse* the *mermaids?*" Magnus demanded.

"I could curse some mermaids," Elyaas said agreeably. "Sure."

Magnus glared at him.

Elyaas shrugged his tentacles. "I'm a demon," he said. "I'll curse a mermaid. I'll curse a cocker spaniel. I don't care about *anything*."

"I cannot believe that I have spent a whole day watching slime rise for no reason at all. If you had told me that the problem was angry mermaids, I could have fixed it without summoning demons to curse them," said Magnus. "I have several contacts in the mermaid community, and failing that, there are always the Shadowhunters."

"Oh, yeah. Magnus is dating a Shadowhunter," Elyaas put in.

"That's personal information I'd thank you not to repeat," Magnus said. "And we're not officially dating!"

"My orders were to summon a demon," Ms. Connor said crisply. "But if you can solve the problem in a more efficient way, warlock, I am all for it. I'd prefer not to curse the mermaids; the customers like looking at them. Perhaps some monetary recompense can be arranged. Do we need to amend your contract, warlock, or are the same terms agreeable to you?"

Magnus felt somewhat tempted to argue for a pay raise, but he was already charging them a satisfyingly outrageous sum of money, and he did want to avoid having a curse fall upon all the mermaids of New York. That seemed like it could get really complicated really fast.

He agreed to sign the amended contract, he and Ms. Connor shook hands, and she departed. Magnus hoped that he would never have to see her again. Another day, another dollar. (Well, another huge pile of dollars. Magnus's special skills did not come cheap.)

Elyaas was looking extremely sulky around the tentacles about being denied the opportunity to cause chaos in Magnus's city.

"Thank you for being totally useless all day," said Magnus.

"Good luck with one of the Angel's chosen, demon's son," said Elyaas, his voice suddenly considerably sharper and less slimy. "You think he will ever do anything but despise you, in his heart of hearts? He knows where you belong. We all know it too. Your father will have you in the end. Someday your life here will seem like a dream, like a stupid child's game. Someday the Great Dark One will come and drag you down and down, with usssss . . ."

His sibilant voice trailed off into a shriek as every candle flame streaked higher and higher, until they licked the ceiling. Then he vanished, with his last cry hanging on the air.

"Should have bought a sssscented candle. . . ."

Magnus proceeded to open every window in the loft. The lingering smell of sulfur and slime had barely begun to clear when the phone in his pocket rang. Magnus pulled it out, not without difficulty—his pants were tight because he felt a responsibility to the world to be gorgeous, but it meant there was not a lot of room in the pocket region—and his heart missed a beat when he saw who the call was from.

"Hey," said Alec when Magnus answered, his voice deep and diffident.

"Why are you calling?" Magnus asked, assailed by a sudden fear that his birthday present had been immediately discovered in some way and the Lightwoods were shipping Alec to Idris because of spells cast on whips by heedless warlocks, which Alec could not explain.

"Um, I can call another time," said Alec, sounding worried. "I'm sure you have better things to do—"

He didn't say it in the way some of Magnus's past lovers would have said it, accusing or demanding reassurance. He said it quite naturally, as if he accepted that was the way of the world, that he would not be anyone's top priority. It made Magnus want to reassure him ten times as much as he would have, had Alec seemed to even slightly expect it.

"Of course I don't, Alexander," he said. "I was just surprised to hear from you. I imagined that you would be with your family on the big day."

"Oh," said Alec, and he sounded shy and pleased. "I didn't expect you to remember."

"It might have crossed my mind once or twice during the day," said Magnus. "So have you been having a wonderful Shadowhunting time? Did someone give you a giant axe in a cake? Where are you, off to celebrate?"

"Er," said Alec. "I'm kind of . . . outside your apartment?"

The buzzer rang. Magnus pressed the button to let him enter, speechless for a moment because he had wanted Alec there, so badly, and here he was. It felt more like magic than anything he could do.

Then Alec was there, standing in the open doorway.

"I wanted to see you," said Alec with devastating simplicity. "Is this okay? I can go away if you're busy or anything."

It must have been raining a little outside. There were sparkling drops of water in Alec's messy black hair. He was wearing a hoodie that Magnus thought he might have found in a Dumpster, and sloppy jeans, and his whole face was lit up just because he was looking at Magnus.

"I think," said Magnus, pulling Alec in by the strings on his awful gray hoodie, "that I could be persuaded to clear my schedule."

Then Alec was kissing him, and Alec's kisses were uninhibited and utterly sincere, all of his lanky warrior's body focused on what it wanted, all of his open heart in it as well. For a long wild euphoric moment Magnus believed that Alec did not want anything more than to be with him, that they would not be parted. Not for a long, long time.

"Happy birthday, Alexander," Magnus murmured.

"Thanks for remembering," Alec whispered back.

The Last Stand of the New York Institute

By Cassandra Clare, Sarah Rees Brennan,
and Maureen Johnson

Magnus felt for a moment as if he had become a storm, black curling clouds, the slam of thunder and slash of lightning, and all the storm wanted was to leap at Valentine's throat. Magnus's magic lashed out almost of its own volition, leaped from both hands. It looked like lightning, burning so blue that it was almost white. It knocked Valentine off his feet and into a wall. Valentine hit the wall so hard that a crack rang out, and he slid to the floor.

—The Last Stand of the New York Institute

KRAK
SLAM

New York City, 1989

The man was far too close. He lingered by the postbox about six feet away from Magnus and ate a sloppy Gray's Papaya hot dog covered in chili. When he was done, he crumpled the chili-stained wrapper and threw it onto the ground in Magnus's general direction, then tugged at a hole in his denim jacket and did not look away. It was like the look some animals gave their prey.

Magnus was used to a certain amount of attention. His clothing invited it. He wore silver Doc Martens, artfully torn jeans so huge that only a narrow shining silver belt prevented them from slipping entirely off, and a pink T-shirt so big that it exposed collarbones and quite a slice of chest—the kind of clothing that made people think about nakedness. Small earrings rimmed one ear, ending in a larger one swinging from his earlobe, an earring shaped like a large silver cat wearing a crown and a smirk. A silver ankh necklace rested at the point over his heart, and he had shrugged on a tailored black jacket with jet bead trimming, more to complement the ensemble than to protect against the night air. The look was completed by a Mohawk boasting a deep pink stripe.

And he was leaning against the outside wall of the West Village clinic long after dark. That was enough to bring out the worst in some people. The clinic was for AIDS patients. The modern plague house. Instead of showing compassion, or good sense, or care, many people regarded the clinic with hate and disgust. Every age thought they were so enlightened, and every age was stumbling around in much the same darkness of ignorance and fear.

"Freak," the man finally said.

Magnus ignored this and continued reading his book, Gilda Radner's *It's Always Something*, under the dim fluorescent light of the clinic entrance. Now annoyed by the lack of reply, the man began to mumble a string of things under his breath. Magnus couldn't hear what he was saying, but he could take an educated guess. Slurs about Magnus's perceived sexuality, no doubt.

"Why don't you move along?" Magnus said, calmly flipping a page. "I know an all-night salon. They can fix up that monobrow of yours in no time."

It wasn't the right thing to say, but sometimes these things came out. You could take only so much blind, stupid ignorance without cracking around the edges a bit.

"*What* did you say?"

Two cops walked by at that moment. They cast their eyes in the direction of Magnus and the stranger. There was a look of warning for the man, and a look of thinly veiled disgust for Magnus. The look hurt a bit, but Magnus was sadly used to this treatment. He had sworn long ago that no one would ever change him—not the mundanes who hated him for one thing, or the Shadowhunters currently hunting him for another.

The man walked off, but there were backward looks.

Magnus shoved his book into his pocket. It was almost eight o'clock and really too dark to be reading, and now he was distracted. He looked around. Only a few years before, this had been one of the most vibrant, celebratory, and creative corners of the city. Good food on every corner, and couples strolling along. Now the cafés seemed sparsely populated. The people walked quickly. So many had died, so many wonderful people. From where he was standing Magnus could see three apartments formerly occupied by friends and lovers. If he turned the corner and walked for five minutes, he'd pass a dozen more dark windows.

Mundanes died so easily. No matter how many times he saw it, it never got easier. He had lived for centuries now, and he was still waiting for death to get easier.

Normally he avoided this street for this very reason, but tonight he was waiting for Catarina to finish her shift at the clinic. He shifted from foot to foot and pulled his jacket tighter around his chest, regretting for a moment that he had chosen based on fashionable flimsiness rather than actual warmth and comfort. Summer had stayed late, and then the trees had turned their leaves quickly. Now those leaves were dropping fast and the streets were bare and unsheltered. The only bright spot was the Keith Haring mural on the clinic wall—bright cartoon figures in primary colors dancing together, a heart floating above them all.

Magnus's thoughts were interrupted by the sudden reappearance of the man, who had clearly just walked around the block and gotten himself into a total state over Magnus's comment. This time the man walked right up to Magnus and stood directly in front of him, almost toe to toe.

"Really?" Magnus said. "Go away. I'm not in the mood."

In reply the man pulled out a jackknife and flicked it open. Their close stance meant that no one else could see it.

"You realize," Magnus said, not looking at the point of the knife just below his face, "that by standing as you are, everyone will think we are kissing. And that is terribly embarrassing for me. I have *much* better taste in men."

"You think I won't do it, *freak*? You—"

Magnus's hand went up. A hot flash of blue spread between his fingers, and in the next second his assailant was flying backward across the sidewalk, then falling and striking his head against a fire hydrant. For one moment, when the man's prone form didn't move right away, Magnus was worried that he had killed the man by accident, but then Magnus saw him stir. He peered up at Magnus with his eyes narrowed, a combination of terror and fury plain on his face. He was clearly a little stunned by what had just happened. A trickle of blood ran down his forehead.

At that moment Catarina emerged. She appraised the situation quickly, went right to the fallen man, and passed her hand over his head, stopping the blood.

"Get off me!" he yelled. "You came from in there! Get off me! You got the *thing* all over you!"

"You idiot," Catarina said. "That's not how you contract HIV. I'm a nurse. Let me—"

The stranger shoved Catarina away and scrabbled to his feet. Across the street some passersby watched the exchange with mild curiosity. But when the man stumbled off, they lost interest.

"You're welcome," she said to the retreating figure. "Jackass."

She turned to Magnus. "Are you all right?"

"I'm fine," he said. "He was the one bleeding."

"Sometimes I wish I could just *let* someone like that bleed," Catarina said, taking out a tissue and wiping her hands. "What are you doing here, anyway?"

"I came here to see you home."

"You don't need to do that," she said with a sigh. "I'm fine."

"It's not safe. And you're exhausted."

Catarina was listing slightly to one side. Magnus grabbed her hand. She was so tired that Magnus saw her glamour fade for a moment, saw a wash of blue on the hand he was holding.

"I'm fine," she said again, but without much heart.

"Yes," Magnus said. "Obviously. You know, if you don't start taking care of yourself, you'll force me to come to your house and make my magically disgusting tuna soup until you feel better."

Catarina laughed. "Anything but the tuna soup."

"Then we'll eat something. Come on. I'll take you to Veselka. You need some goulash and a big piece of cake."

They walked east in silence, over slick piles of wet, crushed leaves.

Veselka was quiet, and they got a table by the window. The only people around them spoke quietly in Russian and smoked, and ate cabbage rolls. Magnus had some coffee and rugelach. Catarina made it through a large bowl of borscht, a large plate of fried pierogi with onions and applesauce, a side of Ukrainian meatballs, and a few cherry lime rickeys. It wasn't until she had finished these and ordered a dessert plate of cheese blintzes that she found the energy to speak.

"It's bad in there," she said. "It's hard."

There was little Magnus could say, so he just listened.

"The patients need me," she said, poking her straw into the ice in her otherwise empty glass. "Some of the doctors—people who should *know* better—won't even touch the patients. And it's so horrible, this disease. The way they just waste away. Nobody should die like that."

"No," Magnus said.

Catarina poked at the ice a moment longer and then leaned back in the booth and sighed deeply.

"I can't believe the *Nephilim* are causing trouble now, of all times," she said, rubbing her face with one hand. "Nephilim kids, no less. How is this even happening?"

This was the reason Magnus had waited by the clinic to walk Catarina home. It wasn't because the neighborhood was bad—the neighborhood wasn't bad. He'd waited for Catarina because it was no longer completely safe for Downworlders to be alone. He could hardly believe that Downworld was in a state of chaos and fear over the actions of a gang of stupid Shadowhunter youths.

When he had first heard the murmurings, just a few months before, Magnus had rolled his eyes. A pack of Shadowhunters, barely twenty years old, barely more than children, were rebelling against their parents' laws. Big deal. The Clave and Covenant and respected-elders shtick had always seemed to Magnus the ideal recipe for a youth revolt. This group called themselves the Circle, one Downworlder report had said, and they were led by a charismatic youth named Valentine. The group comprised some of the brightest and best of their generation.

And the Circle members were saying that the Clave did not deal harshly enough with Downworlders. That was how the wheel turned, Magnus supposed, one generation against the next—from Aloysius Starkweather, who'd wanted werewolf heads on the wall, to Will Herondale, who had tried and never quite succeeded in hiding his open heart. Today's youth thought that the Clave's policy of cold tolerance was too generous, apparently. Today's youth wanted to fight monsters, and had conveniently decided that Magnus's people were monsters, every one. Magnus sighed. This seemed like a season of hatred for all the world.

Valentine's Circle had not done much yet. Perhaps they never would do much. But they had done enough. They had roamed Idris, had gone through Portals and visited other cities on missions to aid the Institutes there, and in every city they'd visited, Downworlders had died.

There were always Downworlders who broke the Accords, and Shadowhunters made them pay for it. But Magnus had not been born yesterday, or even this century. He did not think it was a coincidence that wherever Valentine and his friends went, death followed. They were finding any excuse to rid the world of Downworlders.

"What does this Valentine kid even *want?*" Catarina asked. "What's his plan?"

"He wants death and destruction for all Downworld," said Magnus. "His plan is possibly to be a huge jerk."

"And what if they *do* come here?" Catarina asked. "What would the Whitelaws even do?"

Magnus had lived in New York for decades now, and had known the Shadowhunters of the New York Institute all that time. For the last several decades the Institute had been led by the Whitelaws. They had always been dutiful and distant. Magnus had never liked any of them, and none of them had ever liked Magnus. Magnus had no proof that they would betray an innocent Downworlder, but Shadowhunters thought so much of their own kind and their own blood that Magnus wasn't sure what the Whitelaws would do.

Magnus had gone to meet with Marian Whitelaw, the head of the Institute, and had told her of the reports from Downworld that Valentine and his little helpers were killing Downworlders who were not breaking the Accords, and then the Circle members were lying about it to the Clave afterward.

"Go to the Clave," Magnus had said to her. "Tell them to control their unruly brats."

"Control your unruly tongue," Marian Whitelaw had said coldly, "when you speak of your betters, warlock. Valentine Morgenstern is considered a most promising Shadowhunter, as are his young friends. I knew his wife, Jocelyn, when she was a child; she is a sweet and lovely girl. I will not doubt their goodness. Certainly not with no proof and based on the malicious gossip of Downworld alone."

"They are killing my people!"

"They are killing Downworlder criminals, in full compliance with the Accords. They are showing zeal in the pursuit of evil. Nothing bad can come from that. I would not expect you to understand."

Of course the Shadowhunters would not believe that their best and brightest had become just a little bit too bloodthirsty. Of course they would accept the excuses Valentine and the others gave them, and of course they would believe that Magnus and any other Downworlder who complained simply wanted criminals to escape justice.

Knowing they could not turn to the Shadowhunters, Downworlders had tried to put their own safeguards in place. A safe house had been set up in Chinatown, through an amnesty between the constantly feuding vampires and werewolves, and everybody was on the watch.

Downworlders were on their own. But then, hadn't they always been on their own?

Magnus sighed and eyed Catarina over their plates.

"Eat," he said. "Nothing's happening right now. It's possible nothing *will* happen."

"They killed a 'rogue vampire' in Chicago last week," she said, chopping into a blintz with a fork. "You know they'll want to come here."

They ate in silence, pensive on Magnus's side and exhausted on Catarina's. The check came, and Magnus paid. Catarina didn't think much about things like money. She was a nurse at a clinic with few resources, and he had ample cash on hand.

"Gotta get back," she said. She scrubbed a hand over her weary face, and Magnus saw cerulean trails in the wake of her fingertips, her glamour faltering even as she spoke.

"You are going home and sleeping," Magnus said. "I'm your friend. I know you. You deserve a night off. You should spend it indulging in wanton luxuries such as sleep."

"What if something happens?" she asked. "What if *they* come?"

"I can get Ragnor to help me."

"Ragnor's in Peru," said Catarina. "He says he finds it very peaceful without your accursed presence, and that's a direct quote."

Ragnor was wily enough that Magnus did not worry about him too much. He would never let his guard down anywhere that he did not feel completely safe.

"So it's just us," Catarina said.

Magnus knew that Catarina's heart lay with mortals, and that she was involved more for friendship's sake than because she wanted to fight Shadowhunters. Catarina had her own battles to fight, her own ground to stand on. She was more of a hero than any Shadowhunter that Magnus had ever met. The Shadowhunters had been chosen by an angel. Catarina herself had chosen to fight.

"It's looking like a quiet night," he said. "Come on. Finish up and let me take you home."

"Is this chivalry?" Catarina said with a smile. "Thought that was dead."

"Like us, it never dies."

They walked back the way they had come. It was fully dark now, and the night had taken a decidedly cold turn. There was a suggestion of rain. Catarina lived in a simple, slightly run-down walk-up off West Twenty-First Street, not too far from the clinic. The stove never worked, and the trash cans out front were always overflowing, but she never seemed to care. It had a bed and a place for her clothes. That was all she needed. She led a simpler life than Magnus.

Magnus made his way home, to his apartment farther down in the Village, off Christopher Street. His apartment was also a walk-up, and he took the steps two at a time. Unlike Catarina's, his place was extremely habitable. The walls were bright and cheerful shades of rose and daisy yellow, and the apartment was furnished in some of the items he had collected over the years—a marvelous little French table, a few Victorian settees, and an amazing art deco bedroom set entirely in mirrored glass.

Normally, on a crisp early fall night like this, Magnus would pour himself a glass of wine, put a Cure album into his CD player, crank up the volume, and wait for business to start. Night was often his working time; he had many walk-in clients, and there was always research to do or reading to catch up on.

Tonight he made a pot of strong coffee, sat in the window seat, and looked down on the street below. Tonight, like every other night since the dark murmurs of the bloodthirsty young Shadowhunters had started, he would sit and watch and think. If the Circle did come here, as it seemed that they would do eventually, what would happen? Valentine had a special hatred for werewolves, they said, but he had killed a warlock in Berlin for summoning demons. Magnus had been known to summon a demon himself a time or twenty.

It was extremely likely that if they came to New York, they would come for Magnus. The sensible thing would probably be to leave, disappear into the country. He'd gotten himself a little house in the Florida Keys to while away the brutal New York winters. The house was on one of the smaller, less inhabited islands, and he had a fine boat there as well. If anything happened, he could get in it and speed off into the sea, head for the Caribbean or South America. He'd packed a bag several times, and unpacked it right after.

There was no point in running. If the Circle continued their campaign of so-called justice, they would make the entire world unsafe for Downworlders. And there was no way Magnus could live with himself if he ran away and his friends, such as Catarina, were left to try to defend themselves. He did not like the idea of Raphael Santiago or any of his vampires being killed either, or any of the faeries he knew who worked on Broadway, or the mermaids who swam in the East River. Magnus had always thought of himself as a rolling stone, but he had lived in New York a long time now. He found himself wanting to defend not only his friends but his city.

So he was staying, and waiting, and trying to be ready for the Circle when they came.

The waiting was hardest. Maybe that was why he had engaged the man by the clinic. Something in Magnus wanted the fight to come. He wiggled and flexed his fingers, and blue light webbed between them. He opened the window and breathed in some of the night air, which smelled like a mix of rain, leaves, and pizza from the place on the corner.

"Just do it already," he said to no one.

The kid appeared under his window at around one in the morning, just when Magnus had finally been able to distract himself and start translating an old Greek text that had been on his desk for weeks. Magnus happened to look up and noticed the kid pacing confusedly outside. He was nine, maybe ten years old—a little East Village street punk in a Sex Pistols shirt that probably belonged to an older sibling, and a baggy pair of gray sweatpants. He had a ragged, home-done haircut. And he wore no coat.

All of these things added up to a kid in trouble, and the general streetwise appearance plus a certain fluidity to the walk suggested werewolf. Magnus pushed open the window.

"You looking for someone?" he called.

"Are you Magnificent Bane?"

"Sure," said Magnus. "Let's go with that. Hang on. Open the door when it buzzes."

He slid off the window seat and went to the buzzer by the door. He heard the rapid footfalls on the steps. This kid was in a hurry. Magnus had no sooner opened the door than the kid was inside. Once inside and in the light, the true extent of the boy's distress was clear. His cheeks were highly flushed and stained with dried tear trails. He was sweating despite the cold, and his voice was shaking and urgent.

"You gotta come," he said as he stumbled in. "They have my family. They're here."

"Who are here?"

"The crazy Shadowhunters everyone's freaking about. They're here. They *have my family*. You gotta come *now*."

"The Circle?"

The kid shook his head, not in disagreement but in confusion. Magnus could see he didn't know what the Circle was, but the description fit. The kid had to be talking about the Circle.

"Where are they?" Magnus asked.

"In Chinatown. The safe house." The kid almost shook with impatience. "My mom heard those freaks were here. They already killed a whole buncha vampires up in Spanish Harlem earlier tonight, they said for killing mundanes, but nobody heard of any dead mundanes, and a faerie said they were coming down to Chinatown to get us. So my mom brought all of us to the safe house, but then they broke in. I got out through a window. My mom said to come to you."

The entire story was delivered in such a jumbled, frantic rush that Magnus had no time to unpick it.

"How many are you?" he asked.

"My mom and my brother and sister and six others from my pack."

So nine werewolves in danger. The test had come, and come so quickly that Magnus had no time to really go through his feelings or think through a plan.

"Did you hear anything the Circle said?" Magnus asked. "What did the Circle accuse your family of doing?"

"They said our old pack did something, but we don't know anything about that. It doesn't matter, does it? They kill them anyway, that's what everybody's saying! You *gotta come.*"

He grabbed Magnus's hand and made to pull him. Magnus detached the boy and reached for a pad and paper.

"You," he said, scrawling down Catarina's address, "you go here. You go nowhere else. You stay there. There's a nice blue lady there. I will go to the safe house."

"I'm coming with you."

"Either you do as I say or I don't go," Magnus snapped. "There's no time to argue. You decide."

The boy teetered on the edge of tears. He wiped his eyes roughly with the back of his hand.

"You'll get them?" he asked. "You promise?"

"I promise," Magnus said.

How he was going to do that, he had no idea. But the fight had come. At last the fight had come.

The last thing Magnus did before he left was write down the details: where the safe house—a warehouse—was, what he feared the Circle was planning to do to the werewolves inside it. He folded up the piece of paper into the shape of a bird and sent it, with a flick of his fingers and a burst of blue sparks. The frail little paper bird tumbled in the wind like a pale leaf, flying out into the night and toward the towers of Manhattan, which cut the darkness like glittering knives.

He didn't know why he had bothered to send a message to the Whitelaws. He didn't think they would come.

Magnus ran through Chinatown, under neon signs that flickered and sizzled, through the yellow smog of the city that clung like begging ghosts to passersby. He ran by a huddle of people freebasing on a street corner, and then finally reached the street where the warehouse stood, its tin roof rattling in the night wind. A mundane would have seen it as smaller than it really was, shabby and dark, its windows boarded. Magnus saw the lights: Magnus saw the broken window.

There was a small voice in Magnus's head calling for caution, but Magnus had heard tell in great detail of what Valentine's Circle did to vulnerable Downworlders when they found them.

Magnus ran toward the safe house, almost stumbling in his Doc Martens over the cracked pavement. He reached the double doors, spray-painted with halos, crowns, and thorns, and flung them open wide.

In the main room of the safe house, their backs to the wall, stood a cluster of werewolves, still in human form, most of them, though Magnus could see claws and teeth on some crouching in defensive positions.

Surrounding them was a crowd of young Shadowhunters.

Everybody turned around and looked at Magnus.

Even if the Shadowhunters had been expecting an interruption, and the werewolves had been hoping for a savior, apparently nobody had been expecting all the hot pink.

The reports about the Circle were true. So many of them were heartbreakingly young, a brand-new generation of Shadowhunters, shining new warriors who had just reached adulthood. Magnus was not surprised, but he found it sad and infuriating, that they should throw the bright beginnings of their lives away on this senseless hate.

At the front of the Shadowhunter crowd stood a little cluster of people who, though they were young, had an air of authority about them—the inner circle of Valentine's Circle. Magnus did not recognize anyone who matched the description he'd heard of the ringleader.

Magnus was not certain, but he thought the current leader of the group was either the beautiful boy with the golden hair and the deep sweet blue eyes, or the young man beside him with the dark hair and narrow, intelligent face. Magnus had lived a long time, and could tell which members of a group were the leaders of the pack. Neither of these two looked imposing, but the body language of all the others deferred to them. These two were flanked by a young man and a woman, both with black hair and fierce hawklike faces, and behind the black-haired man stood a handsome curly-haired youth. Behind those stood about six more. At the other end of the room was a door, a single door rather than double doors like the ones Magnus had burst in through, an inside door that led to another chamber. A stocky young Shadowhunter stood in front of it.

There were too many of them to fight, and they were all so young and so fresh from the schoolrooms of Idris that Magnus would never have met them before. Magnus had not taught in the academy of the Shadowhunters for decades, but he remembered the rooms, the lessons of the Angel, the upturned young faces drinking in every word about their sacred duty.

And these newly adult Nephilim had come out of their schoolrooms to do this.

"Valentine's Circle, I presume?" he said, and he saw them all jolt at the words, as if they thought Downworlders did not have their own ways of passing along information when they were being hunted. "But I don't believe I see Valentine Morgenstern. I hear he has charisma enough to draw birds out of trees and convince them to live under the sea, is tall, is devastatingly handsome, and has white-blond hair. None of you fit that description."

Magnus paused.

"And you don't have white-blond hair either."

They all looked shocked to be spoken to in that manner. They were of Idris, and no doubt if they knew warlocks at all, they knew warlocks like Ragnor, who made certain to be professional and civil in all his dealings with the Nephilim. Marian Whitelaw might have told Magnus to control his unruly tongue, but she had not been shocked by his speaking out. These stupid children were content to hate from a distance, to fight and never speak to Downworlders, to never risk for a moment seeing their designated enemies as anything like people.

They thought they knew it all, and they knew so little.

"I am Lucian Graymark," said the young man with the thin clever face at the front of the group. Magnus had heard the name before—Valentine's *parabatai*, his second-in-command, dearer than a brother. Magnus disliked him as soon as he spoke. "Who are you to come here and interfere with us in the pursuit of our sworn duty?"

Graymark held his head high and spoke in a clear, authoritative voice that belied his years. He looked every inch the perfect child of the Angel, stern and merciless. Magnus looked back over his shoulder at the werewolves, huddled at the very back of the room.

Magnus lifted a hand and painted a line of magic, a shimmering barrier of blue and gold. He made the light blaze as fiercely as any angel's sword might have, and barred the Shadowhunters' way.

"I am Magnus Bane. And you are trespassing in my city."

That got a little laugh. "*Your* city?" said Lucian.

"You need to let these people go."

"Those *creatures*," said Lucian, "are part of a wolf pack that killed my *parabatai*'s parents. We tracked them down here. We can now exact Shadowhunter justice, as is our right."

"We didn't kill any Shadowhunters!" the only woman among the werewolves said. "And my children are innocent. Killing my children would be murder. Bane, you have to make him let my children go. He has my—"

"I would hear no more of your whining like a mongrel dog," said the young man with the hawklike face, the one standing beside the black-haired woman. They looked like a matched set, and the expressions on their faces were identically ferocious.

Valentine was not famed for his mercy, and Magnus did not have any confidence in his Circle's sparing the children.

The werewolves might have been partially shifted from human to wolf form, but they did not look ready to fight, and Magnus did not know why. There were too many Shadowhunters for Magnus to be sure he could fight them off successfully on his own. The best he could hope for was to stall them with conversation, and hope that he could inspire doubt in some of the Circle, or that Catarina would come or that the Whitelaws would come, and that they might stand with Downworlders and not their own kind.

It seemed a very slim hope, but it was all he had.

Magnus could not help but look again toward the golden-haired youth at the front of the group. There was something terribly familiar about him, as well as a suggestion of tenderness about his mouth, and hurt in the deep blue wells of his eyes. There was something that made Magnus look toward him as the one chance to get the Circle to turn from their purpose.

"What's your name?" Magnus asked.

Those blue eyes narrowed. "Stephen Herondale."

"I used to know the Herondales very well, once upon a time," said Magnus, and he saw it was a mistake by the way Stephen Herondale flinched. The Shadowhunter knew something, had heard some dark whisper about his family tree, then, and was desperate to prove it was not true. Magnus did not know how desperate Stephen Herondale might be, and he had no wish to find out. Magnus went on, genially addressing them all: "I have always been a friend to Shadowhunters. I know many of your families, going back for hundreds of years."

"There is nothing we can do to correct the questionable judgments of our ancestors," Lucian said.

Magnus hated this guy.

"Also," Magnus went on, pointedly ignoring Lucian Graymark, "I find your story suspect. Valentine is ready to hunt down any Downworlder on any vague pretext. What had the vampires he killed in Harlem done to him?"

Stephen Herondale frowned, and glanced at Lucian, who looked troubled in turn, but said, "Valentine told me he went hunting some vampires who broke the Accords there."

"Oh, the Downworlders are all so guilty. And that is so very convenient for you, isn't it? What about their children? The boy who came to collect me was about nine. Has he been dining on Shadowhunter flesh?"

"The pups gnaw on whatever bones their elders drag in," muttered the black-haired woman, and the man beside her nodded.

"Maryse, Robert, please. Valentine is a noble man!" Lucian said, his voice rising as he turned to address Magnus. "He would not hurt a child. Valentine is my *parabatai*, my best beloved swordbrother. His fight is mine. His family has been destroyed, the Accords have been broken, and he deserves and will have his vengeance. Stand aside, warlock."

Lucian Graymark did not have his hand on his weapon, but Magnus saw that the black-haired woman, Maryse, behind him had a blade shining between her fingers. Magnus looked again at Stephen and realized exactly why his face was so familiar. Gold hair and blue eyes—he was a more ethereal and slender version of a young Edmund Herondale, as though Edmund had come back from heaven, twice as angelic. Magnus had not known

Edmund for long, but Edmund had been the father of Will Herondale, who had been one of the very few Shadowhunters that Magnus had ever thought of as a friend.

Stephen saw Magnus looking. Stephen's eyes had narrowed so much now that the sweet blue of them was lost, and they seemed black.

"Enough of this byplay with demonspawn!" said Stephen. He sounded as if he were quoting somebody, and Magnus bet that he knew who.

"Stephen, don't—" Lucian ordered, but golden-haired Stephen had already flung a knife in the direction of one werewolf.

Magnus flicked his hand and sent the knife dropping to the ground. He glared at the werewolves. The woman who had spoken before stared intensely back at him, as if trying to convey a message with her eyes alone.

"This is what the modern young Shadowhunter has become, is it?" Magnus asked. "Let me see, how does your little bedtime story about how super-duper extra special you all are go again? . . . Ah, yes. Through the ages your mandate has been to protect mankind, to fight against evil forces until they are finally vanquished and the world can live in peace. You don't seem terribly interested in peace or protecting anybody. What is it that you're fighting for, exactly?"

"I am fighting for a better world for myself and my son," said the woman called Maryse.

"I have no interest in the world you want," Magnus told her. "Or in your doubtless repellent brat, I might add."

Robert drew a dagger from his sleeve. Magnus was not prepared to waste all his magic deflecting daggers. He lifted a hand into the air, and all the light in the room was quenched. Only the noise and neon glow of the city spilled in, not providing enough illumination to see by, but Robert threw the dagger just the same. That was when the glass of the windows broke and dark forms came flooding in: young Rachel Whitelaw landed in a roll on the floor in front of Magnus, and took the blade meant for him in her shoulder.

Magnus could see better in the dark than most. He saw that, past all hope, the Whitelaws had come. Marian Whitelaw, the head of the Institute; her husband, Adam; and Adam's brother; and the young Whitelaw cousins whom Marian and Adam had taken in after their parents' deaths. The Whitelaws had already been fighting tonight. Their gear was bloodstained and torn, and Rachel Whitelaw was clearly wounded. There was blood in Marian's gray bob of hair, but Magnus did not think it was hers. Marian and Adam Whitelaw, Magnus happened to know, had not been able to have their own children. The word was that they adored the young cousins who lived with them, that they always made a fuss over any young Shadowhunters who came to their Institute. The Circle members must have been peers of the Whitelaw cousins, brought up together in Idris. The Circle was exactly designed to win the Whitelaws' sympathy.

The Circle was, however, in a panic. They could not see as Magnus could. They did not know who was attacking them, only that somebody had come to Magnus's aid. Magnus saw the swing and heard the clash of blades meeting, so loud it was almost impossible to hear Marian Whitelaw's shouted commands for the Circle to stop and drop their weapons. He wondered which of the Circle even realized who they were fighting.

He conjured a small light in his palm and searched for the werewolf woman. He had to know why the werewolves would not attack.

Someone knocked into him. Magnus stared into the eyes of Stephen Herondale.

"Do you never have doubts about all this?" Magnus breathed.

"No," Stephen panted. "I have lost too much—I have sacrificed too much to this great cause ever to turn my back on it now."

As he spoke, he swung his knife up toward Magnus's throat. Magnus turned the hilt hot in the young man's hand until he dropped it.

Magnus suddenly did not care what Stephen had sacrificed, or about the pain in his blue eyes. He wanted Stephen gone from this earth. Magnus wanted to forget he had ever seen Stephen Herondale's face, so full of hate and so reminiscent of faces Magnus had loved. The warlock summoned a new spell into his hand and was about to hurl it at Stephen, when a thought arrested him. He did not know how he could face Tessa again if he killed one of her descendants.

Then Marian Whitelaw stepped into the light from the spell shimmering in Magnus's palm, and Stephen's face went blank with surprise.

"Ma'am, it's you! We shouldn't— We're Shadowhunters. We shouldn't be fighting over them. They are *Downworlders*," Stephen hissed. "They will turn on you like the treacherous dogs they are. That's their nature. They are not worth fighting for. What do you say?"

"I don't have any proof these werewolves broke the Accords."

"Valentine said," began Stephen, but Magnus heard the uncertainty in his voice. Lucian Graymark might believe they only hunted Downworlders who had broken the Accords, but Stephen at least knew they were acting as vigilantes rather than Law-abiding Shadowhunters. Stephen had been doing it, just the same.

"I do not care what Valentine Morgenstern says. I say that the Law is hard," Marian Whitelaw replied. She drew her blade, swung, and met Stephen's.

Their eyes met, glittering, over their blades.

Marian continued softly, "But it is the Law. You will not touch these Downworlders while I or any of my blood live."

Chaos erupted, but Magnus's darkest imaginings had been proved wrong. When the fight was joined, there were Shadowhunters on his side, fighting with him against Shadowhunters, fighting for Downworlders and the Accords of peace they had all agreed to.

The first fatality was the youngest Whitelaw. Rachel Whitelaw lunged at the woman called Maryse, and the sheer ferocity of the attack took Maryse aback so much that Rachel almost had her. Maryse stumbled and collected herself, fumbling for a new blade. Then the black-haired man, Robert, who Magnus thought was her husband, lunged at Rachel in his turn, and ran her through.

Rachel sagged, the point of the man's blade like a pin piercing her, as if she were a butterfly.

"Robert!" said Maryse softly, as if she could not believe this was happening.

Robert unsheathed his sword from Rachel's chest, and Rachel tumbled to the floor.

"Rachel Whitelaw was just killed by a Shadowhunter," shouted Magnus, and even then he thought Robert might cry out that he had been defending his wife. Magnus thought that the Whitelaws might put away their blades rather than spill more Nephilim blood.

But Rachel had been the baby of the family, everyone's special pet. The Whitelaws as one roared a challenge and hurled themselves into the fray with redoubled ferocity. Adam Whitelaw, a stolid white-haired old man who had always seemed to simply follow his wife's lead, charged at Valentine's Circle, whirling a shining axe over his head, and cut down all those who stood before him.

Magnus edged toward the werewolves, to the woman who was the only one who remained human, even though her teeth and claws were growing apace.

"Why aren't you fighting?" he demanded.

The werewolf woman glared at him as if he were impossibly stupid.

"Because Valentine's here," she snapped. "Because he has my daughter. He took her through there, and they said if we moved to follow her, they would kill her."

Magnus did not have an instant to reflect on what Valentine might do to a helpless Downworlder child. He lifted a hand and blasted from his feet the stocky Shadowhunter at the single door at the far end of the room, and then Magnus ran toward the door.

He heard the cries behind him, of the Whitelaws demanding, "Bane, where are you—" and a shout, Magnus thought from Stephen, saying, "He's going after Valentine! Kill him!"

Behind the door Magnus heard a low, awful sound. He pushed the door open.

On the other side of the door was a small ordinary room, the size of a bedroom, though there was no bed, only two people and a single chair. There was a tall man with a fall of white-blond hair, wearing Shadowhunter black. He was stooped over a girl who looked about twelve. She was fastened to the chair with silver cord, and was making a terrible low sound, a cross between a whine and a moan.

Her eyes were shining, Magnus thought for a moment, the moonlight turning them into mirrors.

His mistake lasted for the briefest of instants. Then Valentine moved slightly and the gleam of the girl's eyes resolved in Magnus's vision. The gleam was not her eyes. The moonlit shine was silver coins pressed to the girl's eyes, tiny wisps of smoke escaping from beneath the bright discs as the tiny sounds escaped from between her lips. She was trying to suppress the sound of her pain, because she was so scared of what Valentine would do to her next.

"Where did your brother go?" demanded Valentine, and the girl's sobbing continued, but she said nothing.

Magnus felt for a moment as if he had become a storm, black curling clouds, the slam of thunder and slash of lightning, and all the storm wanted was to leap at Valentine's throat. Magnus's magic lashed out almost of its own volition, leaped from both hands. It looked like lightning, burning so blue that it was almost white. It knocked Valentine off his feet and into a wall. Valentine hit the wall so hard that a crack rang out, and he slid to the floor.

That one act also used up far too much of Magnus's power, but he could not think of that now. He ran over to the girl's chair and wrenched the chain off her, then touched her face with painful gentleness.

She was crying now, more freely, shuddering and sobbing beneath his hands.

"Hush, hush. Your brother sent me. I'm a warlock; you're safe," he murmured, and clasped the back of her neck.

The coins were hurting her. They had to come off. But would removing them do more damage? Magnus could heal, but it had never been his specialty as it was Catarina's, and he had not had to heal werewolves often. They were so resilient. He could only hope she would be resilient now.

He lifted the coins as gently as he could, and threw them against the wall.

It was too late. It had been too late before he'd ever entered the room. She was blind.

Her lips parted. She said, "Is my brother safe?"

"As safe as can be, sweetheart," said Magnus. "I'll take you to him."

No sooner had he said the word "him" than he felt the cold blade sink into his back and his mouth fill with hot blood.

"Oh, will you?" asked Valentine's voice in his ear.

The blade slid free, hurting as much on the way out as it had on the way in. Magnus gritted his teeth and gripped the back of the chair harder, kept himself arched over and protecting the child, and turned his head to face Valentine. The white-haired man looked older than the other leaders, but Magnus was not sure if he was actually older or if cold purpose simply made his face seem carved from marble. Magnus wanted to smash it.

Valentine's hand moved, and Magnus only just managed to catch Valentine's wrist before he found Valentine's blade in his heart.

Magnus concentrated and made the clasp of his hand burn,

blue electricity circling his fingers. He made the contact burn as the touch of silver had burned the girl, and he grinned as he heard Valentine's hiss of pain.

Valentine did not ask his name as the others had, did not treat Magnus as that much of a person. Valentine simply stared at Magnus with cold eyes, the same way anyone might stare at a loathsome animal in their path and impeding their progress. "You are interfering in my business, warlock."

Magnus spat blood into his face. "You are torturing a child in my city. Shadowhunter."

Valentine used his free hand to deal Magnus a blow that sent Magnus staggering back. Valentine wheeled and followed him, and Magnus thought, *Good.* It meant that he was moving away from the girl.

She was blind, but she was a werewolf, smell and sound as important to her as sight. She could run, and find her way back to her family.

"I thought we were playing a game where we said what the other person was and what we were doing," Magnus told him. "Did I get it wrong? Can I guess again? Are you breaking your own sacred Laws, asshole?"

He glanced at the girl, hoping she would run, but she seemed frozen to the spot with terror. Magnus did not dare call out to her in case it attracted Valentine's attention.

Magnus lifted a hand, sketching a spell in the air, but Valentine saw the spell coming and dodged it. He leaped into the air and then bounded off the wall, Nephilim-swift, to lunge at Magnus. He scythed Magnus's legs out from under him, and when Magnus landed, Valentine kicked him brutally hard. He drew a sword and brought it down. Magnus rolled so that it caught him a glancing blow along the ribs, cutting through shirt and skin but not hitting vital organs. Not this time.

Magnus dearly hoped he was not going to die here, in this cold warehouse, far from anyone he loved. He tried to rise from the floor, but it was slippery with his own blood, and the scraps of magic he had were not enough to heal or fight, let alone both.

Marian Whitelaw stood in front of him, her blades drawn and new runes shining on her arms. Her hair shone silver in his blurred vision.

Valentine swung his sword, and cut her almost in half.

Magnus gasped, salvation lost as quickly as it had been found, then turned his head toward the sound of more footsteps on the stone.

He was a fool to have hoped for another rescue. He saw one of Valentine's Circle, standing in the doorway with his eyes fixed on the werewolf girl.

"Valentine!" Lucian Graymark shouted. He ran for the girl, and Magnus tensed, coiled himself for a leap, and then froze as he saw Lucian pick the girl up and wheel on his master. "How could you do this? She's a child!"

"No, Lucian. She's a monster in the shape of a child."

Lucian was holding the girl, his hand in her hair, soothing and stroking. Magnus was starting to think he might have really misjudged Lucian Graymark. Valentine's face was as white as bone. He resembled a statue more than ever.

Valentine said slowly, "Did you not promise me unconditional obedience? Tell me, what use have I for a second-in-command who undermines me like this?"

"Valentine, I love you and I share your grief," said Lucian.

"I know you are a good man. I know if you stop and think, you will see that this is madness."

When Valentine took a step toward him, Lucian took a step back. He curved his hand protectively over the werewolf girl's head as she clung to him with her small legs locked around his waist, and his other hand wavered as if he might go for his weapon.

"Very well," Valentine said gently, at last. "Have it your way."

He stood aside to let Lucian Graymark pass through the door and out into the corridor, and back into the room where the werewolves had thought they might be safe. He let Lucian bring the werewolves' daughter back to them, and followed him at a distance.

Magnus did not trust Valentine for an instant. He would not believe the girl was safe until she was in her mother's arms.

Lucian Graymark had bought Magnus enough time to gather up his magic. Magnus concentrated, felt his skin knit even as his power drained away.

He pulled himself up from the floor, and ran after them.

The fight in the room they had left was quieter, because there were so many dead. Someone had managed to turn the lights back on. There was a wolf lying dead on the ground, transforming inch by inch into a pale young man. Another young man lay dead beside him, one of the Circle, and in death they did not look so different.

Many of the Shadowhunters in Valentine's Circle were still standing. None of the Whitelaws were. Maryse Lightwood had her face in her hands. Some of the others were visibly shaken.

Now the shadows and the frenzy of battle had receded, and they were left in the light to look at what they had done.

"Valentine," Maryse said, her voice imploring as her leader approached. "Valentine, what have we done? The Whitelaws are dead. . . . Valentine . . ."

They all looked to Valentine as he approached, clustered up to him like frightened children rather than adults. Valentine must have gotten hold of them very young, Magnus thought, but he found himself unable to care if they were brainwashed or deluded, not after what they had done. It seemed like there was no pity left in him.

"You have done nothing but try to uphold the Law," said Valentine. "You know that all traitors to our kind must pay one day. If they had chosen to step aside, to trust us, their fellow children of the Angel, all would have been well."

"What about the Clave?" said the curly-haired man, a note of challenge in his voice.

"Michael," murmured Maryse's husband.

"What of them, Wayland?" Valentine asked, his voice sharp. "The Whitelaws died because of rogue werewolves. It is the truth, and we will tell the Clave so."

The only one of Valentine's Circle not desperately listening was Lucian Graymark. He made his way to the werewolf woman, and placed the little girl into her arms. Magnus heard the woman's indrawn breath as she saw her daughter's eyes. He heard her begin to cry softly. Lucian stood beside the mother and daughter, looking deeply distressed, then crossed the floor with a suddenly determined tread.

"Let's go, Valentine," he said. "All this with the Whitelaws was . . . was a terrible accident. We can't have our Circle suffering for it. We should go now. These creatures aren't worth your time, not any of them. These werewolves are just strays who broke off from their pack. You and I will go hunting in the werewolf encampment where the real threat lies tonight. We will bring down the pack leader together."

"Together. But tomorrow night. Come back to the house tonight?" Valentine asked in a low voice. "Jocelyn has something to tell you."

Lucian clasped Valentine's arm, clearly relieved. "Of course. Anything for Jocelyn. Anything for either of you. You know that."

"My friend," said Valentine, "I do."

Valentine clasped Lucian's arm in return, but Magnus saw the look Valentine gave Lucian. There was love in that look, but hate as well, and the hate was winning. It was as clear as a silvery shark's fin in the dark waters of Valentine's black eyes. There was death in those eyes.

Magnus was not surprised. He had seen many monsters who could love, but only a few who had let that love change them, who had been able to alchemize love for one person into kindness for many.

He remembered Valentine's face as the Circle's leader had cut Marian Whitelaw into bloody halves, and Magnus wondered what it would be like, living with someone like Valentine, wondered what it was like for his wife, who Marian had described as lovely. You could share your bed with a monster, lay your head on the same pillow next to a head filled with murder and madness. Magnus had done it himself.

But love that blind did not last. One day you lifted your head from the pillow and saw you were living in a nightmare.

Lucian Graymark might be the only one of the lot worth bothering with, and Magnus would bet he was as good as dead.

Magnus had been so terribly wrong to let the past deceive him; he'd been wrong to think that the one with depths of goodness in him was Stephen Herondale. Magnus looked at Stephen, at his beautiful face and his weak mouth. Magnus had a sudden impulse to tell the Shadowhunter that Magnus knew and loved his ancestor, that Tessa would be so disappointed in him. But he did not want Valentine's Circle to remember or go after Tessa.

Magnus said nothing. Stephen Herondale had chosen his side, and Magnus had chosen his.

Valentine's Circle withdrew from the warehouse, marching like a little army.

Magnus ran to where old Adam Whitelaw lay in a pool of blood, his shining axe lying, dull and still, in the same dark pool.

"Marian?" Adam asked. Magnus went to his knees in the pool, hands searching to find and close the worst of the wounds. There were so many—too many.

Magnus looked at Adam's eyes, where the light was going out, and knew Adam read the answer on his face before Magnus could think to lie to him.

"My brother?" Adam asked. "The—the children?"

Magnus looked around the room at the dead. When he looked back, Adam Whitelaw had turned his face away and set his mouth so that he would not betray either pain or grief. Magnus used all the magic he had left to ease the man's pain, and in the end Adam lifted a hand and stilled Magnus's, rested his head against Magnus's arm.

"Enough, warlock," he said, his voice rasping. "I would

not—I would not live if I could." He coughed, a wet terrible sound, and shut his eyes.

"*Ave atque vale*, Shadowhunter," Magnus whispered. "Your angel would be proud."

Adam Whitelaw did not seem to hear. It was only a very short time later that the last of the Whitelaws died in Magnus's arms.

The Clave believed that the Whitelaws had been killed by rogue werewolves, and nothing Magnus said made any difference. He had not expected them to believe him. He hardly knew why he spoke out, except that the Nephilim so clearly preferred that he be silent.

Magnus waited for the Circle to return.

The Circle did not come to New York again, but Magnus did see them one more time. He saw them at the Uprising.

Not long after the night in the warehouse, Lucian Graymark disappeared as if he had died, and Magnus assumed he had. Then a year later Magnus had word of Lucian again. Ragnor Fell told Magnus there was a werewolf who had once been a Shadowhunter, and that he was spreading word that the time had come, that Downworld had to be ready to fight the Circle. Valentine unveiled his plan and armed his Circle at the time when the Accords of peace between Nephilim and Downworlders were to be signed again. His Circle cut down Shadowhunters and Downworlders alike in the Great Hall of the Angel.

Thanks to Lucian Graymark's warning, Downworlders were able to rush into the Hall and surprise Valentine's Circle. They'd been forewarned and also heavily forearmed.

The Shadowhunters surprised Magnus then, as the Whitelaws had surprised him before. The Clave did not abandon the Downworlders and turn to join with the Circle. The vast majority of them, the Clave and the Institute leaders, made the choice the Whitelaws had made before them. They fought for their sworn allies and for peace, and Valentine's Circle was defeated.

But once the battle was done, the Shadowhunters blamed Downworlders for the deaths of so many of their people, as if the battle had been Downworld's idea. The Shadowhunters prided themselves on their justice, but their justice for Magnus's kind was always bitter.

Relations between the Nephilim and Downworld did not improve. Magnus despaired that they ever would.

Especially when the Clave sent the last remaining members of the Circle, the Lightwoods and another Circle member called Hodge Starkweather, to Magnus's city, to atone for their crimes by running the New York Institute as exiles from the Glass City. The Shadowhunters were scarce enough after the massacre, and could not be replenished without the Mortal Cup, which seemed to have been lost with Valentine. The Lightwoods knew that they had been treated mercifully due to their high connections in the Clave, and that if they slipped up once, the Clave would crush them.

Raphael Santiago of the vampires, who owed Magnus a favor or twenty, reported that the Lightwoods were distant but scrupulously fair with every Downworlder they came into contact with. Magnus knew that sooner or later he would have to work with them, would learn to be civil to them, but he preferred that it be later. The whole bloody tragedy of Valentine's

Circle was over, and Magnus would rather not look back on the darkness but look forward and hope for light.

For more than two years after the Uprising, Magnus didn't see any of Valentine's Circle again. Until he did.

New York City, 1993

The life of warlocks was one of immortality, magic, glamour, and excitement through the ages.

Sometimes, though, Magnus wanted to stay in and watch television on the sofa like everyone else. He was curled up on the sofa with Tessa, and they were watching a video of *Pride and Prejudice*. Tessa was complaining at some length about how the book was better.

"This is not what Jane Austen would have wanted," Tessa told him. "If she could see this, I am certain she would be horrified."

Magnus uncurled from the sofa and went to stand by the window. He was expecting some Chinese to be delivered, and he was starving from a long day of idleness and debauchery. He did not see a deliveryman, though. The only person on the street was a young woman carrying a baby wrapped up tight against the cold. She was walking fast, no doubt on her way home.

"If Jane Austen could see this," Magnus said, "I assume she would be screaming, 'There are tiny demons in this little box! Fetch a clergyman!' and hitting the television with her parasol."

The doorbell rang, and Magnus turned away from the window.

"Finally," Magnus said, grabbing a ten-dollar bill from a table near the door, and he buzzed the deliveryman in. "I need some beef and broccoli before I face any more Mr. Darcy. It's a truth universally acknowledged that if you watch too much television on an empty stomach, your head falls off."

"If your head fell off," Tessa said, "the hairdressing industry would go into an economic meltdown."

Magnus nodded and touched his hair, which was now in a chin-length sweep. He opened the door, still in his pose, and found himself staring at a woman with a crown of red curls. She was holding a child. She was the woman he had seen on the street moments ago. Magnus was startled to see someone at his door who looked so . . . mundane.

The young woman was dressed in sloppy jeans and a tie-dyed T-shirt. She lowered her hand, which had been raised as if to knock on the door, and Magnus saw the flicker of faded, silvery scars on her arm. Magnus had seen far too many of those to ever be mistaken.

She bore Covenant Marks, carried the remnants of old runes on her skin like mementos. She was not mundane in the least, then. She was a Shadowhunter, but a Shadowhunter bearing no fresh Marks, not dressed in gear.

She was not here on official Shadowhunter business. She was trouble.

"Who are you?" Magnus demanded.

She swallowed, and replied, "I am—I was Jocelyn Morgenstern."

The name conjured up memories years old. Magnus remembered the blade going into his back and the taste of blood. It made him want to spit.

The monster's bride at his door. Magnus could not stop staring.

She was staring too. She seemed transfixed by his pajamas. Magnus was frankly offended. He had not invited any wives of crazed hate-cult leaders to come around and pass judgment on his wardrobe. If he wished to forgo a shirt and wear scarlet drawstring pajamas patterned with black polar bears, and a black silk bed jacket, he could do so. None of the others who had been lucky enough to see Magnus in his bedroom attire had ever complained.

"I don't remember ordering the bride of an evil maniac," said Magnus. "It was definitely beef and broccoli. What about you, Tessa? Did *you* order the bride of an evil maniac?"

He swung the door open wider so Tessa could see who was there. Nothing else was said for a moment. Then Magnus saw the blanket-covered lump in Jocelyn's arms stir. It was in that moment that he remembered there was a child.

"I have come here, Magnus Bane," Jocelyn said, "to beg your aid."

Magnus gripped the edge of the door until his knuckles went white.

"Let me think," he said. "No."

He was stopped by Tessa's voice, soft. "Let her in, Magnus," she said.

Magnus wheeled around to look at Tessa. "Seriously?"

"I want to speak with her."

Tessa's voice had taken on a strange tone. Also, the delivery person had just appeared in the hall carrying their bag of food. Magnus nodded Jocelyn inside, handed over the ten dollars, and shut the door on the confused man's face before he had a chance to hand over the food.

Now Jocelyn stood awkwardly by the door. The tiny person

in her arms kicked its feet and stretched its legs.

"You have a baby," Magnus said, pointing out what was now obvious.

Jocelyn shifted uncomfortably and clutched the baby to her chest.

Tessa padded toward them silently and stood by Jocelyn. Even though she wore black leggings and an oversize gray T-shirt that read WILLIAM WANTS A DOLL, she still always carried an air of formality and authority about her. The shirt, as it happened, was a feminist statement that boys liked to play with dolls and girls with trucks, but Magnus suspected she had chosen it partly because of the name. Tessa's husband had been dead for long enough that his name brought back happy, faded memories instead of the raw agony she had felt for years after his passing. Other warlocks had loved and lost, but few were as hopelessly faithful as Tessa. Decades later she had not allowed anyone else to even come close to winning her heart.

"Jocelyn Fairchild," Tessa said. "Descended from Henry Branwell and Charlotte Fairchild."

Jocelyn blinked as if she had not been expecting a lecture on her own genealogy.

"That's right," she said cautiously.

"I knew them, you see," Tessa explained. "You have a great look of Henry."

"*Knew* them? Then you must be . . ."

Henry had been dead for the better part of a century, and Tessa looked no older than twenty-five.

"Are you a warlock too, then?" Jocelyn asked suspiciously. Magnus saw her eyes drift from the top of Tessa's head to her feet, searching for a demon's mark, the sign that would indicate to Shadowhunters that she was unclean, inhuman, and to be despised. Some warlocks could hide their marks under their clothes, but Jocelyn could look at as much of Tessa as she wished and never find a mark.

Tessa did not draw herself up obtrusively, but it was clear suddenly that Tessa was taller than Jocelyn was, and her gray eyes could be very cold.

"I am," said Tessa. "I am Theresa Gray, daughter of a Greater Demon and Elizabeth Gray, who was born Adele Starkweather, one of your kind. I was the wife of William Herondale, who was the head of the London Institute, and I was the mother of James and Lucie Herondale. Will and I raised our Shadowhunter children to protect mundanes, to live by the Laws of Clave and Covenant, and to keep to the Accords."

She spoke in the way she well knew how, in the manner of the Nephilim.

"Once, I lived among the Shadowhunters," Tessa said softly. "Once I might almost have seemed like a person to you."

Jocelyn looked lost, in the way that people did when they learned something so strange that the whole world seemed unfamiliar.

"I understand if you find my crimes against Downworlders unforgivable," Jocelyn said, "but I—I have nowhere else to go. And I need help. My daughter needs your help. She is a Shadowhunter and Valentine's daughter. She cannot live among her own kind. We can never go back. I need a spell to shield her eyes from all but the mundane world. She can grow up safe and happy in the mundane world. She never needs to know what her father was." Jocelyn almost choked, but she lifted her chin and added, "Or what her mother did."

"So you come begging to us," Magnus said. "The monsters."

"I have no quarrel with Downworlders," Jocelyn said at last. "I . . . my best friend is a Downworlder, and I do not believe he is so changed from the person I always loved. I was wrong. I'll have to live forever with what I did. But please, my daughter did nothing."

Her best friend, the Downworlder. Magnus supposed that Lucian Graymark was still alive, then, though nobody had seen him since the Uprising. Magnus thought a little better of Jocelyn for claiming him as her best friend. People did say she and Lucian had planned to defeat Valentine together, though Jocelyn had not been there to confirm the rumor after the battle. Magnus had not seen Jocelyn during the Uprising. He had not known whether to believe the claim or not.

Magnus had often considered that Shadowhunter justice was more like cruelty, and he did not want to be cruel. He looked at the woman's weary desperate face and the bundle in her arms, and he could not be cruel. He believed in redemption, the inchoate grace in every person he met. It was one of the few things he had to believe in, the possibility of beauty when faced with the reality of so much ugliness.

"You said you were married to a Herondale." Jocelyn appealed to Tessa, voice as faint as if she could already see the weakness of this argument but she had none other to make. "Stephen Herondale was my friend—"

"Stephen Herondale would have killed me if he'd ever met me," said Tessa. "I would not have been safe living among people like you, or like him. I am the wife and mother of warriors who fought and died and never dishonored themselves as you have. I have worn gear, wielded blades, and slain demons, and all I wished was to overcome evil so that I could live and be happy with those I loved. I'd hoped I had made this a better, safer world for my children. Because of Valentine's Circle, the Herondale line, the line that was my son's children's children, is finished. That happened through you and your Circle and your husband. Stephen Herondale died with hate in his heart and the blood of my people on his hands. I can imagine no more horrible way for mine and Will's line to end. I will have to carry for the rest of my life the wound of what Valentine's Circle has done to me, and I will live forever."

Tessa paused, and looked at Jocelyn's white despairing face, and then said, more gently, "But Stephen Herondale made his own choices, and you have made other choices besides the one to hate. I know that Valentine could not have been defeated without your help. And your child has done no wrong to anybody."

"That does not mean she has a right to our help," Magnus interrupted. He didn't want to reject Jocelyn, but there was still a nagging voice inside him that told him she was an enemy. "Besides which, I am not a Shadowhunter charity, and I doubt she has the money to pay for my help. Fugitives are so seldom well funded."

"I'll find the money," said Jocelyn. "I am not a charity case, and I am not a Shadowhunter any longer. I want nothing more to do with the Shadowhunters. I want to be someone else. I want to raise my daughter to be someone else, not bound to the Clave or led astray by anybody. I want her to be braver than I was, stronger than I was, and to let nobody decide her fate but herself."

"Nobody could ask for more than that for their child," Tessa said, and edged closer. "May I hold her?"

Jocelyn hesitated for a moment, holding the tightly wrapped bundle of the child close. Then slowly, reluctantly, her movements almost jerky, she leaned forward and placed her baby with enormous care into the arms of a woman she had just met.

"She's beautiful," Tessa murmured. Magnus did not know if Tessa had held a baby in decades, but she moved the child to her hip, held fast in the circle of her arm, with the instinctive loving and casual air of a parent. Magnus had seen her once, holding one of her grandchildren in just this way. "What's her name?"

"Clarissa," said Jocelyn, looking at Tessa intently, and then, as if she were telling them a secret, she said, "I call her Clary."

Magnus looked over Tessa's shoulder and into the child's face. The girl was older than Magnus had thought, small for her age, but her face had lost the roundness of babyhood: she must be almost two, and already looked like her mother. She looked like a Fairchild. She had red curls, the same color Henry's had been, clustering on her small head, and green eyes, glass-clear and jewel-bright and blinking around curiously at her surroundings. She did not seem to object to being handed to a stranger. Tessa tucked the baby's blanket more securely around her, and Clary's small fat fist closed determinedly around Tessa's finger. The child waved Tessa's finger back and forth, as if to display her new possession.

Tessa smiled down at the baby, a slow bright smile, and whispered, "Hello, Clary."

It was clear that Tessa at least had made up her mind. Magnus leaned in, his shoulder resting lightly against Tessa's, and peered into the child's face. He waved to catch her attention, moving his fingers so all his rings sparkled in the light.

Clary laughed, all pearly teeth and the purest joy, and Magnus felt the knot of resentment in his chest ease.

Clary wriggled in a clear and imperious signal that she wanted to be let down, but Tessa handed her to Jocelyn so that Clary's mother could decide whether she should be put down or not. Jocelyn might not want her child roaming a warlock's home.

Jocelyn did look around apprehensively, but either she decided it was safe or small, intently squirming Clary was stubborn and her mother knew she would have to let her go free. She put Clary down, and Clary went toddling determinedly off on her quest. They stood and watched her bright little head bob as she grabbed up, in turn, Tessa's book, one of Magnus's candles (which Clary chewed on thoughtfully for a moment), and a silver tray Magnus had left under the sofa.

"Curious little thing, isn't she?" Magnus asked. Jocelyn glanced toward Magnus. Her eyes had been anxiously fastened on her child. Magnus found himself smiling at her. "Not a bad quality," he assured her. "She could grow up to be an adventurer."

"I want her to grow up to be safe and happy," said Jocelyn. "I don't want her to have adventures. Adventures happen when life is cruel. I want her to have a mundane life, quiet and sweet, and I hoped she would be born not able to see the Shadow World. It is no world for a child. But I've never had much luck with hope. I saw her trying to play with a faerie in a hedge this afternoon. I need you to help me. I need you to help her. Can you blind her to all that?"

"Can I tear away an essential part of your child's nature, and twist her into a shape that would suit you better?" Magnus asked her. "If you want her mad by the end of it."

He regretted the words as soon as he had spoken. Jocelyn stared at him, white-faced, as if she had just been hit. But Jocelyn Morgenstern was not the kind of woman who wept, not the kind of woman who broke, or Valentine would have broken her long since. She held herself tall and asked, her voice level, "Is there anything else you can do?"

"There is . . . something else I could try," said Magnus.

He did not say that he would. He kept his eyes on the little girl, and thought of the young werewolf girl Valentine had blinded, of Edmund Herondale stripped of his Marks centuries ago, and of Tessa's Jamie and Lucie and all they had borne. He would not give up a child to the Shadowhunters, for whom the Law came before mercy.

Clary espied Magnus's poor cat. The Great Catsby, who was getting on in years, lay prone upon a velvet cushion, his fluffy gray tail spilling over it.

The adults all saw that disaster was imminent. They took a step forward, as one, but Clary had already firmly pulled the Great Catsby's tail, with the regal assured air of a countess reaching for the bellpull to summon her maid.

The Great Catsby gave a piteous meow to protest the indignity, turned, and scratched Clary, and Clary began to scream. Jocelyn was on her knees beside Clary the next instant, her red hair like a veil over her child, as if she could somehow screen Clary from all the world.

"Is she part banshee?" Magnus asked over the piercing wail. Clary sounded like a police siren. Magnus felt as if he were going to be arrested for the twenty-seventh time. Jocelyn glared at him through her hair, and Magnus lifted his hands in mock surrender. "Oh, pardon me for implying that the bloodlines of Valentine's child are anything less than pure."

"Come on, Magnus," Tessa said quietly. She had loved so many more Shadowhunters than Magnus ever had. She went and stood beside Jocelyn. She put a hand against Jocelyn's shoulder, and Jocelyn did not shake her hand off.

"If you want the child safe," said Magnus, "she doesn't need only a spell to hide her own Sight. She needs to be protected from the supernatural as well, from any demons who might come crawling to her."

"And what Iron Sister and Silent Brother will do that ceremony for me without turning Clary and me over to the Clave?" Jocelyn demanded. "No. I can't risk it. If she knows nothing of the Shadow World, she will be safe."

"My mother was a Shadowhunter who knew nothing of the Shadow World," said Tessa. "That didn't keep her safe."

Jocelyn stared at Tessa in open horror, obviously able to infer the story of what had happened: that a demon had gained access to an unprotected Shadowhunter woman, and Tessa had been the result.

There was a silence. Clary had turned curiously to Tessa as Tessa had approached, her screams forgotten. Now she lifted her chubby little arms out to Tessa. Jocelyn let Tessa take Clary again, and this time Clary did not try to wriggle away from her. Clary wiped her small tearstained face against Tessa's T-shirt. It seemed to be a gesture of affection. Magnus hoped nobody would offer Clary to him in her current sticky condition.

Jocelyn blinked and began, slowly, to smile. Magnus noticed for the first time that she was beautiful. "Clary never goes to strangers. Maybe—maybe she can tell that you're not a stranger to the Fairchilds."

Tessa gazed at Jocelyn, her gray eyes clear. Magnus thought, in this case, Tessa was seeing more than he did. "Maybe. I will help you with the ceremony," she promised. "I know a Silent Brother who will keep any secret, if I ask him to."

Jocelyn bowed her head. "Thank you, Theresa Gray."

It occurred to Magnus how outraged Valentine would have been, to see his wife beseeching Downworlders, to think of his child in a warlock's arms. Magnus's thought of responding to Jocelyn's appeal with cruelty receded even further. This seemed the kind of revenge worth getting—to prove, even after Valentine's death, how wrong Valentine had been.

He walked over to the two women and the child, and he glanced at Tessa, and he saw her nod.

"Well, then," Magnus said, "it seems we are going to help you, Jocelyn Morgenstern."

Jocelyn flinched. "Don't call me that. I'm—I'm Jocelyn Fairchild."

"I thought you weren't a Shadowhunter anymore," Magnus said. "If you don't want them to find you, changing your last name seems a fairly elementary first step. Trust me, I'm an expert. I've watched a lot of spy movies."

Jocelyn looked skeptical, and Magnus rolled his eyes.

"I was also not born with the name 'Magnus Bane,'" he said. "I came up with that one all on my own."

"I actually was born Tessa Gray," Tessa said. "But you should choose whatever name seems right to you. I've always said there is a great deal of power in words, and that means names, too. A name you choose for yourself could tell you the story of what your destiny will be, and who you intend to become."

"Call me Fray. Let me join together the names of the

Fairchilds, my lost family, and the Grays. Because you are . . . a family friend," said Jocelyn, speaking with sudden firmness.

Tessa smiled at Jocelyn, looking surprised but pleased, and Jocelyn smiled down at her daughter. Magnus saw the determination in her face. Valentine had wanted to crush the world as Magnus knew it. But this woman had helped crush him instead, and now she was looking at her daughter as if she would make another world, shining and brand new, just for Clary, so Clary would never be touched by any of the darkness of the past. Magnus knew what it was to want to forget as badly as Jocelyn did, knew the passionate urge to protect that came with love.

Perhaps none of the children of the new generation—not this small stubborn redheaded scrap, or half-faerie Helen and Mark Blackthorn at the Los Angeles Institute, or even Maryse Lightwood's children growing up in New York far from the Glass City—would ever have to learn the full truth about the ugliness of the past.

Jocelyn stroked her little girl's face, and they all watched as the baby smiled, lit up with the sheer joy of living. She was a story in herself, sweet and full of hope, just beginning.

"Jocelyn and Clary Fray," said Magnus. "It's nice to meet you."

The Course of True Love (And First Dates)

By Cassandra Clare

Alec's eyes were a little wide. Magnus suspected that he had been acting on reflex and had not actually intended to use force meant for demon foes against a mundane.

The redheaded guy squawked, revealing braces, and flapped his hands in what seemed to be either urgent surrender or a very good panicked duck impression.

—The Course of True Love (And First Dates)

CRACK
AAAH!
DUDE! I'M SORRY! SERIOUSLY! I DIDN'T KNOW YOU WERE A NINJA!
I'M NOT A NINJA.
BLINK

It was Friday night in Brooklyn, and the city lights were reflecting off the sky: orange-tinted clouds pressing summer heat against the sidewalks like a flower between the pages of a book. Magnus walked the floor of his loft apartment alone and wondered, with what amounted to only mild interest, if he was about to be stood up.

Being asked out by a Shadowhunter had been among the top ten strangest and most unexpected things that had ever happened to Magnus, and Magnus had always endeavored to live a very unexpected life.

He had surprised himself by agreeing.

This past Tuesday had been a dull day at home with the cat and an inventory list that included horned toads. Then Alec Lightwood, eldest son of the Shadowhunters who ran the New

York Institute, had turned up on Magnus's doorstep, thanked him for saving his life, and asked him out while turning fifteen shades between puce and mauve. In response Magnus had promptly lost his mind, kissed him, and made a date for Friday.

The whole thing had been extremely odd. For one thing, Alec had come and said thank you to Magnus for saving his life. Very few Shadowhunters would have thought of doing such a thing. They thought of magic as their right, due whenever they needed it, and regarded warlocks as either conveniences or nuisances. Most of the Nephilim would as soon have thought of thanking an elevator for arriving at the right floor.

Then there was the fact that no Shadowhunter had ever asked Magnus out on a date before. They had wanted favors of several kinds, magical and sexual and strange. None of them had wanted to spend time with him, go out to a movie, and share popcorn. He wasn't even sure Shadowhunters *watched* movies.

It was such a simple thing, such a straightforward request—as if no Shadowhunter had ever broken a plate because Magnus had touched it, or spat "warlock" as if it were a curse. As if all old wounds could be healed, made as though they had never been, and the world could become the way it looked through Alec Lightwood's clear blue eyes.

At the time, Magnus had said yes because he wanted to say yes. It was quite possible, however, that he had said yes because he was an idiot.

After all, Magnus had to keep reminding himself, Alec wasn't even all that into Magnus. He was simply responding to the only male attention he'd ever had. Alec was closeted, shy, obviously insecure, and obviously hung up on his blond friend

Trace Wayland. Magnus was fairly certain that was the name, but Wayland had reminded Magnus inexplicably of Will Herondale, and Magnus didn't want to think about Will. He knew the best way to spare himself heartbreak was not to think about lost friends and not to get mixed up with Shadowhunters again.

He had told himself that this date would be a bit of excitement, an isolated incident in a life that had become a little too routine, and nothing more.

He tried not to think of the way he'd given Alec an out, and how Alec had looked at him and said with devastating simplicity, *I like you*. Magnus had always thought of himself as someone who could wrap words around people, trip them up or pull the wool over their eyes when he had to. It was amazing how Alec could just cut through it all. It was more amazing that he didn't even seem to be trying.

As soon as Alec had left, Magnus had called Catarina, sworn her to secrecy, and then told her all about it.

"Did you agree to go out with him because you think the Lightwoods are jerks and you want to show them you can corrupt their baby boy?" asked Catarina.

Magnus balanced his feet on Chairman Meow. "I do think the Lightwoods are jerks," he admitted. "And that does sound like something I'd do. *Damn* it."

"No, it doesn't really," said Catarina. "You're sarcastic twelve hours a day, but you're almost never spiteful. You have a good heart under all the glitter."

Catarina was the one with the good heart. Magnus knew exactly whose son he was, and where he came from.

"Even if it was spite, no one could blame you, not after the Circle, after all that happened."

Magnus looked out the window. There was a Polish restaurant across the street from his house, its flashing lights advertising twenty-four-hour borscht and coffee (hopefully not mixed together). He thought of the way Alec's hands had trembled when he'd asked Magnus if he wanted to go out, about how glad and astounded he had seemed when Magnus said yes.

"No," he said. "It's probably a bad idea—it's probably my worst idea this decade—but it had nothing to do with his parents at all. I said yes because of him."

Catarina was quiet for a few moments. If Ragnor was around he would have laughed, but Ragnor had disappeared to a spa in Switzerland for a series of complicated facials meant to bring out the green in his complexion. Catarina had the instinct of a healer: she knew when to be kind.

"Good luck on your date, then," she said at last.

"Much appreciated, but I don't need good luck; I need assistance," said Magnus. "Just because I'm going on this date does not mean it will go well. I'm very charming, but it does take two to tango."

"Magnus, remember what happened the last time you tried to tango. Your shoe flew off and nearly killed someone."

"It was a metaphor. He's a Shadowhunter, he's a Lightwood, and he's into blonds. He's a dating hazard. I need an escape strategy. If the date is a complete disaster, I'll text you. I'll say 'Blue Squirrel, this is Hot Fox. Mission to be aborted with extreme prejudice.' Then you call me and you tell me that there is a terrible emergency that requires my expert warlock assistance."

"This seems unnecessarily complicated. It's your phone, Magnus; there's no need for code names."

"Fine. I'll just text 'Abort.'" Magnus reached out and drew

his fingers from Chairman Meow's head to his tail; Chairman Meow stretched and purred his enthusiastic approval of Magnus's taste in men. "Will you help me?"

Catarina dragged in a long, annoyed breath. "I will help you," she promised. "But you've called in all your dating favors for this century, and you owe me."

"It's a bargain," said Magnus.

"And if it all works out," said Catarina, cackling, "I want to be best woman at your wedding."

"I'm hanging up now," Magnus informed her.

He had made a bargain with Catarina. He had done more than that: he had called and made reservations at a restaurant. He had selected a date outfit of red Ferragamo pants, matching shoes, and a black silk waistcoat that Magnus wore without a shirt because it did amazing things for his arms and shoulders. And it had all been for nothing.

Alec was half an hour late. The probability was that Alec's nerve had broken—that he had weighed his life, complete with his precious Shadowhunter duty, against a date with a guy he didn't even like that much—and he was not coming at all.

Magnus shrugged philosophically, and with a casualness he did not quite feel, padded over to his drinks cabinet and made himself an exciting concoction with unicorn tears, energizing potion, cranberry juice, and a twist of lime. He'd look back on this and laugh one day. Probably tomorrow. Well, maybe the day after. Tomorrow he'd be hungover.

He might have jumped when the buzzer sounded through the loft, but there was nobody but Chairman Meow there to see. Magnus was perfectly composed by the time Alec ran up the stairs and hurtled through the door.

* * *

Alec could not have been described as perfectly composed. His black hair was going in every direction, like an octopus that had been dropped in soot; his chest was rising and falling hard under his pale-blue T-shirt; and there was a light sheen of perspiration on his face. It took a lot to make Shadowhunters sweat. Magnus wondered exactly how fast he had been running.

"Well, this is unexpected," said Magnus, raising his eyebrows. Still holding his cat, he had flung himself lightly on the sofa, his legs hooked over one of the carved wooden arms. Chairman Meow was draped over his stomach and meowing in perplexity about the sudden change in his situation.

Magnus might have been trying a bit too hard to appear louche and unconcerned, but judging by Alec's crestfallen expression, he was really pulling it off.

"I'm sorry I'm late," Alec panted. "Jace wanted to do some weapons training, and I didn't know how to get away—I mean, I couldn't tell him—"

"Oh, Jace, that's it," said Magnus.

"What?" said Alec.

"I briefly forgot the blond one's name," Magnus explained, with a dismissive flick of his fingers.

Alec looked staggered. "Oh. I'm—I'm Alec."

Magnus's hand paused mid-dismissive-flick. The gleam of city lights through the window reflected off the blue jewels on his fingers, casting bright blue sparks that caught fire and then tumbled and drowned in the deep blue of Alec's eyes.

Alec had made an effort, Magnus thought, though it took a trained eye to spot it. The light-blue shirt fit him considerably better than the unholy gray sweatshirt that Alec had been wearing on Tuesday. He smelled vaguely of cologne. Magnus felt unexpectedly touched.

"Yes," said Magnus slowly, and then he smiled slowly as well. "Your name I remember."

Alec smiled. Maybe it didn't matter if Alec did have a little thing for Apparently-Jace. Apparently-Jace *was* beautiful, but he was the sort of person that knew it, and they were often more trouble than they were worth. If Jace was gold, catching the light and the attention, Alec was silver: so used to everyone else looking at Jace that that was where he looked too, so used to living in Jace's shadow that he didn't expect to be seen. Maybe it was enough to be the first person to tell Alec that he was worth being seen ahead of anyone in a room, and of being looked at longest.

And silver, though few people knew it, was a rarer metal than gold.

"Don't worry about it," said Magnus, swinging himself easily off the couch and pushing Chairman Meow gently onto the sofa cushions, to the Chairman's plaintively voiced dismay. "Have a drink."

He pushed his own drink hospitably into Alec's hand; he hadn't even taken a sip, and he could make himself a new one. Alec looked startled. He was obviously far more nervous than Magnus had thought, because he fumbled and then dropped the glass, spilling crimson liquid all over himself and the floor. There was a crash as the glass hit the wood and splintered.

Alec looked like he had been shot and was extremely embarrassed about it.

"Wow," said Magnus. "Your people are really overselling your elite Nephilim reflexes."

"Oh, by the Angel. I am so—I am so sorry."

Magnus shook his head and gestured, leaving a trail of blue sparks in the air, and the puddle of crimson liquid and broken glass vanished.

"Don't be sorry," he said. "I'm a warlock. There's no mess I can't clean up. Why do you think I throw so many parties? Let me tell you, I wouldn't do it if I had to scrub toilets myself. Have you ever seen a vampire throw up? Nasty."

"I don't really, uh, know any vampires socially."

Alec's eyes were wide and horrified, as if he was picturing debauched vampires throwing up the blood of the innocent. Magnus was prepared to bet he didn't know any Downworlders socially. The Children of the Angel kept to their own kind.

Magnus wondered what exactly Alec was doing here in Magnus's apartment. He bet Alec was wondering the same thing.

It might be a long night, but at least they could both be well-dressed. The T-shirt might show Alec was trying, but Magnus could do a lot better.

"I'll get you a new shirt," Magnus volunteered, and made his way to his bedroom while Alec was still faintly protesting.

Magnus's closet took up half his bedroom. He kept meaning to enlarge it. There were a lot of clothes in it that Magnus thought would look excellent on Alec, but as he riffled through them, he realized that Alec might not appreciate Magnus imposing his unique fashion sense on him.

He decided to go for a more sober selection and chose the black T-shirt that he had been wearing Tuesday. That was perhaps a little sentimental of Magnus.

The shirt admittedly had BLINK IF YOU WANT ME written on

it in sequins, but that was about as sober as Magnus got. He tugged the shirt off its hanger and waltzed back into the main room to find that Alec had already taken his own shirt off and was standing around somewhat helplessly, his stained shirt clenched in his fist.

Magnus stopped dead.

The room was illuminated only by a reading lamp; all the other light came from outside the windows. Alec was painted with streetlights and moonlight, shadows curling around his biceps and the slender indentations of his collarbones, his torso all smooth, sleek, bare skin until the dark line of his jeans. There were runes on the flat planes of his stomach and the silvery scars of old Marks snaked around his ribs, with one on the ridge of his hip. His head was bowed, his hair black as ink, his luminously pale skin white as paper. He looked like a piece of art, chiaroscuro, beautifully and wonderfully made.

Magnus had heard the story of how the Nephilim were created many times. They had all left out the bit that said: *And the Angel descended from on high and gave his chosen ones fantastic abs.*

Alec looked up at Magnus, and his lips parted as if he was going to speak. He watched Magnus with wide eyes, wondering at being watched.

Magnus exercised heroic self-control, smiled, and offered the shirt.

"I'm—sorry about being a lousy date," Alec muttered.

"What are you talking about?" Magnus asked. "You're a fantastic date. You've only been here ten minutes, and I already got half of your clothes off."

Alec looked equal parts embarrassed and pleased. He'd told Magnus he was new to all this, so anything more than mild flirting might scare him off. Magnus had a very calm and normal date planned: no surprises, nothing unexpected.

"Come on," said Magnus, and grabbed a red leather duster. "We're going to dinner."

The first part of Magnus's plan, getting the subway, had seemed so simple. So foolproof.

It had not occurred to him that a Shadowhunter boy was not used to being visible and having to interact with the mundanes.

The subway was crowded on a Friday night, which was not surprising but did seem to be alarming to Alec. He was peering around at the mundanes as if he had found himself in a jungle surrounded by menacing monkeys, and he was still looking traumatized by Magnus's shirt.

"Can't I use a glamour rune?" he asked, as they boarded the F train.

"No. I'm not looking like I'm alone on a Friday night just because you don't want mundanes staring at you."

They were able to grab two seats, but it didn't appreciably improve the situation. They sat awkwardly side by side, other people's chatter rushing all around them. Alec was utterly silent. Magnus was fairly sure he wanted nothing more than to go home.

There were purple and blue posters staring down at them, showing elderly couples looking sadly at one another. The posters bore the words WITH THE PASSING YEARS COMES . . . IMPOTENCE! Magnus found himself staring at the posters with a sort of absent horror. He looked at Alec and found that Alec could not tear his eyes away either. He wondered if Alec was aware that Magnus was three hundred years old and whether

Alec was considering exactly how impotent one might become after that much time.

Two guys came onto the train at the next stop and cleared a space right in front of Magnus and Alec.

One of them began to dance by swinging himself dramatically around the pole. The other sat cross-legged and started beating time on a drum he'd carried in with him.

"Hello, ladies and gentlemen and whatever else you got!" the dude with the drum called out. "We're gonna perform now for your entertainment. I hope you'll enjoy it. We call it . . . the Butt Song."

Together they began to rap. It was quite obviously a song they had written themselves.

"Roses are red, and they say love's not made to last,

But I know I'll never get enough of that sweet, sweet ass.

All that jelly in your jeans, all that junk in your trunk,

I just gotta have it—one look and I was sunk.

If you ever wonder why I had to make you mine,

It's 'cause no other lady has a tush so fine.

They say you're not a looker, but I don't mind.

What I'm looking at is the view from behind.

Never been romantic, don't know what love means,

But I know I dig the way you're wearing those jeans.

Hate to see you leave but love to watch you go.

Turn back, then leave again—baby do it slow.

I'm coming right after, gonna make a pass,

Can't get enough of that sweet, sweet ass."

Most of the commuters seemed stunned. Magnus was not sure if Alec was just stunned or if he was also deeply scandalized and privately commending his soul to God. He was wearing an extremely peculiar expression on his face and his lips were very tightly shut.

Under normal circumstances Magnus would have laughed and laughed and given the buskers a lot of money. As it was, he was profoundly grateful when they reached their stop. He did fish out a few dollars for the singers as he and Alec left the train.

Magnus was reminded again of the extreme disadvantages to mundane visibility when a skinny freckled guy slipped by them. Magnus was just thinking that he might have felt a hand snaking into his pocket when the guy gave a combination howl and screech.

While Magnus had idly wondered if he was being pickpocketed, Alec had reacted like a trained Shadowhunter: he grabbed the guy's arm and threw him up in the air. The thief flew, outstretched arms limply wagging, like a cotton-stuffed doll. He landed with a crack on the platform, with Alec's boot on his throat. Another train rattled by, all lights and noise; the Friday night commuters ignored it, forming a knot of bodies in tight shiny clothes and artful hair around Magnus and Alec.

Alec's eyes were a little wide. Magnus suspected that he had been acting on reflex and had not actually intended to use force meant for demon foes against a mundane.

The redheaded guy squawked, revealing braces, and flapped his hands in what seemed to be either urgent surrender or a very good panicked duck impression.

"Dude!" he said. "I'm sorry! Seriously! I didn't know you were a ninja!"

Alec removed his boot, and cast a hunted glance around at the fascinated stares of the bystanders.

"I'm not a ninja," he muttered.

A pretty girl with butterfly clips in her dreadlocks put her hand on his arm. "You were amazing," she told him, her voice fluting. "You have the reflexes of a striking snake. You should be a stuntman. Really, with your cheekbones, you should be an actor. A lot of people are looking for someone as pretty as you who'd do his own stunts."

Alec threw Magnus a terrified and beseeching look. Magnus took pity on him, putting a hand on the small of Alec's back and leaning against him. His attitude and the glance he shot at the girl clearly communicated *my date*.

"No offense," said the girl, rapidly removing her hand so she could dig in her bag. "Let me give you my card. I work in a talent agency. You could be a star."

"He's foreign," Magnus told the girl. "He doesn't have a social security number. You can't hire him."

The girl regarded Alec's bowed head wistfully. "That's a shame. He could be *huge*. Those eyes!"

"I realize he's a knockout," Magnus said. "But I am afraid I have to whisk him away. He is wanted by Interpol."

Alec shot him a strange look. "Interpol?"

Magnus shrugged.

"Knockout?" Alec said.

Magnus raised an eyebrow at him. "You had to know I thought so. Why else would I agree to go on a date with you?"

Apparently Alec had not known for sure, even though he'd said Isabelle and Jace had both commented on it. Maybe the vampires had all gone home and gossiped about the fact Magnus thought one of the Shadowhunters was a dreamboat. Magnus possibly needed to learn subtlety, and Alec possibly was not allowed access to mirrors at the Institute. He looked startled and pleased.

"I thought maybe—you know you said you weren't unsympathetic—"

"I don't do charity," said Magnus. "In any area of my life."

"I'll give the wallet back," piped up a helpful voice.

The red-haired mugger interrupted what might have become a nice moment by scrambling to his feet, digging out Magnus's wallet, and then dropping Magnus's wallet on the ground with a pained yelp.

"That wallet bit me!"

That'll show you not to steal warlocks' wallets, Magnus thought, bending down to retrieve the wallet from a forest of sparkling high heels on the concrete.

Aloud he said, "This just isn't your lucky night, is it?"

"Your wallet bites people?" Alec asked.

"This one bites people," said Magnus, pocketing it. He

was glad to have it back, not only because he liked money but because the wallet matched his red crocodile-skin pants. "The John Varvatos wallet bursts into flames."

"Who?" said Alec.

Magnus gazed at Alec sadly.

"Totally cool designer," chipped in the girl with butterfly clips. "You know, they give you designer stuff free when you're a movie star."

"I can always flog a Varvatos wallet," agreed the red-haired mugger. "Not that I'd steal and sell anything belonging to anyone on this platform. Specially not you guys." He shot Alec a look that bordered on hero worship. "I didn't know gay dudes could fight like that. Like, no offense. It was badass."

"You have been taught two important lessons about tolerance and honesty," Magnus informed him severely. "And you still have all your fingers after trying to mug me on a first date, so this was the best outcome you could expect."

There was a murmur of sympathy. Magnus stared around and saw Alec looking a little wild-eyed and everyone else looking concerned. Apparently the crowd they had gathered truly believed in their love.

"Aw, man, I'm really sorry," said the mugger. "I wouldn't want to mess up anybody's first date with a ninja."

"WE ARE LEAVING NOW," said Magnus, in his best High Warlock voice. He was worried that Alexander was planning to fling himself into the path of an oncoming train.

"Have fun on your date, boys," said Butterfly Clips, stuffing her card into the pocket of Alec's jeans. Alec jumped like a startled hare. "Call me if you change your mind about wanting fame and fortune!"

"Sorry again!" said their former mugger, waving a cheerful good-bye.

They left the platform amid a chorus of well-wishers. Alec looked as if he wished only for the sweet release of death.

The restaurant was on East 13th and 3rd, near an American Apparel store and among a row of tired-looking redbrick buildings. It was an Ethiopian and Italian fusion restaurant run by Downworlders. It was on the shady, shabby side, so Shadowhunters did not frequent it. Magnus had strongly suspected that Alec would not want to risk any Nephilim seeing them together.

He'd also brought many mundane dates there, as a way of easing them into his world. The restaurant wanted mundane custom but in the main the clientele were Downworlders, so glamours were used but fairly minimal.

There was a large graffitied dinosaur obscuring the sign. Alec squinted at it, but he followed Magnus inside the restaurant readily enough.

The moment Magnus stepped into the restaurant, he realized he'd made a terrible mistake.

The second the door closed behind them a terrible silence fell around the big, low-lit room. There was a crash as one diner, an ifrit with flaming eyebrows, dove behind a table.

Magnus looked at Alec and realized what they saw: even if he wasn't wearing gear, his arms bore runes, and his clothes showed signs that he was wearing weapons. *Nephilim.* Magnus might as well have walked into a Prohibition-era speakeasy flanked by police officers holding tommy guns.

God, dating sucked.

"Magnus Bane!" hissed Luigi, the owner, as he scurried over. "You brought a Shadowhunter here! Is this a raid? Magnus, I thought we were friends! You could at least have given me a heads-up!"

"We're here socially," said Magnus. He held his hands up, palms out. "I swear. Just to talk and eat."

Luigi shook his head. "For you, Magnus. But if he makes any moves toward my other customers . . ." He gestured at Alec.

"I won't," Alec said, and cleared his throat. "I'm . . . off-duty."

"Shadowhunters are never off-duty," said Luigi darkly, and dragged them to a table in the remotest part of the restaurant, the corner near the swinging doors that led to the kitchen.

A werewolf waiter with a wooden expression that indicated either boredom or constipation wandered over.

"Hello, my name is Erik and I will be your server this eve—Oh my God, you're a Shadowhunter!"

Magnus closed his eyes for a pained moment. "We can leave," he told Alec. "This may have been a mistake."

But a stubborn light had come into Alec's blue eyes. Despite his porcelain looks, Magnus could see the steel underneath. "No, that's fine, this seems . . . fine."

"You're making me feel very threatened," said Erik the waiter.

"He's not doing anything," Magnus snapped.

"It's not about what he's doing, it's about how he's making me *feel*," sniffed Erik. He slammed down the menus as if they had personally offended him. "I get stress ulcers."

"The myth that ulcers are caused by stress was debunked years ago," said Magnus. "It's actually some kind of bacteria."

"Um, what are the specials?" Alec asked.

"I can't remember them while my emotions are under this kind of strain," said Erik. "A Shadowhunter killed my uncle."

"I've never killed anyone's uncle," said Alec.

"How would you know?" demanded Erik. "When you're about to kill someone, do you stop and ask them if they have nephews?"

"I kill *demons*," Alec said. "Demons don't have *nephews*."

Magnus knew this to be only technically true. He cleared his throat loudly. "Maybe I should just order for both of us, and we can share?"

"Sure," said Alec, throwing his menu down.

"Do you want a drink?" the waiter asked Alec pointedly, adding *sotto voce*, "Or do you want to stab someone? If you absolutely have to, maybe you could stab the guy in the corner wearing the red shirt. He tips terribly."

Alec opened and shut his mouth, then opened it again. "Is this a trick question?"

"Please go," said Magnus.

Alec was very quiet, even after Erik the annoying waiter was gone. Magnus was fairly sure he was having a horrifying time, and could not blame him. Several of the other customers had left, casting panicked glances over their shoulders as they paid hurriedly.

When the food arrived, Alec's eyes widened when he saw Magnus had ordered their *kitfo* raw. Luigi had put in an effort: there were also luscious *tibs*, *doro wat*, a spicy red onion stew dish, mashed lentils and collards, and all of it laid out atop the thick spongy Ethiopian bread known as *injera*. The Italian part of Luigi's heritage was represented by a heap of *penne*. Alec did make short work of the food, and seemed to know he was supposed to eat with his fingers without being told. He was a New Yorker, Magnus thought, even if he was a Shadowhunter too.

"This is the best Ethiopian I've ever had. Do you know a lot about food?" Alec asked. "I mean, obviously you do. Never mind. That was a dumb thing to say."

"No, it wasn't," Magnus said, frowning.

Alec reached for a bite of *penne arrabiata.* He immediately began to choke on it. Tears streamed from his eyes.

"Alexander!" said Magnus.

"I'm fine!" Alec gasped, looking horrified. He snatched at his piece of bread first and only realized that it was bread when he tried to dab his eyes with it. He dropped the bread hastily and grabbed his napkin up instead, hiding both streaming eyes and scarlet face.

"You are obviously not fine!" Magnus told him, and tried a very tiny bite of the *penne.* It burned like fire: Alec was still wheezing into his napkin. Magnus made a peremptory gesture for the waiter that might have included a few blue sparks snapping and crackling onto other people's tablecloths.

The people eating near them were edging their tables subtly away.

"This *penne* is much too *arrabiata*, and you did it on purpose," said Magnus when the surly werewolf waiter hove into view.

"Werewolf rights," Erik grumped. "Crush the vile oppressors."

"Nobody has ever won a revolution with pasta, Erik," said Magnus. "Now go get a fresh dish, or I'll tell Luigi on you."

"I—" Erik began defiantly. Magnus narrowed his cat's eyes.

Erik met Magnus's gaze and decided not to be a waiter hero. "Of course. My apologies."

"What a pill," Magnus remarked loudly.

"Yeah," said Alec, tearing off a new strip of *injera*. "What have the Shadowhunters ever done to him?"

Magnus lifted an eyebrow. "Well, he did mention a dead uncle."

"Oh," said Alec. "Right."

He went back to gazing fixedly at the tablecloth.

"He's still a total pill, though," Magnus offered. Alec mumbled something that Magnus could not make out.

It was then that the door opened and a handsome human man with deep-set green eyes came in. His hands were in the pockets of his expensive suit, and he was surrounded by a group of gorgeous young faeries, male and female.

Magnus slunk down in his chair. Richard. Richard was a mortal who the faeries had adopted in the way they did sometimes, especially when the mortals were musical. He was also something else.

Magnus cleared his throat. "Quick warning. The guy who just walked in is an ex," he said. "Well. Barely an ex. It was very casual. And we parted very amicably."

At that moment, Richard caught sight of him. Richard's whole face spasmed; then he crossed the floor in two steps.

"You are scum!" Richard hissed, and then picked up Magnus's glass of wine and dashed it in his face. "Get out while you can," he continued to Alec. "Never trust a warlock. They'll enchant the years from your life and the love from your heart!"

"Years?" Magnus spluttered. "It was barely twenty minutes!"

"Time means different things to those who are of faerie,"

said Richard, the pretentious idiot. "You wasted the best twenty minutes of my life!"

Magnus grabbed hold of his napkin and began to clean off his face. He blinked through the red blurriness at Richard's retreating back and Alec's startled face.

"All right," he said. "It's possible I was mistaken about the amicable parting." He tried to smile suavely, which was difficult with wine in his hair. "Ah well. You know exes."

Alec studied the tablecloth. There was art in museums given less attention than this tablecloth.

"Not really," he said. "You're my first ever date."

This wasn't working. Magnus didn't know why he had thought it might work. He had to get out of this date and not hurt Alec Lightwood's pride too much. He wished he could feel satisfaction that he had a plan in place for this, but as he texted Catarina under the table what he felt was a sense of enveloping gloom.

Magnus sat there silently, waited for Catarina to call, and tried to work out a way to say, "No hard feelings. I like you more than any Shadowhunter I've met in more than a century, and I hope you find a nice Shadowhunter boy . . . if there are any nice Shadowhunter boys besides you."

His phone rang while Magnus was still mentally composing, the sound harsh in the silence between them. Magnus hastily answered. His hands were not entirely steady, and he was afraid for a moment that he would drop the phone as Alec had dropped his glass, but he managed to answer it. Catarina's voice filtered down the line, clear and unexpectedly urgent. Catarina was clearly a method actor.

"Magnus, there's an—"

"An emergency, Catarina?" Magnus asked. "That's terrible! What's happened?"

"An actual emergency happened, Magnus!"

Magnus appreciated Catarina's commitment to her role but wished that she would not shout so loudly right into his ear.

"That's so awful, Catarina. I mean, I'm really busy, but I suppose if there are lives at stake I can't say n—"

"There are lives at stake, you blithering idiot!" Catarina yelled. "Bring the Shadowhunter!"

Magnus paused.

"Catarina, I don't think you fully understand the point of what you're meant to do here."

"Are you drunk already, Magnus?" Catarina asked. "Are you off debauching and getting one of the Nephilim—one of the Nephilim who is under twenty-one—*drunk*?"

"The only alcohol that has passed my lips is the wine that was thrown in my face," said Magnus. "And I was totally blameless in that matter as well."

There was a pause. "Richard?" said Catarina.

"Richard," Magnus confirmed.

"Look, never mind him. Listen carefully, Magnus, because I am working, and one of my hands is covered in fluid, and I'm only going to say this once."

"Fluid," said Magnus. "What kind of fluid?"

Alec goggled at him.

"Only going to say this once, Magnus," Catarina repeated firmly. "There is a young werewolf in the Beauty Bar downtown. She went out on the night of a full moon because she wanted to prove to herself that she could still have a normal life. A vampire called this in and the vampires are not going to be of any help because the vampires never are. The werewolf is changing, she is in an unfamiliar and crowded place, and she will probably lose control and kill somebody. I cannot leave the hospital. Lucian Graymark has his phone off, and the word from his pack is that he is in a hospital with a loved one. You are not in a hospital: you are out on a stupid date. If you went to the restaurant you told me that you were going to, then you are the closest person I know who can help. Will you help, or will you continue to waste my time?"

"I'll waste your time another time, darling," said Magnus.

Catarina said, and he could hear the wry smile in her voice, "I bet."

She hung up. Catarina was often too busy to say good-bye. Magnus realized he did not have all that much time himself, but he did waste a moment looking at Alec.

Catarina had said to bring the Shadowhunter, but Catarina did not have a great deal to do with the Nephilim. Magnus did not want to see Alec cut off some poor girl's head for breaking the Law: he did not want someone else to suffer if he made a mistake in judgment, and he didn't want to find himself hating Alec as he had hated so many of the Nephilim.

He also did not want mundanes to be killed.

"I'm so sorry about this," he said. "It's an emergency."

"Um," Alec said, hunching his shoulders, "it's okay. I understand."

"There's an out-of-control werewolf in a bar near here."

"Oh," said Alec.

Something inside Magnus cracked. "I have to go and try to get her under control. Will you come and help me?"

"Oh, this is a real emergency?" Alec exclaimed, and

brightened immeasurably. For a moment Magnus felt pleased that a maddened werewolf was ravaging downtown Manhattan, if it made Alec look like that. "I figured it was one of those things where you arranged to have a friend call you so that you could get out of a sucky date."

"Ha ha," said Magnus. "I didn't know people did that."

"Uh-huh." Alec was already standing up, shrugging his jacket on. "Let's go, Magnus."

Magnus felt a burst of fondness in his chest; it felt like a small explosion, pleasant and startling at the same time. He liked how Alexander said the things that other people thought and never said. He liked how Alec called him Magnus, and not "warlock." He liked how Alec's shoulders moved under his jacket. (Sometimes he was shallow.)

And he was cheered that Alec wanted to come. He'd assumed that Alec might be delighted for the pretext to exit an uncomfortable date, but perhaps he'd read the situation wrong.

Magnus threw money down on the table; when Alec made a demurring noise, he grinned. "Please," he said. "You have no idea how much I overcharge Nephilim for my services. This is only fair. Let's go."

As they went out the door they heard the waiter yell "Werewolf rights!" at their backs.

The Beauty Bar was usually crowded at this time on a Friday night, but the people spilling out of the door were not doing it with the casual air of those who had meandered outside to smoke or hook up. They were lingering under the shining white sign that had BEAUTY written in spiky red letters and what seemed like a picture of a golden Medusa's head underneath.

The whole crowd had the air of people who were desperate to escape, yet who hovered, pinned in place by a horrified fascination.

A girl clutched Magnus's sleeve and gazed up at him, her false lashes dusted with silver glitter.

"Don't go in," she whispered. "There's a monster in there."

I am a monster, Magnus thought. *And monsters are* his *specialty*.

He didn't say it. Instead he said, "I don't believe you," and walked in. He meant it, too: the Shadowhunters, even Alec, might believe Magnus was a monster, but Magnus didn't believe it himself. He'd taught himself not to believe it even though his mother, the man he'd called his father, and a thousand others had told him it was true.

Magnus would not believe the girl in there was a monster either, no matter what she might look like to mundanes and Nephilim. She had a soul, and that meant she could be saved.

It was dark in the bar, and contrary to Magnus's expectations, there were still people inside. On a normal night the Beauty Bar was a kitschy little place full of happy people getting manicures from the staff, perched in the chairs that looked like old-fashioned hairdresser's chairs with massive hairdryers set up on the chair backs, or dancing on the black-and-white tiled floor that suggested a chessboard.

Tonight nobody was dancing, and the chairs were abandoned. Magnus squinted at a stain on the chessboard floor and saw that the black and white tiles were smeared with bright red blood.

He glanced toward Alec to see if Alec had noticed this too and found him shifting from foot to foot, obviously nervous.

"You all right?"

"I always do this with Isabelle and Jace," said Alec. "And they're not here. And I can't call them."

"Why not?" Magnus asked.

Alec blushed just as Magnus realized what he meant. Alec couldn't call his friends because he didn't want them to know he was on a date with Magnus. He especially did not want Jace to know. It was not a particularly pleasant thing to think about, but it was Alec's business.

It was also true that Magnus certainly didn't want any more Shadowhunters in the mix intent on dealing out their rough justice, but he saw Alec's problem. From what he'd seen of Jace and Alexander's showy sister, he was sure that Alec was used to protecting them, shielding them from their own rash actions, and that meant Alec was used to defending and not attacking.

"You'll do great without them," Magnus encouraged. "I can help you."

Alec looked skeptical about that, which was ridiculous since Magnus could do actual magic, something Shadowhunters liked to forget when they were deep in contemplation of how superior they were. To Alec's credit, though, he nodded and moved forward. Magnus noted, with slight puzzlement, that whenever Magnus tried to edge ahead, Alec put out an arm or moved slightly faster, staying in front of Magnus in a protective stance.

The people still in the bar were flattened against the walls as if pinned there, unmoving with terror. Someone was sobbing.

There was a low, rattling growl coming from the back lounge of the bar.

Alec crept toward the sound, Shadowhunter-soft and swift, and Magnus followed.

The lounge was decorated with black-and-white pictures of women from the 1950s and a disco ball that obviously provided no useful light. There was an empty stage made of boxes and a reading lamp that provided the only real illumination. There were couches in the center of the room, chairs at the back, and shadows all around.

There was a shadow moving and growling among all the other shadows. Alec prowled forward, hunting it, and the werewolf gave a growl of challenge.

And there was suddenly a slender girl with her hair in long dark coils, trailing ribbons and blood, dashing straight at them. Magnus leaped forward and caught her in his arms before she could distract or be attacked by Alec.

"Don't let him hurt her!" she screamed while at the same time Magnus asked, "How badly did she hurt you?"

Magnus paused and said, "We may be at somewhat of an impasse. Yes or no questions now: Are you badly hurt?"

He took hold of her shoulders gently and looked her over. She had a long, deep scratch all the way up one smooth brown arm. It was welling with blood, falling in fat drops to the floor as they spoke; she was the source of the blood on the floor outside.

She glared at him and lied, "No."

"You're a mundane, aren't you?"

"Yes—or I'm not a werewolf or anything else, if that's what you mean."

"But you know she's a werewolf."

"Yes, dumbass!" snapped the girl. "She told me. I know all about it. I don't care. It's my fault. I encouraged her to go out."

"I'm not the one encouraging werewolves to go out at the full moon and attack people on the dance floor," Magnus said.

"But perhaps we can settle which of us is the dumbass at a better time when there are not lives at stake."

The girl clutched his arm. She could see Alec, visible as Shadowhunters almost never were to the mundanes. She could see his weapons. She was bleeding too much, and yet her fear was all for someone else.

Magnus held on to the girl's arm. He would have done better with ingredients and potions, but he sent blue crackling power twining around her arm to soothe the pain and stop the bleeding. When he opened his eyes he saw the girl's gaze fixed on him, her lips parted and her face wondering. Magnus wondered if she had even known that there were people who could do magic, that anything but werewolves existed in the world.

Over her shoulder he saw Alec lunge and join battle with the wolf.

"One last question," said Magnus, speaking rapidly and softly. "Can you trust me to see your friend safe?"

The girl hesitated, and then said, "Yes."

"Then go wait outside," said Magnus. "Outside the bar, not this room. Go wait outside and clear out everyone that you can. Tell people it's a stray dog that wandered in—give people the excuse they will all want to dismiss this. Tell them you're not badly hurt. What's your friend's name?"

She swallowed. "Marcy."

"Marcy will want to know you're safe, once we've got through to her," said Magnus. "Go for her sake."

The girl nodded, a sharp jerky movement, and then fled from Magnus's grip. He heard her platform heels hitting the tiles as she went. He was able, finally, to turn back to Alec.

He saw teeth flash in the dark and did not see Alec, because

Alec was a blur of motion, rolling away, then coming back at the wolf.

At Marcy, Magnus thought, and at the same time he saw that Alec hadn't forgotten that Marcy was a person, or at least that Magnus had asked him to help her.

He wasn't using his seraph blades. He was trying not to hurt someone who had fangs and claws. Magnus did not want Alec to get scratched—and he definitely did not want to risk Alec getting bitten.

"Alexander," Magnus called, and realized his mistake when Alec turned his head and then had to back up hurriedly out of the way of the werewolf's vicious swipe at him. He tucked and rolled, landing in a crouch in front of Magnus.

"You have to stay back," he said, breathlessly.

The werewolf, taking advantage of Alec's distraction, growled and sprang. Magnus threw a ball of blue fire at her, knocking her back and sending her spinning. Some yells rose up from the few people still left in the bar, all of whom were hurrying toward the exits. Magnus didn't care. He knew Shadowhunters were meant to protect civilians, but Magnus was emphatically not one.

"You have to remember I'm a warlock."

"I know," Alec said, scanning the shadows. "I just want—" He wasn't making any sense, but the next sentence he spoke unfortunately made perfect sense. "I think," he said clearly, "I think you made her mad."

Magnus followed Alec's gaze. The werewolf was back on her feet and was stalking them, her eyes lit with unholy fire.

"Those are some excellent observational skills you have there, Alexander."

Alec tried to push Magnus back. Magnus caught hold of his black T-shirt and pulled Alec back with him. They moved together slowly out of the back lounge.

The werewolf's friend had been as good as her word: the bar was empty, a glittering shadowy playground for the werewolf to stalk them through.

Alec surprised Magnus and the werewolf both by breaking away and lunging at Marcy. Whatever he had been planning, it didn't work: this time the werewolf's swipe caught him full in the chest. Alec went flying into a hot pink wall decorated with gold glitter. He hit a mirror set into the wall and decorated with curling gold fretwork with enough force to crack the glass across.

"Oh, stupid Shadowhunters," Magnus moaned under his breath. But Alec used his own body hitting the wall as leverage, rebounding off the wall and up, catching a sparkling chandelier and swinging, then dropping down as lightly as a leaping cat and crouching to attack again in one smooth movement. "Stupid, sexy Shadowhunters."

"Alec!" Magnus called. Alec had learned his lesson: he didn't look around or risk getting distracted. Magnus snapped his fingers, a dancing blue flame appearing from them as if he had snapped on a lighter. That caught Alec's attention. "Alexander. Let's do this together."

Magnus lifted his hands and cast a web of lucent blue lines from his fingers, to baffle the wolf and protect the mundanes. Each of the shimmering strings of light would give off enough of a magical charge to make the wolf hesitate.

Alec wove around them, and Magnus wove the light around him at the same time. He was surprised at the ease with which

Alec moved with his magic. Almost every other Shadowhunter he had known had been a little wary and taken aback.

Maybe it was the fact that Magnus had never wished to help and protect in quite this way before, but the combination of Magnus's magic and Alec's strength worked, somehow.

The wolf snarled and ducked and whimpered, her world filled with blinding light, and everywhere she went, there Alec was. Magnus kind of knew how the wolf felt.

The wolf flagged and whimpered, a line of blue light cutting across her brindled fur, and Alec was on it. His knee pressed into the wolf's flank, and his hand went to his belt. Despite everything, fear flashed cold up Magnus's spine. He could picture the knife, and Alec cutting the werewolf's throat.

What Alec drew out was a rope. He wrapped it around the werewolf's neck as he held her pinned down with his body. She struggled and bucked and snarled. Magnus let the lines of magic drop and murmured, the magic words falling from his lips in fading puffs of blue smoke, spells of healing and soothing, illusions of safety and calm.

"Come on, Marcy," Magnus said clearly. "Come *on*!"

The werewolf shuddered and changed, bones popping and fur flowing away, and in a few long, agonizing moments Alec found himself with his arms wrapped around a girl dressed only in the torn ribbons of a dress. She was very nearly naked.

Alec looked more uncomfortable than he had when she was a wolf. He let go quickly, and Marcy slid to a sitting position, her arms clutched around herself. She was whimpering under her breath. Magnus pulled off his long red leather coat and knelt to wrap it around her. Marcy clutched at the lapels.

"Thank you so much," said Marcy, looking up at Magnus

with big beseeching eyes. She was a fetching little blonde in human form, which made her giant, angry wolf form seem funnier in retrospect. Then her face tightened with anguish, and nothing seemed funny at all. "Did I . . . please, did I hurt anybody?"

"No," said Alec, his voice strong, confident as it only very rarely was. "No, you didn't hurt anyone at all."

"There was someone with me . . ." Marcy began.

"She was scratched," Magnus said, keeping his voice steady and reassuring. "She's fine. I healed her."

"But I hurt her," Marcy said, and put her face in her blood-stained hands.

Alec reached out and touched Marcy's back, rubbing it gently as if this werewolf stranger was his own sister.

"She's fine," he said. "You didn't—I *know* you didn't want to hurt her, that you didn't want to hurt anyone. You can't help being what you are. You're going to figure it all out."

"She forgives you," Magnus told Marcy, but Marcy was looking at Alec.

"Oh my God, you're a Shadowhunter," she whispered, just as Erik the werewolf waiter had, but with fear in her voice instead of scorn. "What are you going to do to me?" She shut her eyes. "No. I'm sorry. You stopped me. If you hadn't been here—whatever you do to me, I deserve it."

"I'm not going to do anything to you," said Alec, and Marcy opened her eyes and looked up into Alec's face. "I meant what I said. I'm not going to tell anyone. I promise."

Alec had looked the same when Magnus had spoken of his childhood at the party when they had first met. It was something Magnus hardly ever did, but he had felt spiky and defensive about the advent of all these Shadowhunters in his house, at Jocelyn Fray's daughter, Clary, showing up without her mother and with so many questions she deserved answers to. He had not expected to look into a Shadowhunter's eyes and see sympathy.

Marcy sat up, gathering the coat around her. She looked suddenly dignified, as if she had realized she had rights in this situation. That she was a person. That she was a soul, and that soul had been respected as it should have been.

"Thank you," she said calmly. "Thank you both."

"Marcy?" said her friend's voice from the door.

Marcy looked up. "Adrienne!"

Adrienne dashed inside, almost skidding on the tiled floor, and threw herself to the ground and enveloped Marcy in her arms.

"Are you hurt? Show me," Marcy whispered into her shoulder.

"It's fine, it's nothing, it's absolutely all right," said Adrienne, stroking Marcy's hair.

"I'm so sorry," said Marcy, cupping Adrienne's face. They kissed, heedless of the fact that Alec and Magnus were standing right there.

When they broke apart, Adrienne rocked Marcy in her arms and whispered, "We'll figure this out so it never happens again. We will."

Other people followed Adrienne's lead and came in by twos and threes.

"You're pretty snappily dressed for a dogcatcher," said a man Magnus thought was the bartender.

Magnus inclined his head. "Thank you very much."

More people swirled back in, cautiously at first and then in far greater numbers. Nobody was asking where exactly the dog had gone. A great many of them seemed to want drinks.

Perhaps some of them would ask questions later, when the shock had worn off, and this night's work would become a situation that needed clearing up. But Magnus decided that was a problem for later.

"That was nice, what you said to her," said Magnus, when the crowd had completely hidden Marcy and Adrienne from their sight.

"Uh . . . it was nothing," said Alec, shifting and looking embarrassed. The Shadowhunters did not see much to approve of in kindness, Magnus supposed. "I mean, that's what we're here for, aren't we? Shadowhunters, I mean. We have to help anyone who needs help. We have to protect people."

The Nephilim Magnus had known had seemed to believe the Downworlders were created to help *them*, and to be disposed of if they didn't help enough.

Magnus looked at Alec. He was sweaty and still breathing a little hard, the scratches on his arms and face healing quickly thanks to the *iratzes* on his skin.

"I don't think we're going to get a drink in here; there's much too long a line," said Magnus slowly. "Let's have a nightcap back at my place."

They walked home. Though it was a long way, it was a nice walk on a summer night, the air warm on Magnus's bare arms and the moon turning the Brooklyn Bridge into a highway of shining white.

"I'm really glad your friend called you to help that girl," Alec confessed as they walked. "I'm really glad you asked me along. I was—I was surprised you did, after how things were going before."

"I was worried you were having a terrible time," Magnus told him. It felt like putting a lot of power in Alec's hands, but Alec was honest with him and Magnus found himself possessed by the strange impulse to be honest back.

"No," said Alec, and went red. "No, that's not it at all. Did I seem— I'm sorry."

"Don't be sorry," Magnus told him softly.

Words seemed to explode out of Alec in a rush, though judging by his expression he wished he could hold them back. "It was my fault. I got everything wrong even before I showed up, and you knew how to order at the restaurant and I had to stop myself laughing at that song on the subway. I have no idea what I'm doing and you're, um, glamorous."

"What?"

Alec looked at Magnus, stricken, as if he thought he'd got everything wrong again.

Magnus wanted to say, *No, I was the one who brought you to a terrible restaurant and treated you like a mundane because I didn't know how to date a Shadowhunter and almost bailed on you even though you were brave enough to ask me out in the first place.*

What Magnus actually ended up saying was, "I thought that terrible song was *hilarious*," and he threw back his head and laughed. He glanced over at Alec and found him laughing too. His whole face changed when he laughed, Magnus thought. Nobody had to be sorry for anything, not tonight.

When they reached Magnus's home, Magnus laid a hand on the front door and it swung open.

"I lost my keys maybe fifteen years ago," Magnus explained.

He really should get around to getting more keys cut. He didn't really need them, though, and it had been a long time since there was anyone he wanted to have his keys—to have ready access to his home because he wanted them there anytime they wanted to come. There had been nobody since Etta, half a century ago.

Magnus gave Alec a sidelong look as they climbed the rickety stairs. Alec caught the glance, and his breathing quickened; his blue eyes were bright. Alec bit his lower lip, and Magnus stopped walking.

It was only a momentary hesitation. But then Alec reached out and caught his arm, fingers tight above his elbow.

"Magnus," he said in a low voice.

Magnus realized that Alec was mirroring the way Magnus had taken hold of Alec's arms on Tuesday: on the day of Alec's first kiss.

Magnus's breath caught in his throat.

That was apparently all the encouragement Alec needed. He leaned in, expression open and ardent in the darkness of the stairs, in the hush of this moment. Alec's mouth met Magnus's, soft and gentle. Getting his breath back was an impossibility, and no longer a priority.

Magnus closed his eyes and unbidden images came to him: Alec trying not to laugh on the subway, Alec's startled appreciation at the taste of new food, Alec glad not to be ditched, Alec sitting on the floor with and telling a werewolf that she could not help what she was. Magnus found himself almost afraid at the thought of what he had nearly done in almost leaving Alec before the evening was over. Leaving Alec was the last thing he wanted to do right now. He pulled in Alec by the belt loops of his jeans, closed all distance between their bodies and caught Alec's tiny needful gasp with his mouth.

The kiss caught fire and all he could see behind his closed eyes were gold sparks; all he was aware of was Alec's mouth, Alec's strong gentle hands that had held down a werewolf and tried not to hurt her, Alec pressing him against the banister so the rotten wood creaked alarmingly and Magnus did not even care—Alec here, Alec now, the taste of Alec in his mouth, his hands pushing aside the fabric of his own worn T-shirt to get at Alec's bare skin underneath.

It took an embarrassingly long time before they both remembered that Magnus had an apartment, and tumbled toward it without disentangling from each other. Magnus blew the door open without looking at it: the door banged so hard against the wall that Magnus cracked an eye open to check that he had not absentmindedly made his front door explode.

Alec kissed a sweet careful line down Magnus's neck, starting from just below his ear to the hollow at the base of his throat. The door was fine. Everything was great.

Magnus pulled Alec down to the sofa, Alec collapsing bonelessly on top of him. Magnus fastened his lips to Alec's neck. He tasted of sweat and soap and skin, and Magnus bit down, hoping to leave a mark on the pale skin there, wanting to. Alec gave a breathy whimper and pushed his body into the contact. Magnus's hands slid up under Alec's rumpled shirt, learning the shape of Alec's body. He ran his fingers over the swell of Alec's shoulders and down the long lean curve of his back, feeling the scars of his profession and the wildness of his kisses. Shyly, Alec undid the buttons on Magnus's waistcoat, laying skin bare and slipping inside to touch Magnus's chest, his stomach, and Magnus felt cool silk replaced by warm hands, curious and caressing. He felt Alec's fingers shaking against his skin.

Magnus reached up and pressed his hand against Alec's cheek, his brown bejeweled fingers a contrast to Alec's moonlight-pale skin: Alec turned his face into the curve of Magnus's palm and kissed it, and Magnus's heart broke.

"Alexander," he murmured, wanting to say more than just "Alec," to call him by a name that was longer than and different from the name everybody else called him, a name with weight and value to it. He whispered the name as if making a promise that he would take his time. "Maybe we should wait a second."

He pushed Alec, just slightly, but Alec took the hint. He took it much further than Magnus had meant it. He scrambled off the sofa and away from Magnus.

"Did I do something wrong?" Alec asked, and his voice was shaking too.

"No," Magnus said. "Far from it."

"Are you sending me home?"

Magnus held up his hands. "I have no interest in telling you what to do, Alexander. I don't want to persuade you to do anything or convince you not to do anything. I'm just saying that you might want to stop and think for a moment. And then you can decide—whatever you want to decide."

Alec looked frustrated. Magnus could sympathize.

Then he scrubbed both hands through his hair—it was already a wreck thanks to Magnus; there was no ruining it any further; it had reached maximum ruination—and paced the floor. He was thinking, Magnus saw, and tried not to wonder what he was thinking of: Jace, Magnus, his family or his duty, how to be kind to himself.

He stopped pacing when he reached Magnus's doorway.

"I should probably go home," said Alec eventually.

"Probably," said Magnus, with great regret.

"I don't want to," Alec said.

"I don't want you to," said Magnus. "But if you don't . . ."

Alec nodded, quickly. "Good-bye, then," he said, and leaned down for a quick kiss. At least Magnus suspected it was supposed to be quick. He wasn't entirely sure what happened after that, but somehow he was wrapped around Alec entirely and they were on the floor. Alec was gasping and clutching at him, and somebody's hands were on someone else's belt buckle and Alec kissed Magnus so hard he tasted blood, and Magnus said, "Oh, *God*," and then—

And then Alec was back up on his feet and had hold of the doorframe, as if the air had become a tide that might rush him back to Magnus if he didn't grab at some support. He seemed to be struggling with something, and Magnus wondered whether he was going to ask to stay after all or say the whole night had been a mistake. Magnus felt more fear and more anticipation than he was entirely able to play off, and he realized it mattered more than it should, so soon.

He waited, tense, and Alec said, "Can I see you again?"

The words tumbled out in a rush, shy and eager and entirely uncertain of what Magnus would answer, and Magnus felt the headlong rush of adrenaline and excitement that came from the start of a new adventure.

"Yes," said Magnus, still lying on the floor. "I'd like that."

"Um," said Alec, "so—next Friday night?"

"Well . . ."

Alec looked instantly worried, as if he thought Magnus was going to take it all back and say that actually he had changed his mind. He was beautiful and hopeful and hesitant, a heart-breaker who wore his heart on his sleeve. Magnus found himself wanting to show his hand, to take a risk and be vulnerable. He recognized and accepted this strange new feeling: that he would rather be hurt himself than hurt Alec.

"Friday night would be fine," Magnus said, and Alec smiled his brilliant, light-up-the-world smile and backed out of the apartment, still looking at Magnus. He backed up all the way to the top of the stairs. There was a yell, but Magnus had already risen and closed the door before he could see Alec fall down the steps, as that was the sort of thing a man had to do in private.

He did lean on the windowsill, though, and watch Alec emerge from his building's front door, tall and pale and messy-haired, and walk off down Greenpoint Avenue, whistling off-key. And Magnus found himself hoping.

He had been taught so many times that hope was foolish, but he could not help it, as heedless as a child straying close to the fire and stubbornly refusing to learn from experience. Maybe this time was different—maybe this love was different. It felt so different; surely that had to mean something. Maybe the year to come would be a good year for both of them. Maybe this time things would work out the way Magnus wanted them to.

Maybe Alexander Lightwood would not break his heart.

The Voicemail of Magnus Bane

By Cassandra Clare, Sarah Rees Brennan,
and Maureen Johnson

"Hi, Magnus. It's Alec. Alexander. Well, you know that. I'm just calling because I think we need to talk. I guess you're busy. Call me back, okay?"

Beep

—The Voicemail of Magnus Bane

RIIIING
RIIIIIIING
RIIIIING
RIIIIING
CLICK
SWEET CHEEKS
slide to answer
BEEP
HI, MAGNUS. IT'S ALEC. ALEXANDER. . .

The Voicemail of Magnus Bane, High Warlock of Brooklyn, in the Days Following a Certain Incident in *City of Lost Souls*

Today 2:00 a.m.

"Hi, Magnus. It's Alec. Alexander. Well, you know that. I'm just calling because I think we need to talk. I guess you're busy. Call me back, okay?"

Beep

Today 2:10 a.m.

"Hi, Magnus. This is Isabelle Lightwood. There seems to have been a small misunderstanding. My brother came home under an impression I'm sure is totally mistaken. Call me or else, and let's get this cleared up! I don't know why I said 'or else.' We're all friends here."

Beep

Today 2:35 a.m.

"Isabelle speaking. Maybe there hasn't been a misunderstanding. Maybe you just made a terrible error. That's okay! People make mistakes. All they have to do is grovel and beg for forgiveness, and then all is well. That's how it can be. I'm prepared to let it go this once, Magnus."

Beep

Today 3:00 a.m.

"Isabelle. Let me just follow up by describing what a big mistake you would be making if you broke up with Alec. The Lightwoods are a seriously hot people. Some people say the Herondales used to be hot, but think about it—not only do we outnumber them, but we took their last hottie and we made him ours. Obviously, we won the victory.

"I have looked back on portraits of our ancestors. Gabriel Lightwood was notably smoking. It is rumored that one Consul agreed with everything my great-great aunt Felicia Lightwood ever said, because when she spoke all he heard was 'Foxy foxy foxy.' If you break up with Alec, you will not only be losing one stone cold fox, but a family of foxes. I will pass down the word to my children's children. No Lightwood is ever going to so much as wink at you in a bar. Think about that. Think about being Lightwoodless and lonely five hundred years from now, in a sad and chilly nightclub on the moon."

Beep

Today 11 a.m.

"Hi, it's Alec. I guess you're still busy. That's okay. I know you have a lot of things to do. Just—call me back when you're free? Whenever you're free, it doesn't matter what time. I'll be awake. I really want to talk to you."

Beep

Today 2:30 p.m.

"Hello, Mr. Bane, this is Hadrian Industries. We're calling to engage your services for a simple ritual, in the same vein as the one you performed for us last February. We would like you to bring a crate of horned toads with you. We shall of course amply compensate you for the toads."

Beep

Today 5:14 p.m.

"Mrrrrrowl. Mrrrrrowl."

"Ow! Ow, stupid cat! Ahem. You told me, 'stop calling, Isabelle,' but I'm not the one calling you. Church is calling you. Mine are merely the fingers that work the phone.

"See, here's something you may not have known before you committed your recent rash acts. Our cat, Church, and your cat, Chairman Meow? They're in love. I've never seen such love before. I never knew such love could exist in the heart of a . . . cat. Some people say that love between two dude cats is wrong, but I think it's beautiful. Love makes Church happier than I've ever seen him. Nothing makes him happy like Chairman Meow. Not tuna. Not shredding centuries-old tapestries. Nothing. Please don't keep these cats apart. Please don't take the joy of love away from Church.

"Look, this is really just a warning for your own good. If you keep Church and Chairman Meow apart, Church will start to get angry.

"You wouldn't like Church when he's angry."

Beep

Today 6:00 p.m.

"Hi, Magnus. This is Clary. Nobody told me to make this phone call.

"Isabelle did ask me to call you, but I said no, and she doesn't know I'm making this one.

"Honestly, when I first met Alec, I thought he was really horrible. Admittedly, I was a little off my game, what with finding out about magic worlds and Mom being kidnapped. That was a bad time, but Alec still was really not my favorite person.

"He was a jerk, but he wasn't a jerk because he's a bad guy. He was a jerk because he was unhappy, and he felt like he had to pretend to be someone he wasn't. I guess he learned that he had to hide things all the time, when he was growing up—that he had to keep secrets or lose people. He's a lot better when he's with you. He's better because he's happier.

"I don't really know how relationships work. Jace is the only boyfriend I've ever had, and I'm told our relationship has not gone along traditional lines. But I guess that's what a relationship seems like to me: that no matter what else is going on, you're happiest when you're together.

"I'm not just calling because I'm worried about Alec. You seemed really happy with him, too.

"I was wondering how you are. I hope you're doing okay."

Beep

Today 8:26 p.m.

"Hi, Magnus. This is Alec. Alexander. I guess you don't want to talk to me. I can understand that. But I really think if we were together . . . if I could just explain . . .

"I'm so bad with words. I'm sorry. But you always seemed to know what I meant. I don't want to lose that. I don't want to lose you. I want to talk to you so badly, but if I can't, I guess I'm calling to say . . .

"I'm really sorry. I just called to say that."

Beep

Today 9:39 p.m.

"Hi, Magnus. It's Simon. You know me. Well, you called me Soames last time we spoke, but we've hung out. I'm calling to, uh . . . to—sorry if this is out of line—suggest that you maybe take Alec back.

"I think it would be good for morale. Honestly, Alec was really horrible to Clary when they first met, and if he turns all cranky again, I don't know what Clary's going to do. In those days, Clary had way fewer weapons and way fewer brothers.

"This time it's different. Her boyfriend is on fire. She's got enough problems. I guess what I'm saying is that we'd all appreciate it if you took one for the team.

"Not that I'm part of a Shadowhunter team.

"Shadowhunters don't let vampires join the team.

"This message probably seems selfish, and also crazy. I honestly do feel bad for Alec. He's a good guy. Much less annoying than Jace. I've always felt like, given the opportunity, we could be friends. Maybe bros. Maybe we could be bros who shoot arrows together.

"It may at this point be obvious that Isabelle forced me to make this phone call. I'm not really sure what I'm supposed to say.

"Here's the thing. Alec looks really bad.

"Ow, Isabelle! I mean, he's looking fine, he's a very handsome guy. Much better-looking than Jace, if you ask me. But he's obviously really down. Anyone can see it.

"I don't really notice how guys look most of the time, but even I can see it. He has black rings under his eyes, and his sweaters seem to be coming apart with despair. His mom is worried because he's not eating, and I heard Jace hinting about hairbrushes yesterday. Of course, for a badass warrior, Jace is kind of prissy.

"I don't know what happened between you guys, but I know when someone is sorry. I can tell you, whatever he did, Alec is sorry.

"If you could give him a break, that would be great. Okay. I guess that's it.

"Please don't ever tell Jace I said he was a badass."

Beep

Today 11:48 p.m.

"No, you listen, with your not-calling-back face! You're making a big mistake! I was the best thing that ever happened to you!

"Uh. Okay, statistically, that's not very likely.

"A lot of stuff has happened to you. A lot of people have happened to you.

"I think that was what made me do what I did. I just wanted to know that I wasn't, you know, low down on a long list. I didn't want to be a pretty mediocre footnote in the story of your life.

"Oh, God.

"Jace. Jace, wake up. Jace, how do you delete messages on someone else's phone?"

Beep

Today 8:11 a.m.

"Mr. Bane, I am authorized to contact you on behalf of my client. It is my opinion, and I consider it will be the opinion of the judge, that your actions vis-à-vis terminating your relationship with one Alexander Gideon Lightwood, Esquire, were unlawful. I have in my office witnesses and documentation to prove that you were in fact common law married, and Mr. Lightwood could claim half of your freehold in Brooklyn.

"All right, fine, it's Isabelle again.

"All right, my lawyer is Church. But I truly believe that we have a case. And Church has never lost a lawsuit.

"Answer the phone, Magnus!"

Beep

Today 10:31 a.m.

"Mr. Bane, I am calling to leave a message on an urgent business matter. One of our representatives called about the matter of the horned toads delivery. He described your manner of answering the telephone as 'curt' and 'extremely harsh,' and your tone as 'wild, not to say maddened.' Is there a problem with the toads? We are very concerned."

Beep

Today 7:52 p.m.

"Listen up, buddy: nobody breaks up with a Lightwood. Nobody! Meliorn thought that he could tell his faerie buddies over cups of mead that he'd broken up with me, and all I'm saying is that Meliorn hasn't seen his faerie steed in a while.

"Once a guy visited the Institute and thought he could leave a 'Dear Jane' letter for me as he walked out the door. Jace found the letter. Ten minutes later that guy had a broken wrist and a concussion. And then I let Jace at him.

"This is Isabelle, by the way."

Beep

Today 8:01 p.m.

"Hello, Bane. I mean, ah, Magnus. Greetings, Magnus Bane, High Warlock of Brooklyn, from Maryse Lightwood of the New York Institute. Um . . . head of the New York Institute. I'm totally the head, and I am calling on Shadowhunter business. Because I am in charge of all Shadowhunter business. The matter on which I am calling is a complex one. Too complex to be discussed over the phone. I think, upon consideration, that it would be best if you visited the Institute so we could discuss this in person.

"Please do not misunderstand me. This is a professional phone call about a purely business matter. I am simply intent on important Shadowhunter business.

"You would naturally be welcome to stay for tea and social conversation with whatever members of the Institute might happen to be present at the time of your visit. After we conclude our business, of course."

Beep

Today 10:29 p.m.

"Greetings to High Warlock Magnus Bane from the New York werewolf clan. This is Maia Roberts. Um, Luke would have called, but he's, uh, in the bathroom.

"What? Shut up! He's been in the bathroom for a really long time, okay? We think it might be food poisoning. He's been in the bathroom for so long that we believe that he is no longer our leader.

"Anyway, the werewolves would like to visit with you. You know, just one of those friendly werewolf on warlock visits. And whoever else happens to show up at the meeting.

"I just want to state for the record that this is stupid and he's never going to buy it!"

Beep

Today 1:06 a.m.

"I'm outside your door, Magnus! I'm going to break it down!"

(pause)

"I would have already broken it down if you hadn't put up stupid warlock spells like a stupid warlock cheater! Answer the door right now or I'll kill you! I know you're in there. I know you broke my brother's heart. I'm not going to stand for it.

"Answer the door right now so I can kill you!"

Beep

Today 2:33 a.m.

"Greetings, Magnus Bane, High Warlock of Brooklyn, from Raphael Santiago of the New York vampire clan, loyal servant of our glorious Queen Maureen, forever may she reign in dark glory, and the future Prince Consort Simon, babelicious rock god.

"We have to begin all our telephone calls in this manner now. Including our nightly call to a place called Hot Topic.

"It would be needless to state, after this introduction, that I consider myself a damned soul.

"I am contacting you because our queen wished to send a summons to 'the shiny man who is Simon's friend.' That is a quote. She adds that she supports you and she is a fan of much 'yaoi manga.' I have no idea what that means, and I never wish to know.

"While I am on the telephone, Lily happened to overhear some not terribly interesting conversation at Taki's between several melodramatic teenagers of your acquaintance. Imagine my surprise when I learned that the ill-advised relationship between yourself and an excessively young male Shadowhunter has been abruptly and unpleasantly concluded.

"I wanted to inform you that your esteemed colleague Ragnor Fell now owes me ten dollars due to a small bet that we made amongst ourselves on the subject of how that absurd liaison would end.

"Of course, Ragnor will never pay me my ten dollars, because he was murdered by the Nephilim, due to a conflict between Nephilim that Downworlders were for some reason embroiled in. Just like the conflict we are currently having, so I suppose you could say that Ragnor died for nothing.

"Shadowhunters. Could their new motto be something like 'Not Worth the Bother'?"

Beep

Today 11:23 a.m.

"Hi, Magnus. This is Isabelle. I'm calling to apologize for attempting to break down your door, for the phone calls and visits that I've been told might have counted as harassment, and for describing you to all your neighbors as a filthy Downworlder love weasel. Though I realize some of the things I said might have seemed threatening, of course as a Shadowhunter I would never inflict physical harm on anyone not engaged in evil or at least being totally annoying.

"I feel I was being pretty reasonable the entire time, and

playing it pretty cool, but I'm told that from an outside perspective it looks like I might have slightly lost my head.

"I admit I do get a bit protective of my big brother. He always protects me.

"The truth is, I don't have to threaten you with anything worse than you've already done to yourself.

"Alec is brave, and he's good, and he's loyal, and like all Lightwoods he has cheekbones you could use to slice salami. You're never going to find anyone as great as my brother or anyone who loves you as much.

"He's one of the best things in my life, and I'm prepared to bet he's one of the best things in yours. You're going to be so sorry when you wake up and realize what you threw away.

"In exchange for my promise to be cool in future, I'd appreciate it if you deleted this sappy message. I have a reputation in this town to keep up."

Beep

Today 4:02 p.m.

"Hi, Magnus. This is Alec. I'm just calling to say that I might have asked a couple of people who you were actually talking to if they could possibly put in a good word for me with you. And it, uh, has now been brought to my attention that a couple of people might have taken things slightly too far.

"So I guess this is me calling to tell you that I'm really sorry. Again.

"I won't call again. I won't text. I'm sorry about all the texts. Especially about the one I sent at three fifteen in the morning on Wednesday. You know the one. Yeah. I'm very sorry about that.

"You can call me or text me, though, if you ever want to.

"I don't expect you will. But I really hope you do. I won't give up hoping."

Beep

Today 5:06 p.m.

"Mr. Bane, this is Hadrian Industries calling to inform you that you are extremely late for the appointment we made. We have been waiting for over an hour. There is no sign of you. There is no sign of the toads. We want to—"

(message cut off)

These records were obtained, with some difficulty, from a cell phone which appeared to have been broken and burned with intense magical fire.